"Julie Beard continues to show her range of talent as she writes fast-paced and character-driven tales that take place in centuries long gone but brilliantly reconstructed."
—*Painted Rock Reviews*

"Beard is writing tales of love and romance that always have happy endings."
—*Chicago Tribune*

More praise for the novels of
national bestselling author Julie Beard . . .

The Duchess' Lover

"Julie Beard writes intelligent romances brimming with emotion and sensuality. *The Duchess' Lover* is a keeper. I loved it!"
—*Joan Johnston*

"A multifaceted read that paints an accurate portrait of a bygone era while tugging on the reader's heartstrings."
—*Publishers Weekly*

"Ms. Beard writes about the love affair between Olivia and Will with such sensitivity and love that it will warm your heart . . . Julie Beard is one of the few writers who take the concept of love and passion right to the brink! Keep up the wonderful writing, Julie. I'm a fan for life!"
—*A Romance Review*

"A courageous and passionate story of a woman reawakened by the love of a younger man."
—*Madeline Hunter*

"Julie Beard does it again. *The Duchess' Lover* is seductive and sensual. A delicious treat to be savored. I couldn't put it down."
—*Kathleen Korbel*

continued . . .

Very Truly Yours

"Charming characters . . . A true delight."   —*Booklist*

My Fair Lord

"A lighthearted and amusing read . . . lively fun."
                                    —*All About Romance*

"An exciting historical romance." —*Painted Rock Reviews*

The Maiden's Heart

"[An] engaging love story."   —*Publishers Weekly*

Romance of the Rose

"Delightful and wickedly witty . . . picturesque portrait of Elizabethan England brimming over with Ms. Beard's special sense of humor and delight in storytelling . . . perfectly irresistible."   —*Romantic Times*

"Experience the passion and pageantry of the Elizabethan world in this wonderfully entertaining story."
                                    —*Susan Wiggs*

"An unforgettable love story, rich in history, cloaked in intrigue, full of contrasting settings all bound together by the vivid, descriptive writing style of this talented author."
                                    —*Rendezvous*

Falcon and the Sword

"Medieval romance at its best. Beard paints a lively and colorful portrait of the thirteenth century with vivid descriptions, sharp narrative and an engrossing, original plot. She is at the top of her form."   —*Romantic Times*

"A sensitive, thought-provoking story with an original plot, fascinating characters, and a vibrant setting. Another best-seller for Ms. Beard."   —*Rendezvous*

A Dance in Heather

"Lively [and] endearing."   —*Publishers Weekly*

"A nice interweaving of medieval British history, pageantry, and love."   —*Library Journal*

"A glorious love story in every sense—alive and vibrant, enthralling, and intriguing . . . I couldn't put it down until the last page."   —*Rendezvous*

Lady and the Wolf

"Fiery passion . . . [An] outstanding tale of the Middle Ages."   —*Rendezvous*

"*Lady and the Wolf* mixes the plague, primogeniture, the Spanish Inquisition, witchcraft, jousts, grave robbing, and some sizzling sex scenes into a brand-new, bestselling, fourteenth-century romance."   —*Chicago Suburban Times*

Titles by Julie Beard

MIDNIGHT ANGEL
THE DUCHESS' LOVER
VERY TRULY YOURS
MY FAIR LORD
THE MAIDEN'S HEART
ROMANCE OF THE ROSE
FALCON AND THE SWORD
A DANCE IN HEATHER
LADY AND THE WOLF

THE CHRISTMAS CAT
(anthology with Jo Beverley, Barbara Bretton, and Lynn Kurland)

CHARMED
*(anthology with Jayne Ann Krentz writing as Jayne Castle,
Lori Foster, and Eileen Wilks)*

Midnight Angel

Julie Beard

BERKLEY SENSATION, NEW YORK

MIDNIGHT ANGEL

A Berkley Sensation Book / published by arrangement with the author

PRINTING HISTORY
Berkley Sensation edition / December 2003

ISBN: 0-425-19439-6

A BERKLEY SENSATION™ BOOK
Berkley Sensation Books are published by The Berkley Publishing Group, a division of Penguin Group (USA) Inc., 375 Hudson Street, New York, New York 10014.
BERKLEY SENSATION and the "B" design are trademarks belonging to Penguin Group (USA) Inc.

PRINTED IN THE UNITED STATES OF AMERICA

10   9   8   7   6   5   4   3   2   1

Acknowledgments

An important part of my story revolves around ideas I read about in Robert Graves's dense and fascinating book titled *The White Goddess: A Historical Grammar of Poetic Myth*. I found Graves's research and conclusions difficult to comprehend but brilliant, and certainly well worth many years of contemplation.

I owe special thanks to my friend and fellow author Shirl Henke. Without her encouragement, insight, and help this book might never have been finished.

Chapter 1

On the streets they called him the Midnight Angel. The prostitutes chattered about him endlessly while they waited for their next customer in the fog where the gaslight sloughed into shadows.

Some said he was a knight in shining armor who would appear any moment on his fancy black stallion to sweep them off to a gleaming castle. Others said he was a myth, that no man could be so noble as this Mr. Morgan, with his tall top hat, spotless white silk cravat, and genteel manners. Others said he was a cripple, for no one had ever seen him alight from his expensive carriage.

The hardened whores dismissed him as a fantasy of working-class girls who hoped to make a few quid on their backs and then turn respectable. The young ones who hadn't yet admitted to themselves that this was the only line of work they would ever have spoke obsessively about

the girls Mr. Morgan had rescued. They believed he plucked
them off the street and took them to Stone House, his shelter
for fallen women. There the girls were cleaned up, taught
manners, and married off to foreign princes, which even the
most naive chits found hard to believe. A few claimed to
have personally bedded Mr. Morgan, and they avowed he
"twaren't no gent-ul-mun." He was just a clever one who
could get his ballocks off without paying for it.

Reginald Shane wasn't sure what he thought about
Mr. Morgan. The twenty-year-old clerk could scarcely
believe he was sitting across from the legendary figure in
his carriage and that he'd been hired to be Morgan's secretary, or man-of-affairs. The job description had been
vague. Morgan had sent word just that day and had
arranged to pick him up at The Scarlet Feather.

That was the most baffling part of it. The Scarlet Feather
was a brothel for men and only men. Did Mr. Morgan
know Reggie was a homosexual? Did he care? And more
to the point, what precisely were Mr. Morgan's own
predilections? Had he hired Reggie for more than his
clerical skills? After all, the Midnight Angel's genteel
manners might be attributed to more than an upper-crust
upbringing.

"You're staring at me, Mr. Shane," the Midnight Angel
said.

They had just rolled through a low-hanging cloud of
yellowish-green filth belching from a nearby match factory. Reggie cleared his throat and looked out the window,
pretending he could see something—anything—of interest
beyond their suddenly too-close quarters.

"Are you nervous, Mr. Shane?" Morgan spoke in a gruff
half-voice. It sounded as if he'd smoked too many cigars.
But there was not so much as a hint of tobacco lingering on
his black silk cape. In fact, Reggie thought he detected perfume wafting from the gentleman's formal clothing. That
surely meant Morgan preferred women, no matter how
soft-skinned he might appear to be. Reggie hoped it was

true. He was determined to become a respectable clerk and put his days of prostitution behind him.

"I do not mean to stare, sir," Reggie said while he twisted his worn brown bowler in his hands. He pushed a hand through his thick skein of brown hair and sniffed, an unconscious habit that always scrunched up the sea of pale freckles on his nose. He forced a grin. "I am still trying to sort out my good fortune. I don't understand why you chose me. But I'm grateful to you for this job, I am. And I promise I'll do my best."

"You'd better." Morgan smiled, and his dark mustache rose. His eyes glimmered with an almost lavender shade when they passed a bright gaslight. He reeked of quality, but possessed uncommon perceptiveness as well. He was indeed a mystery.

Reggie cleared his throat. "What will my duties entail, sir? And how did you know I was looking for work?"

"A mutual acquaintance told me of your sincere desire to make a better life for yourself. I decided to hire you unseen. If you do not want the job . . . ."

"Oh, no! I'm grateful."

"Good. I want to train you to run Stone House."

Reggie gasped. "Are you serious? That's a tremendous responsibility . . . and, er, honor, of course."

Morgan kept his gaze outward, closely eyeing the whores who lined the streets in countless numbers. *Good lord,* Reggie thought, *was Morgan out to find himself a girl for his own pleasure?* Reggie certainly hoped he wouldn't be expected to tup one as well. Was it possible Morgan didn't know Reggie's leanings?

"I say, sir, where are we going?"

"We're riding, Reginald. Just riding. May I call you Reginald?"

"Of course, sir. Call me Reggie."

"I'm looking for someone."

"Who?"

"Her name is Minnie."

A favorite? Reggie nearly blurted, but bit his tongue. He forced himself to sit back and appear relaxed, though he was anything but. Perhaps the rumors were accurate. Perhaps Stone House wasn't so much a home for wayward women as it was a harem for this mysterious Midnight Angel. Perhaps that's why he had chosen Reggie. He knew Reggie was nothing more than a street bugger and was, therefore, unlikely to report any exploitation of the Stone House girls.

"You don't trust me, Reggie," Morgan spoke unexpectedly.

The clerk reddened. So this bloke was not only perceptive but a mind reader as well. Reggie began to perspire in earnest. "No, sir, it's not that. I—"

"I don't expect you to trust me yet. But I hope you will believe me when I say you have a great future ahead of you if you work hard. I want to open another branch of Stone House in Southwark, and I can't manage both places. I'll need you to handle the day-to-day details, and perhaps to roam the streets as I do. I know you aren't afraid of the streets."

"No, sir," Reggie said, his jaw jutting. "I'm not afraid of the streets."

And that was saying a lot, for there was a great deal to be frightened of on the darkest streets of London, where the Midnight Angel swooped down to save young girls from a life of hell.

Sophie Parnham shoved open the back door of the Chamberlain Music Hall in the East End during the show's rousing finale. A sullen moon shown down unforgivingly on London's ragged skyline. The fetid breath of progress hung overhead, coughed up from chimneys at nearby coal and match factories. Impervious to the ugly surroundings, the fourteen-year-old girl stepped into the alley at the back of the theater where her mother performed every night.

Sophie savored the relative silence. Here the roar of

laughter and applause faded. No performers could come dashing up to her, crying, "Sophie, help! My costume is falling off!" or "Sophie, Miss Canfield is feeling faint. Get the smelling salts," or "Sophie, we're short of stage hands. Draw the curtain. Now!"

She could hear the audience starting to filter into the streets. All too soon it was time to duck back into the music hall. "So soon," she said on a long sigh and reached for the back door. She was stopped by the sound of a polished, upper-class accent.

"Good evening!" a gray-haired man called out from the end of the alley. He wore a top hat and lifted it in her direction.

Sophie snapped up her head, hot with indignation. He had obviously assumed she was a fallen angel. She grabbed for the door and tugged. It was locked!

"Oh, dear." She bit her lower lip, stealing a nervous glance at the gentleman who would soon be upon her. She yanked on the door, but to no avail. Her knuckles rapped the wooden surface, but it would do little good. No one would hear her above the backstage commotion as the actors prepared to go home.

"Good evening, young miss."

He was so close now that his very proper yet distinctly intimate voice crawled around her shoulders. She shivered and shook it off. "What do you want?" she snapped, still tugging on the door. Sophie had learned to hold her own with men. Her mother had taught her well.

"Are you in distress, my dear?"

She squared off and flashed him warning look. "No, sir. Now kindly leave me alone."

He gave her an approving smile.

"There, there, my dear," the man said in a paternal way. "Don't be afraid. I mean you no harm."

"I'm not afraid." She frowned at the shadows that swathed his face, wishing she could make out his features, then quickly knocked again. "I've been locked out. Someone will open in a moment." When he kept a respectable distance, she relaxed a little. "What are you doing here, sir? The thieves will get you."

"I should ask you the same, my dear. I saw you all alone and thought perhaps you might be lost."

"No, sir. I work here at the theater." Sophie pushed back a stray tendril of her crimped blond hair. "I was simply out for a bit of air."

"Ah, did I see you onstage?"

"No, sir. I help with the costumes."

"What is your name, child?"

"Miss Sophie Parnham."

"And who are your parents? Do they know you're all alone on the dangerous streets of London?"

Such personal questions made her uncomfortable, but his concern seemed genuine. "I'm an orphan. But I assure you, sir, I can take care of myself."

"I have no doubt, child, but I'm sure if your parents were alive they would tell you that a proper young girl should not be out alone. There are all manner of pickpockets, thieves, and kidnappers about on a night like this, as you just pointed out."

"I'll be safe." She turned to the door and banged again. "Someone will hear me and let me in. Please, sir, go now."

"As you wish, my dear. And may I say the show was marvelous." He held out a small bouquet of flowers she didn't at first recognize. "It's mistletoe. Go on. Take it."

"Mistletoe!" She reached out for the prize. She'd never seen the plant in bloom. She'd only seen it in winter, with round, white berries and misty green leaves. Her mother had always hung it at Christmas.

She started to hand the bouquet back, but he waved a white glove. "No, no. They're yours, my dear. A gift. I want nothing in return." He touched the same glove to the brim of his top hat and gave her a respectful nod, then turned and strolled away. She watched him retreat down the damp alley and disappear around the corner.

"Open up!" She shouted again, this time banging on the door as if to wake the dead. "It's me! Soph—"

The last syllable of her name never left her lips, for someone had grabbed her from behind.

"Come on, luv," said a coarse voice. An arm wrenched her around the middle, while a hand clamped over her mouth. Her assailant pulled her against his vile-smelling, emaciated body. "If ye know what's bloody good fer ye, ye'll keep real quiet, hear?"

Sophie immediately went limp.

"There ye go. Yer a smart one. Now coom wit me."

When he began to drag her down the alley, she sunk her teeth into his fingers. He jerked his hand from her mouth with a snarled oath. She screamed, but the cries were swallowed by the sounds of the streets. Writhing in his steely grip, she kicked backward, but he held fast, amazingly strong for one so thin. Sophie knew with growing dread that the gentleman she'd just met had spoken truly. The streets were full of pickpockets and thieves. And worst of all—kidnappers.

Not very far away, Reggie and his new employer rode in uncomfortable silence until Mr. Morgan rammed his lion-headed walking stick into the ceiling twice. The coachman immediately shouted an order to the horse, and the carriage slowed. They finally stopped in a mushroom of mist that swirled on the cobblestone pavement in front of a seedy pub called The Queens Head. A paunchy tart with garishly dyed red hair came slinking from the shadows.

"If it ain't the Midnight Angel hisself," she said, approaching the open carriage door. "'Elloo, Mr. Morgan."

"Good evening, Minnie. How are you, old girl?"

The tart gave him a cynical look. "I'm still kickin', ain't I?" She smiled seductively, flashing him a row of rotten teeth. "When ye goin' to take me to yer harem, Mr. Morgan?

That's whot that Stone House is, ain't it? I'm ready for a good tuppin'."

Morgan smiled. "Get in, Minnie. I'll take you there now."

Reggie tugged at his collar, where sweat had pooled uncomfortably, soaking his threadbare cravat. His mind ran wild. What if Morgan had his way with this disgusting creature here in the carriage, as some sort of perverse initiation rite for his new employee? The clerk simply couldn't accept that a gentleman like this would spend his own money to help outcasts, to try to genuinely reform them, just for the moral satisfaction. What did the Midnight Angel get out of this? Why would he bother with a worn-out old hag such as Minnie? Surely she was beyond reform.

Minnie gripped the doorway and hoisted herself in. Instead of taking the seat opposite the men, she plunged down between them. Reggie took one look at her creped and sagging bosom and nearly lost his supper. She had to be fifty years old. Shivering with revulsion, he pitched himself forward to the opposite seat, watching in amazement as the Midnight Angel put his hand on Minnie's knee, not with lust, but with compassion.

"It's time to stop this way of life, Minnie," Morgan said gently. "You know I usually come after the young girls, the ones who haven't wasted a lifetime already, but there is still time for you to rest. Try something new."

Reggie squinted in the shadows to see what sort of a man could speak so kindly outside the boudoir, and to such a haggard soul. He felt guilty for fearing the worst about his new employer. Clearly, Morgan cared a great deal about the women he rescued. For a moment, Reggie thought the old whore would agree. Then she snorted with cynical laughter and eyed him with a practiced leer.

"Ye want me to take yer young fellar there?" Minnie said, then winked at Reggie. "Wants to watch? Or I'll take ye both at th' same time? I can do it fer the right coin."

"No, thank you," Reggie blurted, then let out a nervous laugh that sounded nearly hysterical.

"I'm taking you to Stone House," Morgan said, his kind eyes never wavering from Minnie's. "You can't do this anymore, old girl. I have a friend who will take care of you. Her name is Mrs. Cromwell. She could use your help with the younger girls."

Minnie's eyes hardened. "I ain't no bloody charity case. I ain't never asked fer a quid I didn't earn fair enough layin' on me back. Why would I want 'elp now from the likes o' you, Mr. Morgan?"

"Because I know what happened," he said so softly that Reggie could scarcely hear.

"Ye know what?" Minnie spat defiantly.

"I know your daughter's dead. I know Lollie was beaten to death by a customer last week. A man you had procured for her. She was only sixteen. Too young for such a life, Minnie. And too young to die."

Minnie's bitter glare dissolved into tears. She covered her face, and her upper body shook as piteous sobs filled the cabin. "I shoulda killed 'er meself when she was born! I shoulda, before any bleedin' bloke could end 'er life with the 'ead a 'is walkin' stick! Then me own 'eart wouldn't be tore outta me chest now. Oh, Lollie! Me darlin' Lollie!"

By now the carriage had drawn up in front of a converted factory building. A painted sign that read "Stone House" hung over an arched entrance.

"Escort Minnie in, won't you, Reggie? Mrs. Cromwell will take care of her."

Reggie reached out and found himself helping the weeping whore from the carriage with more ease and skill than he knew he possessed.

Later that night Reggie went home with a peculiar sense of satisfaction. He had genuinely helped someone, and it felt good. And he concluded that Mr. Morgan was unquestionably a gentleman. It would be some time before Reggie realized just how wrong he was.

* * *

At one in the morning, Morgan's carriage pulled up in the alley beside Beaumont House on the Strand. The gray stone palladium mansion had been in the Earl of Beaumont's family for several generations. To call it magnificent would have been an understatement.

Morgan took his circumstances in stride. Stepping out of the carriage, he tipped his hat in thanks to his driver and the carriage rolled away toward the carriage house. Morgan looked both left and right in the mist-shrouded cobblestone alley, then entered through a small door that took three keys to open. He slipped up a narrow and dark staircase three flights until he reached yet another door. This time all he had to do was knock.

"Mr. Morgan," came a gentle voice. "Is that you?"

"Yes."

The door creaked open, and Morgan blinked against the sudden light from gas lamps lining the richly appointed dressing room.

"Come in, come in," said Colette with a warm smile and obvious relief. The sixty-year-old maid motioned him in. She looked tired.

"I shouldn't keep you waiting up on nights like this, Colette."

"I wouldn't have it any other way. I'd worry about you if I didn't see you were back safely after your sojourns."

Morgan shrugged off his coat, handing it to the stooped maid, and frowned down at her white mobcap. "You still seem worried. Is something amiss?"

She didn't seem to hear the question as she straightened the coat and slipped it into the bureau.

"Colette? Is something wrong?"

When she turned abruptly and smiled again, it seemed forced. "No, no, I'm very well. Off with your waistcoat now. Did you rescue any lucky young girls?"

"No young ones tonight." Morgan unfastened his shirt

and cufflinks, then pulled off the white starched linen. "Though I did take an old tart off the streets. Poor thing. Lost her daughter recently."

"I vow, if there were more like you, the world would be a better place."

"Perhaps." Morgan had been haunting the streets for nearly five years, and instead of seeing a decrease in the number of young girls who resorted to prostitution, it seemed the number had multiplied tenfold.

"Up with your arms, if you please." Colette nudged under Morgan's bare upper arms and unfastened a pin that held in place the end of a long roll of bandage material. The maid tugged at it, then reached for the end around Morgan's backside. As she slowly unwound the binding, Colette watched as her employer's full and ripe pear-shape breasts rose up in freedom, the nipples hardening in the cool air.

"There you are, Mr. Morgan." Colette winked conspiratorially. "You're a woman again. Feels better now, does it not?"

"Yes, it does," Lydia replied. With a shiver of relief, she shrugged off the last invisible vestiges of her secret alter-identity.

"Unfortunately, you must dress again."

Lydia looked at her in surprise. "Now? Why?"

Colette frowned. "I didn't want to say anything, but of course I must. Sir Todd and Lady Leach are waiting along with your husband in the library."

"At this hour? Something terrible must have happened." She gave her maid a penetrating look. "What is it?"

"Miss Louise Canfield is here as well." The maid's look was guarded. "They've all been waiting for you."

"Louise Canfield? You mean the actress?"

Colette nodded. She wasn't telling Lydia everything she knew, and Lydia wouldn't force her to be indiscreet. Colette and Henry Armitage had been serving Lydia's husband, the Earl of Beaumont, for thirty years. They knew more about Beau than Lydia did.

"Well, I suppose I must go and find out what is amiss."

Lydia tapped her foot and tried to guess what news awaited her while Colette retrieved her corset. She would have to exchange one form of constraint for another. It was just as well. No matter how reckless and brave she was while conducting her late-night assignations as the Midnight Angel, she simply would not feel comfortable in a woman's dress without a corset. She held up her arms as Colette fit the stiffened material beneath her breasts and laced up the backside.

Lydia examined herself in the full-length beveled mirror. Her thin figure would be boyish except for her sensuously full breasts, which now pooled atop the half-moon cups of her corset. She smoothed her left hand over her short black hair, which she'd slicked straight back from her forehead to her nape with a generous dose of maccassar oil. The sleek lines made her high cheeks seem like precipices, and her mouth appeared fuller and wider than when she dressed appropriately for her sex. Her blue, almost lavender eyes, took in her reflection. She'd spent so much time as Mr. Morgan she scarcely knew who she really was.

"Don't forget the mustache, ma'am," Colette said.

"Oh my, yes." Lydia pulled the false hair from her upper lip with a laugh. "I don't even see it anymore. I certainly don't want to scandalize Sir Todd and Lady Leach by joining them in a dress and mustache." Nor would she want to embarrass herself in front of the famous music hall actress who awaited her in the library.

Colette helped her ladyship into petticoats and a lush cream-colored gown of watered silk. The transformation from Mr. Henry Morgan to Lady Lydia Beaumont was nearly complete. Colette toweled her hair to remove the scented oil, then pinned a fall of Lydia's own hair at the back of her ladyship's head. Last came a squirt of feminine perfume. Finally, the Countess of Beaumont was prepared to receive her visitors.

Chapter 2

By the time Lydia joined the gathering in the earl's library, the fire burned low beneath the ornately carved granite mantel. The clock ticking on its coral-colored surface struck 1:30.

"I'm so sorry you've been waiting," she said, gliding across the dark blue Persian carpet that stretched the length of the oblong room. "I would have been home sooner but a . . . a dear friend is ill and I sat with her until she was better."

"Thank heaven you've arrived," said Clara, accepting the white lie as truth. The trim and primly dressed wife of the barrister Todd Leach had risen as soon as the footman opened the doors. She was now halfway across the room and touching her cheek to Lydia's. "I was worried about you, though obviously your dear husband is used to your gallivanting at all hours of the night." The sharp words were softened by a gentle smile.

"Beaumont trusts my judgment," Lydia said, patting

Clara's shoulder. Then she withdrew from her friend's light embrace and scanned the room. Her husband sat as usual in his wicker wheelchair, his legs stretched out and blanketed. The haunted look in his eyes warned her that something was direly wrong. Clara's husband stood next to him near a chair by the fire. Sir Todd was dapper, plumply handsome, and blond. Normally, he exuded good-natured optimism, but tonight a frown creased his brow. Finally, her gaze settled on the object of her curiosity—the actress.

"My dear," Lydia's husband said, holding out a hand and drawing away her scrutiny.

"Good evening, darling." She kissed his forehead, feeling self-conscious about it for the first time. From the sofa, Louise Canfield watched the tableau with discerning green eyes. She wore a low-cut bodice, which displayed ample breasts, a sparkling emerald necklace, and a dashing cap of lime green feathers. In contrast, her red hair, which looked to be dyed, framed her pale complexion dramatically.

"My dearest," said Lord Beaumont, "allow me to introduce you to Miss Louise Canfield."

Lydia smiled warmly. "It is a pleasure, Miss Canfield."

"Likewise, Lady Beaumont. Though I regret the circumstances."

"What has happened?" Lydia looked from one to the other.

Everyone appeared uncomfortable, refusing to return her gaze. Beaumont could not have done so even if he'd wanted to. Her fifty-five-year-old husband had been blind for two years. He was a handsome, silver-haired rake who had only recently begun to show his age.

"My daughter has been kidnapped," Louise said. She spoke in a throaty, rich manner, as one might expect of a veteran performer. She was clearly used to taking command of the stage, for she had riveted everyone in the room without so much as the flick of a feather boa or a stage prop. "She's gone, and I am desperate to get her back."

"I'm very sorry," Lydia replied, perplexed, sensing the

undercurrents of tension in the room. She took a seat on an ottoman next to Beaumont. "How did it happen?"

Louise explained how Sophie had been abducted from behind the Chamberlain Music Hall earlier that evening. By the time she had finished her tale, Lydia felt ill. She knew better than most what dangers Sophie would face on the streets. And Lydia was more than willing to help search for the child. Was that why Louise Canfield had come here? Did she know this was where the Midnight Angel began and ended every nightly sojourn?

"How may we assist you, Miss Canfield? Lord Beaumont and I understand your distress and will help in any way possible."

The actress smiled, but it was clearly a stalling measure. Her lovely, catlike eyes fluttered in a moment of uncomfortable silence. Then she looked to Beaumont with a familiarity that startled Lydia.

"My dear," he said, squeezing his wife's hand. "I will not mince words. You and I have always been forthright in our dealings with each other. Louise's daughter is also my daughter."

It took a moment for the words to register. Then Lydia looked back and forth between her husband and the actress with dawning understanding. "Oh. I see."

"Louise and I were . . . friends . . . many years ago. I did not know that our association had resulted in the birth of a child."

"I never told his lordship about Sophie," Louise said, "because I was fully capable of taking care of her myself."

Lydia vaguely recalled the newspapers printing something about the actress having a very rich, longtime patron who apparently did not mind her infidelities. She could afford to be independent.

"I'm sorry," Beaumont said contritely to Lydia.

"Don't be, darling. I am happy for you." And she was. She wanted him to have the comfort of knowing he'd left descendants. But the notion took a moment to absorb. It always surprised her when she heard stories of her husband's legendary affairs. That was because her own relationship with Beau had been entirely platonic for the duration of their five-year marriage. "You have been mourning your lack of an heir. Of course you must acknowledge her at once."

"That's very generous of you, Lady Beaumont." Louise's relief was obvious.

"He can recognize her *if* we can find her," Todd said. He drummed his fingers on the mantel. "It won't be easy. For one, Miss Canfield told everyone that Sophie was an orphan."

Lydia shot the actress a frank look of censure.

"I did not want the sting of illegitimacy to touch Sophie. And . . . ." She sighed, meeting Lady Beaumont's eyes with a hint of defensiveness as she added, "I had my career to consider. You do not know how difficult it is for an actress to retain her following. Sophie knows she is my daughter, but I instructed her to tell everyone she was orphaned. I treated her like a beloved niece. She's been my right hand. Everyone at the Chamberlain depends on her. We've been saving to buy our own music hall one day. I wanted her to run the show. You have no idea how capable she is." A note of maternal pride crept into her theatrical voice.

"Does she know that Beau is her father?" Lydia asked.

Louise shook her head and cast her eyes downward. "Sophie is a very perceptive child. She suspects her father was one of my gentlemen admirers, but I've told her nothing. A young girl tends to fantasize about such things, and I did not want her hurt." She glanced at Beau, who remained silent. "I was afraid Beau—rather, his lordship— would either reject her entirely or take her away from me." She turned to Lydia once more. "She knows that I wished to keep her by my side and that I love her very much."

"Thank goodness for that," Lydia said with a sigh. "Well, the search must begin at once. But where shall we start?"

Todd smiled encouragingly. "I believe I know. You've heard of the great Lord Clue?"

Clara's eyes lit up. "Do you think he'd be willing to help?"

"I believe he might."

"Lord Clue?" Lydia's voice rang with dismay. "Isn't that . . . ?"

"Lord Montgomery," Todd said. When Lydia turned a faint shade of green, he added, "Do you know him?"

She swallowed hard. "No. I've never had the pleasure." *Only the pain,* she thought. And the pain apparently was not yet over.

S̲ir Todd Leach looked resentfully out his carriage window as his coachman turned down one of the narrow streets in that seedy, forbidden brick forest of the East End known as Limehouse.

"Wait for me," Todd told his coachman. "I won't be long."

He had searched for Montgomery all day in respectable places—in the nobleman's bachelor apartments, in the clubs, at Scotland Yard. Montgomery's man, Pierpont, had been unusually tight-lipped about his employer's whereabouts. And so Todd had assumed the worst. He'd waited until an appropriately late hour before coming to the den. He crossed the rain-slicked cobblestones to a raw brick building that wore a subterranean stairwell like a jagged scar. The steps were dangerously uneven.

"Into the bowels of the earth," he muttered, catching a handrail when his expensive leather shoes slipped on the treacherous steps.

At the first whiff of the murky, pungent odor of opium, Todd shortened his breath and frowned deeper. What a bloody fool Hugh Montgomery was, especially for such a brilliant man. He had given up on something in life, Todd was sure of it. Why else would he seek comfort here?

Montgomery was twenty-nine years old and strikingly tall, dark, and handsome in a subtle way, as Clara had once quietly but significantly observed. He possessed extraordinary deductive reasoning, which led the commissioner of Scotland Yard to grudgingly turn to him for help on difficult cases. He was a brilliant writer, and his series of books, *Observations on Criminology,* were consumed by readers as avidly as if they were novels. The only area to which he seemed unable to apply his exceptional mind was his personal life.

Hugh Montgomery was bored with his own fame, oblivious to the women who practically threw themselves at his feet, and ignorant of the fact that whatever long ago pain had obliterated his aspirations for love should be put to rest. He was beyond common sense, which lasting love required. Yet it was his uncommon sensibility that enabled him to sort out details ordinary men could not quite grasp.

Todd suspected that the void in Montgomery's life led him over and over to this opium den. Thus far he had been able to control the drug. It was an escape, a forbidden pleasure, but how long would it be before the drug controlled him? Todd had seen that happen all too often.

Montgomery claimed that his tinctures of laudanum, taken in the privacy of his home, killed the pain from an old injury, and the occasional puff from the golden bowl here in Limehouse merely sharpened his logic. Todd was waiting for his friend to realize that quite the opposite was true. Although there might be an hour or two of clarity and contentment, eventually opium would only dull the amateur sleuth's keen sense of discernment.

"Pipe, sir? Pipe?" The Chinese proprietor called out in a jarring voice. All around them men with sallow, yellow complexions and unfocused eyes mumbled about the visions only they could see. Some twitched with the need for another lungful of the drug. Others sat suspended in time and motion, blissfully enjoying hours of oblivion. Only the man who owned the place, who wore a bright red oriental robe and a long black braid, was clear-headed as he repeated "Pipe?" with incongruous cheer.

"No, thank you." Todd walked past him, searching every nook, every tossed pillow in the dark pockets of the opium hive for signs of Montgomery. When Todd saw two long well-dressed legs stretched out from behind a doorway, he sighed with relief.

"Monty, is that you?" Todd widened his stride but stopped abruptly when a blood-curdling cry broke the torpor of the room.

"Help! They're all over me!" A bald man in a crumpled suit ran past him with horror etched on his pasty face. He brushed frantically at his sleeves. "Get them off! Scorpions! Get them off!"

There was nothing, of course. Nothing but a drug-induced hallucination. Todd shook his head sadly.

"Here, here, sir. Relax. Relax," the proprietor said calmly. He smiled broadly and handed the man a pipe. A circle of red fire glowed in the shadows between the men. The bald man stopped screaming.

Todd proceeded. He brushed aside the curtain shielding the doorway and stepped over the long legs he'd seen. "Monty?"

He twisted around and saw Viscount Montgomery sitting upright with his back against the wall below a flickering gasolier. He appeared alert, and there was no sign of lost control, except for his open collar and absent tie. He looked up at Todd with his usual dimpled half-smirk. The barrister blinked in self-doubt. Was the viscount engaged in some sort of undercover investigation? If so, Todd would have to withhold the lecture he'd been rehearsing for the last several hours.

"Toddy," Viscount Montgomery said, "I'm surprised to see you here, old boy. I would have thought better of you."

Todd's amiable mouth compressed to a sliver. "I'm not here to indulge in this vile habit, and you know it."

Hugh let out a long, slow sigh. His broad shoulders rose and fell languorously, and Todd would warrant he had been under the influence earlier in the evening. He had an uncanny ability to bounce back, owing to his remarkable physique.

Hugh was taller than most, very erect of posture, with the strength of an athlete, but the grace of an intellectual. His jaw was square, his straight brown hair was thick as a hedge. He had a narrow waist and lean hips. Todd was far more the sportsman than Montgomery, but little good it did him. He had always suffered from plumpness and was, frankly, envious of his friend's exceptional good looks.

"Get up, you spoiled lout," Todd muttered. "You've wasted every God-given gift with which you were born. With your bearing and breeding and mind I would have been prime minister by now, as you well might have been. But here you sit, indulging in a drug that has ruined more great men than I care to think about. Your mind is still intact, I pray, because it's needed tonight."

Hugh leveled an interested gaze at his friend. "What has happened?"

Hugh did not protest when Todd seized his arms and began to hoist him up. The viscount lifted his long, strong legs and stood unsteadily, staggering against the bare brick wall. In the light of the lamp, which hissed mightily for very little light, Todd could see the pinpoint pupils in Hugh's stormy azure eyes. Yes, he'd been partaking of opium.

"Are you capable of making any sense of a case on which I desperately need help?"

Hugh leaned his head against the wall and pursed his lips. "I believe so."

"Good."

"But I don't want another case," he added petulantly.

Todd nodded. Hugh took every investigation to heart. Although Scotland Yard detectives could treat their successes and failures as part of the job, Lord Montgomery could not. The only reason he continued to help solve difficult cases was because he was good at it—most of the time—and because it seemed to him that so little justice was done in the world. What little he might add would perhaps be his only contribution to society, so to fail at such a purpose was painful.

Todd had learned all this about his old friend after dealing in the courtroom with evidence procured by the famous Lord Clue. As a barrister, Todd had more than a passing familiarity with crimes and criminals. He understood the weaknesses of Scotland Yard detectives, who were more bound to that venerable institution than to any particular case. He knew that his best hope of finding the Earl of Beaumont's illegitimate daughter lay in the labyrinth of Hugh Montgomery's mind.

"We need your help, old chap," Todd said, propping up Hugh when he began to slide down the wall. A stubble of day-old beard shadowed his bloodless complexion. Todd cursed, persevering, "We're looking for a girl."

Hugh's eyes narrowed. "What girl?"

"The illegitimate daughter of Louise Canfield and Lord Beaumont. She's been kidnapped."

His interest now piqued, Hugh asked, "When?"

Todd shared the details with him. By the time he finished, he knew he had Hugh in the palm of his hand. Lord Clue couldn't resist righting an injustice, even though he acted as if he might. But Todd had yet to deliver the *coup de grâce*. "She's fourteen years old, Monty," he said, raising his brows provocatively. *"Fourteen."*

Hugh shut his eyes and grimaced. "I see."

Todd knew this wasn't fighting fair. Over the years, he'd learned much about his friend after too many glasses of wine. And he'd learned during inebriated circumstances about a case that haunted Hugh still. It had involved the daughter of one of his father's servants, a fourteen-year-old girl who had been found dead at the bottom of a cliff that bordered their property. Hugh had been a mere twelve years old, and the mysterious tragedy had left an enduring impression. It was one of the reasons he had studied criminal case histories, which had led to his books on the subject.

"She's fourteen?" Hugh said, straightening to his full height. He slipped out of his lethargy with a stretch of his neck and drew back his shoulders. "Then we must go."

When a flush of color returned to the viscount's face, Todd sighed with relief, then braced himself for the insult that undoubtedly would follow.

Hugh made an attempt to straighten his collar then glared down at his shorter friend with one arched brow. "Come along, Leach. We can't tarry here all night. If only you wouldn't waste yourself in these dens of debauchery."

L ydia looked out one of two long windows that faced the street in her husband's study. The gold tassels dangling from the French-cut maroon velvet curtains nearly brushed the smart pillbox hat that topped her confection of false curls. Any passerby who might glance up would see in the glaring glass the erect and trim form of the dignified Countess of Beaumont. They could not possibly see the dread coiled deep inside her.

"He's here," she said as the carriage rolled to a stop on the pavement below.

"Good," said her husband. "Viscount Montgomery is the best, you know."

She swallowed hard. "Yes, I know."

"I am aware that this is hard for you, darling."

Her eyes fluttered against the sting of tears. Beau had always understood her. His love had always cocooned her, made her feel warm and safe. It had almost even succeeded in making her feel pure again. But nothing could quite do that, and so she had thrown herself into good deeds, into rectifying a very bad world. It was her way of not giving in, of atoning.

"You've always been so kind to me, Beau." She turned from the window, knowing that Lord Montgomery would soon descend from the carriage. She could not bear to watch.

Everything about his planned visit had a surreal quality.

Lord Hugh Montgomery was a stranger to her, and yet he was not. He was the young, earnest man she had known some five years ago, but now he was a famous sleuth. She had seen that morning how her servants bustled about, taking care to ensure that everything was in place, their duties ably fulfilled. Their expressions came alive, and there was more than the usual whispering in the hallways when they thought she was out of sight. They had heard about Lord Clue. All were eager to see him.

It bothered her enormously. She resented him. If only they knew. If only the world really knew what he was like . . . what he had done. But they would learn nothing from her. She could not expose him without ruining herself. And it bothered her that Beau loved her dearly but could not love her in the way that mattered most.

She heard the commotion from the entry hall directly below and retreated to her husband's chaise lounge. She sat on the edge of the red and blue plaid blanket that kept his legs warm. He wore a gold smoking jacket and a pristine white cravat. His cheeks were gaunt, but he was still elegant and handsome. She placed a hand over one of his and squeezed gently.

"You know, Beau, I would not be alive today if it were not for you," she said softly.

"You do not have to be grateful, darling."

"But I am." She was desperate for him to accept this offering. She had never been in love with Beaumont, nor had she pretended to be. Many times she'd wished it were otherwise, but she'd learned long ago the heart is not biddable.

"Lydia," he said, dragging out the word as if he were talking to a recalcitrant child, "don't you know that I would not be alive today either were it not for you?"

A surge of relief shot through her as she realized it was true. She had made his last years on Earth as pleasant as possible. Lord Beaumont was dying of syphilis and had been from the first day they'd met five years earlier. A companionable match was all they could ever have, because consummation would endanger Lydia's life. Beau's health had been declining in recent months, and he did not have long to live. That was another reason why it was important to find Sophie quickly.

"Sir Todd has instructed my solicitor to make Sophie my heir," he said. "Of course, you will retain your dower rights. That will make you one of the wealthiest widows in the country. I hope that is acceptable to you."

"Of course it is." She leaned forward and kissed his cheek. "I'm so happy you have discovered your daughter. I promise you I will take good care of her."

"I know you will."

There was a knock at the door, then the butler appeared. "Sir Todd Leach and Lord Hugh Montgomery are here to see you, sir."

Lydia turned to her husband, biting her lip nervously as she asked, "Are you certain you don't wish to be present when I talk to him?"

Beau smiled, understanding her unease. "We've already discussed this, my dear. You will be fine. I am quite sure of it. Now, go with my blessing."

Squaring her shoulders, Lady Lydia Beaumont went to face her past.

Lydia first approached her own parlor, where she knew Clara awaited her. She was glad that Lady Leach had arrived before her husband. Having Clara at her side would help bolster her courage. Her friend might even keep Lydia from a cold faint once she was finally face to face with Hugh Montgomery.

Oblivious to Lydia's history with Viscount Montgomery, Clara said, "I think you'll be very happy to have him on the case." Arm in arm, the women exited the feminine parlor and traversed the long hall to the main staircase.

"I'm sure I will be," was Lydia's even reply.

"You know he solved the Samurai Slayings."

"Yes."

"Toddy says Scotland Yard detectives could get nowhere with that one."

"I'm sure," Lydia answered woodenly.

"The killer left all his victims near Limehouse," Clara added. "Two of them were quite respectable. He sliced open their abdomens in an L shape, just like a Samurai warrior committing hari-kari."

Lydia shuddered, but said nothing.

"Montgomery discovered that the knife wasn't Japanese at all. It was a very rare Chinese blade. He located the shop where it had been sold and learned that it had been purchased by a baronet from Leeds. He was stark raving mad. And to think that Scotland Yard detectives didn't know there was a difference between Chinese and Japanese swords! They were prepared to arrest a merchant. Without Lord Montgomery's powers of observation, who knows how many more respectable people would have been butchered before the real killer was arrested?"

"Yes, I know all about it, Clara." Lydia paused when they reached the top of the grand staircase. She studied the delicate lace edging on her sleeve, pretending to find a flaw. Anything to delay the inevitable.

"How could you know? You've been such a faithful companion to your husband you never go out in society. When anyone finds out that you are my friend, I'm bombarded with questions about the reclusive Countess of Beaumont."

"I do read the newspapers."

"Oh, of course. I can't wait to meet Lord Clue. He and Sir Todd have been friends for some time, but, like you, he keeps to himself. He's rather obsessed with finding justice, I gather."

"How interesting," was Lydia's ironic reply. "Let us get this over with."

Clara gave her a strange look but followed her down the stairs.

Chapter 3

✤

The first thing Hugh noticed was her voice.

He had been admiring a clock on the mantel, letting the soft ticking lull him momentarily. It was an ornate and bronze ebony clock in which the actual timepiece stood over a sculpture of doors that served as backdrop to a bronzed figure playing the piano. He had just noticed a tiny chip in the surface when he heard her talking in the hall. It was like something out of a dream.

He shut his eyes, thinking he had not shaken the effects of opium or that perhaps he had taken too much of his laudanum tincture that morning. He rubbed the back of his neck, refusing to turn in search of her. How many times over the last five years had he turned in a crowd, thinking he'd heard that rich, lovely sound? How many times had he canted his head right or left to see around a top hat or bowler, certain he'd seen her profusion of dark curls in a crowd, only to be left with an aching sense of disappointment? He'd loved her long, luxurious hair best.

The voice had come through the door. Whoever it belonged to was approaching the drawing room. But it was not her. That much he knew.

"What a clever clock," Hugh said in an even tone that indicated no particular passion.

"Here they are," Todd said, rising from the settee that faced the double doors, which opened as the women entered.

"It's an Antoine-Andre Raviro French Empire mantel clock," Hugh added, brushing a mote of dust from the tiny piano with a long finger. "The very sort that broke the case of the German clock thief."

"Good to see you, Lady Beaumont. Clara, dear, I'm glad you're here."

"It was a most peculiar case," Hugh continued with his back to the others. "An attaché to the German ambassador had just the week before stolen the piece from Buckingham Palace. I told him as much, and he admitted it there on the spot in the middle of a dinner party."

"And how did you know that particular clock had belonged to the Royal Family?" came that voice again.

Hugh froze. It *was* her voice. Only his head turned to regard her. His breath stopped for an endless moment, then resumed deeply. Very slowly his body pivoted until he faced her fully. *My God, it is her.*

"You're dead," he said bluntly.

Lydia almost laughed. How like him. He had had no more use for her five years ago and so he had presumed her dead. "If only it were that easy, Lord Montgomery. Unfortunately, life is not as black and white as it must be in your world of crime. I am very much alive."

Todd looked from one to the other in confusion. "You've met before?"

"Only briefly," Lydia was quick to answer. "It was a lifetime ago. And then I was not the Countess of Beaumont. How good to see you again, Lord Montgomery."

She held out her hand, daring him to touch it. She prayed he wouldn't, for even now she could feel the charge between them. Hugh hesitated, his handsome face still registering shock.

"Is it really you?" he asked incredulously.

Lydia shrugged and gave Clara a teasing smile. "Do I look like a ghost to you, Lady Leach?"

"No, ma'am, you're very much flesh and blood," Clara returned with a smile.

Lydia felt a momentary stab of guilt when she saw a flash of pain in his eyes. Then he flushed red with an emotion she recognized from their brief time together. Frustration. He hated any sign of failure in his powers of reasoning. And what greater failure than not knowing the woman he had once loved, and ruined, had escaped his detection in his very own society—a society to which she had not belonged as an impoverished governess.

And that, more than anything, probably bothered him the most. The innocent young governess his father had forbidden him to marry was now the Countess of Beaumont and would soon be a wealthy woman in her own right. It seemed strange even to her. She sighed out the tension that had held her stiffly in place.

"I regret that you were unable to find me," she said with a dare in her voice that only he would understand.

A slow, ironic half-smile curved his lips. "Life never ceases to amaze and bewilder me, Lady Beaumont." He sauntered forward, caressed her with his gaze, then reached out for her hand, which was concealed in her skirts.

She could do nothing but allow him to take it without creating a scene. When he pressed his lips to the back of it, a frisson of heat shot up her arm and burned her heart.

"If life baffles you," she managed to say blandly, "then you must understand a great deal about death."

He righted himself and held her gaze captive. "No. I fear even that is beyond me. At least I hope it is for some time to come."

"You are not immortal? I am surprised to hear it."

"I am all too human." His jaw muscles tensed as he

seemed to age a decade before her very eyes, but then he laughed, breaking the spell. "Alas, I am merely mortal, Lady Beaumont. No matter what you might read in the papers. I do not solve every mystery that comes across my path."

She tipped up her chin. "Then what good will you do my husband's daughter?"

"I succeed in most cases and plan to do so with this one. I take an especial interest in the plight of children. I can help you, Lady Beaumont."

Lydia sighed. She had to focus on saving Beau's child, no matter the cost to her emotionally. If Montgomery could find Sophie, then she would have to cooperate with him. "Yes, I believe you can," she replied. "Otherwise, I would never have agreed to meet with you."

She turned away, her heart pounding. Lydia felt as if she'd just averted being crushed by a runaway hansom cab. Had she kept her composure while leaping from harm, only to fall apart after the near miss? She went to a chair as far from him as possible, gripping the back of it for support as she asked, "Would anyone care for any refreshments?"

"No, thank you," Hugh said.

She allowed her gaze to move in his direction. His usual ironic half-smirk had returned. She let out a slow breath of relief. Things would go better now. She could never forget that he had given her up because of their class differences. He would not lose sight of that now that he was beyond the impetuosity of youth.

Todd still eyed them curiously but took his cue. "Well, since you know each other, let's dispense with the formalities. Perhaps we should discuss the details of the case."

"Excellent idea," Clara said, taking a chair beside Lydia.

Todd presented all the information they had. Hugh listened carefully. He had returned to the mantel and leaned on it casually with one elbow, stroking his chin with a thumb as he took it in. He asked a number of questions:

What time of night precisely was she taken? Were there any witnesses? Had they been interviewed? What was Sophie's relationship with her mother like? It wasn't until he asked about the child's relationship with her father that Lydia stood up.

"My husband did not know he had a daughter until her mother came to tell him of her disappearance."

Hugh had begun to pace. He stopped and regarded her analytically. "He was not embarrassed by this?"

"No, he was happy to find out that he had a child. Beau has always been an unconventional man. He appreciates women, and I believe he would be just as proud of a daughter as a son, and just as accepting of a natural child as one legitimate. He would like to meet with you, but he is very ill. I will take you to his room if you'd like, but you cannot stay long."

Hugh met briefly and uneventfully with Beaumont, then left. Much later, Lydia went to her husband's room to say goodnight. When she bent down to kiss his forehead, he felt for her hand and gently tugged her down beside him. She often sat at his bedside in this way, recounting the day's events. This time, however, her heart was in her throat and she wasn't sure she could speak.

"How bad was it, darling?" he said, still holding her hand.

She swallowed hard, willing back her tears. "Very bad."

He couldn't look directly at her, but he moved his head in the direction of her voice, which had carried an unusual tremor. "Do you still feel . . . ?"

She nodded, knowing he couldn't see the affirmation. *Yes, I still love him. Yes, my entire body still hums when he enters the room.* "It will be difficult to work with him."

"You don't have to. There are other investigators. We could call in Scotland Yard. However, I once publicly criticized the Criminal Investigation Division, so I doubt the director would put the Special Branch on the case. No less is needed."

"No one will be as thorough as Lord Clue."

"You are such a brave young woman."

"No. Just determined. My feelings no longer matter. I had my chance. Now we have to make sure that Sophie has hers as well. Montgomery offers our best hope, Beau. I know it. I've seen him at work. If anyone can find her, it's him."

Beaumont nodded, clearly ambivalent. "Very well, my darling. But if at any point you change your mind, say so. I don't want you hurt anymore than you have been."

She chuckled jadedly. "I don't think I have those kind of feelings anymore."

"There you are wrong," he said gently. "As time will tell."

Lydia kissed him again, and his words weighing heavily on her mind as she retired to her private parlor. On a whim, she pulled from the locked drawer in her small partners desk an object she had not looked at in five years. Her diary. Opening its flowery cover, she felt as she had when she'd opened the door to the drawing room during Hugh's visit earlier in the day—amazed at the feelings that lingered like ghosts somewhere between heaven and hell. Silently, she began to read.

April 3, 1875

I met the most amazing gentleman today. Though the word *met* seems wholly inadequate, considering the death defying circumstances.

He is Lord Hugh Montgomery. He is my charge's older brother. He must be about my age, four and twenty. So little has been said of him during my first month here at Windhaven, I had begun to wonder if he really existed.

I'd seen his portrait in the gallery. In it he appeared regal and arrogant, like a French nobleman in King Louis XIV's court. I see now it was the fancy of the artist, perhaps executed on the instruction of Lord Montgomery's father, the earl. I can well imagine the dignified, gray-haired Earl of Boxley might want as a son the kind of man shown in the painting. But Viscount Montgomery is far more unique.

I found him strolling through a grove of oaks that stopped just short of a steep ravine at a high point called Devil's Peak at the edge of the estate. I had a day off, as his sister Katherine had gone into London with her father. I hadn't realized how far I'd wandered until I came to the rocky edge of the precipice. I looked down at the jagged trees that grew from the outcropping and then at the clusters of greenery that looked like tufts of emerald cotton far below. It was a monstrous drop-off, and the thought of falling made me queasy.

"Be careful!" he shouted.

I nearly jumped, then caught myself from falling backward. My heart plummeted to my stomach. I whirled around and shaded my eyes from the bright spring sunshine. And there he stood. He wore a tweed coat cut to his knees and brown boots. His tie was loose, and his thick brown hair was bare. He had a squarely cut jaw and patrician nose. All in all, he was as handsome as the rakes I'd read about in novels.

He was a rugged gentleman. A practical genius. These are thoughts that came later. Then I was so struck by his presence that I merely gaped at him, dumbfounded.

"Step away from that cliff," he ordered curtly.

He took a few steps out from the grove, clearly irritated that I had interrupted his contemplation. His distinctive black brows wedged together impatiently beneath the shock of hair that fell haplessly over his forehead. He was badly in need of a haircut.

"I said get away from that cliff!"

For some reason I cannot now fathom, I was rooted to the spot. The wind whipped threateningly around my skirts, flapping the light rose cotton like a sail at sea. An impetuous gust whipped over the treetops and burst against me. I swayed backward but caught my balance with a toe-step forward.

"For God's sake!" he cried out. His body went rigid, then he bolted toward me. "Do you want to kill yourself?"

Irrationally, I was more afraid of him than I was of the wind, which still threatened to toss me over the edge.

"I'm sorry," I mumbled.

"Don't be sorry!" he answered impatiently, striding stiffly toward me.

I saw the fury in his stormy eyes, and even though he was a young man, there was something paternal about him. I no longer feared him, but feared disappointing him. And then—oh, Lord, why?—he reached out to grab me and I stepped back, like the good and modest daughter of a simple country vicar I was.

My heel slipped over the sharp edge of slate. I tried to jump forward, but the slate crumbled beneath my foot. Pieces thudded down the side of the cliff, then tumbled silently to the treetops far below. My frown melted into blind panic, which I saw reflected in his whitened face. His impatience turned to dread, then instantly transformed into determination.

"Take my hand!" he bit out.

When I offered it, he clasped my wrist painfully. But before he could pull me to safety, the edge of the cliff cut out beneath me. I dropped like deadweight and screamed. I thought we would both plunge to our deaths. But he grunted, then slammed into the ground, chest down. He still held my wrist, stopping my fall.

Pain shot through my shoulder, then came more pain when my body slammed against the side of the jagged cliff.

"Help!" I cried out when my breath returned.

"Don't panic," he ordered through gritted teeth. Clearly, he was using every bit of his considerable strength to keep me from plunging to my death. "You must find a place to climb. Put your feet against the rock and push yourself up."

My feet scrabbled against the exposed rock. "There is no place to—ah, there!" I'd found a crevice, and it felt like one in which a sapling had taken rocky root. There were a few jutting edges about twenty feet below a plateau or rock. Other than that, there was nothing between me and certain death. "I've got it!"

"Now push up." He began to inch backward away from the ledge, pulling as he went. Together we managed to get me to safety. He pulled me close, and I clutched him like a kitten with her claws embedded in his sleeves. I don't know how to explain what happened next. When he tried to move us farther from the ledge, the ground suddenly crumbled again, this time beneath Lord Montgomery. He shoved me back as he disappeared over the edge, his face a mask of grim, ironic resignation.

"No!" I cried out, reaching for him. It was too late. Down he went.

There is so much to relay about what transpired next. I'll mention only the most important points from here on. Lord Montgomery landed twenty feet below on that narrow plateau I'd glimpsed while dangling over the edge. It had brutally stopped his fall. His head was bleeding badly. I could see he was unconscious. Instinctively, I knew there was not enough time to run back to the house for help. I had no choice but to go after him. Overcoming my fear of heights, I found a place to lower myself by clinging to the roots of small trees growing from the rock.

When I reached him, I pressed myself against the cliff and pulled his bleeding head into my lap. "My lord, I'm so sorry."

He stirred then and gripped one of my arms, squeezing hard. *Not to worry*. I knew that's what he meant with that touch. I inwardly vowed then I would not let him die.

I ripped my petticoats into a swath of bandage and wrapped it snugly around his bleeding head. In the brief moment I took to catch my breath before climbing back up the precipice for help, I felt a rare exultation. I had heroically saved a man who was a hero himself.

APRIL 6, 1875

Lord Montgomery is recovering nicely from his fall. The doctor said he had a concussion, but nothing was permanently damaged. Apparently ready for visitors, he sent for me today as I'd hoped he would.

I arrived in the earl's study and found his heir stretched out on a chaise, dressed in a charcoal smoking jacket, his legs covered in a blanket. A white bandage swathed his head. He looked rather like a Saracen.

"You're staring, Miss Parker," Viscount Montgomery said, looking up from a book with a mildly tart expression. This apparently was his usual manner, and though I had expected something more in the nature of a recovering invalid, I took it in stride. After what we'd been through together, I felt as if we were blood brother and sister.

"Your bandage, it makes you look . . ." My voice trailed away. It was not the place of a governess to remark on her superior's appearance. But my brush with death made such social rules seem superfluous. Were there class distinctions in the afterlife? "You look rather dashing. Like a hero of the Crimean War."

His expression remained impassive. Then a glimmer of humor lit his eyes. "I'm glad you can find something to admire in my state of disability."

"I'm glad to hear you are expected to make a full recovery."

He made a moue of distaste. "Don't just stand there like a housemaid. Come closer. Take a seat. I want to see how you fared."

I blushed a little at the prospect of being examined, but not as much as I would have before our mishap. I went closer to the chaise and sat in an upright chair. "I'm quite well, thanks to you, sir."

"You're a foolish woman," he pronounced. Then he smiled ever so slightly. "A very brave and foolish woman."

"And you're a foolish man for bothering to save me," I said, volleying the ball back into his court.

He stared a moment. Then frowned. I suspect he'd never heard a governess speak so boldly. I held my breath, fearing I had stepped over a cliff of another sort.

"Will you have supper with me tonight, Miss Parker?"

It was a surprise return volley, and with it he won the game. My eyes widened in amazement. "Yes," I stammered with a glorious smile. "Yes, I will."

April 12, 1875

I haven't written in days. That's because Hugh—. I just caught myself putting that familiar name in writing! There. Anyone who reads this will know what a fool I am. When we are alone—never in front of servants, of course—I call him Hugh and he calls me Addie. I know it's incredible. To Christian name each other is scandalous! But it is different with us, is it not? We literally saved each others' lives. I feel as if I know Hugh better than anyone else in the world, and he me.

We've been very discreet with this new, intense friendship. But I fear that the tie that binds is visible to others. When we are together, it is as if there is a wall cocooning us, shutting out everyone else. I am not aware of acting differently in his presence, but I must be, for I have seen Mrs. Bertram, the housekeeper, skulking around with more than her usual frowns. I know she suspects something. If nothing else, she certainly frowns on the time we spend alone together. No decent woman would act as I have.

Am I decent? I no longer know or care. That near plunge to my death has changed everything. What if I were to die tomorrow? Would I have ever lived? With Hugh, I feel as if I'm alive for the first time. And oh how I want to live life to its fullest!

Lydia closed the diary. The wounds of the past bled anew in her heart. Her chest literally ached. She had indeed lived fully. But what a painful life it had been. Yes, Hugh Montgomery had saved her life, but he had later nearly killed her. Then it was Beaumont's role to rescue her. Rescuer seemed to be the role men played in her life.

She could scarcely remember what circumstances had sealed their fates. The accident at Devil's Peak had started it all. But there were other things that drew them together. He had confided his lifelong fascination with criminology and that he had published a book on the subject at the age of twenty.

That had impressed Lydia enormously, and her esteem had bound him to her. His father disapproved of his intellectual pursuits even though Hugh enjoyed, even then, a growing reputation in criminal investigations. But there had been little personal gratification in his successes. Until Lydia, or Addie as he knew her then, had spoken enthusiastically about them. She had been important to him.

He had loved her once. She had to believe that, or all the mistakes she had made afterward would be unforgivable, and she would not be able to work with him to find Sophie. She had known him so well then. Did she still? There was only one way to find out . . . if she had the courage.

Chapter 4

❦

"I'm here to see Lord Montgomery," Lydia said when she arrived at his rooms. She gave her card to a man who introduced himself as "Pierpont, his lordship's man." She hoped he didn't notice that her hand trembled. He glanced at the script, then met her with neutral eyes, nodding.

"Very good, ma'am. Please take a seat here." He indicated a scarlet-colored divan poised by a slate hearth. The sofa was the only surface that appeared to be clear of clutter. Books, periodicals, and papers were strewn about as if a strong wind had jumbled them all together.

Lydia frowned at the mess. Such disarray must be the natural outcome of Montgomery's single-minded attention to work. Was it possible he hadn't changed that much after all? Apparently not, for the stern-looking, balding gray employee, whose right brow rose triangularly over a jaundiced eye, followed her gaze and sighed heavily. Lydia could well imagine why. Viscount Montgomery could afford to have a fleet of servants, but he liked solitude, and his man very likely had taken on many roles to serve his eccentric master.

"Forgive the disarray, ma'am. His lordship is working on a case."

"Just one?" she inquired, the corners of her mouth lilting upward.

She thought she saw his lips twitch with an aborted smile. He regarded her more carefully. "No, that would make my life much too simple. I'll send in some tea, ma'am. His lordship will be just a moment, I pray."

"Thank you." She relaxed when Pierpont departed. He seemed to have a great deal of insight regarding his employer. He must be as much a companion to Hugh as an employee. How odd to think that he knew Hugh Montgomery far better than she. Their encounter had been so long ago, and she needed to know what kind of man the viscount had become.

She glanced around his chosen environment. It was obviously a small apartment, consisting of few rooms. This area was richly appointed with Persian carpets and flocked wallpaper. Mahogany antiques and exotic porcelains accented the heavy masculine furniture. Because it was the only drawing room, it served a dual purpose as a study.

She circled around a globe stand to examine a bookshelf filled with leather-bound volumes—Dickens, Trollope, Shakespeare, and Plato. He had read them all, she knew. Then she spotted a row of Montgomery's own work. There were four new volumes. He had been busy since she'd last seen him. She couldn't help but be impressed, and her chest flushed with a peculiar mixture of pride and resentment. There were eight books altogether bearing his name. She'd studiously avoided reading articles about him in the newspapers and society columns, so she was surprised by how prolific he had become. But she shouldn't be, she realized. His life had gone on after her. Had there ever been any doubt of that?

She reached out with a gloved hand and streaked a path across the book spines. They were tangible, immortalizing creations. At least she hadn't sacrificed herself for a failure. She'd loved Hugh for his determination, his unceasing quest for truth and justice, which sprang not from a sense of self-righteousness, but from his innate decency and his faith in logic. She'd known from the first that he would become a great man. And he obviously had.

"I hope you're impressed." His soft voice came from behind her.

Lydia curled her hand into a fist as she withdrew it slowly from the books. Taking a deep breath, she turned to face him, unsmiling. "How could I be otherwise? You've succeeded in all the ways that mattered to you most."

A slow blink shuttered his true feelings. "Almost all."

His dark suit was tailored perfectly, emphasizing his impressive figure. The years had made him even more compelling, more masculine. He moved toward her like a skater over ice, stopping too close, as if that were his rightful place. But he had forfeited all rights, she had to remind herself. She stared determinedly at the mother of pearl buttons on his shirt, afraid to meet those coolly mesmerizing blue eyes. The urge to slap him, or insult him, rushed over her.

At the same time, she found herself imagining how it would feel to kiss him. How natural it would be to lift her chin and offer her lips. How easy it would be to lean into the kiss and enjoy once again that indescribable intimacy. *Madness!*

Finally, she forced herself to gaze at him with neutral eyes. "I have always wondered if there really was a God," she said lightly. She pushed past him and took a seat on the divan, carefully smoothing out her skirts. "And now I know there must be. For only a divine being could arrange such an ironic reunion, and only for His own perverse amusement."

"Ironic, yes." He crossed his arms and leaned against the

bookshelf. "I looked for you for three years. I searched desperately, employing all my investigative skills, and yet I failed to find you. Did you know that, Addie?"

The name was a jagged spike piercing her breast. Addie was the young woman who had been naive enough to believe his promises, who had given herself like a lamb to the slaughter, who had thought that hell could not exist for those who truly loved, only to learn that there was a very particular kind of hell created just for those foolish enough to give up their hearts.

"Please don't call me that. Addie Parker died the day she left your father's estate."

Hugh's mouth thinned with irony. "My sister is dead as well."

"Katherine? No! How did it happen?"

"A fever. Two years ago."

"I'm so sorry."

"Are you?" He cast her a bleak look. "Why did you leave?"

Ignoring the anguish in his voice, she echoed, "Why?"

"I loved you. I wanted to marry you," he protested.

Such sweet words. So earnest. So familiar. Did he really think she would fall for them again after all that had happened?

"Your father said you did not want me. He made an insulting offer to buy me off, then he sent me packing."

"And you believed him?" His voice rose in anger. "You knew what sort of relationship I had with my father. Why, for God's sake, why did you accept his word? Why didn't you come to me before you left?"

"I waited by the fish pond for nearly twelve hours, until I lost every last shred of pride."

"He kept me from coming to you, Addie. Didn't that possibility occur to you?"

"Did he hold you prisoner?"

"Yes, he did!"

"Oh, come Montgomery!"

"I was held captive at Windhaven for a week. By the time I could search for you it was as if you'd vanished from the face of the Earth. If you'd only kept faith. Why were you so quick to believe I'd abandon you?"

"What was I to assume? I was a governess. You were a rich and powerful lord."

"I wasn't a lord!" He spat the words at her. "You weren't a governess!"

He strode angrily across the room until he towered over her. "We had saved each others' lives! How could you not know how rare, how genuine that was? How could you throw it away because of my father?"

Lydia tried to push aside a tendril of hair that had fallen onto her temple, but her hand shook too badly. Instead, she balled her fingers, burying her hands in her lap. She could think of no reply as she watched the florid color drain from his face and the fury flashing in his eyes give way to remorse. He let out a deep breath and sank onto the opposite end of the divan.

"I am sorry. I'm sorry for so much." After a moment, he stared at her in his unblinking way and said quietly, "I loved you. You loved me—or at least I believed you did."

Lydia gulped and squeezed her eyes shut against a rain of tears. Oh, how she had loved him! She had loved him more than was humanly possible. She had reinvented the world with their love, dismissing all the known laws of the universe. They had truly been one. There had been nothing between them. She had thought nothing ever would come between them. So quickly she'd been proven wrong.

But he was right. To know love, to be loved, to have that privilege was a sacred thing. Had she been horribly mistaken to doubt him? Had she, dogged by self-doubt, given up too easily and lost so much?

Tears seeped from her lids and streaked down her cheeks. She brushed them away with her fingertips and took a deep breath. "I am sorry." Her simple yet vague statement was as unclear to her as it was to him. Was she sorry for having doubted him? Or merely sorry for crying?

"Addie, I . . ." he said uncertainly.

She held up the palm of one hand, cutting him off. She hated weepy women. How much better it was to be angry. Yes . . . and safer, too. "How frustrating it must be," she lashed out, "knowing that your powers of investigation failed when it mattered most. The only reason you didn't find me was because you never expected I could be among your own class. You would never have guessed that I had married an earl."

"That's unfair."

Ignoring the plea in his voice, she pressed on. "Is it? Where precisely did you look for me?"

He took a kerchief from his pocket and dabbed his forehead. The windows were closed, but it was not warm in the room. Her accusations stung, she noted with satisfaction. With the inscrutable Lord Clue, that was quite an accomplishment.

"I looked . . . everywhere. I started with your family, who were of no help at all. I put advertisements in papers in all the major cities. I interviewed dozens of governesses who claimed to fit your description. I worked with Scotland Yard detectives, and even struck up a friendship with the commissioner. During my search for you, I found evidence that helped him solve a decades-old murder case. I had to have something to throw myself into after months of searching for you along the wharves and in back alleys."

Her spine went straight as a hat pin. "How dare you! What made you think you would find me such ghastly places? We both know what sort of women linger by the river."

"Bodies wash up there," he said softly. "I feared you were dead. How else could I explain your disappearance? I know you loved me, Addie."

"Dead!" she said, shocked, then newly fortified with indignation. "Did you think I would throw myself over a bridge pining for you?"

"I thought it possible. I knew your father was a vicar. He said he'd turned you out, the rotter."

All the memories came rushing back, too painful to bear. She whispered, "He did," then released a slow, pent-up breath. When she met his eyes, she could see compassion and remorse, but it was not enough. She would never let it be. Her wounds were ragged and had healed badly. Nothing would ever be the same between them.

"If your father disowned you, how did you survive?" he persisted.

She snapped her head away. He was exceeding the bounds now. He was asking too much. Far too much. "I do not consider that any of your business, sir. But I will tell you that my dear husband saved me from the life of destitution to which you had condemned me."

"But I loved yo—"

"Love doesn't matter all that much, does it, when one's reputation has been ruined?" There was finality in her words. And sadness.

He had no ready answer. He swallowed the rest of his brandy as if it were medicine, then set the glass down with a quiet thud. "No, I suppose not. What is done is done. All that we need to determine now is whether you care to have me on this case. I will not interfere if it pains you, and it seems clear that it does. God knows I've caused you enough pain already."

"But you must be on the case!" She moved to the edge of the divan. Just as she had been rescued by her husband, she was determined to rescue others. The role had become so ingrained it was as natural to her as breathing. "We're talking about a fourteen-year-old girl. She's innocent, unlike us. We must do everything we can to save her before it's too late."

He nodded in agreement. Then his eyes filled. The muscles in his jaw flexed with emotion. "I still love you, Addie."

And I still love you. She turned away before he could

read her face. He must never know her true feelings. Could they work together? Or would she be courting disaster all over again? She would rather die than be unfaithful to Beaumont. How on Earth could she do this? The viscount was too dangerous.

But then the solution came to her.

Lydia turned back to him. "We have both made mistakes, Montgomery. We both have regrets. But that doesn't change the present. I intend to find my husband's daughter. I agree, it would be difficult for you and me to work together, considering what we've already been through. I will send Beaumont's agent to you. You can work with him. I think it best if you and I keep our distance, don't you agree?"

He sighed, and his shoulders slumped in resignation. "Yes. What is the man's name?"

"Morgan. Mr. Henry Morgan. You may trust him entirely. My husband does. And of course, so do I. When he speaks," she said, smiling inwardly, "you can trust he speaks for me. He's quite an angel."

"Good. I could use an angel on my side, what with all the devils nipping my heels."

Lady Clara Leach strolled through the potted trees and bushes in the conservatory at Beaumont House, anticipating the arrival of a Mr. Henry Morgan. It was an airy room, high-ceilinged and flooded with sunlight that winked through floor-to-ceiling panes of glass that encompassed the octagonal space. Finches flitted from branch to branch in the tall tropical trees that rose to the high domed tin ceiling.

Prior to her marriage to Todd, Clara had been a very independent woman. An old maid, really, who had relied on her own intellect to cling to the edge of the middle class. She'd long been involved with the Ladies' National Association, working for the repeal of the Contagious Diseases

Acts, and had fought for the rights of factory workers. However, after falling in love with Todd, she'd been so blissfully happy that her desire to save the world had greatly diminished. More than anything, she now wanted to be a mother.

Unfortunately, that was one accomplishment beyond her reach. After two nearly fatal miscarriages, Clara had been ordered by her doctor to abstain from relations with her adoring husband. Although she could not abandon hope of giving Todd an heir, she feared it might be impossible. That was why she decided to resume her political activities and looked forward to helping the Beaumonts find Sophie.

Clara hoped this visit with Mr. Morgan would put her thoroughly in the middle of the investigation. She had no idea who Mr. Morgan was or why he had written to her on Lady Beaumont's stationery. Assuming this had something to do with the search for Sophie Parnham, she had readily agreed to the late-afternoon rendezvous.

"Lady Leach, how good of you to meet with me."

She turned toward the entry and saw an elegant, almost effeminate man approaching her. "Hello." She stepped out from the thicket of potted trees, her heels clicking softly on the white tile floor. "I presume you are Mr. Morgan."

"Yes." He paused and glanced over his shoulder as the footman closed the double doors, leaving them to their privacy. Clara noted his lean frame, his long neck, his slicked black hair, and his high cheeks. He reminded her of an actor. When the doors were secured, he turned to her with a conspiratorial wiggle of the eyebrows.

"There," he said, "now we can speak privately."

"I take it, Mr. Morgan, that you wish to discuss the search for Miss Parnham."

"In a manner of speaking." His voice was breathy and low. He smoothed his hand over his hair and glanced nervously at her. "You see, Lady Leach . . . er, rather, Clara—."

Her eyes went wide at this shocking familiarity. "Do I know you, sir?"

"Intimately."

"What!"

Morgan moved closer, wringing his trim hands. "You see, I'm not everything I would appear to be, Clara."

Again, the use of her first name shocked her, and she took a step backward. "I don't understand. You'd best explain yourself, sir."

Morgan shot another glance over his shoulder, then looked at her apologetically. "It's me, Clara." His voice was clear now, bell-like, and oddly familiar.

"Who? I don't quite—"

"It's *me*. Lydia. Lady Beaumont."

Clara's jaw dropped. She blinked slowly. The raspiness had cleared entirely. It *was* Lydia's voice. Clara squinted, blurring out the male clothing, to better examine his—or her—face. There were the familiar high cheeks, the pale amethyst eyes, the night-colored hair. Yes, the features all belonged to Lydia. But the hair was so short! And a mustache!

Clara recoiled in horror. "Good heavens, it is you! But your hair! And . . . and that black thing above your lip."

"Haven't you ever seen a mustache?" Lydia giggled with a burst of relief, then clapped her hands together and pressed them to her mouth, stifling her giddiness. "Oh, my dear friend, I am so sorry to shock you this way. But it worked! I fooled you, didn't I? Tell me I did!"

"Yes, you did. Never in a million years would I have assumed you'd do anything so . . . scandalous! What on Earth—"

"I can explain everything." And she did. She took Clara by the hand, laughing when her friend at first recoiled, then sat down on the wicker divan. She explained that she was the Midnight Angel who roamed London's streets in search of young girls who were about to embark on lives of prostitution.

"But why? How?" Clara asked in a tone half amazed, half disbelieving.

"Like you, dear friend, I've never been content to accept

life as it is. You and I both are practical by nature. We married far above our stations. I would never be content to do nothing but play cards and crochet, would you?"

"No, of course not." Clara's crystalline eyes sparkled with excitement. "But I must say, Lydia, as bold as I have been, I would never have the courage to do what you have done. What is it like? How does it feel to dress and act like a man?"

Lydia stared pensively out the windows to the small walled-in garden beyond the conservatory. Then she turned to her friend with a mischievous grin. "It's been marvelous. For the first time in my life, I've been able to accomplish things without making sure to give credit to a man. I've been able to act decisively outside my own home without having to consult anyone else. And most important of all, I've been able to do good for others, directly, and I've been able to see the benefit of my accomplishments with my own eyes."

"How have you kept it secret?"

"I have loyal servants. And Mr. Morgan never leaves the carriage. And he ventures forth only in the evening. That's why I presented myself to you, Clara. I need to know if I can take my double identity out into the open. I want to work closely with Lord Montgomery, but it must be under the guise of the Midnight Angel. Therefore, I need to make sure my costume and demeanor are believable in the light of day."

"But why did you turn to me for guidance?"

Lydia pressed her hand warmly. "Not only do I trust you, Clara dear, but I know that you have seen more of the world than most women of our station. Beau told me that you actually met George Sand."

Clara nodded enthusiastically. "Yes, I had the pleasure of chatting with the novelist shortly before she died."

"What was she like?"

"She was possibly the most amazing person I have ever met." She gave Lydia a teasing sidelong look. "Now I'm not so sure. I was introduced to George by a mutual friend who worked with me on a special committee for the Ladies' National Association. The night we met she was surrounded by admirers. Many of them were artists and aspiring writers. She wore absolutely no cosmetics. Her hair was bluntly cut and short. And she smoked a pipe! With her voice chafed by smoke, I would never have guessed she was a woman if I hadn't known better."

"How did she manage to be so . . . individual?"

"Because she didn't give a damn what anyone thought of her."

Lydia blinked in surprise. She'd heard more than her share of curse words from women, but never among her own set. She laughed and gave Clara a quick hug. "Oh, I'm so lucky to have you as a friend."

"Now, mind you, George wasn't trying to pretend to be anything other than herself, and you are."

"True. But it would help a great deal if I knew how she managed to dress like a man and not have the whole world turn on her."

"She simply accepted herself completely as she was."

The bubble of excitement burst, and Lydia's expression fell. "I see." Self-appreciation had never been her strong suit, a fact of which she'd been painfully reminded by Hugh Montgomery.

"Most men do as they please," Clara continued. "They pay little heed to looks. When they wrinkle, they don't care. They still hold the reins of power and are considered distinguished, while we poor fools spend hours plastering and painting our faces trying to cling to youth. You see, we've all agreed to play the game by their rules, and, therefore, we can no longer even distinguish true beauty with our own eyes. You know the Marquess of Rockford?"

"Yes." Lydia's mouth tugged with a smile, knowing where she was going.

"If you look closely at him, you must honestly say he looks like a bulldog. But because he's close with the Royal

Family, there are any number of young women who think he's simply divine."

"That's partly because he exudes such presence. It makes one question one's own eyes."

"Precisely. It all boils down to confidence."

"And indifference to the opinion of others."

"Yes."

"I should be more like the marquess," Lydia said pensively.

"But why? I think you're perfectly marvelous the way you are." Clara took a closer look at Lydia's angular cheeks and well-defined temples. "Come to think of it, why must you disguise yourself in order to work with Lord Clue? Beaumont is such an unconventional husband, I can't imagine he cares what anyone thinks of his wife spending time with another man if it's part of an investigation."

Lydia stood and strolled to the greenery. She inhaled the thick smell of potted soil, which mingled with evergreen, then turned and put her hands behind her back. With her legs set far apart, she felt like a man. She wished she could control her feelings like one. She'd never told anyone, other than her husband, about her affair with Hugh. Now that the past had come back to haunt her, she wanted to speak to someone, to try to make sense of it.

"Lord Montgomery and I . . . ." She swallowed hard and swept both hands over her hair. She shook her head and returned to Clara's side, sinking down beside her. Would Clara condemn her? Who wouldn't? "I was a fool, Clara. I—"

"Shhh," Clara quickly interjected. She shook her head sharply. "No, don't say another word. I understand."

"It was years ago."

"I understand."

"We—"

"There is no need to explain."

Lydia was dumbfounded. She had rehearsed this confession many times to an unknown confessor, and this was not the response she'd prepared herself for. She searched Clara's eyes, wondering at her lack of condemnation.

Clara's flawless, cameo face creased with compassion. "I know what it is like to love a callow young nobleman and have him betray your dreams. I, too, have a hidden past. Todd . . . he . . . his love saved my life."

Tears pooled in Lydia's eyes. It touched her deeply to know that Beaumont wasn't the only man who could be so forgiving of a wife's indiscretions.

"Beau saved my life as well." Her mouth twisted with bitter self-reproach. "How I hate myself for betraying him still. You see, I still have feelings for Montgomery. I do not trust myself in his presence. Isn't that simply awful?"

"No," Clara said flatly. "It's wise. I think Beaumont must be very grateful that you're willing to search for his daughter on his behalf, and to put your tender heart at such risk in the process. Now don't waste another moment blaming yourself. We must simply arm you with the best disguise possible. If Lord Montgomery doesn't know who you are, he will not burden you with his charm. Let me see how you walk."

Lydia cleared her throat of emotion. She lifted her chin and strode as confidently as possible across the room, then turned, awaiting Clara's verdict.

"Not bad. This time widen your stride. Men do not have to worry about tearing undergarments. So stretch your legs a bit. And lead with your forehead, as if you have somewhere important to go. Most men think everything they do is terribly important."

Lydia strode back, feeling as if her forward motion would hurtle her through the conservatory windows. She stopped abruptly at Clara's side, teetering a moment on her toes to regain her balance.

Clara smiled approvingly. "You're almost there, Lydia. Didn't that feel better?"

"I certainly felt more confident. About what, I haven't the vaguest notion."

Clara laughed. "You certainly look the part, though I do mourn the loss of your beautiful hair."

Lydia smoothed a hand over the sleek mane that had been bluntly cut at the base of her skull. "It had to go. I pin it up by day, and of course I add false curls, which my maid fashioned from my own shorn hair."

"What does Beaumont think of all this?"

Lydia smiled fondly. "He is proud of me. He is the only person beside my personal maid and her husband who know of my disguise. And now there's you. Please don't tell Todd."

Clara frowned. "I've never kept a secret from Toddy before."

"You must. He is friendly with Montgomery, and I fear the truth will slip out. You see, Clara, Lord Clue doesn't realize just how helpful I can be. I've seen a great deal on the streets of London, even from the safety of my carriage. I know I can help, but I must do so as the Midnight Angel."

Clara nodded solemnly. "Of course you must. The life of a child is at risk."

Lydia heaved a sigh. "I knew you would understand."

"Will you do me a return favor?"

At the sound of trepidation, Lydia pierced her with a look. "Of course. What is it?"

"I need a companion on a secret mission."

Lydia lifted a brow, her eyes coming alive. "That's my specialty. Why the secrecy?"

"I want to be examined by a doctor at the Little Shepherd's Ladies' Clinic. It's in a terrible part of town. Just being seen there would create a scandal." Clara licked her lips and added in lower tones, "The doctor there does *internal* examinations. She uses the same sort of examining tools used in the lockdown wards where prostitutes are examined for disease."

"You needn't be ashamed. Any doctor worth his salt knows that's the best way to find out what's wrong with a woman's internal organs. There should be no place for modesty in a doctor's examining room."

"Yes, but there are some who still believe women shouldn't be examined in such a manner. My own doctor holds that view."

"Then he's terribly old-fashioned."

"Nevertheless, I don't want Todd to know I've been seen by someone else. At least until I have more information to share with him."

Lydia suddenly realized why Clara wanted to see the doctor. "Oh, my dear. I've only been thinking of my own troubles. This is about your miscarriages, isn't it?"

Clara swallowed hard. "Yes. I have to know if there is any hope of having a child."

Lydia sat beside her and squeezed her hand. "Of course I'll go with you. I know the clinic well. All the girls I pick up under the guise of the Midnight Angel go there for examinations. And I visit quite often during the day to help the clinic's board raise money, dressed as Lady Beaumont, of course. I'd be happy to take you. Just name the time."

"It can wait. You must first meet with Hugh Montgomery. Poor little Sophie is waiting for rescue, and time is wasting."

Chapter 5

✤

"What clues do we have so far?" Hugh asked distractedly as he eyed his glass of water, holding it in front of his nose. He stood by a sideboard in his cozy study. He'd just filled his glass halfway, pouring from a scientist's beaker, and wanted to make sure he had just the right amount before he added the tincture of laudanum.

"The commissioner of Scotland Yard has written, saying that the C.I.D. is on the case," Pierpont replied, scouring his notes as he spoke. "He was rather insulted, I gather, that he first heard about the case from you and not from Lord Beaumont. Nevertheless, he says that you needn't worry about Sophie Parnham."

"Poppycock," Hugh said lightly as he reached for the opiate solution that sat tantalizingly in a small brown bottle on a white doily covering the stained oak sideboard.

Pierpont let out a martyr's sigh. "But sir, the commissioner says detectives and the entire police force are looking for Miss Parnham. He suggests that if you involve yourself in the case he'll call off the search."

"Bloody hell." Hugh set down the water glass and the bottle of laudanum, then rested his hands on the bureau, shooting his man-of-affairs a scathing look. "You know what he really means by that, don't you?"

"Yes, sir." Pierpont eyed the laudanum disapprovingly.

Hugh noticed the look, but as usual ignored it. "It means he's still fuming over the fact that I solved the Samurai Slayings when his entire force was running in circles. And this is how my old friend thanks me."

"Might I suggest, sir, that you follow the commissioner's advice and let the Yard handle this case?"

"No, you may not." Returning his focus to the heavenly bottle of distilled opium and alcohol, he tipped it sideways and silently counted the drops as he poured. Just then the front door bell rang. "Ignore it. I'm not home. What else have you found out?"

"Sir Todd sent a note saying he's working closely with detectives on a citywide search, and that you should focus on what you do best—examining the fine details."

"What else?" Hugh asked as he twirled the soothing liquid in the glass, savoring this moment with ritualistic fervor.

"The Earl of Beaumont sent a very cordial letter thanking you for your work on the case."

"Good." Still clutching the brown bottle, Hugh touched the glass rim to his lips and drank deeply. He exhaled with satisfaction, immediately feeling the medicine's calming effects. "I want you to pay a visit to the usual cast of characters to make inquiries on the streets. Oh, and be sure to chat with Sir Malcolm Dunbar. He keeps a virtual family tree of romantic affairs betwixt members of the *ton*. I want to learn more about Louise Canfield's many paramours."

"Very good, sir."

"And as much as I hate to, I'll discuss the case with my father. He might have heard something. One witness said

Sophie was seen being carried away by a well-dressed footman, so perhaps the perpetrator sits in the House of Lords, or is at least a rich gentleman. One cannot suppose a footman would be so stupid as to commit a crime in his master's colors, unless he was mad or acting on behalf of said master. If we—"

"I beg your pardon."

Hugh stopped his rapid-fire ruminations to look in astonishment at his unexpected visitor.

"I rang," the man said by way of apology as he stood hesitantly in the doorway. "No one answered the door."

"So you let yourself in and found your way back to my private parlor?" Hugh arched one brow. "Perhaps there was a good reason no one answered the door."

"I'm sorry, sir, but it's urgent. I come on behalf of Lord and Lady Beaumont."

"Ah! You must be Morgan."

The mustachioed, thin man looked from Hugh to the bottle of laudanum, which he still clutched in his hand.

Hugh looked at the damning evidence as well, seeing it through Morgan's eyes. "I'm sorry you had to wait, Morgan, but my man-of-affairs here has a taste for laudanum." He added sotto voce, "I had just indulged him and was about to send him on his way."

"What?!" Pierpont said indignantly. "Why, I never—"

"Yes, that's right," Hugh returned, daring him to rebut the accusation. "I practically had to wrestle the bottle away from him, poor fellow. Now enough of that, Pierpont. I won't have you indulging in laudanum while you're conducting your duties. Although it's perfectly legal, we all know its use signifies moral weakness. Please show this gentleman to the parlor, won't you? I'll be in shortly. That is, if you have your wits about you enough to do my bidding."

Pierpont fairly growled with indignation. He took a deep breath and inclined his head as he propelled himself out of the room. "As you wish, sir."

* * *

In what she hoped was a manly stride, Lydia paced slowly in the parlor as she waited for Hugh. She had taken a risk letting herself into his apartment, then boldly walking to his private rooms. But the impromptu plan had worked. She'd taken him off-guard, which was hard to do with the savvy Lord Clue. He'd seemed flustered, and she would bet a great deal of money he had been too distracted to observe anything in particular about her. By the time he joined her, he would have recovered his composure, and first impressions would already be cemented.

Of course, the only reason she'd been able to walk in at all was because he went without a nobleman's usual phalanx of servants. All the better. The fewer eyes observing her, the easier the chance of maintaining her disguise.

"Well, well, this is better," Hugh said from the doorway.

She turned slowly, as if she were in control of time itself. "Yes, again my apologies."

"Not to worry. Let us start all over again." He held out his hand for a shake. "I am Viscount Montgomery."

Lydia hesitated for only the slightest second, then thrust hers out, squeezing hard enough to distract him from the diminutive size of her hand.

"Morgan. Mr. Henry Morgan. I am Lord Beaumont's agent."

"Ah, yes. I was expecting you, but . . . ." Hugh's face bore his usual bored, skeptical pose, yet she could see the confusion just beneath the surface.

Panic flashed through her. Although she could disguise herself, she knew he sensed something familiar about her. It was hard to erase the intimacy lovers shared. She pulled a letter from her knee-length black coat, offering it to him, and hurried on with her business.

"Lord Beaumont sends you his greetings. He thanks you

again for your help in the investigation, and he leaves me at your complete disposal."

Hugh glanced at her small gloved hand a moment before relieving it of the envelope. Then he broke the seal and scanned the enclosed letter with his intense eyes, absorbing the wordy letter speedily, then inserting it back in the envelope and placing it on a nearby table.

"Please thank Lord Beaumont for his generosity." Hugh folded his arms, shifting his weight, while he scrutinized her more closely. "Now tell me precisely, Mr. Morgan, how it is that you believe you can aid the great Lord Clue?"

His patent arrogance tried her patience, and her nostrils flared. She could not believe he was so frank in sharing his overblown opinion of himself with a stranger. Fortunately, she had bragging rights of her own, though he would never know it was Lydia who boasted, and not the fictitious Morgan.

"You've heard of the Midnight Angel?" she said.

He smiled indulgently. "Naturally. I made him famous."

She laughed. "*You* made the Midnight Angel famous? And how, pray tell, did you do that?"

"I wrote about him in my most recent book. I thought he deserved credit for all the good he's done for the fallen angels who pitiably plague London's streets."

She gave him a tight smile and tried to keep the sarcasm from her voice, saying, "How magnanimous of you."

"Not really. I was also hoping to deflect some curiosity from myself. It is a great burden, Mr. Morgan, to be considered the Robin Hood of the justice system, stealing clues from the rich so they might be put in jail."

"Do you know who the Midnight Angel is?"

He looked up with a bored expression. "Does it really matter?"

Anger flashed through her. Her disguise had proved to be a greater benefit than she'd anticipated. It allowed her to see a different side of Hugh. How bloated his ego had become. He was a disappointment, incapable of seeing her worth, even when she was dressed as a man.

"It matters to me, sir," she said sharply. "You see, I am the Midnight Angel."

His expression went blank, and she knew a moment of triumph. She'd stunned him! Incredulity danced behind his eyes, then his adroit mask of indifference pulled the curtains on his true feelings. He hadn't known. He had not guessed the Midnight Angel's identity, even though he'd written about the elusive figure. She'd thought that surely someone during the last five years had watched Morgan slip into the alley by Lord Beaumont's mansion. And someone had surely tied that person to Stone House and the Midnight Angel's numerous good deeds. But although the great Lord Clue was aware of the phantom savior, he had not put two and two together.

"Are you telling me," he said, "that Lord Beaumont's agent—you—are working in disguise? Why?"

"I don't want to take credit—or blame—for my good deeds. You've heard the old saying, 'no good deed goes unpunished'?"

"Yes, but surely your employer wouldn't mind taking credit for his funding of Stone House? It has cost him a great deal. I assume you are working on his behalf in this matter."

"His lordship never cared about the esteem of his peers. He likes his privacy. In his youth he was a reckless roué. He is used to being just out of bounds of the best circles. And now he is unfashionably conscientious for a member of the nobility. Kindness is such a middle-class aspiration, don't you think?"

"Damn the peerage! But why not tell the rest of the world about his good deeds? He's setting a good example."

"He feels such public knowledge of his charity would somehow diminish its true worth. He does not need accolades to help others in need." She paused when the truth nagged her. Suddenly she thought it prudent to tell Hugh the whole truth about her husband. It might spur him in his search for Sophie. "Lord Beaumont is dying. That's why I have come, to find his daughter before it is too late."

All Hugh's arrogance vanished in the blink of an eye. He looked profoundly shaken by this news. "I'm very sorry to hear it."

She felt the sting of tears and turned away. "He's been dying for a very long time," she said in her gruffest voice. "He has accepted his mortality. But he can't accept the fact that the daughter he never knew he had is now suffering. Because his lordship is physically unable to search for her, I must do it in his stead."

"I understand. If I agree to let you assist my investigation, what kind of help can you offer me?"

"I know the streets. You are a gentleman and a nobleman. I am neither. You seem to believe that the truth can be found in fine details and polite drawing rooms. I have found the greatest measure of justice, and injustice, in the back alleys where no gentleman would be caught dead. I can help. You must believe me."

He ground his teeth together, looking down his nose at her, while he ruminated over his options. "Why is it so important to you?"

"I owe Lord Beaumont my life. The least I can do for him is save the life of his daughter."

He blinked rapidly and appeared humbled by this. "Very well. We shall work together. This is not my usual *modus operandi,* but I hold your employer's wife in the greatest esteem. I will do all I can to solve this terrible mystery."

Her knees went wobbly with relief, and she sank down into a nearby chair as he began to pace. "Thank you, sir."

He clasped his hands behind his back. "Tell me who you believe committed this abduction, Mr. Morgan."

"I believe that this crime is sexual in intent, sir," she said.

"I believe you're right. What is your reasoning?"

"Syphilis. It's such a scourge in London that a gentleman can no longer risk the pleasure of a common whore. Sophie was condemned by her virtues. She was a virgin;

therefore, not tainted with disease. She was young, but not too young. At the age of fourteen, she is legal tender."

"True. But why abduct her?" he pressed. "If she is of the age of legal consent, why not seduce her and toss her back on the street? Why turn this into a crime by kidnapping her?"

"I don't know. One thing is clear," she said, looking to him for agreement, "the abductor did not know of Sophie's connection to Lord Beaumont."

Hugh gave her a dazzling, white-toothed smile of cynicism. "Or he knew and did not care."

"How could he know? Sophie called her own mother Miss Canfield. Not even Lord Beaumont knew he had a child. Everyone at the theater thought she was an orphan."

Hugh didn't respond right away. He seemed preoccupied with his thoughts. He ambled to the mantel over the fireplace and plucked a cut sprig of mistletoe from among the objets d'art assembled there. He studied it in his astute way, then held up the long, oval leaves and wilted scarlet blossoms for her consideration.

"Do you recognize this?" he inquired.

"It's mistletoe."

"Quite so. I found it when I examined the place where Miss Parnham was last seen."

She sat forward. "Outside the theater?"

He nodded.

"Nothing grows behind the Chamberlain Music Hall, except for mold and rats."

"Exactly. That's why I've concluded this little bit of nature was left as a talisman."

"An intentional clue?" When he nodded, she argued, "But why would any rapist or abductor want to leave a calling card?"

"To take credit for the deed."

"Or blame."

He tossed the greenery back onto the mantel with a jaded chuckle. "That's the problem. If the perpetrator sits in the House of Lords, there will be no blame. Not even if Sophie Parnham is found murdered."

She could not argue, for he spoke the truth. "What makes you think someone from the highest reaches of society would stoop so low as to commit such a heinous crime?"

He smiled enigmatically. "I'll tell you when I am able to draw more conclusions. In the meantime, I have a meeting with Scotland Yard. I'm going to talk to investigators about a social society called the Brotherhood of Botanical Inquiry, otherwise known as the Botanicals. I have a few other appointments to keep as well. Let's meet again, shall we? Let's say, at midnight?"

This time it was her turn to smile elusively. "The Midnight Angel should be happy to oblige."

She rose and left the room with wide, purposeful strides. The moment the door clicked shut behind her, Hugh turned and shouted for his loyal servant.

"Pierpont!"

The dignified man-of-affairs hurried in at the sound of urgency. "Yes, milord? What is it?"

"Follow her!"

"Her? I don't understand. Follow who?"

"Lady Beaumont, you blithering idiot."

"Lady Beaumont?"

"Run down the stairs now and tell me what sort of carriage she came in. Hurry! Before she gets away."

"Lady Beaumont—oh! Do you mean Mr. Morgan was actually—"

"Yes, yes! Thank God Sophie Parnham's life doesn't depend on *your* powers of observation. Now go!"

Chapter 6

Reginald Shane climbed out of Mr. Morgan's carriage and trotted across the street through a light drizzle. His boots scuffled over uneven cobblestones as he looked uneasily at the imposing gray stone edifice in front of him. He glanced over his shoulder at the Midnight Angel, who looked encouragingly at him from the dry confines of the carriage.

Reggie forced a smile and tipped his bowler in acknowledgment. Yes, he would knock on Lord Montgomery's door, as he had been instructed to do, though the prospect made him queasy. Why? Why was he always so ill at ease with his social superiors? He was no longer a street bugger. His work required more social interaction.

He was actually doing good in the world and getting paid for it, Reggie reminded himself. He'd just spent the carriage ride from Beaumont House updating the Midnight Angel about the goings-on at Stone House. He'd slipped into the operation like a well-oiled hand into a glove.

Mrs. Cromwell, the formidable housekeeper, had told him just that morning how pleased she was to have the assistance of a man who knew how the world worked.

And there was so much more he wanted to do for the girls at Stone House. Reggie believed they were entitled to proper treatment, which included everything from pretty petticoats to a healthful diet. Feeling as if he were on a mission, he'd bargained with cloth merchant Saul Eberhardt to obtain a dozen bolts of serviceable white linen for female unmentionables. From One-Eyed Jimmy, leader of the East End costermongers, he had negotiated good terms for fresh fruit to supplement the limited variety of food the Stone House cooks prepared.

In many ways he knew he had become invaluable to his mysterious employer, but he felt wholly inadequate when his job called for mingling with the upper crust. He didn't mind dealing with Morgan, because the Midnight Angel seemed not to belong to any class at all. He was a strange one. Neither man nor woman, neither upper class nor low. There was something queer about him, and Reggie meant to discover what it was . . . eventually.

Right now, however, he had to make his first entreaty at the home of a nobleman, and the prospect had him in a cold sweat. Still hesitating in front of Lord Montgomery's apartment, Reggie's heart began to race as he replayed his conversation with Morgan before alighting from the carriage.

"Well, at least it ain't Regent Street," he had muttered more to himself than to his employer as he straightened his tie.

"Don't worry, Reggie," Morgan said in his raspy voice. His small hands were tucked in white gloves and curled around the head of his ornate pewter walking stick. "Lord Montgomery won't bite. You'll likely just meet his man, though one can never tell with Montgomery. He is rather unconventional. They call him Lord Clue, you know."

"Great," Reggie drawled, pulling on his brown bowler. "He'll be on to me in the bat of an eye."

"You'll be fine, Reggie. Your past doesn't matter. Only the future."

"I'd rather be helping the girls at Stone House."

"You are helping. One girl in particular. Sir Todd is working closely with Scotland Yard on the search for Sophie Parnham, but I think our chances are better with the unconventional Lord Clue."

Reggie nodded in resignation. "Best get on with it then."

With that he had set out to follow his employer's instruction. Swallowing for courage, he took the stairs to Lord Clue's apartment two at a time. Moments later he stood at the door. The hallway smelled of furniture polish and flowers. After Reggie knocked, the door opened abruptly and the scent of pipe tobacco whirled into the mix. He swallowed hard and looked up at a man who was taller, older, and clearly superior to him in every way. Reggie dug in his heels lest he turn and run.

"Yes?" the taller man said, somehow managing to sweep the entire musical scale with that one word.

"Good evening, sir. My employer, Mr. Henry Morgan, is here to call for Lord Montgomery." He offered Morgan's calling card, then was struck by a disquieting notion. "Are . . . are *you* Lord Montgomery?"

The black suited man's beaked nose flared. "No, foolish fellow. Lord Montgomery would not answer his own door!"

"But Mr. Morgan said his lordship was—."

"Don't listen to anything you hear about the infamous Lord Clue. No sooner will you pass on the gossip than you'll find out it was utterly false and that the truth is infinitely more fascinating. Come in."

He plucked Morgan's calling card from Reggie's hand and nodded toward the parlor. "His lordship might want to question you, so have a seat. I'm sure Mr. Morgan will understand."

Reggie wasn't so sure. He hadn't been a man-of-affairs long, but he thought his first duty should surely be to inform Morgan that Montgomery would be late.

"I beg your pardon, sir, but I'll just inform Mr. Morgan—"

"You'll do nothing of the kind. His lordship will be here momentarily. I'm sure Mr. Morgan won't worry."

"Well, I suppose—"

"You haven't been in service long, have you?"

Reggie ran two fingers along the inside of his collar, and his expression wilted. "No, I haven't. How did you know?"

The upper servant's gray brows puckered. "You have neither the confidence nor the humility of one who has been in service. You weren't born into the profession, that much is obvious. You'll have a great deal to learn."

Reggie's lips thinned, and he frowned truculently. "I don't hear Mr. Morgan complaining."

"You won't, I can assure you. You'll just be left without a position, holding a half-hearted commendation."

"I say, Pierpont, you're going to scare the poor lad."

Reggie's gaze shifted toward the pleasing sound of an elegant voice. It came from a very upright and purposeful figure who strode into the room. Reggie knew at once that this was Lord Montgomery.

"Good evening, sir," he said without waiting for acknowledgment. This earned him a scrutinizing glance from the famous sleuth.

Lord Montgomery brushed a hand over his thick brown hair, tugging it aside as he assessed Reggie. "I see no problem with him, Pierpont. Don't forget you yourself were a young servant once." He turned to a pile of papers scattered on a chaise. "Where in blazes are my notes from the Pomander case?"

"I have no idea, my lord. I simply can't keep up with your notes. And the housekeeper, as you know, has thrown up her hands in despair."

"She can do whatever she likes with her hands as long as she keeps them off my notes. Now where the devil are they?"

"You'll have to find them yourself."

Reggie's jaw nearly dropped. Was this how an employee spoke to the nobility?

"Do as I tell you, not as you see me do, young man," Pierpont said. "I'm quite sure Mr. Morgan has none of his lordship's unfortunate habits. Therefore, he must be treated with the utmost respect, unlike Lord Clue."

Ignoring Pierpont's barbed sagacity, Montgomery continued digging through a pile of papers. "Ah, here we go!" he exclaimed, plucking one from the pile with a self-satisfied grin.

"What do the notes from the Pomander case have to do with Lord Beaumont's missing spawn?" Pierpont archly inquired.

"Nothing." Montgomery folded the scrap of paper and slipped it into his waistcoat, then regarded Reggie conspiratorially. "What do you say, er—what is your name?"

"Reginald. Reggie Shane," the younger man offered. He was entranced by the fierce concentration of this unusual gentleman. He didn't seem to notice or care that Reggie didn't fit in. It was unheard of for a gentleman to treat servants so familiarly. Then again, a viscount who sullied his hands with criminal investigations already had cast aside conventions.

"What do you say, Shane?" Lord Montgomery's eyes danced. "Shall we join the Midnight Angel while we send Pierpont on a few errands?"

"Oh, dear," Pierpont intoned. "What now, milord?"

"I want you to stop by Mrs. Trueberry's."

"You mean *the* Mrs. Trueberry? The whorehouse madam?"

"Yes. Question her as you know I would regarding possible sightings of Sophie Parnham."

"Must I?"

"Yes, old boy, she knows all the ins and outs, as it were, of London's lowlife."

"Well, if that is all—"

"It isn't. Do your best to locate One-Eyed Jimmy. There are some questions I have to ask him."

"One-Eyed Jimmy!" Reggie blurted out.

Pierpont scowled. "Do not speak unless you're spoken to, young man."

"You know the costermonger?" Montgomery said.

"Yes, sir!" Reggie looked contritely to the servant. "Was that acceptable, Mr. Pierpont? His lordship did speak to me."

Magnanimously ignoring the clever rebuke from his inferior, Pierpont waved a hand. "Quite so."

"I could deliver that letter for you, Lord Montgomery," Reggie said, now almost confident. He loved having a purpose. "That is, if Mr. Morgan says it's all right."

"Very good, then. Pierpont, that's one less task for you."

Pierpont shifted. "Perhaps you'll be of some use after all, Mr. Shane. I have always detested that blasted rogue. No respect for his betters," he added pointedly before he quit the room.

"Wait here," Montgomery ordered Reggie. "I'll get my coat and we'll be off."

Reggie found himself suddenly alone and exhilarated. He'd acquitted himself admirably. He flushed with the sense of infinite possibilities. How much more could he accomplish for the girls at Stone House if he could confidently deal with a viscount? Morgan would be so proud.

He clasped his hands behind his back and strutted slowly around the room, admiring the objets d'art and curio pieces. And not once did he even feel the slightest urge to filch them! He had come a long way indeed.

He paused when he reached a small glass case hanging on the green and maroon wallpaper. It contained a miniature silhouette of an elegant woman, an ivory comb, a cameo ring, and a brilliant diamond brooch fashioned in the shape of a butterfly. He frowned.

"What is wrong?" Lord Montgomery said.

Reggie jumped with a start. "Oh, milord, I didn't know you had returned. Forgive me." He started for the door.

"Not so fast," Montgomery said, stopping Reggie's anxious retreat by thrusting his walking stick in the way.

The viscount held his top hat in the other hand. A light cape dressed his shoulders. He lowered the walking stick and placed a hand on Reggie's shoulder, guiding him back to the curio case. Together they gazed at the diamond brooch. "It's beautiful, isn't it?"

Reggie's heart dropped to his stomach. Did Lord Montgomery think he was planning to steal the jewelry? His mouth went dry as he croaked, "Aye, sir, it's . . . lovely. But I would never—"

Shaking his head in dismissal, the viscount said, "I know, Reggie. Be at ease. It belonged to my mother. Worth fifty-thousand pounds. You have refined taste," he added dryly.

Lord Clue didn't seem to distrust him at all. He began to breathe easier as Montgomery continued speaking.

"Why did it catch your eye?"

"It reminded me of something," Reggie said honestly.

Montgomery leveled him with a sharp gaze. "Oh?"

That one word was worth volumes in any other man's vocabulary. Reggie cleared his throat, but nothing came out. Montgomery's eyes narrowed, and Reggie felt as if they were drilling through his skull. Like Mr. Morgan, this gentleman was too bloody perceptive.

"It will do no harm to tell me about it."

"You see, it's . . . a club of sorts." Reggie smiled weakly. "That's all." He swallowed hard, feeling his Adam's apple bob and stick in his throat.

"What sort of club?" Lord Clue persisted.

Reggie focused on the diamonds, too embarrassed to face the nobleman. They glittered and winked hypnotically in the gaslight. A sour taste twisted on his tongue. The taste of cheap gin. He'd drunk so much of it the last time he had been there he'd become sick. He remembered his head spinning and the proprietor's mocking laughter.

"It's a secret club," he said at last, knowing it was important not to betray Montgomery's trust, yet ashamed of the reason he had been there. *That was in another life,* he reminded himself. "The patrons meet only on certain nights in an abandoned building. There is no sign over the door, but the gents who go there call it the Diamond Forest. The owner wears a bejeweled butterfly much like that brooch, and not a whole lot else." Would the viscount ask him why he was there? "He also wears a diamond oak leaf exactly where Adam wore his fig leaf."

"Ah. So it's that sort of club."

"Yes, sir."

"How very interesting. I've never heard of it. I suppose that's not so surprising because, as you say, it's a secret."

The viscount chuckled and clapped him on the shoulder. The room lightened and the uncomfortable memory of Reggie's last visit to the Diamond Forest vanished like smoke through an open flue.

"I didn't think there was anything I didn't know," the viscount added wryly. "Well, Reggie, we shouldn't keep Mr. Morgan waiting any longer."

It's about bloody time," Lydia muttered to herself when Reggie climbed into the carriage. She motioned for him to take the seat beside her as Montgomery climbed in. He was left with no choice but to take the opposite seat. He did so gracefully.

"Good evening, Mr. Morgan."

"Lord Montgomery." When their gazes collided, she flinched, then coughed to cover it. "I thought you'd never come."

"Reginald and I had a very interesting conversation."

She glanced at her man for explanation, but he, too, stared at her with unusual intensity. *Really, old girl,* she railed inwardly, *don't fall apart now. They know nothing.*

She leaned back against the brass-studded leather seat, thrusting out her flattened chest. "How kind of you to join us for our nightly sojourn, Lord Montgomery. Where shall I tell the coachman to take us?"

His lips curled with a challenge. "I rather thought you could be our guide tonight. You made a great point of telling me how familiar you are with the streets. After all, I am simply a spoiled viscount playing at criminal investigations."

She frowned. "I did not mean to imply anything of the kind. I admitted we need your help."

"Very well. We shall take turns, just as we would for an evening of cards." His cobalt eyes sparked from the shadows. His slow certainty made her uneasy.

"So you think this is a game." Her voice was breathier than usual. He had always had that effect on her. He stole her breath, stopped her heart, and made her skin prickle with awareness. He was so close. And she remembered. For the first time in years she remembered the strong, supple feel of his body on hers. She recalled his blazing kisses, his murmured words of love, as they thrashed on perspiration-soaked sheets. Unable to face him while holding such thoughts in her mind, she looked out the carriage window.

"All of life is a game, Morgan. First, you shuffle the deck and deal, then I will. Shall we see what sort of hand you've dealt us?"

She turned her lavender gaze back to him. No matter how many costumes she might don, no matter how thickly woven the veil that hid her, he could see her as he always had. His regard jolted her. Her eyes fluttered. He didn't know. He couldn't. She simply had to act the way Louise Canfield performed on stage.

"Well, Mr. Morgan?"

At his impatient tone, she concluded he hadn't guessed her identity and wasn't playing her like a toy. He was simply being his eccentric and unvarnished self.

"Very well," she rasped. "There is a place called the Dolly Mop Tea House. And from what I hear, the only one who has the leisure or inclination to drink tea is the bawd who runs the place."

She leaned forward to speak out the open carriage door to Collette's husband. Mr. Armitage stood with his pudgy hands behind his back, patiently rocking on his heels. He always went beyond duty for the Midnight Angel, acting as footman as well as driver. His belly extended well beyond the confines of his livery coat. His ruddy cheeks almost glowed in the late-night fog. He smiled warmly when he saw his employer.

"Yes, sir?"

"Take us to Leicester Square, Mr. Armitage."

Lydia insisted on going into the Dolly Mop Tea House alone while the men waited by the carriage. It was important to prove herself to both of them—and more important, to prove to herself that she could do this. She quickly made arrangements, then hurried back to the carriage, which sat in a pool of moonlit mist. The horses' hooves clomped on pavement she couldn't see.

Reggie had been pacing and hurried to meet her. "What happened?"

"We'll go in together," she said in an authoritative manner. "The bawd's name is Mrs. Lampwick. She obviously laces her tea with brandy or opium, so her reactions should be slow. She has a nose for quid, so pay her off at every turn if need be. Reggie, use the money I gave you."

Reggie nodded excitedly, but Lydia could feel Hugh's worry surround her like a snug cloak. She shrugged it off, trying to focus instead on their surroundings. This would be so much easier if she weren't attuned to his every mood.

The night seemed to swallow them whole where they stood by the decaying building. Lydia was grateful. The deepening fog seeped into her lungs, and she relished the moisture, for her mouth had gone dry the moment she'd stepped inside the Dolly Mop. She knew it would be sordid, but seeing it firsthand had been a nightmare.

"I take it you have reason to believe Sophie Parnham is here?" Hugh said, breaking into her troubling reverie. "If not, I do not think you should risk this charade."

What does he mean by charade? *Could he know?* She forced herself to meet his gaze unflinchingly. "You need not worry about me, sir. I am old enough to understand the risks I'm facing. Rather, I should think you might consider staying behind. You'll be risking your reputation."

He laughed mirthlessly. "My reputation was lost long ago."

"No, sir," she returned, "a nobleman's reputation is never lost. It is only we commoners who ever truly pay for our sins." She could scarcely believe she had blurted out such a revealing statement. A very long silence followed. Not even the horses fidgeted.

"Well, then, I need not fear," Hugh said at length. This time his laugh was less bitter, almost sad. The spell was broken.

"The girls are in the parlor," she said. "I'd warrant a few are as young as nine." She stopped when her voice quivered.

"She's not here, Morgan," Hugh said softly. "Don't make yourself go back in there. This is a shot in the dark. You have no evidence she's here."

She hated his certainty. Resented his empathy. "How do you know? Don't you understand I can leave no stone unturned? We're looking for his lordship's only child."

Hugh put his hands in his pocket and took a step closer, turning his body so Reggie could not hear what followed. Speaking low, he said, "Mrs. Lampwick doesn't deal with the same class of people as the Botanicals."

She bit her lower lip and nodded, unable to argue with that. "But you don't know the Botanicals were responsible."

"I don't know *yet*."

How self-assured he was! She shook her head disparagingly. "If there is a chance, however slim, that Miss Parnham is inside, we must search now." Life was so simple for one who saw things in black and white, who was guided by logic instead of a tender and bruised heart. How could he possibly know how many shades of gray there were when he had not suffered enough to truly open his eyes? She noticed a fleck of dirt on his lapel and could not resist the urge to brush it off.

The air between them crackled as he watched her do it, but he made no reply. Only stood very still.

"Perhaps you *are* a spoiled nobleman," she said finally. "Or perhaps you're simply afraid to go in there. Yes, I believe that's it." She smiled smugly. "Then we'll have to go in without you, Lord Montgomery. Come along, Reggie."

"Wait."

Hugh's voice stopped her in her tracks. She turned to find him regarding her with a look she remembered from long ago. The sarcasm, even the teasing light, had vanished from his eyes. They shimmered instead with a dark intensity. Fear? For her? His jaw clamped tightly. She was alarmed to see him so concerned for another man—a virtual stranger. Why, if he did not know her identity . . .

"I won't let you go in without me."

"Why not?"

"Because I'm afraid to stay out here all by myself." He gave her a cheeky grin, but his eyes remained dark. "Let me go in first. I'll keep her distracted."

"That's a capital idea," Reggie said. "I'll warrant she's seen your photograph in the newspapers, milord. She'll be impressed by that."

Hugh nodded. "I'll regale her with details of some of my famous cases while you two search."

Even Lydia had to welcome the offer without condition. "Good. When talking to Mrs. Lampwick, I implied that we're in some sort of perverse arrangement and that we wanted to pick just the right girl to please us all."

Reggie snorted in disgust. "No doubt Mrs. Lampwick has selected one very carefully."

Lydia repressed a shiver. "The sick old woman's eyes actually lit up."

Reggie nodded. "I can well imagine. What about the bully boy who let you in? The big lout looked like he had hams for fists."

"He did. And a nose as large and red as a small apple. I slipped him a few quid to buy another bottle of gin. That should keep him out of sight."

Reggie tapped up the rim of his brown bowler with a touch of a knuckle, grinning broadly. "My hat is off to you, sir. That was smart."

"What are you going to do while I'm charming Mrs. Lampwick?" Hugh asked.

"I've already surveyed the parlor where many girls are on display. If you can get Mrs. Lampwick into her private sitting room, Reggie and I will go room to room searching."

"We'd best be ready to make a fast exit," Reggie said. "There will be a right fine ruckus if we barge into the private rooms. The blokes who come to a place like this pay a pretty penny for a young virgin."

Lydia took a deep breath and nodded. "Shall we?"

The Midnight Angel led the way, entering through the red door when it opened at the hands of the stocky porter. Crying came from one of the rooms. It sounded like a very young girl. Lydia froze. Could it be Sophie?

Before they could investigate, muffled footfalls sounded on the creaking floorboards as a fat sot of a woman dressed in a low-cut gown of stained scarlet satin wove her way toward them.

"My dear Mrs. Lampwick," Hugh said charmingly as the bawd approached. "How very good it is to see you again."

Her rouged cheeks puckered against the pouches beneath her eyes as she squinted, trying to focus on the gentleman in front of her. Mrs. Lampwick momentarily lost her balance and had to push off the narrow hallway wall. Straightening to a full five feet of height, she frowned at Hugh suspiciously. " 'Ave we met, sir?"

"How could you possibly forget, my dear?" He reached

out and plucked her slack hand from her side, bending to kiss it. "I am Lord Montgomery."

"Lord Montgomery?" Her frown deepened.

Hugh motioned with his head for the others to start the search as he led the bawd toward the open door from which she had emerged. Lydia and Reggie slipped away unnoticed.

Mrs. Lampwick's eyes opened wide with greed. "Oh, you're the famous Lord Clue!" That was all it took. She began gushing and flirting, acting like a schoolgirl, though she had to be at least fifty.

As soon as Hugh closed the door behind them, Lydia and Reggie set to work, checking room by room. Inside the one they'd heard the sobs coming from, Reggie found the unfortunate young girl Mrs. Lampwick had chosen for them hovering on a sagging mattress in the corner. She couldn't have been more than thirteen. Her face was painted, and her long blond hair had been crimped. She looked at Reggie dully, the tears on her cheeks now dried in resignation. He wondered if she was an opium eater. That was the best way for a bawd to control her whores.

"'Ello, luv," she said in a froggy, surprisingly mature voice that made Reggie wonder momentarily if she were a dwarf. But she barely had breasts. She was simply young. "Whot 'appened to yer friends?"

"One's chatting with Mrs. Lampwick, and the other one is looking for a new girl. Sophie Parnham. Have you heard of her?"

The girl shook her head. Then she ran her hands down her sides in an incongruously sensuous gesture, playing the role she'd been assigned. The poor child looked like a bad actress who had been miscast and didn't know it.

She puckered her mouth and said, "'Ow do ye want it, luv?"

Reggie's mouth dropped open, then he nearly shouted like a stunned father, "How do I want what?"

The girl stood and began to remove her robe.

"Oh, no you don't, little lady." Reggie leapt forward and slipped the garment back on her shoulders. "Absolutely not!"

"Ye wants to be on top?"

The question sickened him, even though it was the very question he'd asked clients a lifetime ago. "No, I want you in my carriage."

"What?" Her practiced expression of lust vanished in a moment of confusion. It was the first time she looked her age. "Ye're not taking me away from 'ere," she said fearfully.

Here and your source of opium, I'll bet, Reggie thought. "Look, sweetheart, I'm taking you to Stone House. You'll be much better off."

"Like bloody 'ell! Mrs. Lampwick takes good care o' me."

There was a quick knock on the door. "Reggie, hurry up," whispered Morgan sotto voce.

Reggie picked up the girl by the waist. When she started to scream, he clapped a hand over her mouth. She bit him, and he cursed, then dragged her to the door while she howled like a cat in heat.

"Quiet, or you'll get us all killed."

But that warning came too late. When he entered the hall, Morgan was already at the back door and the viscount held it open, frantically motioning for Reggie to hurry up. His exit was speeded along when he heard Mrs. Lampwick careening down the hall after him.

Wielding an old rusty saber, she shrieked, "Where do ye think yer going! Come back! I'll 'ave ye arrested, if I don't kill ye first. What do ye mean, stealin' me girls?"

Reggie dragged the child out into the alley where the driver anxiously held open a door to the carriage. Throwing the girl inside, he scrambled after her, tumbling down beside the Midnight Angel and Viscount Montgomery. By then the coachman cracked the whip and they started off with a violent lurch, vanishing into the mist. All could hear the porter chasing after them and Mrs. Lampwick threatening their very lives.

"Come back with that girl! I'll call the police!"

"Oh, the police will be called, all right—by us," Montgomery said as he assisted Mr. Morgan and Reggie from the floor where the girl still crouched in terror. Breathing a sigh of relief, he smoothed back his tousled mop of shiny dark hair. "It's well past time Scotland Yard learned about the children serving the redoubtable Mrs. Lampwick, wouldn't you say, Mr. Morgan?"

Their eyes met and held in the flickering gaslights from the street. At length, Lydia smiled grimly and nodded. "Yes, it is. Now it's your turn to deal, milord. Let's hope the cards fall better this time around."

Chapter 7

❦

Champagne. The image of a sparkling crystal glass filled with bubbling champagne flitted through Hugh's mind during the entire carriage ride from the Dolly Mop Tea House to the Diamond Forest. Certainly, he had a taste for the drink. Something about this night made him want to celebrate. But it was the color of Addie's skin that made him think of the bubbly. She had tried to dull her natural pink complexion with beige cosmetics. What resulted was a healthy, ginger glow.

Addie was so beautiful, even when her attempts to look like a man of the world resulted in the vague appearance of a prepubescent boy. Did she really think she'd fooled the great Lord Clue? Or was this just one more layer of pretense? Perhaps the only way she could allow herself to be with him was to masquerade as someone else. Someone other than his beloved Addie.

No, not Addie. He had to think of her as Lydia now. He no longer had the right to call her by her true name. He had lost that privilege five years ago and must now join in the charade. But which one? There were so many.

Here sat Addie Parker, who now called herself Lydia, Countess of Beaumont, who dressed as a man named Henry Morgan, who paraded as the Midnight Angel. Yes, Hugh definitely needed champagne, if for no other reason than to soothe his befuddled brain.

The night had been eventful enough without the distraction sitting primly across from him. Under great protest, with kicking, biting, and curses of compelling creativity, the girl they'd rescued from Mrs. Lampwick's den of vice had been subdued, but it took both men to do it. Hugh wondered idly if Reggie noted how carefully his employer had held back lest "his" disguise be undone. The girl had been forcibly taken from the place where she had been given shelter, food, and enough spirits and opium to keep her docile. She was terrified.

Only the Midnight Angel's calming low voice had finally quieted her hysteria. Once Betsy Omers had learned who was behind her sudden abduction, she had quieted at once, her eyes shining with adoration for her savior. They had deposited her in Mrs. Cromwell's capable hands at Stone House and gone on their way.

Remembering the girl's response to Lydia, the great Lord Clue was forced to admit his own feelings of adoration for the Midnight Angel. A rueful smile twisted his mouth sadly. Then Reggie's voice interrupted his reverie.

"We're almost there, milord." He had to duck his head to see out the window over Lydia's shoulder. She stared at the passing scenery, then glanced Hugh's way.

Their gazes locked. His heart swelled. He wanted to be alone with her. No one else could mesmerize him so completely with one simple look. Those amethyst eyes of hers could see into his very soul with a passing glance. He and his Addie were two halves of one whole, and they'd been ripped apart by a capricious and cruel fate.

"It doesn't take much to ruin heaven, does it, Mr. Morgan?"

Her eyes fluttered like the wings of a butterfly. She had to filter every thought through all this pretense. "I'm sure I don't know what you mean," she rasped, unaware of how sensual she sounded in her pretend voice.

"I'm sure you do. But we'll save that discussion for another day."

The carriage slowed and then came to a heavy, squeaky stop in front of what looked like an abandoned building.

"Are you sure this is it?" she asked.

Reggie nodded. "I'm sure." He tugged on his bowler. "Now, I don't want you to be shocked, Mr. Morgan, but you might see a few things here that are peculiar, to say the least."

She looked affronted. "Why aren't you worried about him?" She cocked a thumb in Hugh's direction.

Reggie looked nonplused. "Lord Clue? Why, he's seen it all, I'm sure."

"And the Midnight Angel hasn't?" she persisted.

Hugh smothered a smile. She had always diminished her own worth in certain obvious ways—accepting class differences too easily, for example. But in other ways she was bold as brass, hard-headed, and just plain proud.

Reggie's face was flaming. He cleared his throat as he carefully chose his words. "Mr. Morgan, sir, you've seen a great deal of the fallen angels littering London's streets. I'm not sure, sir, you've seen . . . boy tarts. And men who like to, well, dress up as . . . women."

Her eyes exploded with mirth. "What?! I can't imagine why anyone would want to do that."

"Perversity, sir, plain and simple."

They all exchanged tense glances, each awaiting shock and horror from the other. When nothing of that nature was forthcoming, Lydia began to laugh. Soon Reggie joined in, bursting with relief. Even Hugh let out a chuckle from deep in his belly. He couldn't say what they were laughing about, but it felt right. They were a team tonight. They had to be.

The door flew open, and Mr. Armitage lowered the steps. "Here you are, sirs."

"Shall we?" Reggie asked, then stepped into the misty, sordid night.

Lydia felt distinctly uneasy as the trio began their surreal sojourn to the Diamond Forest, a very secret place, to be sure. Once they'd abandoned the safety of the carriage, they followed Reggie's lead, traveling through a maze of hallways in an abandoned building. The cold brick and plaster walls seemed to sweat, secreting a nasty scent that hung sourly on the miasmic air.

When they finally reached the entrance, it was a narrow archway ten feet deep guarded on the front end by two tall men dressed like members of the Queen's Guard at Buckingham Palace. They each wore a genuine bright red tunic and a tall puffy black bearskin cap. They differed from the real thing only in that their faces were garishly painted with women's makeup and their uniforms were tattered castaways, not at all the neatly kept attire worn by those who guarded the queen. Nevertheless, Queen Victoria's late husband Prince Albert would turn over in his grave if he saw a great symbol of the monarchy being used in such a fashion.

Uneasily, Reggie spoke sotto voce with the guards. It was apparent they knew him. After slipping them a fistful of money, he managed to gain entrance for his obviously upper-class companions, but not until they all agreed to wear the half-masks provided by the club. Lydia and her conspirators fitted the borrowed pieces over their eyes. She shuddered, imagining the men who must have worn her mask before her. What would she see beyond the darkness?

They felt their way through the seemingly endless tunnel, moving toward a faint flicker of light. The sounds of music and coarse, drunken laughter echoed down to them. At last they pushed through a curtain of beads straight into a great, churning mass of dancing, chattering, laughing men and women. But which was which?

At first all seemed normal. She saw a man dressed in formal tails and white waistcoat, a very dapper gentleman with a neatly trimmed auburn beard. He danced cheek to cheek with a woman in a long gown. But the woman had no breasts to speak of, and she was taller and far more muscular than the man. When the Amazonian dancer turned sideways, revealing an arm that was hairier than an ape's, Lydia concluded that *she* was a *he*.

"Oh, dear," she whispered as her companions came to stand beside her.

"How very interesting," Hugh purred.

"I don't see the proprietor, milord," Reggie said to Hugh. "That's who you want to see, ain't it? The man in the diamond butterfly mask?"

"Yes, but not to worry. I'll look around."

There was much to see. On closer examination, Lydia found bare-breasted women smoking and laughing with male companions, a few females dressed like men, and a great many bearded ladies decked out in their finest. All were safe here, for half-masks hid their identities. Even if one recognized someone else, who would want to admit it? Secrecy was assured because of guilt by association.

After overcoming her initial shock, Lydia focused on the colorful setting. There was an enormous stained-glass chandelier that hung from the domed ceiling. A painted blue bar stretched the length of one wall. Sienna and gold Aztec wallpaper adorned the walls, and two pillars sat in the middle of the dance floor. They were carved like ancient oak trees, with the wood etched like bark and branches twisting up to the ceiling. They reminded Lydia of something out of a druidic forest.

In contrast, a fresco adorned the ceiling, done in the early sixteenth-century Renaissance style. At first glance, it looked like a copy of Michelangelo's masterpiece in the Sistine Chapel. But this painting contained a few details

Michelangelo had omitted in his commission by Pope Julius II. All the figures in this "heavenly" portrait were completely naked, and everyone was joined in sexual union with someone else in the montage—angels with angels, men with devils.

Lydia gasped. She sensed Reggie's "I told you so" nod of the head and frowned to conceal her incredulity. "Well, Reggie, I'll grant this place is unusual, but it takes more than this to scare me off."

She felt a shadow tower over her, and she turned with a jump that belied her declaration of bravery. "Oh, Montgomery, it's only you."

He gazed down at her with kindness . . . and something more, much more. He had a way of looking at people that obliterated everyone else in the room, she reminded herself. That did not mean he suspected her identity. She sighed away the tension that had unconsciously been gripping her. "What do you think, Lord Clue? Shall we stay? If Reggie doesn't have reason to believe that these people are directly connected to Sophie's case, we can't waste time here."

Hugh casually put a hand on her shoulder. She stared at it, wondering how and why it seemed to be burning a hole through her coat.

"Give me a few minutes," he said, scanning the room. "I want to see if I recognize anyone belonging to the Botanicals."

"How could you possibly recognize anyone with all these masks? And who are the Botanicals precisely?"

Hugh removed his heavy, warm hand from her shoulder to snatch a glass of champagne off a tray that passed in the hands of a server—a fat woman dressed like Attila the Hun. She wore long, gold braids made of yellow yarn and a Viking helmet and carried a battle-ax on the heavy leather belt girding her ample waist. The costume would have appeared more formidable if not for her pendulous breasts, utterly bare and lolling on several layers of gelatinous white flesh. This time Lydia's jaw dropped unabashedly.

"Here," Hugh said with paternal reassurance as he handed her the champagne goblet and swiped up a second one for himself, "I think you'll need it before the night is through."

When Attila moved on, Lydia finally closed her jaw to drink and positively swilled her champagne. "Ah, that's better," she said, dabbing her lips with a backhand.

Hugh sipped more cautiously. "To answer your question, the Botanical Society is a fraternal organization ostensibly devoted to the study of Nature, with a capital n."

"You mean . . . birds, plants, that sort of thing?"

He nodded. "You noticed the oak pillar as an obvious tribute to nature. And the cornices adorned with oak leaves and acorns."

"What else do you know about them?"

"They're a group of men who meet two evenings a month at the homes of various members, all belonging to high society. Even the Prince of Wales attends on occasion."

Lydia whistled low and was quite proud of the effect. She'd worked hard on acquiring the basic male affectations, such as striking a match without flinching to light a cigar, or subtly tugging on her pants when she rose, to reposition her nonexistent male anatomy. Her whistle of amazement was a special talent.

"But the prince always leaves before midnight," Hugh added significantly as he pursed his beautifully formed lips around the glass for another sip.

His fingers gracefully gripped the goblet stem. They were long and strong. How well she remembered. *I cannot think of that.* She shifted her mood deliberately, asking with a sly grin, "What happens at midnight? Do the Botanicals turn into mice?"

"That's when the core members of the group retire to a room filled with young virgins."

Lydia's mood sobered at once. "How young?"

He shrugged. "Many are well below the age of consent. But it doesn't matter to these *noblemen*." He stressed the word with a disgusted curl of his lips. "They would never pay for the crime of deflowering a child. Everyone knows a gentleman must be able to have sex without risking his life. That's why the Contagious Diseases Acts were passed, so the police could imprison diseased whores. They would never think of arresting the men who hired these poor tramps."

"Why don't any of these so-called gentlemen make love to their own wives?" Lydia asked, unable to contain the white hot fury bubbling up inside her.

"Most of these men think their wives are too pure to be sullied with sex, except for the occasional attempt to procreate."

Lydia sighed and shook her head, letting go of her anger. "Fools. They're all bloody fools."

"Most of the girls have been bought by the Botanicals, virtually sold by impoverished parents. The poor girls have no advocate."

"They should have!" she shot back indignantly. "You've apparently known about this for some time, but you've done nothing to stop it."

He tipped back his glass for the last few precious sips of the very fine French champagne, then looked at her with patient amusement. "Do not get yourself in a dither, Mr. Morgan. I've been trying for years to find a witness, or at least enough evidence to bring down the Botanicals. But it hasn't been easy. The prince's sponsorship has protected the group from Scotland Yard inquiries. Perhaps I'll find something pertinent tonight."

She turned to him with urgency and gripped his arm, unaware of how feminine a gesture it was. "Do you think they have Sophie? I know you found the sprig of mistletoe by the theater, but . . . could she be here? Tonight?"

He took a measured breath. It was growing exceedingly difficult for him to keep up his facade of indifference when she touched him. "I doubt we'll find Sophie. But let us roam around a bit and ask a few questions. Make them aware that we're interested in what they do. That's the only way to put pressure on them. They might make a mistake."

"Or they might just kill us," Reggie interjected as he eyed the room nervously.

The triumvirate split up for the next twenty minutes and wandered about, making observations, looking for signs of backroom activities. Hugh drew many stares, partially because of his height and doubtless there were those who recognized him in spite of his mask. He was used to being recognized and ignored it. All the better if his presence upset someone. But he did not want Lydia endangered. He riveted his gaze on her and found she had unwittingly become the object of another man's affections—a man so effeminate he would make Lilly Langtree look masculine. The poor fellow followed her through the crowd like a puppy dog. *Well, at least she is safe with him,* Hugh thought with an ironic laugh. *Safer than she'd be with me.*

He forced himself to concentrate on the case, scanning the crowd. The only member of the Botanicals he saw was Lord George Bradon. His thick broom mustache and buck teeth gave him away. Otherwise Hugh might not have recognized him. He was dressed in a sequined gown that narrowed at the feet like the tail of a mermaid, and his flat, mealy lips were painted into a plump red bow.

Hugh skimmed the long carved oak bar. His gaze passed Reggie, who drank with an acquaintance, doubtless pumping the fellow for information. Hugh's eyes stopped abruptly when they fastened on a man who wore a glittering butterfly mask over his eyes and looked vaguely familiar.

From the waist up he was well dressed in a fine twill suit, but he wore no trousers. Not even undergarments. In fact, the only thing that hid his anatomy was a glittering gold and diamond leaf the size of a hand. Hugh didn't even want to know how he had managed to attach it to his male anatomy.

So this was the proprietor. Hugh tried not to stare, but

the many faceted jewels dazzled and leapt with rainbow colors in the light of a nearby gasolier. The way the club owner stood, casually leaning on the bar, observing others, with none daring to speak to him, and the way he put his cigar to his mouth with elegant grace, led Hugh to understand he was in charge here. And he was a gentleman, if not a nobleman.

Hugh moved toward the bar. When he was close enough to see the man's cleft chin, his mind jerked with recognition. *Trevor Dobson.* Sir Trevor Dobson was the baronet who lived in a manor next to his father's palatial mansion, called Windhaven, northwest of Oxford. Hugh had been on many a fox hunt with Dobson. He weighed his options, then sidled through the crowd until they were face to face.

"Good evening, Sir Trevor," Hugh said.

The aging baronet turned his head slowly toward Hugh, let out a puff of cigar smoke, and regarded his neighbor's son with wry amusement. "Good evening, Montgomery. What brings you to the Diamond Forest?"

In his mind, Hugh turned over a number of answers. "I'm trying to determine if any of your patrons are kidnappers," or, "I wanted to find out why you named your club after a piece of jewelry worn by my mother until her untimely death," or, "I'm curious to find out just precisely what sort of sexual perversion you practice, because there are obviously so many variations in this seedy place." All too forward to achieve his ends. Instead, he decided on the neutral, "I was in the neighborhood and thought I'd stop in."

Dobson snorted a laugh. "I'm glad you did." He stubbed out his cigar in an ashtray on the oak bar, then motioned for one of the bartenders to give the viscount a double shot of the finest brandy.

"Thank you," Hugh said, accepting the balloon snifter with a mock toast in the air and an appreciative sip. "I gather you aren't spending much time in the country these days."

"No." Dobson grinned, revealing a row of tobacco-stained teeth. "I prefer my entertainments in town."

Hugh glanced sardonically at the lower half of his body. "So I see."

"What really brought you here, Lord Clue? You don't have to pretend with an old neighbor."

"I'm looking for a girl."

Dobson's grin broadened, and he waved his cigar at the crowd. "There are a few here, I believe, though the overwhelming population of the Diamond Forest consists of males, mostly those who favor the . . . er, company of their own sex, and a great many who simply prefer women's clothing."

Well, he was utterly honest. Hugh was glad that his father's old friend wasn't going to try to hide the obvious. Although Hugh was a grown man, he still thought of the silver-haired Dobson as an authority figure. As far as he had known, Dobson was family-oriented, a devoted husband. How wrong he had been.

"Do you want me to find someone for you?" Dobson continued. "There is a back room available."

Hugh considered that he might learn something by taking Dobson up on the offer. Still, the odds were too long. He decided on a direct course. "I'm searching for a girl who has been kidnapped. Her name is Sophie Parnham. She was taken outside the Chamberlain Music Hall two days ago. I have reason to believe someone was after her virginity."

"Smart move," Dobson said dryly.

"What the fool didn't know, however, was that she's the illegitimate daughter of the Earl of Beaumont."

Dobson's head snapped his way. Then he guffawed. "Oh, that is prime! Poor devil. Whoever it was will get his comeuppance, that is if Beaumont lives long enough to do anything about it. I understand the earl's life of debauchery has finally caught up with him."

Hugh was surprised Dobson knew Beaumont's well-kept secret but made no comment about it. Instead, he said casually, "I thought the culprit might be one of the Botanicals."

"Possible," Dobson replied noncommittally. "Have you any candidates?"

"Do I recognize Bradon over there—dressed like a mermaid?"

"Yes, but he isn't your man. Women do nothing for him. Bradon has a thing for fishermen. He likes the bugger boys from the wharf. Wants them to dress like whaling ship captains and tie him up with anchor lines."

"Lord!" Hugh said in disgust.

The older man pulled another cigar from his jacket pocket and offered it to Hugh, who declined. Dobson then stuck it in his mouth to chew. "I'll tell you what, Montgomery. How about one favor for another between old neighbors? I'll keep my eye out for Miss Parnham. I'll even ask around for you. I'll send word if I hear anything."

"And in return?"

Dobson shrugged. His pencil-thin gray mustache curled with irony. "You simply pretend you were never here. And you've never heard of the Diamond Forest. I wouldn't want any of your friends at Scotland Yard to pay me a visit."

Hugh finished his brandy. It was a bargain he could strike for now. He nodded.

"But I will tell you, Monty, that I'm not afraid of you, no matter how clever you are. Do you know why I say that?"

Hugh shrugged.

Dobson smiled enigmatically. "Ask your father."

"We're not speaking. I haven't seen him in five years."

"Ask your father," he repeated with a knowing look that made Hugh uncomfortable.

Lydia had finally succeeded in discouraging her besotted admirer by dumping a glass of champagne over his greasy head. Not wishing to draw further attention to herself, she vanished into a crush of jostling bodies on the dance floor. Where the deuce were Hugh and Reggie? She was too short to see over the press.

Suddenly she found herself being swept into the arms of a man who felt blessedly familiar. She stumbled against him, felt the instant heat, and looked up quickly into two piercing blue eyes.

"Oh, Montgomery! It's you." She fell into dancing, relieved to see her former admirer at the edge of the floor slinking off in defeat. Only then did she realize she was dressed as a man and dancing with a man. "Montgomery! What are you doing?"

She shoved him away and raked him with an indignant glare. "How dare you! Simply because we're with a passel of perverts doesn't mean I've lost my morals," she hissed.

"Oh, shut up," he said with a chuckle, pulling her back into his arms. "Haven't you heard the phrase, 'When in Rome . . . '?"

"The men in Rome didn't dance together. That was in Greece."

He stopped her protests with a quick twirl. They waltzed to a tune being played by a four-string quartet in a balcony. In spite of her embarrassment, all Lydia's anxiety gave way to pleasure. She loved to dance and hadn't done so in years. She'd never known that Hugh was so deft on his feet, but she should have. Was there anything he couldn't do, curse the man?

"What have you found out?" she gruffly inquired.

He pulled her in closer, ostensibly to murmur secret findings in her ear. But she could scarcely hear his response because his hot breath tickled down her neck and sent blazing tendrils of excitement scurrying across her skin. Her head thundered with her own pulse.

"I found the proprietor," he said, bending down and pressing his cheek to her temple.

Lord, she thought, *he is certainly acting the part!* "You mean the man with the butterfly mask and the blazing display of diamonds affixed to his genitals?" She was proud of the way she said the last word so naturally.

Hugh barked out a delighted laugh. "The very one. Turns

out he is Sir Trevor Dobson. Does that name ring a bell?"

"Yes, but I can't remember why." When he nestled his rough chin in her hair, she sucked in a breath. He was making her shiver with desire. *Get a hold of yourself.*

"Dobson lived next to Windhaven. I used to hunt at his place."

Of course! She'd visited his house when she was governess at Windhaven. "Never heard of him," she replied.

He grinned down at her with such amusement that it worried her. "You're a clever one, Morgan."

She wasn't sure if it was a compliment or an accusation. When Hugh whirled her around, she caught sight of Reggie at the bar. He looked at her strangely, and she felt self-conscious about dancing with Hugh. She didn't want Reggie to think Morgan was enjoying himself. And he was, she thought, as she allowed herself to nestle her cheek a moment against Hugh's strong chest.

Morgan was enjoying himself very much indeed.

They were unusually quiet during the ride home. Reggie leaned his head against the backboard and shut his eyes. Hugh looked pensively out the window, very handsome in his top hat and evening wear. Lydia simply drank in every detail of his splendid body. She wished to be in his arms again, but she did not dare. The dance—unorthodox as it was—had been the only opportunity for intimacy she could permit. It was not safe in his arms.

"What are you thinking?" she asked, trying to distract herself.

He didn't look at her immediately. He was lost in one of his deep bouts of thinking. When he finally turned toward her, he was all seriousness. "I just realized something that has been torturing my mind since we left the club."

"What?" She sat a little straighter. When Lord Clue made connections, that often meant he was close to solving a case.

"The Botanicals have nothing to do with Sophie's kidnapping."

"What?" Disappointment rang in her voice. "How do you know?"

"Seeing Lord Bradon reminded me of something. The symbol adopted by the Botanicals is a branch of holly, not mistletoe. I'd forgotten that. Bloody idiotic of me."

"Don't blame yourself. You wanted to see a connection with a known organization, and your mind leapt to conclusions. It's very natural. Without such an important lead, however, we are lost."

She sounded forlorn, and he turned to her with his burning intensity. "I'm sorry. I fear I'm being distracted by a personal matter. My mother owned a brooch that looked very much like the diamond mask worn by Trevor Dobson."

A potent silence followed this puzzling statement. At last she whispered, "You think there is some connection between your mother and Sir Trevor?"

"There has to be." His eyes met hers and she knew. She knew he knew who she really was. The horses clomped onward. The carriage rocked and squeaked. Time seemed to stand still. The air closed in around them. Her thoughts whirled in the thickening silence. How should she react? What should she say?

Nothing! Say nothing. Do not acknowledge it. But there it was, this dangerous new awareness shimmering between them. How long had he known she was pretending to be Morgan? She dared not think of it, lest it undo her utterly. Instead, she asked in a strained whisper, "Do you think . . . Trevor Dobson . . . had anything to do with your mother's death?"

He nodded slowly. "Yes, I fear so."

The carriage came to a stop. Reggie woke from his light sleep.

"Ah, here we are," he said with forced joviality. He had obviously been uncomfortable reentering his old life albeit briefly. He opened the door and let down the steps, then practically jumped out to chat with the coachman.

Lydia stared intently at the two men outside, trying not to look at Hugh. But then he deftly crossed to her seat. He sat at the edge, one hand propped against the back of it. He'd taken off his hat and looked down at her with scorching intensity. She inhaled his masculinity, waiting a moment, letting the intimacy build.

"You remember Windhaven, don't you?" His voice was soft as velvet in the night.

She swallowed hard, answering in her real voice, "Yes. I remember too much. The accident at Devil's Peak, the ritual, the . . . the gossip—"

"Don't remember that," he murmured, then tipped up her chin with a finger and covered her mouth with his own, stopping short her sentence. His lips were hot, tender, firm, seeking, giving. So much. He didn't part her lips. But his closed-mouth kiss held years of pent-up passion. She remained stiff at first, thinking she could just take it, enjoy it, without admitting it or paying for the sin. But then her own passion, her undeniable love for Hugh, broke loose, and she leaned into him, surrendering.

Reggie gave Mr. Armitage directions to his place, then stepped back to the carriage. He was still nervous about having his employer and the great Lord Clue see the sort of places in which he had so recently done business. But that was past, and he had a job to do. He had to see the gents on their way. It was very late. He poked his head in the cabin, then froze.

There Lord Montgomery and Mr. Morgan sat, locked in a passionate embrace.

Chapter 8

W hat is wrong, milady?" asked Colette. She straightened the Morgan suit and hung it in the bureau, then turned and gazed at Lydia's reflection from over her ladyship's shoulder.

Lydia made no reply, frowning at herself in the oblong, free-standing mirror. She took no note of her thin, nearly naked figure adorned only in a corset and stockings. Her physical body troubled her never so much as the gloomy future that stretched endlessly ahead of her.

After the kiss with Hugh in the carriage, her world had changed irrevocably. How could she ever go back to the secure, staid life she'd fashioned for herself as the countess? How could she give up Hugh yet a second time? Shaking her head to dismiss such painful thoughts, she turned her attention to the implications of her Midnight Angel disguise being penetrated. She and the viscount had not revealed her identity to the stunned Reggie, but how long before the clever fellow fit the pieces together?

The three of them had awkwardly parted company after that, and she returned directly to Beaumont House. She'd trembled the whole way home, completely undone by the strange turn of events.

Hugh knew who she was. Had he known all along? The thought sent a deep shiver of apprehension snaking down her spine. She hated being found out. She'd thrived living vicariously in a man's disguise. Was she prepared to be herself and nothing else? And now Reggie would find out as well. Could she trust either of them to keep her secret? Lydia was shaken to realize how dependent she had become on her alter identity.

"Now, then, milady, you're as quiet as a mouse. You can tell Colette what's bothering you."

Lydia forced herself to look at her maid's worried, kindly expression in the mirror.

"So much has happened, I can't really say what disturbs me most," Lydia replied. She commenced to bite her thumbnail.

"Well, whatever it is, don't try to solve your problems now, ma'am. Put your worries to bed, along with yourself, and everything will seem brighter in the morning."

That would be only a few hours from now. Lydia doubted she would sleep at all. She kept remembering Hugh's kiss.

It was all there. The fire had never burned out. I love him just as much as ever. But does he love me? Did he ever?

While Colette retrieved her sleeping gown and began to put it over her head, a new worry seeped into Lydia's already troubled thoughts. If people learned that she was the infamous Midnight Angel, it would doubtless be splayed all over the papers. Reporters loved smearing the peerage with ugly gossip. Once her photograph appeared in print, someone would recognize her as Addie Parker.

Lydia had very carefully hidden her identity from her husband's set, staying away from the social affairs most aristocrats attended, using her husband's declining health as an excuse. But if the world found out her sordid history, she would become a pariah, utterly alone when her husband was no longer alive to protect her. And worse, she would always be alone.

The fear that Reggie might not keep her secret now forced her to admit a forbidden desire she'd been harboring even from herself.

I want to be with Hugh. I want to be his wife.

She wanted to be his lover and friend. They belonged together. Once they had saved each other's lives. Could they do it again? He did not look well. She intuited that something was wrong with him and felt deep in her woman's heart that she could make him better. But that would be impossible if he learned the truth about her. For although he knew she was Addie Parker, the governess he had seduced, he did not know what she had become afterward, in that horrible time before Beaumont saved her.

Suddenly the door flew open, interrupting her ruminations. Both women turned with a start. Then Colette let out a scream. There stood a man, staring at Lydia in her state of dishevel.

"Reggie!" Lydia finally managed to choke out. "What are you doing here?"

He said nothing for a long, tortured moment. He simply stared dumbfounded at her trim figure tucked in the frilly corset. His puppy-dog brown eyes met hers, and she could see the recognition flash there. Then his gaze glazed over in confusion, fixed at the site of her breasts cupped neatly and bulging over the top of her corset, before Colette collected her wits enough to seize a robe and throw it over her mistress's body.

"Bloody hell," he cursed, shaking his head. "You fooled me but good, didn't you?"

"Reggie, how did you get in here?"

He frowned sullenly. "After I saw you and the viscount . . . well, I wanted to know what was what. After you dropped me off, I hailed a cab and followed you here. I caught the backdoor before it shut behind you. I came up the stairs, but I never expected to see . . . *this*."

"We have to talk," Lydia said while jamming her arms into the robe and belting it. "But not here."

"Tell me who you are!" he shouted.

"I am the Countess of Beaumont," she said as calmly as she could.

His face lost all expression. He looked as if he would pitch up his dinner any moment.

"Reggie, let Colette get you something to drink."

"Bloody hell," he rasped. "And I thought this was an honest job. You lied to me!"

He began to sway, and she thought he might faint. He staggered back into the narrow, secret hallway, then closed the door.

"Quick, Colette! Go after him. Take him to my private parlor. And give him a good dose of brandy."

"Aye, ma'am," the maid said, leaving Lydia to dress herself for what promised to be an incredibly difficult interview.

At 10 o'clock the next morning, Lydia accompanied Clara to the Little Shepherd's Ladies' Clinic in the East End. Because Clara wanted this to be an anonymous visit, they hired a hansom cab instead of taking either of their personal carriages.

"You seem pensive, Lydia," Clara said when they had nearly reached their destination. "I hope you don't regret agreeing to come with me."

"No, of course not," Lydia said warmly, pressing her hand. "Not at all. It's simply that I have a great deal on my mind. Both Reggie and Montgomery discovered the real identity of Mr. Morgan last night."

"Oh, no! And you worked so hard at your disguise. What happened?"

"I've had very little sleep and could not possibly recount it all. But let it suffice to say that Montgomery knew me too well for any disguise to work with him. And Reggie realized something was wrong when he saw Montgomery kissing me."

Clara drew in an audible gasp. Then she laughed at the image her mind created.

"Don't say a word," Lydia pleaded. "I feel horrible. Naturally, I plan to tell my husband."

"Oh," Clara said, sobering. "I'd quite forgot how he might feel."

"I haven't. I simply cannot betray him behind his back. And I assure you it will never happen again. Meanwhile, Reggie feels terribly hurt by my deception. We had a long talk, and he's agreed to keep my secret."

"Can you trust him?"

"I think so. In a way, my confession has bound him more closely to me. He feels important. Still, his fantasies of working for a proper gentleman have been shattered. He wants so very much to be a legitimate employee. I don't think working for a woman fits in with that plan," she said dryly. "But he has agreed to stay on, at least until we find Sophie. I couldn't bear to face Montgomery this soon, so he is pursuing some leads on his own."

"That is why you had time to go with me today." Clara considered the situation, then said, "I should think when the shock wears off Reggie will realize how fortunate he is to be working for a countess."

Lydia nodded, although Clara's words gave her a pang of discomfort. She was such a fraud. How long would it be before her charade was revealed?

"Enough about me. Let's talk about you," she said with forced brightness. By then the carriage had stopped in front of an ancient brick building with crumbling mortar. It sat like a great hulking mass, shadowed by teeming tenements and factory buildings belching sooty filth into the morning sky. Clara's shoulders sagged momentarily. But the sign above the door was clean and professional looking.

Lydia patted her hand. "Don't be discouraged by the setting. The doctor is marvelous. Now let's find out precisely what she has to say."

They found the interior of the clinic to be clean and efficiently run by a woman everyone referred to as Nurse Petrie. Her command post was situated behind a tall counter from which she issued directions in a stern voice. The waiting room was filled with indigent patients, women whom life had defeated. They were dressed in none too clean tattered clothes that reflected the weary hardship etched on their faces. Many of the younger ones had children clinging to their skirts. The elderly and seriously ill hobbled to a makeshift infirmary in the back.

At the sight of Lydia, Nurse Petrie came around from her station and welcomed them warmly, ushering them to the doctor's office. There Lydia and Clara sat until Dr. Abigail Smith joined them to discuss Clara's fertility problems. She wore a utilitarian navy blue dress and white collar. She was rather stern looking, but that was understandable considering how many poor women waited in line for her services, and considering how difficult it must have been for her to survive the male-dominated medical system. She had little time left over for charming pleasantries. As a patron of the clinic, Lydia had witnessed over the years how much Dr. Smith cared about her patients.

Dr. Smith personally escorted the nervous Clara to an examining room, where she was to be probed vaginally with a speculum, a tool that had roused the distrust of respectable women because it was regularly used during forced examinations on prostitutes. Dr. Smith assured Clara that the speculum was necessary for a thorough diagnosis.

While her friend was receiving the physical examination, Lydia anxiously paced in the office. A half-hour later, a pale Clara rejoined her, and moments later Dr. Smith returned, closing the door of her inner sanctum. "Well, Lady Leach, the news is not all bad," she said, tossing down her notes and sinking into her chair with a weary sigh.

"Really?" Clara's cheeks flushed with normal color. She exchanged a hopeful look with Lydia.

"There is nothing permanently wrong with your reproductive organs."

"That's excellent news," Clara said, moving to the edge of her chair. "Isn't it?"

"I'm afraid, however, that your use of the corset has disturbed the natural placement of your female organs."

Clara stiffened back against her chair as if the physician had slapped her. All she could manage to say was, "Oh?"

The doctor continued, "I believe you can successfully carry a child to term, but you must give up the use of the corset immediately and allow your insides to fall back into their natural place."

There was a long, stunned silence. How could Clara possibly give up on an undergarment that was necessary for virtually every acceptable fashion? Only the most Bohemian of women abandoned that cinching contraption. Conversely, many women whom Clara associated with in the Ladies' National Association believed that corsets were essential to a woman's independence because they encouraged self-constraint and an upright self-image. These thoughts were written, along with shocked dismay, all over Clara's face.

"I simply can't go without," she replied. "I must think of my husband's career."

"Yes, you can," Lydia said. "Think of what your husband would want. Do you think he'd care about social niceties if abandoning them meant producing an heir? You once said you weren't as brave as I am, but that's simply not true. What does it matter what others think of your appearance as long as you have your precious child?"

The doctor nodded as Clara digested Lydia's words. Was she so bold? Certainly any social scandal was secondary to providing Todd with the child they both desired so

devoutly. Gradually the shock and fearfulness dropped
away like rusty shackles, and the light returned to Clara's
lovely blue eyes. "You're right, Lady Beaumont. It's a
small sacrifice to make if it means I can give my husband a
son. Very well. I'll do it."

While Clara and the doctor further discussed the intimate details of her new regimen, Lydia returned to
the lobby. There she observed the clinic's bustling activity
with her usual fascination and sadness. How beaten and
forlorn these women were. She could only imagine the
bleakness of their lives, forced to labor at strenuous jobs
for a pittance, old before their time, often sick with preg-
nancies that followed much too closely one after another.

Turning her attention away from such gloomy specula-
tions, she soon found her attention riveted on the young
girl cleaning the floor. She attacked it with such methodi-
cal, almost ritualistic strokes of her broom that the dirt
went flying in clouds. Such was her fixation that Lydia
wondered if the girl's mental faculties were intact. Frequently, such encumbered people were given menial tasks
in institutions.

When the girl at length raised her head, Lydia could see
part of her face for the first time. For a moment, her heart
skipped. She thought it might be Sophie. Like Sophie, this
girl was young, blond, and blue-eyed. However, this girl
didn't have Beaumont's distinctive high cheeks, while
Sophie did. At least she appeared to in the photograph
Lydia had seen.

"Nurse Petrie," Lydia said as the nurse passed by on an
errand, "is this a new girl? I've never seen her before."

"That's our May," said Nurse Petrie. "I put her to work a
week ago. Pretty girl, isn't she?"

"Yes, she is." The more Lydia stared at May, the more
she wondered about the poor child's circumstances. The
girl's bearing and features seemed to indicate that she was

not born into the lower class. But if she was as intelligent as her discerning eyes would indicate and was from the middle class, why was she sweeping the floor? Why hadn't she been given a more important task?

"She looks so unhappy."

"Yes, that's true enough," the nurse said in her clipped manner. "But until she starts to talk, we can't do much else with her."

"She's mute?"

"She stumbled into the clinic a year ago, on May 5. She said only two words—*May Day*. That's why we call her May. She stayed with us for two weeks and then vanished. A week ago she came in unannounced as if she'd never been gone. There was no explanation, of course, because she won't talk. I felt sorry for her and put her to work." Nurse Petrie lowered her voice. "When she first came here she'd been molested, poor thing."

"What kind of man could do such a thing?"

"You should rather say, ma'am, what sort of *men*," the nurse said, giving her a significant look.

"A pack of cowardly dogs," Lydia replied indignantly.

"Yes. Quite a large pack, too. At least, that's what the doctor concluded upon examining her. May never said a word. And because she can't or won't tell us where she's from, we can't return her to her rightful home. Dr. Smith has been kind enough to allow her to stay here."

Lydia frowned thoughtfully. "Do you suppose she was molested on May Day?"

"Dr. Smith says that would be about right, based on the evidence, which had partially healed by the time she arrived here last year."

"How odd that she would come back to the clinic a year later just in time for May Day. It's a little less than three weeks away." Lydia's heart went out to the poor thing. She reached for her pocketbook. "Would it be acceptable if I gave her a little money of her own to spend?"

"That would be right lovely. Now, if you'll excuse me,

your ladyship, we have a girl going into labor in the back."
Just then a howl of gurgling pain echoed down the hall,
and Nurse Petrie hurried away.

Lydia approached the girl. "May?" she asked tentatively.
The girl looked up sullenly. "May, I'd like to give you
some money so you can buy something for yourself."

The girl stared down at the sovereign Lydia offered, and
her eyes widened in astonishment. Then she stepped back,
clutching her broom to her frail chest.

"Don't be afraid, child," Lydia said. "I don't want anything in return. Except perhaps for a smile."

May frowned even harder. She was stubborn. That was
good. She'd need some starch in her spine to survive life's
blows. May reached out for the coin, and Lydia pressed it
into the palm of the still-frowning girl. Lydia recognized
her feelings—she wanted and needed the money, and hated
that she did. Lydia had once hated needing help, too.

Suddenly, an image of Sophie's photograph entered
Lydia's mind, and she wondered if Sophie was still innocent, or had she in a few days endured enough trauma to
damage her spirit as May's had been?

May regarded her dolefully. Lydia glanced down at their
joined hands and saw something that startled her—a distinctive scar on the girl's inner wrist.

Lydia frowned, and May snatched her hand away, blushing. She was clearly embarrassed by the permanent,
crudely drawn image that had been carved into her wrist.
She hurried away, leaving Lydia to wonder at the remarkable image she had just seen. The girl's wrist had been
emblazoned with the image of a butterfly.

Chapter 9

❧

Lydia dropped Clara at her home, leaving her friend with much to consider. The promise of a bright new future and possible motherhood lay before Clara and Todd. But such good fortune was not in her own future, which appeared bleak indeed. The only salvation she could imagine was to find Sophie for her husband before it was too late.

As she rode back to Beaumont House, Lydia sat in her carriage turning over in her mind what she had stumbled upon at the clinic. She knew it was important to tell Hugh about the butterfly scar on May's wrist. Perhaps she was too focused on finding symbolic meaning in everything, but such a disfigurement must surely be more than coincidence.

Hugh would know what to make of it. But she couldn't face him again until she confessed her infidelity to her husband. Before courage deserted her, she dismissed her driver at the front entry and headed straight to Beau's bedroom. Dr. Benson stepped out of the room just as Lydia reached the top of the stairs. Her heart lodged in her throat as she looked at his grave expression.

Beau could not be gone! Her mind refused to accept it as the portly physician walked slowly toward her. He smiled sympathetically and stroked one of his bushy gray mutton-chops with his sausage fingers.

"Ah, Lady Beaumont, I was hoping to speak with you. Is there somewhere private . . . ?"

Lydia ushered him into a small sitting room directly down the hall and offered him a seat. Swallowing for courage, she took a firm grip on the edge of her chair and asked, "How is he?"

He shook his head soberly. "I fear he may have only a few days more to live."

"A few days?" she echoed numbly as all the breath left her body. She had known the day would come since she had wed Beau, but now it all seemed so horribly cruel, so sudden. Then the thought struck her—*how could they possibly find Sophie in this short a time?* Especially when Lydia wanted to be by Beau's side in his final hours. "Isn't there anything you can do?"

"It's in God's hands, ma'am. I've taken the liberty of finding you a nurse. She is trained to oversee his lordship's care and will make certain he does not suffer."

Lydia nodded, but could say nothing. Words stuck in her throat. The doctor bade her farewell and quietly left. When she opened the door to her husband's room, the nurse was sitting by the bed. Dressed in a crisp and serviceable gown of dark cotton, she was tall and almost mannish looking with a long, horsey face that only softened when she looked down at her patient. Lydia liked her at once.

After they introduced themselves, Nurse Galsworth asked direct questions about her patient's sleeping patterns, preferences as to diet, and other details his wife was most likely to know. Then she explained about the medications Dr. Benson had prescribed to make his lordship's final hours more comfortable. "He will sleep a great deal, but that is a blessing."

Lydia nodded, knowing it was true yet feeling a dreadfully

selfish need to speak with her husband, to tell him so many things she had never been able to fully express during their years together. She owed him everything . . . and now she had to confess how she had betrayed his trust. Looking at Nurse Galsworth, she said, "I would like a few moments alone with my husband. I will summon you when I'm ready to leave."

"Very good, Lady Beaumont." The nurse turned and left the room soundlessly.

"Beau?" Lydia sat on the edge of the four-poster bed and took his hand in hers. It was cold as ice. She felt his wrist for a pulse. It was there, though faint. As a chill swept over her, she knew the doctor had spoken accurately. Her beloved husband did not have much longer. "Beau, I'm home," she repeated softly, massaging his hand as if to restore the warmth of life to it.

He tried to lift his eyelids, but they merely fluttered. He smiled wanly and nodded. She twisted her position so she could lay down beside him and pressed her cheek to his shoulder.

"Beau, I have a confession to make."

"Shhhh," he whispered.

She looked up at his face once more, so white and lined with premature aging. His eyes were completely open now. "I must tell you—"

"No," he whispered faintly, "you mustn't. You . . . and . . . Montgomery have my . . . blessing."

She sat up, stunned, uncertain at first that she'd heard correctly. "No, darling, you don't understand. In my heart, I've been unfaith—"

"Live, Lydia," he whispered. "Live as if there is no tomorrow. For me, there isn't. But you are young. So is Hugh." He shut his eyes again, but a tiny smile seemed to touch his mouth.

"Oh, Beau, I love you," she whispered as tears streamed down her cheeks. What had she done to deserve such a man as this? He did not stir as she watched him doze again.

In the silence that followed, she listened to the ticking of the clock on the mantel and pondered his words. What if there were no tomorrow? How would she act today? Would she hold herself in reserve? Would she deny her heart contentment?

"I'll . . . be . . . gone . . . soon, Lydia."

She looked down at him, kissing his temple, then searching his face again for the great truth she suspected he held especially for her. "I wish things did not have to be this way. Please, Beau."

He shook his head. "Can't . . . help . . . it. Live, darling. Look in your heart, and live before it's . . . too . . . late. Good-bye, Lydie."

She pressed her forehead to his and wept, seized with the impossible desire to keep him alive. She held him tight and shook against him, trying to stifle the sound. *How self-ish of me to weep,* she thought. *I should be strong for him. He is ready to go. I can't hold him back.* She washed his face with her tears and cried herself into accepting silence. He had to go. She had to let him.

At last, when she had collected herself, she whispered in his ear, "It's all right, dear. I'll be fine. Go. Go in peace."

The words seemed to be the benediction he sought, for he fell into an unbroken slumber after that. She held him for a long time, losing track of the hours.

He finally stirred. "Sophie," he said. "Lydia, I . . . Sophie—"

"I'll find her, Beau. I swear. She'll be safe. I'll do it for you." She kissed his forehead. "Now go to sleep. You can rely on me."

"I . . . always knew I could," he murmured. Then he drifted back into unconsciousness.

She remained by his side until his sleep was deep and restful. Once satisfied that he would not awaken anytime soon, she summoned the nurse to take over the vigil. Lydia now knew that her search for Sophie could not flag. She would take no rest until Beau's child had been found and restored to her rightful place.

Even her painful past with Hugh paled to insignificance by comparison.

She ordered the carriage for her trip to Hugh's apartment, then went to her bedroom to freshen up while she waited for the coachman. Colette had the day off, so Lydia was left to her own devices. She soaked her face with cold cloths, then powdered her nose and secured the pins that held her false curls in place at the back of her head.

Peering at her reflection in the vanity mirror, Lydia thought she was starting to look old. Or perhaps it was merely the violent emotions that had left her looking and feeling undone. If only she knew what Beau meant by living. He made it sound so simple, but she knew in her heart that it could not be. Her husband, too, knew nothing in her life had ever been simple.

She thought of May, the poor young girl in the clinic. How old she looked as well! Her face was smooth, but her eyes were as washed out as old coals. Surely she'd been gay and carefree at some point in her life just as Lydia had been. But when? It had been so long ago.

She turned to her desk, feeling a sudden urge to read more of her diary. Until the other day, she hadn't opened it in years. But something buried deeply in her subconscious nagged at her, insisting that she once again open that heavy book in spite of all the painful memories it would unleash. What was it? Some clue related to finding Sophie?

She retrieved her key, unlocked the drawer, pulled out her diary, and began to flip through the vellum pages, uncertain exactly what she was looking for . . . until she found it:

APRIL 31, 1875

"Hugh, look at this," I said when I rushed into the library. Of course, I waited until I shut the door firmly behind me lest any of the myriad servants passing along the hall were to hear me. I clutched a large book to my chest that felt as if it weighed a stone. I hurried across the carpet and plunked down the dusty tome on the mahogany desk where he worked in rolled-up shirtsleeves on his next publication.

"What is it, Addie? You look as if you've just beat Ponce de Leon to the fountain of youth."

I caught his teasing grin, the dimpled cheeks, and those powerful, bottomless blue eyes of his twinkling at me. I felt like the most fulfilled and powerful woman in the world. Here I was, sharing knowledge with the most intelligent man I had ever met. And he treated me as an equal.

"This is a book titled *Pagan Traditions of the British Countryside* by a man named Thurber R. Frances."

"Never heard of him."

"I didn't expect you had," I said wryly. "But he seems to be an antiquarian of some renown. Now hush and listen carefully. I think you'll find this very interesting."

I sat on a chaise lounge covered in burgundy leather and brass buttons and pulled the book into my lap, groaning from the weight of it.

"Are you reading to exercise your mind or your arms?" he jested.

I smiled and shook my head, though I kept my eyes schooled on the page numbers as I intently flipped through, looking for the place I had marked. "Neither. When Katherine fell ill again, I decided to look for a good book here in the library so I could read to her. I stumbled upon this. Listen:

" 'Today's citizens know of May Day as a time when merry young men and women frolic around the maypole. Few realize the truly pagan origins of this simple country pastime. Nor are they aware that this supposedly harmless celebration, which is considered an innocuous rite of spring, follows an even older tradition that is still practiced here and there in secrecy by a few small villages that haven't given up their country ways to the industrial revolution.' "

Hugh leaned back, stretched his long legs under the

desk, propped his elbows on the arms of his chair and his chin on his hand, and regarded me with mock severity. "Young lady, you had best be going someplace very interesting with this."

I rolled my eyes. "You have absolutely no patience or imagination, sir. Just listen, will you please?"

He spread his hand out as if to say, "Be my guest."

"On the eve and early morning hours of May Day, a tradition called Beltaine was observed in great numbers up until the seventeenth century and is still observed in various pockets of the country to this day."

"Yes?" he asked, drawing out the word. "The seventeenth century is long past."

"This book was written two years ago! The author states that the rites are still being practiced," I said, frowning, then cleared my throat and continued:

" 'In particular, there have been recent reports of Beltaine ceremonies being conducted in Wales, Scotland, the Isle of Skye, and in the Cotswolds.' "

"We live in the Cotswolds."

"Oh, that's brilliant, milord," I replied with a laugh.

"Well, that's your point, isn't it?"

"Yes!"

"And I hope you have others."

He was teasing me because he knew I could give as good as I got. "Yes. I don't have time to read the entire book to you, but I can tell you the gist of it. It's incredible." I blushed at all the implications I'd read. "It seems that May Day is little more than a passed-on celebration from pagan days when tree-worshippers cavorted in the woods. This author states that the May Pole thrust into the earth and adorned with garlands around which young maidens dance is a symbol of the . . ." I moistened my lips, my mouth suddenly dry. However could I get through this? Squaring my shoulders, I finished boldly, "It is a symbol of the . . . male phallus."

His eyes danced at this, and the corners of his lips

twitched upward. He was thoroughly enjoying my obvious discomfort, but I persevered anyway. "It's a fertility rite whose original purpose was to encourage fecundity—the growth of crops and the increasing of the herds."

He leaned forward on his desk, almost piercing me with his unusually strong concentration. "Do continue, my dear."

"I'm not so interested in May Day as I am in the eve of that holiday," I continued, struggling to sound coolly logical. "In the Celtic tradition it was called Beltaine, after Bel, a pagan god who is burned in effigy on Beltaine. Sometimes revelers dance around a bonfire, and young men leap over the flames, enacting the role of Bel, or Baal-Zebub, a strongman worshipped in the old religions and later dubbed Beelzebub, which became another word for the devil when Christianity began to demonize earlier religions. The author says that in the old tradition, marriage vows were put aside on Beltaine, and drunken revelers would fall into an orgiastic fit. The babies who were delivered nine months later were called Pan's children, because all men were pagan gods on this night. I suppose the idea was that if the people were fertile, so would be the crops."

"Very intriguing," he murmured.

At his intimate tone, my eyes lifted and I found him staring so intently at me my pulse began to drum in my ear. Then he reached out and placed a hand over one of mine, which was resting on the desk. A lick of flame seemed to shoot up my arm. I trembled from the heat and tension that crackled between us yet I did not pull away, although the logical part of my brain told me to do so. That voice seemed all too distant and small.

I held my chin steady and regarded him calmly, although my imagination ran wild, envisioning this dark-haired intellectual stripped of his clothing, bare chested and brawny. He appeared before me, half-man and half-horse, staring me down on a dark woodland path, stomping the mulched earth impatiently with his hooves.

"Go on," he murmured.

I opened my mouth to speak, but nothing came out. Just a little squeak. I cleared my throat and forced myself to continue—anything but admit he had me thoroughly undone. "So you see, this celebration is happening still in this area, according to this author."

Hugh rubbed his thumb slowly back and forth over the top of my hand. That simple but forbidden gesture—our ungloved hands touching—felt as outrageously sinful and delightful as the fornications at a Beltaine ritual. I exhaled a breath and shut my eyes, no longer pretending he wasn't affecting me profoundly.

"If these pagan rituals are still being conducted—even as a nostalgic reenactment—why haven't I heard about them?"

I pulled my hand away, reminding myself to focus on the reason I initiated this most embarrassingly intimate conversation. "You haven't heard about them because no one would want to be seen behaving so scandalously. Although Charles Darwin says the biblical account of creation is incorrect, there are many in the religious establishment, Church of England and Nonconformists alike, who would argue otherwise. And even if one didn't care about religion, decent society could never abide such sexual license. Anyone who still celebrates Beltaine would do so with utmost secrecy."

Hugh leaned back, breaking the spell he had cast over me, and cupped his entwined fingers at the back of his head, his elbows winging outward. "Suppose you're right, Addie. Why has this phenomenon captured your interest?"

At last! Now I could explain. I sat at the edge of my seat, thrilled to think I might help him unravel the unsolved mystery that haunted him. "Don't you remember what you told me about the death of that servant girl? You saw her body at the bottom of the cliffs. That was on May Day, wasn't it?"

He nodded.

"When you looked up at Devil's Peak above, you saw the remaining trails of what appeared to be a bonfire, although you could never find it when you went searching. You thought it strange that anyone would set a fire out in the middle of nowhere. What if that was precisely the reason the fire was set there—because no one was supposed to see it? It was a secret. A sacred ritual."

He narrowed his eyes speculatively. "So you think that a fourteen-year-old milkmaid had been taking part in a Beltaine ritual and somehow was cast over the edge."

"Or she fell."

He let out a sigh and gave me a quick smile. "Interesting theory, my dear, but hardly conclusive."

"Yes, but what of the butterfly? You said the likeness of a butterfly had been carved into her wrist."

Now I had his complete attention. "What do you suppose that signified?"

"Mr. Frances says many of the pagan myths revolve around the idea of transformation—shape-shifters and magic cauldrons. Doesn't the butterfly typify the very essence of transformation? You have a creature that starts its life as an ugly caterpillar and turns into a beautiful butterfly in the cocoon."

"Very well thought out, Addie." His eyes blazed with pleasure. "These are very difficult connections to make— very astute of you." He leaned forward. "So you think she was part of a pagan ritual."

"Yes. It's the only explanation you haven't considered."

"And why didn't I? I'm very impressed, Addie."

I flushed with pride from head to toe, and I know my face showed it, for Hugh grinned, saying, "And I suppose you've thought this all out to its logical conclusion. What do you want me to do with this information?"

"I want you to examine the place where you thought you saw smoke trailing up to the sky."

"I searched that area thoroughly shortly after the girl died." He scratched his chin thoughtfully. "But that was a long time ago. I suppose a new examination with fresh eyes would be worthwhile. When do you want to do this?"

"Now."

He glanced out the window at the setting sun. "Can't it wait until morning?" he said with a bark of disbelieving laughter.

"No!" I nearly shouted, knowing I had finally brought him around. He had been so busy writing that he'd utterly lost track of the days. His ability to concentrate frequently meant he shut out the entire world. "Hugh, look at your calendar."

He did, then frowned, startled. "April 31," he whispered in amazement.

I nodded. "Yes, the eve of May Day. Beltaine!"

Later we found ourselves back at the place where we had first met—Devil's Peak. It was nearly midnight, and we could hear some sort of drum pulsing on the wind. The sound evoked the image of a primitive animal hide stretched over a large wooden barrel being beaten with a stick.

Whirling around us was a breeze unique to spring— vividly fresh, rife with the elusive scent of lime green buds and grass, the combination of tantalizing warmth and a hint of winter's biting last gasp. Myriad brilliant stars danced overhead in the black velvet of the night. With the cliff not far away on one side and the drum beat of what promised to be some pagan ritual emanating from the other way, I felt wholly vulnerable to nature.

And exhilarated. I was here alone with Hugh! What would we find?

My mind conjured images of druids—cloaked figures emerging out of dense, dark woods to gather around a mighty oak, their sacred deity. There was something appealing about the image of a simpler culture and time, before factory smoke choked the skylines and polluted the rain, and before the country folk migrated to cities, hungry and desperate for work. I could well imagine our Celtic ancestors living contentedly among the great gnarled oaks that provided shelter, that reached from the life-giving fertile earth to the water- and warmth-giving sky. What more did anyone really need?

Foolishly, I ignored the fact that the druids were also said to have practiced human sacrifice!

Thurber Frances wrote that at first, in matriarchal times, the druids consisted of shape-shifting women called "priestesses of Artemis," whose souls dwelled in the trees. Women apparently once ruled the earth because of their procreative abilities. Later, when men dominated societies, the druids were thought to be male priests who formed an elite class of bardic wizards. They defined their intimate, earthy world by keeping alive all the ancient myths in long ballads they memorized and passed down as oral history from generation to generation.

Could I hear their voices on the wind now—these ancient women and men of the trees? If Hugh and I were to walk toward that almost carnal drum beat, would we find hooded priests and priestesses dancing around a tree spirit? Or perhaps even preparing a human sacrifice to the sacred oak?

Hugh grabbed my hand and squeezed reassuringly. I gazed up at him, and excitement glowed in his eyes. We were in this together. It was a great adventure. Almost surreal. For although I had hoped the book I'd discovered might point to some evidence of pagan rites, I didn't really think we'd come face to face with it on our first try. Then again, this was the traditional date for Beltaine. When else would it happen?

"Shall we see what we've stumbled upon?" he said, smiling down at me with curiosity blazing in his face, and something more . . .

We followed the drum beat until we reached a sparsely wooded landscape marked by sloping hills and sink-holes from underground caves. There were perhaps a dozen small stone openings marking the hillside. Each apparently led to underground pathways. Hugh said they fed into various caves. He had explored them when he was younger but found all the entries quickly reached dead ends. If a grand cave was hidden in this hillside, it had gone undiscovered thus far. He joked that only pixies and faeries could make their way through the narrow passageways.

And yet it seemed certain that the drum beat that had drawn us thus far emanated from one of these entrances. We approached several of the holes in the stony hillside and listened. When we found the right entrance, it was obvious. The drum beat seemed to echo down a long tunnel straight into our ears.

"This is it!" he said. His eyes gleamed fiercely in the moonlight. "I would have sworn no one could get through any of these passages."

"But someone has," I replied. My heart pounded with uncontrollable excitement.

"You wait here," he said. "I'll see who is making all that racket."

I grabbed his arm, staying him. "I'm coming with you," I insisted boldly. When he looked as if he'd argue, I countered logically, "It wouldn't be safe for me to remain out here in the woods all alone, would it?"

He grinned. "Ah, Addie, my brave and clever girl. Follow me."

He knelt and wriggled through the tiny aperture with me directly behind him. We found ourselves in the kind of dense, overwhelming darkness unique to caves. A faint rustling noise from above us made me shiver, and he reached back to give my hand a squeeze. "A bat," he whispered.

That did not reassure me, but I persevered, trying not to think of the ichor that might lay beneath our very feet. A strong, ammoniac aroma made my eyes burn, but before I could think of what it surely meant, Hugh spoke.

"We have to follow the sound of the drum. Don't think of anything else until we see light at the end of the tunnel, for it will be where they're celebrating."

We felt our way through the moist, black cave. The cold air blowing up from some underground well was a blessing for our noses. Then suddenly a flicker of light indicated an exit. My breathing now was shallow, tense. We walked through the opening and found ourselves in the midst of a magnificent set of standing stones. There were three—tall, slender, and ancient. A fire burned nearby in the middle.

So excited had we been by our discovery of the light that we failed to realize the drums had gone silent. The place was utterly deserted. I gazed at the strange scene, trying to make sense of it. A bonfire leapt high in the air, a blistering, smoky orange splitting the darkness. The fire certainly had not started itself with spontaneous combustion, and it had clearly been fed to a roaring height by someone. There was a large kettle over a smaller fire of seething coals, apparently some sort of brew or stew. Wooden cups had been abandoned, as if the drinkers had left in a hurry.

"This is damned eerie," Hugh said, looking around at the towering stones outlined by flickering flame.

Confusion and a slow, cold wave of fear dropped like a soaking cape about my shoulders. Who had made the fire? Where had they so suddenly gone? Then my mind registered the incredible sight before me. Here was an ancient cluster of monolithic stones, not as large as Stonehenge, but still impressive. How had humans in any age managed to erect such monoliths?

"You didn't tell me this was here," I admonished in a whisper.

"I didn't know it was," he replied in awe.

How could he not know? I wondered. Surely this place must be legendary. It was a magnificent monument to a past civilization, right here at the edge of his own property. "We didn't imagine the drums, did we?" I asked.

"No. We did not."

I heard uncertainty in his voice—for the first time since I'd known him. Suddenly, I was afraid for our lives.

Sensing my disquietude, he said, "They knew we were coming. Someone must have been on watch and somehow warned the gathering of our presence. Let's get out of here."

No sooner had we turned than the mysterious fire builders were upon us.

Lydia closed the diary. She didn't need to read to remember what happened next. Her journal had opened the floodgates. She and Hugh were knocked unconscious with blows to the head.

They awakened just before dawn in a meadow not far from Windhaven and quickly made their way home. A physician had been summoned to stitch their head wounds. Their bandages became badges of dishonor. Everyone in the surrounding area knew that they had been out together alone at night. No one believed their claim to have found a circle of three megalithic stones that probably dated back to the Bronze Age. Hugh had never been able to locate them again. The cave entrance they'd used seemed to have disappeared overnight.

Thus, Addie Parker's reputation as an upright young woman had been ruined. Hugh's reputation as a reliable investigator had been called into question.

But she could not dwell on that. It was past and done. What was important now was the memory triggered by that long-ago attack. Suddenly an image leapt out from her memory, one she had not thought of since that night. It had been dancing just beneath the surface of her unconscious since their visit to the Diamond Forest Club. Now connections were clicking into place.

She'd glimpsed her attacker in the split second before he'd struck her. He was entirely cloaked in a hood, so his identity was unknown. She remembered thinking he was a druid of some sort, knowing at the same time it was surely just a costume. But there was something else. A flash of brilliant light that reflected golden fire. In such complete darkness, what could have glittered so distinctly from inside a pitch black hood?

"Diamonds!" she cried aloud. A diamond mask.

Chapter 10

J ust a minute! Just a minute!" shouted Pierpont through the front door of Hugh's apartment in answer to the racket Lydia had somehow managed to raise with her gloved knuckles on the thick wooden door. "Possess your soul in patience. I'm coming. Are you trying to wake the dead?"

Lydia's eyes widened in shock when the door opened. Hugh's man was fastening the sash on his robe, clad in carpet slippers—with a hole in one toe! He frowned like a flustered owl.

Regaining her composure before she burst out laughing, she brushed past him with the admonition, "You really ought to have more servants, Pierpont." She scanned the apartment in search of Hugh, then said, "Where is he? I have to speak to him about the standing stones."

When he did not reply, she whirled around in the center of the room, her lavender linen skirt belling slightly around her, revealing a tiny glimpse of fashionable high-heeled boots.

She demanded an answer with imperiously raised eyebrows. But it was clear that she'd left the man speechless.

He frowned, fighting not to shuffle his feet in consternation, but unable to keep from staring dumbly at her—a woman who knew no bounds. She'd come alone to a single man's home dressed first as a man and now as an unchaperoned lady. What of her reputation? And she a countess! It was incomprehensible. Inexcusable!

"Well, don't just stand there and stare at me," she snapped. "I tried to get Reggie to come with me so this would be more proper, but he has no interest in playing chaperone for a woman, no matter if she is a countess."

Pierpont recovered enough of his sanguinity to let his upper lip curl slightly at this.

"I'm quite certain you understand his reservations," she said dryly as she glanced down the hall.

"Quite," he managed to choke out, still rooted in place.

"If you won't call Lord Montgomery, I'll be forced to do it myself."

When she started for the bedrooms, Pierpont dashed around her and nearly plastered himself over the doorway. "He's not here, madam!" he yelped.

"Then why are you protecting the door?" she asked logically.

He blinked at this, then straightened, collecting his composure. "You are quite correct," he said, stepping aside. "If you would simply follow the basic rules of society, I wouldn't lose my head. Would you care for a brandy, ma'am? I certainly would." Without waiting for her reply, he walked straight to the sideboard.

"No, thank you. It is a bit early in the day for me," she remarked dryly, observing this further evidence of Pierpont's status in Hugh's household. When he poured himself a neat glass, then tossed it down in one gulp, he showed himself to be much more than an all-purpose servant or secretary. He clearly had Hugh's full confidence, or he would not be helping himself to the brandy.

"Mr. Pierpont," she said changing tack from demanding to pleading, "you must tell me where he is."

"I can't," the erudite servant stated flatly, meeting her eyes now, not unsympathetically.

Lydia's stomach pitched uneasily. "He's with a woman."

Pierpont's eyelids twitched. She couldn't tell whether she'd hit the mark or was so far off he'd momentarily considered telling her the truth.

"You can rest assured, ma'am, that I will tell his lordship you stopped by. Now you really should go, for your own sake."

"That's all well and good," came a familiar voice from the still-open doorway, "but she'll still need an address so she can find his lordship immediately."

Lydia turned in surprise to see Reggie, hat in hand, drenched in rain and sweat as if he'd run the whole way from his tenement. "Reggie! You came after all."

He nodded, blushing with a touching mixture of regret and pride. "I have me a job to do, sir—er, rather, ma'am, and I intend to do it. Now look here, Mr. Pierpont, with all due respect, you have to give the countess what she's after. The life of a young girl is hanging in the balance."

Pierpont looked down at his feet. "Yes, I know." He poured another brandy and clutched the glass in a death grip. "I wish I could tell you where he is, but I can't. For your sake, ma'am."

Lydia and Reggie exchanged looks. She held out her hands in a *je ne sais quois* gesture. "I don't know quite how to convince you, Pierpont, but it would be most difficult to shock me."

"Perhaps," he said with an air of omniscience that sent a chill of foreboding down her spine. "But I fear it would be all too easy to disappoint you."

"If you mean he's with a woman, I assure you—"

"No," Pierpont said flatly. "I wish that were the case." He sighed with a peculiar blend of regret and exasperation, then headed for the back rooms. "Very well. I'll take you there myself. But first allow me dress? Unless you do not deem that necessary?"

Lydia wisely suppressed a smile at this sharp bit of sarcasm. Not for the first time she sensed that Pierpont might be one of the few people on Earth capable of understanding just how much Hugh Montgomery had put her through.

An hour later, Lydia stood between Reggie and Pierpont as they gazed down at the body of Lord Hugh Montgomery. He was passed out cold in one of the most dreadful opium dens of London. She and Reggie had no success in rousing him from his drug-induced torpor. Horrified and frightened, Lydia glanced around at the other lethargic opium eaters lying like broken toys in the murky, smoke-filled interior of this hellhole. Many looked respectable, dressed as gentlemen such as Hugh. Others were too far gone, their clothing filthy and tattered, their skins waxy yellow and eyes filmed over, dull and gray like blind men . . . or dead men.

Lydia's mind could not take in the enormity of Hugh in this ghastly place. She felt as if they were at his wake, remarking how lifelike he looked for one who was dead. He had always been so filled with life, never in repose, always restless, his mind ever working. He did not belong here any more than he belonged in a mausoleum.

"He won't regain consciousness for some time," Pierpont said disapprovingly. He was obviously experienced with his employer's vice. "I'm sorry you had to see this, your ladyship, but you insisted."

She nodded, suddenly overcome with the same feelings she'd experienced when Hugh had fallen over the cliff. "Leave us for a moment." When neither of her companions moved, she added, "Please. We're alone here in the corner. I'll be safe. Wait for me at the entrance. I won't be long."

"It will do no good," Pierpont replied with regret, even sympathy in his voice.

But Reggie nodded to her, then turned and walked away. She was gratified that he trusted her judgment. Perhaps it was because he had at first come to think of her as a man. Pierpont followed unwillingly.

"Hugh?" she said. He didn't move so much as an eyelash. She knelt on the dozen cushions that pillowed his sprawled and motionless form. Taking his hand, she blinked back tears.

Oh, Hugh, what has become of you? How could you have let this happen? Couldn't you have been stronger? For me? I've hated you for so long, and I wanted to see you suffer as I had. But now that I see you this way, I ache for you.

She reached under his neck and pulled him closer. His finely chiseled jaw fell against her knee. She stroked his cheek and shut her eyes tight, remembering when she had done that with perfect love.

Oh, I loved you, Hugh. She bent and placed her lips to the small, jagged white scar that zagged across his right temple. That was the only visible wound from their encounter on the cliffs. She had saved his life that day and would do so again without a second thought.

But damn him! How dare he throw his life away in an opium den! Didn't he know people had placed their trust in him? She certainly had. After mustering her courage to depend on him once again, she would not permit him to let her down a second time.

She gripped his head in both hands, leaning close over his face. "Damn you, Hugh Montgomery, I won't let you fail me again. Do you hear? Do you?!" She fought the urge to pound his insensate skull into the pillows, but then succumbed and cradled it once more in her lap, murmuring, "You owe me so bloody much, and I mean to collect it. If not for my sake, then for my dear, dear husband's. And for Sophie's—that poor young girl. We have a job to do, Hugh.

One last mystery to solve together. And we will solve it!"

He moaned at this but did not rouse. Lydia sighed in defeat, then stood up and hurried toward the front door. There she found the two men anxiously awaiting her.

"Bring him to my house, Mr. Pierpont," she ordered in a tone that would brook no argument. "Reggie and I will take a cab ahead of you. A hot bath, a pot of steaming coffee, and a meal will be waiting for him. And for you as well." Her frown softened to warm understanding. "And thank you."

"You are welcome, madam," he said, bowing.

Yes, she had an ally in Pierpont. And she would need one, for Hugh was going to require a great deal of attention, much to her amazement. She wondered how many other surprises were in store for her. For so long she had lived in a world of good and evil, black and white, judging herself and others with such clear-cut standards. Now this gray, vision of life was unveiling itself before her in a subtle manner she found difficult to grasp.

Hugh was proving himself to be worse in some ways— and in other ways not nearly as bad—as she remembered him. She would have to adjust her point of view in order to deal with his weakness. They must act quickly, as a team, for the clues she had found might very well require reading between the lines. And she desperately required Lord Hugh Montgomery to help her decipher them.

The smell of eggs and oatmeal filled his stuffy nostrils and made his stomach lurch with dread. "I'm not hungry," he mumbled, leaning back against what felt like an extremely comfortable and expensive feather bed.

Where the devil am I? Hugh wondered. *The last thing I remember is chatting with Chin Ho, just after he'd given me a large bowl to smoke. I blissfully went into a dream world far, far away from reality. But then Addie appeared in my dreams. She was sad, then angry. And now here I am, back to reality, but someplace I don't recognize.*

He managed to crack open one eye and found two hazy figures standing over him.

"He's coming about," said his man-of-affairs. "Here you are, Lord Montgomery. A good breakfast to get you back on your feet. Can you come to the table?"

"What time is it?" Hugh rasped in a scratchy voice.

"Two in the morning," Pierpont cheerfully replied.

Hugh grimaced. "Where am I?"

"At Beaumont House," came a feminine reply.

Hugh blinked some more until he could see Lydia standing there like a vision in lavender. She was so beautiful, with her dark hair swept up and pulled back tightly from her fair and delicate face. His stomach twisted in a knot. Or was that the effect of the drug? Oh, how he had failed her. Damn it!

He had looked forward to seeing her as Lydia Beaumont. He had planned to subtly make her squirm over her subterfuge as Henry Morgan. He had even hoped he might kiss her again, for it was clear from their brief encounter in the carriage she was still hot-blooded and not immune to his touch. But she had trumped him on every score by seeing him at his worst. Pierpont must have taken her to the opium den. Yes, that was it. Hugh shot him an accusing look, and his man reddened with guilt.

"I'm sorry, milord, but she insisted," Pierpont said quietly.

Hugh simmered at this but could hardly blame him. The viscount was just beginning to realize how determined the countess could be. "I'm sorry, Lady Beaumont."

"For what?" she asked icily.

"For your having to witness what you did tonight."

In the long, uncomfortable silence that followed, Pierpont excused himself. "Call me if you need me," he said, slipping out of the room.

"Why don't you eat?" she asked to fill the subsequent void. "There is a breakfast tray on the table."

He lifted his head and saw the steaming food he'd

smelled moments ago. His stomach protested once more. "Can't. Not yet."

"Coffee then?"

"Definitely. I never say no to that."

With a natural grace that seemed to have grown in the intervening years, she went to the table where a silver coffeepot sat. She poured a steaming cupful and dropped in the cream and sugar she knew he liked. When she came to his bedside, he wanted to knock the china from her hand and pull her into his arms, to plant a long, deep kiss on her mouth. But when he held out his hand to take the saucer from her, his hand trembled from the effects of opium. He realized he was in no condition to manhandle anyone. And of all women, Lydia deserved better—far better than a miserable excuse of a man such as he.

"Sit up," she ordered, disgust evident in her voice. "Prop yourself up on a pillow."

He did so with all the vim and vigor of a seventy-year-old. "Don't say a word," he mumbled as he struggled with the pillow. "I know what you're thinking. The drug is going to send me to an early grave."

"I'll give you credit for keen intelligence, but you score frightfully low on common sense. If you understand how destructive for you this habit is, how did you allow yourself to start in the first place?"

He leaned back into the pillow with a groan. "I don't know." It was a lie, but one he knew was white in nature. He would not admit the truth.

With a stern look of reproval stamped on her face, she lifted the cup from the saucer and put it to his lips, as coolly unemotional as a nurse with a patient. But he could feel the sudden hot river of desire singing between them the moment he placed his hands over hers, guiding her as he swallowed. Now he was trembling for a far different reason than the residual effects of opium.

Lydia Beaumont was a far more potent drug. Then he felt the faint tremors begin in her hands as she leaned so closely to him. Hugh allowed himself to savor the emotion for as long as he dared. After several slow sips, he felt steady enough to take the cup into his own hands, drinking deeply. He dared not meet her eyes, nor she his. He knew she was still angry and shocked over the way she'd found him. How could he blame her?

After finishing the coffee, he worked up his courage and asked her, "Why did you come after me? You have many wonderful qualities, Lydia, but you're not Florence Nightingale. You must require my help with some new information regarding Sophie."

He knew he'd hit the mark when she at last met his gaze. Then the corners of her mouth turned up in a grudging smile, the first sign of forgiveness. "You're right. Whatever your faults, Hugh—"

"And there are many," he supplied.

"—I'll admit you know me well . . . and yourself, too."

He returned her smile, relieved to be back on familiar and far less emotionally risky ground. "You're a hound on the scent just as I am."

Lydia stiffened and started to protest, but he cut her off.

"Don't mistake what I say. I know you care deeply about your husband's daughter, but you also love a good mystery. If I hadn't met you, I might have ended up a drunkard at the racetracks, or in an asylum as my mother did," he admitted, then added quickly, "Instead, for all my failings, I've become a world-famous sleuth."

Hugh looked down at the empty cup, appalled at what he'd revealed to Lydia, regretting he'd brought up the Countess of Boxley. He'd loved his mother dearly and always felt like he was gossiping about her when he mentioned the frightfully sad ending of her life. She'd committed suicide. The doctors said she'd gone mad after the birth of her daughter, Katherine. Because of women's supposedly frailer constitutions, the ordeal of childbirth sent some such as Lady Boxley spiraling into hysteria, then an irrevocable withdrawal from the world around them. But now,

Hugh wondered if it had been that simple. Was it more than childbirth that had depressed her? And did she have something more than a diamond butterfly in common with Trevor Dobson?

Lydia's face softened at the mention of his mother. Hugh frowned to cover his vulnerability on this topic . . . and his vulnerability to her. "You were the only one to recognize the importance of my investigative work. I thank you for it."

"Then repay me now by helping me put together the latest clues."

She scooted closer to him, perching on the side of the bed. Her warmth would have bowled him over if he hadn't already been propped against the headboard. He could feel his pulse again begin to pound. Unable to resist, he let his gaze wander down her ivory neck to the swell of her breasts. Already he knew the effects of the opium had dissipated under the spell of her nearness. He fought the urge to reach out and take her in his arms. Best to change the tenor of their conversation, and that right quickly.

"Will I be helping the Countess of Beaumont or Mr. Henry Morgan?" He grinned teasingly.

Lydia's eyes flashed. "Does it matter? Either way I'm the Midnight Angel. And either way, we're both frauds, are we not? To think, all this time I believed you were the upright and perfect gentleman. Really, Hugh, it's a shame to think what you might have done with your life—"

"If I hadn't lost you," he admitted.

She cast her eyes down and scowled. "We won't discuss that. Do you understand?"

The earlier spell was well and truly broken. He nodded reluctantly.

"Because if you don't, after we find Sophie I will leave and never come back."

"I understand," he replied after a long and painful pause. Then, pulling himself together, he said briskly, "Now let's talk about the case. What do you have?"

"I've been thinking a great deal about the clues we have so far."

"Yes?" He rose in a nightshirt borrowed from Beaumont and went to pour himself another cup of coffee, surprised she didn't retreat to the other side of the room. She did not look at him, but neither did she move from the edge of the mattress. Once again he was vividly struck by memories of their former intimacy. Perhaps there was hope for them yet. How he had loved this woman. And how his life might have been different if he hadn't let her slip from his fingers.

"Sir Todd visited me before I came to your place." Was her voice a bit hoarse? He hoped so.

"How is old Todd?" he asked gamely.

She watched Hugh stir his coffee and marveled at the steadiness and grace of his hands. He was recovering from his debauch with amazing speed in spite of his appalling habits. She could not tear her gaze from those hands. How well she remembered them caressing every inch of her body, raising her to the very peak of ecstasy.

"Todd is fine," she said with an unsteady swallow. *I must focus on the issues.* "Unfortunately, the search on the streets has been unsuccessful, and newspaper advertisements requesting leads in the kidnapping have yielded few clues. However, he appears to be making great progress with Scotland Yard. He has finally pressed the commissioner on the Botanicals."

"Bearing a note from me," Hugh couldn't help but add as he raised his cup to his lips. He was never one to give up credit where it was due. "I told the commissioner that there was evidence the Botanicals were involved with Sophie's kidnapping."

"A special team has been assigned to interview members of the society."

"Unfortunately, as I mentioned in the carriage, I'm now convinced the Botanicals are no longer even suspect." He waited a beat, looking at her from the corner of his eye. She surprised him with her reply.

"Yes, I've thought about that, and I think you're right."

Hugh raised one eyebrow. "Really? What have you found out?" He dug into his eggs as if they were the elusive suspect.

"I wanted to tell you earlier, but I . . . I wished to speak first with Beaumont. I went to a clinic in the East End. It's run by a marvelous female doctor—but that's beside the point. In the clinic I found a young girl who was about fifteen years of age. The nurse explained to me that she had come in the year before after being molested by a group of men. She was virtually mute, too traumatized to be able to explain precisely what had happened. All the staff could elicit from her was something about May Day, and so they started calling her May. She stayed a few weeks, then disappeared, and recently returned without explanation."

"She'd been molested on May Day?" Hugh speculated. "Usually victims who have been traumatized by some ghastly event fixate on the circumstances, the dates, or the environment surrounding their abuse."

"Or perhaps the eve of that holiday."

"Beltaine."

When he said it, the word shivered between them, and memories from that long ago night grew vivid once more, like living things, unearthed from a deep sleep—sleep perhaps best left undisturbed . . .

Lydia bit her lip, then said quietly, "Hugh, May had a butterfly carved into her wrist."

He leaned back quickly, as if she'd dealt him a stunning blow. "My God," he breathed and shook his head. "We've talked about this once before. Do you remember? The milkmaid found at the bottom of the Devil's Peak was scarred with the image of a butterfly."

"Yes. I reread my diary about that time when we . . . when you and I . . . found the standing stones. Do you remember?"

"How could I forget?" He scowled at the memory and began eating again. He could not recall that event without great sorrow over Lydia's lost reputation. Moreover, finding the standing stones was the one great unresolved mystery that had nearly ruined his reputation. Hugh had insisted he'd made a great archaeological discovery, but no one had ever believed him because he could not locate the site again in spite of months of diligent searching. Lydia had been the only other person to see the stones. When she left Windhaven, there was no one to corroborate his story.

"The butterfly might have had something to do with the standing stones," she said. "What if the girl in the clinic was there last year at Beltaine? We heard the drums, Hugh. Remember? We know some sort of ritual was taking place at that time of year. Rituals by definition repeat themselves."

"But why would we stumble on two victims in such disparate places?"

"May was taken around the time of Beltaine, as was the servant girl you found. And so was Sophie. When we were attacked at the monoliths, I saw a dark, cloaked figure just before I was struck unconscious. I thought he wore a sparkling mask—perhaps of a butterfly?"

Hugh blinked, then daubed his lips with the napkin, leaning back to consider the matter. "You suspect Trevor Dobson."

"I don't know. I'm just now beginning to make the connections. His club is called the Diamond Forest. There was oak imagery all over the place. The druids were said to conduct their sacred rites in holy circles of giant stones. The man who knocked us unconscious wore a hooded robe—like the ones you see in the lithograths of ancient druid societies."

"So you think Sir Trevor is a druid?"

"I think he might be pretending to be one. Hugh, we saw with our own eyes that he has a highly perverted penchant for costumes and drama. Perhaps he enjoys ancient rituals, too."

"Yes. You're right about the forest imagery. That is much more emblematic of druids than the Botanicals, who are more interested in the cultivation of certain species of flowers and shrubs. But if Dobson claims to be a druid, it could be more than pretense. There are druidic societies even today, mostly artistic groups that have nothing in common with the druids but for a romantic notion of natural inspiration. Purely harmless, as I understand them."

"But look here," she persisted, walking to the side table against the wall to retrieve a newspaper. "Sir Todd brought this by. He says Scotland Yard detectives flagged this advertisement in the *Times*. They were struck by the references to nature, which you had mentioned in connection with the Botanicals."

Hugh held the paper, which had been folded into quadrants, up to the gaslight, and read, "Willow, Furze, Dwarf Elder, Hawthorn, Yew, White Poplar. Dwarf Elder. Bel 31." His voice trailed away as he drummed the fingers of his right hand on the tablecloth. "Bel . . . Bel."

"Beelzebub," she offered excitedly. "The pagan god. I read to you about the Celtic Beltaine rituals, remember?"

"And April 31 is the eve of May Day. But what does the rest mean?" he speculated, then concluded, "It's a code, obviously."

"We must break this code," she said determinedly.

His eyes caught hers and kindled. "That might not be so simple."

"Someone is sending this message to someone else. Do you think it's Dobson?"

"I don't know."

"What good are you then?!" she shot back.

He saw the taunting, teasing glint in her eyes. And the anger. The seriousness of her mission darkened her lovely eyes. He snatched her hand in his own from where it lay on the table and squeezed it warmly. Flames seemed to lick between them, peeling away their skin, their past, leaving only the heated, needy present. "Don't insult me, Countess," he said softly.

"Then break the code! Find Sophie," she implored him.

In spite of the gravity of the situation, she could not resist a faint smile to soften her harsh demands.

The door opened suddenly, and Pierpont hurried inside. Lydia snatched back her hand as if it had been scalded.

"Sir, I must speak with you."

Hugh slouched back in his chair as if nothing were amiss between him and the countess. "Go on then," he said to Pierpont. He let his eyes stray back to Lydia, watching how deeply she blushed. He did not intend to embarrass her . . . but damnation, he wanted her!

Pretending to ignore the obvious interplay between the two, Pierpont said, "I was speaking with Mr. Shane just now, and we were reviewing clues on the case."

"I hope you've had better luck than I have," Hugh replied wryly. "Any ideas?"

"Mr. Shane thought this would be worth interrupting your . . ." He glanced uncomfortably at Lydia, then hurried on. "I wanted to tell you earlier. While you were gone, I received a note from Sir Malcolm Dunbar. Being the infamous gossip that he is, and in response to my inquiries made on your behalf, he said he knew quite a bit about Sophie's mother. He mentioned a number of her lovers, and among them was none other than Sir Trevor Dobson."

Lydia's hands flew up in shock. She knocked over a juice glass, and the liquid went puddling onto the carpet. "Trevor Dobson and Louise Canfield? Oh, my God!"

Pierpont's brow arched with satisfaction over the reaction to his revelation. "Dunbar says this was long ago, but they've remained close to each other.

Hugh said, "If he was close with Miss Canfield—"

"Then he might have known Sophie was her daughter," Lydia said, finishing his thought. "She might have even let slip that Beaumont was the father."

Hugh stroked his chin. "Hmmm. That doesn't make sense. He wouldn't risk kidnapping a child who has important relatives."

"Then perhaps he's not going to harm her. Perhaps he has extortion in mind."

"So far, there's no evidence of that."

"Nevertheless," she insisted "he's the one, Hugh. He has to be. It all fits together somehow—the butterfly, the circle of stones, the dates. And now we find Dobson might have known Sophie's mother. Sophie's still safe. She has to be!"

"Only until Beltaine. Let's go." Hugh stood abruptly and hurried toward the door. "The Diamond Forest will undoubtedly still be open at this hour. Like cockroaches, the patrons only come out at night. We must speak to Dobson."

"Hugh, wait!" she said sharply.

He turned. "What for?"

"You're wearing night clothes."

"Bloody hell," he cursed, looking down at his bare legs and feet. Then he heard her smother a chuckle. "This would be perfect for Dobson's crowd, wouldn't it?"

She grinned at him with unabashed warmth. "Indeed, it would, but I recommend you quickly change."

"I'm glad to be working with you again, Lydia," he said earnestly.

She sobered, then nodded. "Yes, Hugh. I am, too." They were a team once again . . . if only for a short while.

Chapter 11

On the way to the Diamond Forest, as the coach rolled
slowly but steadily through the murky mists of late-
night London, Lydia expressed her fears that the club
would be closed for the night.

"No chance of that, ma'am," snorted Reggie. "It's nearly
three-thirty in the morning. That's when the place really
becomes lively."

Reggie proceeded to tell her, Lord Montgomery, and
Mr. Pierpont of some of the more bizarre individuals who
frequented the club. There were chuckles and occasional
gasps all around, but Reggie's voice trailed away when
they pulled up in front of the building. "Something is
wrong." He sounded dumbfounded.

The club lay deep in the bowels of the abandoned building, so it was not surprising that the windows and empty
shop fronts were dark. But unlike the last time they were
here, the street was virtually empty. There wasn't so much

as a single carriage, other than their own, in sight. Nor were there any passersby.

"Let us have a look inside," Hugh suggested, looking to Lydia for assent.

"Yes," she agreed. "I'm eager to see the garish royal guards again, just to make sure I hadn't dreamed them up in my nightmares."

Reggie led them through the darkened hallways, up a stuffy stairwell, to the entrance of the club. It was clear then that the place was entirely abandoned.

"Lord!" Reggie exclaimed. "Are my eyes deceiving me?"

"I don't know what you mean, Mr. Shane," Pierpont said. "I see nothing at all but a dark passageway."

"Precisely my point," Reggie replied impatiently. He led the way through the tunnel entrance. Once inside, they could see the club was as dark and empty as the street below. A skylight allowed for moonshine, and they could just see the silhouettes of a few overturned chairs and tables. But otherwise, all furniture had been removed.

Hugh lit a match and held it before him and explored the private rooms. He returned, shaking out the match. "No one is here."

"It's as if the place never existed," Reggie said in amazement, his voice echoing in the empty hall.

"Everything that could be taken out was," Lydia remarked. "And obviously very quickly. Sir Trevor has apparently decided to close down his operation."

"It was because of our visit." In the dim light from the sky-light Hugh exchanged a meaningful look with Lydia. "It seems Sir Trevor is indeed the man of the hour. I would never have thought the mystery could be unraveled so quickly."

"Where do you suppose he went?"

"Sir!" Reggie called from the empty oak bar. "There appears to be a note." He waved a piece of paper in the air and hurried to Hugh's side. "I can't understand a single word."

Hugh took it and held it up to the skylight but couldn't make out the cryptic note until Pierpont lit a match for him. "Aha!" Hugh said excitedly.

Lydia gripped his elbow. "What does it say?"

"More of the same gibberish we found in the newspaper: Hazel, Elder, White Poplar, Vine, Furze, Elder, Ash, White Poplar, it says on the first line. On the second: Ivy, Silver Fir, Elder, Oak, White Poplar, Ash."

"It's the code!" Lydia cried. "So it was Dobson who put the advertisement in the paper."

"Or someone close to him."

The low-burning match nearly blistered Pierpont's fingers, and he quickly shook it out. "What do you suppose the note says, sir?"

"He's telling us where we can find Sophie."

Sophie Parnham finished the lamb stew her keeper, Mrs. O'Leary, had brought for the evening meal. The girl pushed aside the pewter plate unsatisfied, although the fare, as usual, had been delicious. How could one enjoy even the finest meal while being held captive?

Granted her prison—a cellar built deep in the ground— was large and comfortable enough. She had a soft bed, plenty of blankets, candles, matches, books, knitting, even a makeshift privy, which Mr. O'Leary cleaned daily. But she was still a prisoner.

That point had been confirmed two days ago when she'd tried to escape during one of Mrs. O'Leary's thrice-daily food deliveries. The old woman's husband had been standing guard outside the wooden door, which was embedded in the ground at an angle. As soon as Sophie had scrabbled up the wooden steps and saw the first glimpse of blinding white sunlight she'd seen in days, she also saw the barrel of a gun aimed at her forehead. The wiry, gray-haired, but still spry Mr. O'Leary had threatened to shoot if she didn't behave herself.

As best Sophie could tell, she had been brought here blindfolded at night after being kidnapped outside the theater. She suspected she'd been drugged, for she had no idea how long or far she'd traveled from London—if she had left the city at all.

Suddenly the door at the top of the stairs creaked open. She jumped back, nearly knocking over her chair. "Who is it?" she hissed. The O'Learys wouldn't come back for her evening dishes until morning.

She heard voices. The only one she recognized was Mrs. O'Leary's, and it was surprisingly submissive.

"Oh, aye, sir, aye," she gushed. "Miss Parnham's here, and plump as a little cherry, just as you ordered."

Mrs. O'Leary must be speaking to someone important. She never spoke so respectfully to her husband. But why were they talking about Sophie's weight? She unconsciously crossed her arms over her mid-section. More than once she'd wondered with grim humor if her keeper had been plying her with such good food to fatten her up, like the old witch in the story of Hansel and Gretel.

"Thank you, Mrs. O'Leary," came a very deep and dignified voice. "You must treat her very carefully. She has a very special . . . ."

The wind picked up, and Sophie couldn't hear the rest of the sentence. "Blast," she cursed to herself. She'd give anything to know why she was here. She'd stopped crying for her home days ago, accepting that her situation was dire but still tolerable. But not knowing her fate nearly had her nerves at the snapping point. Even if she was going to die, she would feel better knowing it. Not knowing was the worst.

She jumped to her feet and crept quietly to the bottom stair. Looking up the short flight that led to the discreet entrance, she could see legs silhouetted against a haunting, azure dusk. The air was refreshingly rife with woodland scents. Then the legs moved forward, and an expensive black leather shoe hit the top stair.

Oh, God, he's coming down. Sophie skittered backward, bumping into the table. The corner gouged her hip.

"Ow!" She bent over and bit her lip in pain but managed to rouse herself back into a semblance of composure by the time the stranger reached the bottom stair. He wore a very finely woven knee-length coat, waistcoat, ascot, and top hat. And he was rich as Croesus. She didn't know how she knew this, for the small candle burning beside the staircase gave little light, certainly not enough to show the texture of cloth. Perhaps it was the way his clothing was cut.

"Good evening, m'dear."

As soon as she heard that voice up close, she gasped. This was the gentleman who had spoken to her in the alley. She squinted to see him better. At the same time, his hand snaked out, and he snubbed out the candle with his thumb and forefinger. Darkness sucked the last of the meager light. The only remaining illumination came from a narrow air vent at the top of the cellar.

So he doesn't want me to see him. An ominous chill coursed down her arms. This man meant no good. Until now she hadn't associated him with her capture, for it was a footman who had snagged her. She'd caught a glimpse of his livery before she'd lost consciousness. But now she realized it must have been this man's servant who did the deed.

"What do you want from me?" Her voice trembled with fear that froze her muscles, rooting her to the spot.

"I think you know the answer to that," he purred.

She swallowed thickly, unwilling to speculate, even in her thoughts. She didn't want to give him any wicked notions that hadn't already occurred to him. She would hope for the best. Perhaps he had found out that she was Louise Canfield's daughter. Perhaps he wanted to use Sophie to force her mother to accept his amorous intentions. It had happened before, although Louise was always very careful to keep Sophie ignorant of her affairs.

"Do you know who my mother is?" she said, clearing the lump of fear lodged in her throat. *I must remain calm. I must*

not show him I'm afraid. Louise always said men were like
dogs. They won't attack if you don't let them see your fear.

"Of course I know who your mother is." He reached out
and touched under her chin, forcing it up with his index
finger. "And I know who you are. You are Cerridwen."

Sophie's eyes fluttered. "What? No, I—" She stopped
abruptly with a joyous thought. He had captured the wrong
person. He thought she was someone else. This Cerridwen
person. Once he realized his error, he would let her go.
"No, sir, you are mistaken. My name is Sophie Parnham."

"Hush, Cerridwen."

"No, it's true. My mother is really Louise Canfield—the
famous actress. I have never told anyone that before, but—"

"Your mother is the moon," he said.

His voice was intense and monotone, as if he'd gone into
a trance. She would give anything to see his face, but the
shadows hid him. He made no sense. Was he jesting? Trying to scare her?

"Your mother is the moon," he continued with quiet passion. "And your father is the sun."

"I don't even know who my father is," she blurted out on
a sob. How she wished she had a father to save her now.
"My mother is Miss Canfield! The famous stage actress!
She'll pay dearly for my return. I swear."

"Don't mention that whore's name!" he commanded in a
gravelly voice. "You are not born of her despoiled loins.
You are perfect. You are a virgin. The white goddess."

He reached out with a trembling hand and sifted through
her hair with a sensuality that made her shiver with revulsion. "You are the witch who turns into a mare . . . a night
mare. *He socht tha Mare, he fond tha Mare, he bond tha*
Mare wi' her ain hare. That's an old fourteenth-century
poem, Cerridwen. It's about you. Oh, your hair is so beautiful. Just like I knew it would be."

"Don't touch me," she spat at him, whipping her hair
back from his grasp.

His empty hand went rigid, then balled into a fist, and

slowly lowered to his side. In a clearer and colder voice he said, "As you wish, Cerridwen. For now. But you must prepare yourself for the sacrifice. It's coming soon."

He turned and started back up the stairs.

"But I want to go home. Please. *Please!*"

He did not seem to hear. He knocked on the door. When it opened and then shut after his retreating figure, Sophie broke into hysterical sobs. "Get me out of here!" she cried to the empty room. "I want to go home! Do you hear me? Take me home!"

This is a nightmare, her mind screamed. *Help me, Lord. Please, help me.*

"Nightmare," she choked through her tears. Night mare. He had called her the night mare. The white goddess. He was mad. Utterly insane. Then she stopped suddenly as this horrible man's words came to mind. *Prepare yourself for the sacrifice.* But what did that mean? *Something evil.*

She would have plenty of time to ponder the mystery. Alone in her prison, she would have nothing but time.

Hugh paced an already-worn path on his Turkish carpet in the same wilted clothing he'd worn for the past twenty-four hours. The sun had come up some time ago, yet he had never gone to bed after their fruitless journey to the Diamond Forest. Lydia had sent a messenger over with terrible news less than an hour after they'd parted company in the dawning light of day.

My husband is dead. You must find Sophie without me. Then Beau can rest in peace.

Lydia's husband had died sometime during their early morning sojourn to the club. Hugh couldn't imagine the grief and guilt Lydia must be feeling. He hugged himself as he paced, feeling exhausted, yet almost too tired, and certainly too worried about Lydia, to sleep.

"I need to go to her," he muttered as much to himself as to the ever-faithful Mr. Pierpont.

"No, sir, you cannot do that." The fifty-year-old former butler poured two cups of steaming black tea with a steady hand, which was covered with a faint tracery of veins. His hair was now fully gray—which he blamed on Hugh—but once had been a dusty brown. "You must think of the countess's reputation. How would it appear if you were suddenly there by her side consoling her?"

"Reputation?" Hugh groused. "What does that matter now? Lydia needs me."

"The Countess of Beaumont," Pierpont said pointedly, "needs time to mourn the death of her husband. I gather, sir, you have history with her ladyship. But although you might share a past, that does not give you the right to force a present upon her, especially at a time like this."

"I simply want to support her, Pierpont, not make love to her."

"You must leave her alone, sir. Write a note. But you cannot go to her. It's out of the question."

"Bloody hell!" Hugh cursed, raking both hands through his hair. Pierpont spoke the truth. He had no right to share her intimate feelings at a time like this. He'd lost that privilege long ago. Aching frustration made him eye his bottle of laudanum. It had been hours since he'd taken anything to soothe his nerves. He'd wanted a clear head to think, but now everything seemed all too clear. How could he not be with Lydia? He longed to take her in his arms and hold her, to let her know she would not be alone. Never again.

He knew she loved Beaumont, but he also knew in his heart of hearts that her marriage wasn't passionate in nature. Beaumont had been the father Lydia had lost because of her affair with Hugh. God, she had lost so much because of him. "I just want to tell her not to worry, that she'll never have to be alone again. I owe her so much. I ruined her life. And losing her destroyed my chance of happiness as well. She—"

"She? Who?"

At the sound of Sir Todd Leach's voice, Hugh looked up

raggedly with a light of hope gleaming in his bloodshot eyes. "Leach! What news do you bring?"

"Lady Beaumont is holding up well," Todd said as he hung his hat in the hall and smoothed his dapper suit. "Lord, you look like hell, Monty. When was the last time you slept?"

"He hasn't slept a full night since he again met Lady Beaumont."

"Ah." Todd dragged the word out thoughtfully. "So that's what this is all about. I knew something was going on, but I didn't dare presume. And Clara has been noticeably mute on the subject. No doubt out of loyalty to her friendship with Lady Beaumont."

Hugh picked up the bottle of laudanum, caressing the caramel-colored glass. "Your wife took Lady Beaumont to a clinic for indigent women. Do you know anything about that?" Hugh asked distractedly.

"Lady Leach required moral support in order to visit a doctor there," Todd said as he accepted a cup of tea from Pierpont. "As a result of their secret mission, my wife is no longer wearing a corset. She says she feels better already."

"I say!" Pierpont said in a shocked whisper.

"Your ears are turning red, Pierpont, but mine won't," Todd said amiably. "This doctor says the corset has been interfering with our efforts to have a family. If that's the case, she can jolly well do without. Why, some ladies even wear bloomers these days."

"I would hardly call them ladies. The things that go on in society these days!" Pierpont muttered, then left the room.

"You've shocked Pierpont. You really shouldn't torment the old chap," Hugh said, wiping a sheen of perspiration from his upper lip with the back of one hand while he examined the bottle in the other. "I would be lost without him. And I don't have time to train his replacement. Not in this lifetime anyway."

"Are you going to drink from that hideous bottle or make love to it?"

"Why can't I do both?" Hugh replied with a rasp of bitter laughter. His gleaming eyes caught Todd's.

"You know the answer to that better than I do. If you lose yourself now, you'll never be able to help the countess."

"That's the damnedest thing about an addiction, Toddy, old boy. You can't live with it, and you can't live without it. I'm on a pendulum, and I'm no good on either side, just somewhere in the middle. Too much of the drug and I fall into a stupor. Not enough and my body is wracked in pain. One day I'll quit."

"When?"

"When I have the time. Right now I have a case to solve."

"By the by," Todd said, "I met with the commissioner this morning. The Metropolitan Police have swept over every criminal, every bawd, and every pervert from Limehouse to Cremorne Gardens. There is absolutely no word about Miss Parnham in the underworld. The person who took her is likely working for someone outside. That means your best hope of finding her lies in good, old-fashioned detective work. Scotland Yard detectives have gone over the *London Times* with a fine-toothed comb. There doesn't seem to be any record of who took out that advertisement that mentioned all those trees. So you must rely on your own ability to crack the code."

"I'm working on it," Hugh said wearily. "Amazingly, all clues are pointing to one man—Sir Trevor Dobson, an old neighbor."

"Good heavens!"

Hugh described the evidence gathered thus far. "I just need a bit more proof before I can justify asking the authorities to arrest Dobson."

"And an arrest won't necessarily mean he'll reveal Miss Parnham's whereabouts."

"Pray God Sophie's not dead already." Hugh finally put down the bottle of laudanum, breaking the spell it held over him. But he couldn't keep from perspiring. His body craved opium, even if his mind was strong enough to resist. He pressed his broad palms against his temples and smoothed back the moisture beaded at his hairline. "I seem to have lost my touch. Perhaps I care too much this time. Or perhaps I'm simply getting old."

"At thirty? Lord, I should hope not." Todd's expression was genuinely concerned.

"But my mind isn't what it used to be even ten years ago."

Todd looked pointedly at the bottle Hugh held but said nothing.

Hugh loosened his tie further until it drooped on his chest. Then he popped the stud on his collar and sank down onto a chaise lounge, sprawling his long legs out as he sank onto the back rest. "I want to go to her, Leach. I'll simply pay my respects."

"Do you mean Lady Beaumont? Certainly not before the funeral."

"No. Now." *I don't know what happened to her. I want to know how she suffered. I wanted to marry her. I would have. If only she hadn't left! If only Father hadn't sent her away. The bloody bastard!*

He groaned, and his stomach muscles clinched hard. His body craved opium.

Ask your father. What had Dobson meant by that cryptic advice? Suddenly Montgomery was seized by the need to know. There must be a clue that the earl could give him. "Pierpont! Pierpont!"

The older man came to the doorway. "Yes, sir?"

"Contact my father. Tell him I want to meet with him."

"Lord Boxley?" Pierpont asked in amazement.

"Yes. And tell him it's urgent."

"Very good, sir."

With this decision, Hugh recovered some semblance of control. He stood, straightening his upturned collar, but the blood plummeted from his head to his feet and his knees buckled. He staggered back into his seat.

"Milord!" Pierpont rushed to his side. "You simply must

sleep. You cannot possibly help Lady Beaumont find the girl if you're dead yourself."

Hugh waved him off. "It's nothing." He took a few deep breaths, pulling himself up into a sitting position with considerable effort. *Opium. Opium. Opium.* The internal chant had begun, but he would not hear it. He had to think. He had to solve this damned riddle. *Lydia. Lydia. Lydia.*

Her love was the drug he'd really been craving all these years. The lack of her had driven him into the depths and to superhuman heights. His mind had taken over where his heart had failed. That muscle had atrophied for want of use, and his brain had strengthened instead. He'd searched for knowledge, wanting there to be some purpose in life, even after he had made a mess of it, but what he'd really longed to find was lasting love.

"It's time, sir," Pierpont said, already at the sideboard mixing the tincture of laudanum. When it was obvious that Hugh could not go any longer without it, his faithful attendant always dispensed with his disapproving looks and prepared the mixture himself.

"No." Hugh rose unsteadily. "Something just occurred to me, Leach. There is a . . . a book on the shelf. I haven't looked at it in years, but it just occurred to me . . . ."

"Drink this, sir," Pierpont persisted, coming forward with the precious glass.

Hugh eyed it with hatred, and longing, then drank the contents in six loud gulps. Almost immediately, the laudanum soothed his frayed nerves, returned his sense of peace, and made his muscles relax. He sank back onto the chaise.

"Leach, be a good fellow and fetch me that book up there on the top shelf. I swear I couldn't get up myself even if a fire were blazing around me."

Sir Todd did as he was asked. "Which one is it?"

"I believe it's at the very end. The burgundy leather with the gold imprint."

He shut his eyes. His eyelids were heavy as boulders. He

couldn't sleep now. He just knew the solution to everything lay in that book. Why hadn't he thought of it before? He forced his eyes open and watched through a swirling haze of fading consciousness as Todd pulled the book from the shelf.

The barrister blew on the top cut of the gold-lined pages, and a plume of dust rose. He handed it to Hugh, saying, "Is this what you wanted? You obviously haven't read it in a while."

Not for five years, Hugh thought.

Hugh didn't think he even had the energy left to read the title aloud. But he managed a glance. And just before the book slipped out of his fingers and thudded on the floor, before he fell into a deep and much-needed slumber, he registered the words with a sense. of triumph, knowing he would now have the answers he needed. For this was the book written by Thurber R. Frances, *Pagan Traditions of the British Countryside,* the book that Lydia had read to him the day they found the standing stones.

Lydia sat in the upright chair ten feet away from her husband's coffin, which was on display in the ballroom. She wore black from head to toe, from outer to undergarment. Her tight corset forced her to sit very straight, and she was glad. If she was able to slouch, she was certain her spine would melt. Her entire body would dissolve into a puddle on the floor. She knew she had to be strong, but she had no feelings at all it seemed, and so she must rely on ritual and duty to keep her on course.

It was as if she was suspended in a kind of strange limbo. Knowing that her husband was mortally ill, she had been preparing herself for this day for five years. Yet her life had changed utterly the moment Beaumont died in ways she could in no way prepare for. Where would she go? Who would she be? What would become of her? What would become of her life, her days, her heart? With Beau, she had had a purpose—to comfort him and to save others from her own downfall. But now what?

I must find Sophie. I promised Beaumont I would. And I will.

But not today. Today she would keep vigil by the man who had transformed her life. He was the one who had taught her that there were many kinds of love. Passion was only one of them. Tears came to her eyes every time she thought of the miracle the Earl of Beaumont had been in her life—still more proof that there was a benevolent Creator.

Lydia sat for hours, recalling all the pleasant times she'd shared with her husband. She'd cried hard when she first learned of his death. Now she wanted to celebrate every detail of his life. At 10 o'clock, when Colette crept into the ballroom and urged her to get some much-needed rest, Lydia acquiesced. She let Beaumont's valet take over the vigil. She didn't realize how exhausted she was until she crawled into bed with her diary and willingly recalled, at long last, the hardest memories, the ones she'd tried to forget. Until now.

SEPTEMBER 31, 1875

I don't know what to make of what appears to be incredible good fortune. The pen with which I write these words is priceless. The ink flows like a river. And to think that yesterday I had nothing with which to write at all.

I haven't written in so long because I was too distraught, as well as destitute. I left Windhaven in a torrent of emotions after being sent away by the earl. Even though I am a fallen woman, I thought my father would forgive me and take me in. I thought he might blame Hugh Montgomery and have pity on me. Instead, he accused me of luring Hugh into our clandestine affair.

I remember many hours of my father's sermons on forgiveness, and I had believed every word. And I believed that he believed them as well. But after a single night in his home, when I confessed my predicament, he put me out and said I was never to return. Though Papa says he loves me still, he cannot risk my wicked influence on my younger sisters.

Without references, I could not get work in any respectable home. I had enough money saved to buy a train ticket to London and to rent a boarding room. The only work I could find was as a seamstress. I did slop work at night in a dreadful shop by the river. We would have to stitch outside by the streetlight because the proprietor wouldn't purchase candles.

Many of the young women I worked with said they had either just quit working as prostitutes, or were going to start soon because respectable work didn't pay enough to keep body and soul together. They said it so matter-of-factly. I was unable to hide my shock and dismay. I declared that I would rather die than sell my body.

Heavens, that seems so long ago. Moral superiority is no longer a luxury I can afford. One night, after I realized that my low wages would no longer cover the cost of my squalid room, I slept on the pavement outside a tobacconist's shop. I curled up in my coat on the front stoop and folded my arms around my rail-thin belly. It no longer gurgled for want of food, like a neglected child who no longer cries for affection she knows she won't get. There is simply a gnawing ache where food should be. Or is that my heart that still hurts so?

Somehow I managed to sleep, even though carriages clattered by on the rain-slick cobblestones five feet away from me and a persistent costermonger cried his wares on the corner as factory workers milled past. "Git ye're apple 'ere—a ripe, fine red 'un 'ere."

I could tell even from a distance they were bruised and rotten.

And although I could see him and his customers, they did not see me. I had witnessed this phenomenon many times in my short tenure in London. Those more fortunate walked past the starving and the dying as if they did not exist. Now I was one of those invisible creatures. I no longer had the strength to work. Though I was cold at night, I did not even have the energy to look for a fire in an alley or a heat vent at one of the factories.

With a persistent cough that I knew would soon turn into something worse, I was prepared to die here. No one would be able to say I had demeaned myself in order to survive. I would show them. In death, I would triumph.

And then she came to me. Mrs. Ella Fenniwig. I stirred from my nearly comatose repose and found her staring at me through the open door of her gilt, ornate carriage. With her rustling silk gown and spectacular hat she looked like a peacock in full plumage, and just as colorful.

"Who is that one there?" she said in a very elegant and melodic voice that carried the distance. It was distinctive enough to rouse me, which took enormous effort. When you are so terribly hungry, you want to do little else but wait for sweet, eternal slumber.

A footman jumped off the dickey in the back of her carriage and trotted to my side. I had no strength to recoil. He bent close to study my face. "She's sick, mum," the young man in livery said over his shoulder.

"What's wrong with her?" Mrs. Fenniwig asked.

The footman pushed back my shoulder with his boot until he could see more of me. "Looks hungry."

"Is that all?"

"I ain't no doctor, but I knows 'em starvin' when I sees 'em."

"Well then, pick her up."

I felt the young man's arms scoop under me, and the next thing I knew I was sitting in a plush carriage with a woman who smelled like a luscious bouquet of spring flowers. She was gorgeous, and she had a kind smile. I felt the first stirring of relief, although I didn't know why.

Ella Fenniwig took me home, bathed me, fed me, and clothed me. She welcomed me into her charming townhouse and put me into an effusively feminine bedroom all my own. She treated me as warmly as a daughter. She was delighted to learn that I was educated and well spoken. She fawned over my apparent good looks, although she allowed I was a bit scrawny and promised to fatten me up. For weeks I lived in a fairy tale world with my benefactress. She seemed like a queen or a sorceress, for how could a woman live so freely, alone, and so luxuriously without a man directing her life?

I assumed she was a widow or an heiress. How very wrong I was. A month after I arrived at Mrs. Fenniwig's home, I learned that she was a bawd—a very high-class one, but a bawd nonetheless. And I was expected to be one of her high-class *girls*.

Chapter 12

Under Mrs. Fenniwig's tutelage, I have just completed a period of very thorough training, which included lessons in comportment, French, seduction, and lovemaking—all areas required for a courtesan, and all areas in which I'd already proved myself proficient. My education had included French, as well as Latin. As for comportment, I have a natural elegance—at least that is what Mrs. Fenniwig says. Although I had not consciously seduced Lord Montgomery, I had certainly made love to him. And in this strange world where all social rules were broken regularly, I have begun to lose my sense of shame about that as well.

I was relieved to learn that Ella wanted to groom me as a companion for a wealthy gentleman and not use me as a common whore.

How odd it felt writing that last sentence. A month ago I would rather have starved to death than sell my body to

survive. But near starvation taught me a lesson. I want to
live. Hugh Montgomery did not take that right away from
me when he took away my reputation. Seeing the very well-
bred and politically connected gentlemen who visit Miss
Fenniwig's parlor, I now understand the hypocrisy eating
at our society like a cancer. Why should men stray from
their marriage vows without calamity striking? Why should
men be allowed to visit prostitutes without punishment,
while the poor dolly mops and street walkers who catch
syphilis from them are imprisoned like criminals?

No, I shall be a much-admired courtesan, although I
must admit my training has been a bit unusual and even
humorous at times. Ella said it was important for me to be
prepared for any patron, no matter what size or shape he
comes in. Therefore, she had me observe several of her
special girls through the hidden portal in the Royal Chamber, which is her room for important short-term clients.
Here particular customers, who are known for their kindness, generosity, and good health, are allowed to spend a
single night with one of the girls who are not engaged in a
companionable arrangement.

Watching the peculiar lovemaking habits of various
gentlemen was more entertaining than attending the theater, and at times I could scarcely hold back my laughter.
The first lesson I observed was presented by Carlotta, a
lovely Spanish courtesan who had been working for Ella
for years. She was a voluptuous thirty years of age and had
long black hair and dark, exotic eyes. Her client, the
Marquis de Mortier, was seventy if he was a day. When
Carlotta sprawled her lovely black frilled dress across the
bed and smiled seductively, the marquis methodically dis-
robed, layer by layer, until his pallid prune-dry body was
bare. He looked ready for the grave. But to my amazement,
he had a prodigious member, which he put to good use for
at least an hour. I could only assume that Carlotta's cries of
ecstasy were well rehearsed, but I was not altogether sure.

My next lesson came while observing Caitlin, a younger

girl from Wales. She had an angelic spray of reddish-blond hair and a doll-like face with wide green eyes. She was assigned to a decent-looking young manufacturer from York. He had broad shoulders and compact muscles, and I thought surely Caitlin had been far luckier than Carlotta. But when Caitlin very skillfully and seductively lowered the manufacturer's trousers, she could scarcely find what she was looking for.

I assume she did, for he threw her down on the bed, half ripping off her garments, and went at it for a mad minute. When he strained with his climax and collapsed on the bed, I felt cheated. I could only imagine how Caitlin felt. Then again, she might have been relieved it was over nearly before it had begun. But again, I was not sure.

I did feel certain about one thing. I had been very lucky to have fallen in love with Hugh Montgomery. His love-making had been divine. And I had loved him. Surely that was required for genuine pleasure. But I was not through with my lessons quite yet.

After watching enough of the goings-on in the Royal Chamber, I decided I wanted to test my skills there myself. Ella quickly agreed it was a good idea. Her customers come to her because of her healthy, yet experienced, girls. Once I accepted a patron and became a courtesan, I would be stuck with my choice—good, bad, or indifferent—possibly for years. Ella prided herself on making good and lasting matches. It would be better to test my preferences now.

I soon found myself in the room alone with Don Carlo Alvaretto San Lorenzo. When he turned to me with his knowing dark eyes, my spine started tingling at once, which I should have known was a clear signal of trouble. Carlo started by handing me a bouquet of luscious pink roses. Rather, I should say he swept them forward with panache and grace and a charming smile that would melt icecaps from the North Pole. He was a swarthy Italian with dazzling black eyes, long black lashes, and a muscular body that exuded masculinity.

It was not long before he began to nibble at my lips like a skillful bee nuzzling for honey. When I tensed, he smoothed his magic fingers up my back and forced me to relax, pressing me against his warm, firm chest. When I demurred, he spoke low Italian endearments, and soon his reassuring heat had penetrated my last defenses.

Carlo was a passionate and athletic lover. He handled me like a conquistador, somehow making me feel as if my submission was all part of the plan. His hot, muscular body covered every inch of me. He found my most tender points and brought them to fulfillment with just the perfect combination of tenderness and firmness. He entered at the perfect moment and rode me with sly skill and supreme strength until I cried out with traitorous pleasure. And as I soon learned, with Carlo, once was never enough.

We made love all night long. My natural reticence vanished. We tried every position until I eventually collapsed in exhaustion. When he left the next morning, I was satiated yet most disheartened. He seemed to have proved my theory false—that love was required for great lovemaking. Obviously the human body responds without need of that tender emotion. But what kind of a woman did that make me? Had I really loved Hugh? I was too confused to know.

Carlo visited me every night for the next month, much to Ella's disapproval. She was glad to know I was learning to appreciate the sport of sex. And of course she taught me how to avoid pregnancy. But Carlo was not a rich man and would not make a suitable patron. I persuaded her that there was much more he could teach me. It was then that I learned the last important lesson from Ella Fenniwig.

One night when Carlo was making love to me with his usual ecstasy-inducing skill, I looked up into his entranced face and realized I was bored. Even as I cried out my release, I was bored. I did not love Carlo. Our affair was over.

Ella understood. When I told her I wanted a patron whom I could *not* love, she agreed that was wise. He need not be handsome or charming, merely kind and rich.

Unfortunately, I did not quite realize how much my experience with Carlo had changed me. I now knew the difference between love and lust, and I thought I understood the distinctions between love and need. Freed of the illusions of dependence I had harbored with Hugh, I was now impatient for something altogether different and more honest. I did not realize that honesty was not highly prized by very many of the men who sought out Mrs. Fenniwig's services.

During my first interview with the patron Mrs. Fenniwig had chosen for me, we had lunch in Ella's private drawing room. Sir Edward Day had recently inherited his title of baronet, which he clearly wished had been viscount or marquess instead. He ambitiously meant to impress society in every way possible and wanted to sport a courtesan on his arm at certain affairs. This clearly had become fashionable among the elite since the Prince of Wales was seen in public with one mistress after another.

Unfortunately, Sir Edward did not understand the distinction between a simple fallen angel and a companion. He quite lost his composure over lunch, and before he knew the least little bit about me he had the audacity to start groping my breasts. I did what any vicar's daughter might—I stabbed him with a fork.

L ydia let her diary lower into her lap as she sank back into her pillow. With a smile on her face, she closed her eyes as that event replayed in her mind. She'd forgotten about her adventures with Mrs. Fenniwig. She'd tried hard to forget. But looking back on it now, Lydia realized she would never have had the courage to help others under the guise of the Midnight Angel if it hadn't been for the tough lessons she'd learned from Ella. And she would never have met her dear, dear husband if the uncouth Sir Edward hadn't accosted her at that very moment.

She flipped the page of the diary and read on.

NOVEMBER 5, 1875

It has been a week since I last wrote. And what a week! I want to record every detail so I do not forget. After I stabbed Sir Edward's arm with the pointy tines of my salad fork, he cried out in shock and then again in outrage. He turned bright red, stood abruptly, threw his napkin on his plate, and stormed from the room, straight into Ella's parlor.

"I have never seen such outrageous behavior," I could hear him shouting as I hurried after him. When I entered the parlor, he turned with a look of loathing and pointed at me. "This young *lady* stabbed me with a fork!"

All eyes turned to me. Ella's commanding gaze fixed on me. She had the address of a royal princess, and I had often wondered if perhaps she had been one of Prince Edward's many paramours, for she was so well connected in high society. Also regarding me was a visitor whom I had never seen before. He was dignity personified. He was tall and slim, dressed immaculately in a black suit and gray striped ascot. He had black hair with gray wings, an aristocratic nose, and a sardonic mouth. He filled a high-back carved wing chair with enough style and grace to indicate he would be just as comfortable as if he were having tea with the queen.

"Is this true?" Ella inquired. "Did you stab Sir Edward, Adelaide?"

We had decided to use my full name, not Addie. For a moment I thought she was speaking to someone else.

"Yes, it's true," I replied. "He tried to . . . to touch me. I thought it was an incredible display of poor judgment and bad manners."

The dignified visitor chuckled softly and regarded me with admiration. "You're quite right, my dear. It was."

Sir Edward sent him a blazing look of disdain. "I am a very rich man, sir. But I do not throw good money after bad. I expect to get what I pay for." He recovered some of his composure and turned more civilly to Ella. "If I wanted a prude, madam, I would *marry* the chit, not merely *fuck* her."

I gasped, but after that there was no other sound, other than the ticking of the clock on the mantel. The room went deadly still. At last Ella stood and assumed her most professional smile.

"I am so very sorry, Sir Edward. But you are not at all the gentleman I had imagined. I cannot possibly recommend you to Miss Adelaide. I hope you will accept my apologies. I trust you can see yourself out?"

The next day Ella called me into her private parlor again. I assumed she expected my thanks, which I intended to give profusely. But I was surprised to see the same handsome gentleman I had seen the night before, and who had witnessed my debacle with Sir Edward, sitting in the same high-back chair. This time he wore a very distinguished tan wool jacket and a brown and white checked waistcoat.

The early afternoon light streaming through Ella's bay window revealed more age in the gentleman than I had seen the night before. He looked to be in his mid-fifties, and although he clearly had been quite the swell in his younger days, I could now see dark circles under his lively eyes. He did not look well.

"Come in, Adelaide," Ella said, her naturally warm features especially vibrant. "I want to introduce you to the Adrian Tyrell, the Earl of Beaumont."

Startled, I looked at the handsome stranger. I had no idea he was an earl. I blushed and immediately dropped into a curtsey. "A pleasure, your lordship," I mumbled.

"The pleasure is all mine, my dear," he said as he stood.

"Adelaide, Lord Beaumont wants to ask you a very special and particular question. I will leave you alone. Just bear in mind that I thoroughly approve of his proposition. Call me when you have made your decision."

I licked my lips, and my breath caught in my throat. I could only assume that the earl had taken a fancy to me and wanted to keep me as a mistress. And after the debacle with Sir Edward, I had decided I could not stand being kept by any man. But how could I turn down one who was so gracious and important?

The Earl of Beaumont proved himself to be sensitive to my moods, saying, "I understand your hesitation, my dear. All I ask is that you listen to what I propose."

I assumed the graceful smile I had learned from Ella and nodded. "Of course."

Ella nodded approvingly and quietly departed.

"Won't you be seated, Miss Parker?"

I sat on the edge of the chaise. He watched me settle, then smiled warmly at me. "I admired how you handled yourself yesterday with that most ill-bred baronet."

I suppressed a smile. "Thank you. I assure you I would not normally stab any gentleman."

"Of course not. He was no gentleman." The earl clasped his hands behind his back and paced thoughtfully a few feet. "I'll come to the point straight away. I came here today to ask you if you would marry me."

I stared after him, certain I had misheard. Then he stopped and looked at me, clearly waiting for an answer.

"What?" I whispered.

His cheeks creased with a well-worn and easy smile. "I know this must come as a shock. But I am utterly serious. I want to make you my wife. Naturally, you will assume the title of Countess of Beaumont, although I don't think I'll be able to manage an audience with the queen for you."

An audience with the queen? Was he mad?

"I have no heirs, much to my dismay. I was the only child of an only child. I will leave you everything when I die."

I had stopped breathing by now and grew lightheaded.

"Do continue to breathe, Miss Parker. I do not want you to decease before I do. I am fifty-five, your senior by a number of years. It's only right that I should pass first."

"Why?" was all I could manage to utter. No nobleman wanted his worldly goods and memory left in the hands of a disreputable commoner.

He blinked several times, searching for words, and his elegant demeanor was tinged with sadness. "I am dying. I have syphilis. I may live for only a few years. One never knows about these things. I've been infected for some time. My doctor says the disease is progressing."

"Oh," I exhaled, my heart going out to him at once. Then I grew alarmed. If I became his wife . . . .

"I'm sorry for speaking so crudely, Miss Parker," he continued, "but I must be honest. I've never married. I loved women too much and no one woman in particular enough. But I do not want to die alone. And it seems a waste to have so much and no one to whom I can leave it. Miss Fenniwig told me about your circumstances. I hope I don't presume too much by thinking I might be a friend to you."

I didn't know what to say.

"I will respect you, Miss Parker, as I have already begun to do. I will not expect conjugal relations—I would never risk your life. All I want is a companion."

Dare I believe him? Somehow, I did. Still, there were other matters to consider. "My reputation, sir," I argued. "It's one thing to claim me as a mistress, but a wife! Surely someone will learn of my time here with Miss Fenniwig."

"Not necessarily. I come from a very old line of the nobility dating back to William and Mary—old enough that I needn't try to please anyone. I keep to myself these days. I won't ask you to so much as host a tea party. Simply be my companion. You're intelligent and lovely. I would consider myself fortunate simply to share your company." When I still remained speechless, he added, "Besides, I wouldn't be the first gentleman of the *ton* to marry a mistress."

"Are you always this impulsive, sir?"

"No, but the closer to death I come, Miss Parker, the less I care about anything but pleasing myself. I have had my share of women. I'm now paying the price. Perhaps in my past as a roué I broke a heart or two. Perhaps I might have even left a bastard in my wake, though I am not aware of having done so. If I can make your life more pleasant, it will be my way of paying penance, in some small portion."

He sat down beside me, and I inhaled a whiff of his cologne. I did not recognize it, but it was obviously expensive, for it had an ephemeral quality, like fine wine.

I looked in his eyes and saw such kindness, such worldliness, that I briefly regretted I could not have known him when he was in his prime. Of course my mind wanted to compare him to Hugh, as I compared every man I met. Lord Beaumont was far smoother and more at ease with life. Yet he and Hugh seemed to share intelligence and a humility that allowed them both to see something of value in me, despite my lowly circumstances. I was surprised to realize that part of me—the most foolish part—wanted to say no. I was still in love with Hugh in spite of everything.

Then the earl placed his hand on mine. His long, graceful fingers were warm and soothing. It was a paternal gesture, and the part of me that still ached from my father's rejection breathed a sigh of relief. I was, at last, breathing normally again. I could finally think straight. And there was clearly only one answer I could give him.

"Yes, Lord Beaumont, I accept your proposal."

Lydia pressed the diary to her breasts and hugged it hard, as if embracing her dear sweet husband for the last time.

"Oh, Beau, I shall miss you," she said as tears flooded her eyes.

Then peace overcame her. Lydia had always wondered how she could repay him. She'd never accepted that her companionship was reward enough for Beaumont. Now she could do for him in death what she could not do in life. She could save his daughter just as he had saved her. She would cast off her widow's weeds and set out on the search as soon as he was buried.

Although social custom held that she should sit at home in black for two years, she would have none of it. She would search for Sophie, and she would do so, at long last, dressed as herself—Adelaide Lydia Beaumont, née Parker. No more charades. No more subterfuge. Society be damned.

Chapter 13

Hugh arrived in a hansom cab at the Montague Club just as the sun set behind the overcast skyline. Slivers of salmon light and yellow tufts of sulphur-tinged fog gave the chimney-spiked skyline an eerie look and a foul stench. It was the smell of the city. He scarcely noticed. Only when he returned from the country did it offend him.

When he stepped down onto the cobblestones, he tugged his hat forward against a sudden drizzle. He had just crossed the street when a hand grabbed his upper arm. Hugh turned sharply, suspecting someone was trying to distract him from a sly pickpocket.

"It's me, sir. Didn't mean to startle you."

A grin tugged at Hugh's lips. "Reggie! How did you find me?"

The shorter man nodded toward another cab that was rolling away in the rain. "I followed you from your place. I arrived just as you were leaving. Her ladyship sent me."

Hugh gripped the young man's shoulder, asking urgently,

"What is it? Has something happened? Does she need me?"

Reggie's freckled face paled under Hugh's intense scrutiny. When Montgomery released him he stepped back, saying, "Don't know about that, sir. All I know is that his lordship is being buried tomorrow, and she wants to see you immediately after—to get on with the investigation."

Hugh blinked a moment in stunned silence. "She can't meet with me then. Her period of mourning—"

"It's over, sir. Before it began," the young man said uncomfortably.

"It's supposed to last two years!" Hugh stood flummoxed as Reggie continued his unhappy recitation.

"She's going to bury the earl, then she's heading straight out. She doesn't care what anyone says. I've never seen anything like it. She's even giving up on the Midnight Angel. She says whatever good she does she intends to do it as herself, and the world be damned."

"Does she now?" A slow, wistful smile curved Hugh's lips. He was touched to the heart with emotions he couldn't name, much less understand. "My darling Lydia," he murmured to himself, then collected his wits once again and turned to Reggie. "Tell the countess she should be ready to pay a visit to Mr. Thurber Frances, the author. I've made an appointment for the day after tomorrow, and I'm sure she won't want to miss it."

"Very good, sir," Reggie replied, but the troubled expression on his face indicated that he believed the situation was anything but good.

Hugh approached the gentleman's club where his father's butler said the earl would be drinking with his cronies. To his surprise, his belly roiled uneasily. He thought he'd succeeded in obliterating all feeling for the old man, but hatred died a slow death, especially when there was so much to hate.

Hugh hadn't seen Charles Montgomery, Sixth Earl of

Boxley, since the earl had sent Addie away. It had been five years, and it would have been fifty more if Hugh didn't want to know why some disparate pieces were falling together in one strange puzzle.

He found his father on the first floor, holding a very expensive cigar in one hand and cradling a brandy in the other. He was gray haired, gray suited, and gray souled. Grouped around him were several fellow members, indulging in a hand of whist. As they played the cards with desultory attention, Hugh watched the old man exchanging quips with a companion.

Although Lord Boxley's wits were razor-keen, his reflexive smile faded the moment it reached his eyes. He was always thinking. There had been need for that when he inherited the title and had to rescue the family's estates from his father's profligate spending. The sixth earl had restored luster to the Boxley title that had been tarnished by the fifth earl. His incisive mind had made him a valued adviser to the prime minister, and it was said he even had the ear of the queen. Whereas the fifth earl had been a drunken debaucher, the sixth earl had been the typical Victorian gentleman—polite, unemotional, and, above all, proper.

Hugh unconsciously ran a hand through his hair, which had frizzled in the rain. He was sure he looked like something the cat had dragged in. That's what his father would see anyway.

"Good evening, Lord Boxley," he said to his father when there was a lull in the conversation between the men gathered around the card table.

The group of gentlemen, all of whom belonged to the House of Lords, looked up at the intruder, some with blank expressions, one or two with hostility. Who was this brash intruder? As recognition set in, a palpable tension filled the air.

Lord Boxley's sharp eyes narrowed. "Montgomery, what brings you here?"

"Well, bless me, if it isn't the infamous Lord Clue," said the man on his father's right.

"Good evening, Avesbury," Hugh said warmly. The Marquess of Avesbury had spent many a holiday with Hugh's family, and Hugh held him in fond regard. He saw more affection in the doddering old man's rheumy eyes than he did in his father's cool, gray ones.

"I keep reading about you in the papers, young man," Avesbury croaked. "Most impressive. Your mother would be proud of you, I'm sure. Working on any cases now?"

"Don't encourage him," his father said coldly. "When he gets bored I'm hoping he'll find a more suitable occupation for his intelligence and connections than gallivanting around the seamier sides of London."

"Strange that you should mention connections, sir," Hugh said. "I was hoping to use yours to help me solve a new case."

"I should have known you'd want something from me or you wouldn't have sought me out." Boxley stood and looked regretfully at his companions. "If you'll excuse me, gentlemen. I fear I must attend to family business."

Hugh followed him into a quiet corner where they settled into two high-backed chairs. He accepted a cigar from a silent servant who discreetly retreated, then took his time trimming the tip as he debated what to tell his father. Naturally, he would make no mention of finding Addie. The earl had already done his best to destroy her and had nearly destroyed Hugh in the process.

He most certainly would not bring up their violent last encounter. Nor would he rail at the earl for his meddling. Because the old man had made no effort to reconcile over the last five years, it was clear he remained unrepentant.

"Well?" Boxley steepled his fingers and regarded his son with thinly veiled disdain. "What is this case?"

"That can wait," Hugh replied. "I have something much more important to ask you."

"Go on."

"Was my mother having an affair with Sir Trevor Dobson before her death?"

There was a long silence as the smoke from their cigars coiled between them and eventually merged in the shadows hovering near the tin ceiling.

Then the earl leaned forward in his chair, his eyes glowing with barely leashed fury. "Are you mad? Your mother and Dobson!" He looked quickly around them to make certain no one had overheard. A slight sigh escaped his mouth when he was certain no one had.

Just as suddenly, he slumped back and puffed his cigar, a look of disgust falling over his features as he said, "I should've known there's no hope for you. That you'd actually dare to judge your own mother that way. Small wonder, considering the low type of company you keep these days. The Countess and I respected and loved each other until the day she died. Frankly, I find your question as offensive as it is pathetic."

Hugh swirled the brandy around in his snifter. "Is that why you had her committed to that awful asylum in the middle of nowhere? Was she going to embarrass you by leaving you?"

"No!" Boxley's voice was simmering now.

"Then why did you commit her?" Hugh persisted relentlessly.

The earl put down his brandy with a clank of the glass. "You know very well I had no choice. Every doctor I consulted said there was no other possibility. After your sister was born, she became melancholy. Then suicidal. I had to do it for her own good."

"Some good it did her!" Hugh tightened his grip around the balloon glass, remembering that time etched indelibly in his memory. He had come home from boarding school one Christmas, and his mother had been perfectly sane. Six months later she had been committed and soon after hung herself. He watched the old man's whole body appear to crumple for an instant before he masked his pain. Much as Hugh had reason to hate his father, he knew the earl felt guilty about her death. As well he should, but that was long ago and beside the point now. He tried another approach.

"I know this must be painful for you, sir, but I must ask you one thing in particular. Where did my mother get her diamond butterfly brooch?"

"You know very well where it came from," the earl snapped impatiently. "I inherited the piece from my mother. It dates back to Queen Elizabeth's era."

"So she didn't get it from Dobson?"

"Of course not!"

"It's a curious piece, don't you think?"

"Not really."

"If it dates back that far, I should think it would more likely be the Tudor rose, or something from the family crest. Why a butterfly? It's not a terribly historic symbol."

"If you had ever bothered to listen to my lectures on the family history, Montgomery, you would have remembered what I told you about the First Earl of Boxley. He had a way with the ladies and did nothing to restrain his ardor, which was not an uncommon practice in Elizabeth's court. His affections were so fickle that the queen dubbed him her butterfly, because he flitted so easily from blossom to blossom to blossom, deflowering them all. All except for the virgin queen, of course."

Hugh's hard features softened as he imagined that bawdy era, which so contrasted with the reign of the prudish Queen Victoria.

"Do you know," Hugh asked, "that Trevor Dobson possesses a crystal mask that looks almost identical to mother's brooch?"

"Really?" The earl did not seem particularly interested.

"He even has a club called the Diamond Forest where he wears the mask."

His eyes widened. "How do you know that?"

"I was there. I wouldn't have thought you would be familiar with such a place."

"I've tried to have the place shut down. It's a blight on London's reputation." Boxley looked over his shoulder, then leaned forward, whispering, "You'll ruin your reputation in a place like that."

"That's all you think about, isn't it, Father? Reputations." Hugh smiled contemptuously. "How many lives have you sacrificed on that hard, cold altar?"

"You're still angry about that governess, aren't you?"

Hugh gave a hollow laugh. "You don't even remember her name, do you?"

"I did it for your own good," his father replied.

Hugh's brows drew together fiercely. "You killed the patient to the cure disease. Do you know that?"

"You seem perfectly healthy to me. One day you'll thank me for it. I'm surprised you haven't already."

Hugh surprised them both by slamming down his fist on the table. The earl's drink leapt and clattered. All sound in the club silenced, then slowly resumed. "Look, you stubborn old man," Hugh hissed through clenched teeth. "I did not come here to rehash that wretched time. You know very well my feelings on the matter. I simply want to know why Dobson told me to come see you."

"I have no idea!" The earl took a deep breath and let it out slowly. "What are you investigating?"

"The illegitimate daughter of the Earl of Beaumont and the actress Louise Canfield has been kidnapped. I thought one of Dobson's associates in the Botanicals might have done it."

"The Botanicals?" he replied with disingenuous surprise.

Hugh snarled, "Don't give me that look, Father."

"The Prince of Wales belongs to that club!"

"We both know the prince is unaware of the true purpose of the club—the sexual trade in virgins that goes on after all the respectable members have gone home to their wives or mistresses."

The earl's eyes glinted dangerously. "You'd best watch what you say, my son. Not even the infamous Lord Clue could get away with accusing the esteemed members of the Botanicals of conspiring to rape young women. I've heard the rumors, but I've been a member for more than thirty years and have seen no evidence of such debauchery. You know how hard I've worked to restore dignity to our family name. Do you think I would dare to belong to any group engaged in such despicable behavior?"

Hugh leaned back, a cynical smirk on his face. "Perish the thought. As it so happens, I no longer suspect the Botanicals of being involved with Miss Parnham's disappearance."

The earl tilted his head curiously. "Why not?"

"Mistletoe," was Hugh's cryptic reply.

"You're talking gibberish."

"The Botanical's symbol is holly, and mistletoe was left at the scene of Miss Parnham's abduction. I believe Dobson might belong to another group that might be guilty of the crime. Or perhaps he's acting alone."

"But you don't know."

Hugh shook his head, staring at the play of candlelight on his brandy. "No. Why did Dobson send me to you?"

The earl shut his eyes in an apparent moment of indecision. Then he thrust out his chin and shook his head. "I never wanted to tell you."

Hugh's head snapped up. "Tell me what?"

The earl shook his head again, and made a moue, as if the whole subject tasted bitter on his tongue. "Trevor Dobson is . . . he's your uncle."

Now it was Hugh's turn to be dumbfounded. *"What?"*

"He's my half-brother. You are well aware that your grandfather would bed anything wearing a dress. He left bastards from here to Timbuktu."

Hugh was momentarily speechless, then he said ironically, "I don't recall seeing anyone bearing my likeness in the local village."

"That's because my father hated my mother and rarely

visited Windhaven. He was attracted to the lowest sorts of women imaginable—the mangiest prostitutes he could drag off the streets. Only once did he have a true love affair—with Dobson's mother. At least she was from the middle class. He didn't legitimize their son, but he made him wealthy."

"Trevor Dobson?"

"Yes. Father arranged a baronetcy for the boy. When he was young, Dobson's mother moved into Tremaine Way so she could be near Windhaven. She claimed to be a widow. I certainly didn't want to dispute her claim because my father had embarrassed my mother enough already. So we all pretended to be cordial neighbors."

"I suppose there is some likeness between you and Sir Trevor. I never saw it before."

"You were never looking for it."

"So Dobson inherited the butterfly mask? And you inherited the butterfly brooch?"

"One can only assume the mask came from my father. His mother gave me the brooch as a wedding gift. The fifth earl left me very little, as you know. In fact, the only real thing of value he bequeathed to me was the one thing he had to give me by law—the title. For all I know, Dobson might be rolling in the family jewels. If there were any left after my father tried and failed to pay off his creditors, that is."

"But you're friends. You and Dobson."

"We are neighborly. I never wanted to raise curiosity by engaging in an unexplained feud with my closest neighbor. He's a good enough fellow, but I'd stay away from him, if I was you. He's been a bit odd these past ten years since his wife's passing. And this club of his is simply beyond the pale. I do not want anyone to know he is related in any way to our family, Montgomery. I am concerned that he should have raised the issue with you. He's always been discreet until now."

"I'm sure he was simply letting me know that if I exposed his perversities, he could expose something in return. I stumbled on his place quite by chance."

"Nothing happens by chance," the earl said in a jaded tone.

Hugh gave him a half-smile. "Perhaps not." He thought of Lydia's encounter with May, the girl whose situation could be the same as the one facing Sophie Parnham. How had May acquired a scar in the shape of a butterfly? "Sometimes when I write my books I leave out certain details, even though they're true, because I know they're so unbelievable that someone will accuse me of writing fiction, not fact."

"Leave Dobson alone, Montgomery. For the sake of our family name."

"I can't, sir. He had an affair with Sophie's mother. There has to be a connection. And I have to pursue it."

The earl digested this, then nodded stiffly. "I know you will do whatever you want. You always have, and the rest of the world—and your family—be damned. Best beware, though. Dobson might be dangerous."

Hugh nodded. For the first time in five years, father and son agreed on something.

Sophie heard the iron ring on the outside of the door moving and awakened to utter darkness. She'd let the candles burn out and lay in a fetal position on her bed. After the visit from the gentleman she'd met in the alley, her hope of rescue had withered to a dried husk. He had strange notions, and she doubted she could appeal to his conscience.

Worse yet, if he was a wealthy gent, no one would suspect him—least of all her mother. Louise would be searching places like Haymarket and Cremorne Gardens.

The door creaked open, revealing a pewter sky and the silhouettes of budding trees. Sophie blinked at the light, and her body tightened with a dual surge of hope and fear. She still didn't know why she'd been kidnapped. She supposed she was going to be deflowered. But why was her kidnapper dragging it out? He could have raped her if that was his only intention.

"Miss Parnham?" An unfamiliar voice floated down into the cellar.

"Yes?" she replied. She sat up and tucked strands of her blond hair behind her ears.

Feet appeared, and a man descended with a lantern in hand. Sophie had never seen him before. "Who are you?"

He put the lantern on the table and smiled kindly, almost apologetically. "I am a doctor."

"A doctor?" Sophie answered, bewilderment ringing in her voice.

"My name is Dr. Keeley. I've come to make sure you are healthy and safe, my dear. You needn't be afraid."

Her mind raced as she tried to absorb this new twist in her circumstances. At the same time she squinted against the uneven light to see him more closely. Dr. Keeley wasn't much taller than Sophie. He was thin and wiry with black hair that fell unexpectedly down his forehead. Although he clearly was used to being treated with respect, and although he had a broad, ready smile used to reassure his patients, there was a worn and haunted look in his eyes. His face appeared to be sallow and gaunt. She recognized the symptoms of an opium eater.

He pulled up a chair beside her bed, and Sophie scooted away, not sure whether to trust him.

"Now, my dear, how are you feeling?"

Her eyelids fluttered in disbelief. "Horrible! I've been kidnapped. Please, sir, get me out of here. My mother has money, sir. She's famous. She'll do anything to get me back. Anything."

"But you're an orphan!"

"I lied. My mother is Louise Canfield. Ask her. Don't ask anyone else, because no one else knows." He looked at her sympathetically. "I'm not making it up. It's true."

"Are you getting enough to eat?" he asked, as if she weren't a trembling mass of fear. He looked in his black bag, adding casually, "You know, that famous investigator, Lord Clue? He's looking for you. I read it in the paper."

"He is?" Sophie hissed, leaning forward. "Are you sure? Well, he'll find me then, won't he? He solves all the famous crimes."

The doctor chuckled ruefully as he pulled out a shiny instrument she didn't recognize. "Oh-ho, no, he won't find you, dear girl. You are in the middle of nowhere."

"Where? Tell me! Where am I?"

"Now this might be a bit . . . uncomfortable, Miss Parnham."

Sophie twisted around and tore at her bedding until she found a note she'd hidden under the pillow. "I've written a letter to Louise. Will you give it to her? Please?"

"Now, Miss Parnham—"

"You must have mercy, sir. It doesn't tell her where I am, because I don't know. But it will let her know I'm alive. She must be worried sick. She'll give you free tickets to the theater, I'm sure. *Please.*"

A pained look flashed over the doctor's thin, sallow face. Perhaps the remnants of a professional conscience? She didn't know, but for the first time in days she knew hope.

"Please, sir."

"I'll make a deal with you, my dear. I will take the letter and think very hard about giving it to your mother. But you must do something in return for me."

"What? Anything!"

"You must lie down on your back and be very still. You might feel a little pain, but it won't last. But you must lie still and not fight me, or you might be permanently injured." He held up the frightening clawlike contraption.

"What is it?" she said as her skin turned cold.

"It's a speculum."

"What are you going to do you do with it?"

"I'm going to examine you, Miss Parnham, to make sure you are healthy and pure."

Pure. Her blood froze in her veins. Did he intend to do what she suspected? Sheer humiliation washed over her. Could she endure such an awful thing?

Sensing her hesitation, he said in a soothing voice, "Please lie down. This won't take long."

She realized then she'd made a bargain with the devil, and she wasn't even sure he was going to hold up his end of it. But what other hope did she have? She did as he asked and stared up at the ceiling, biting her lower lip. Her hands clawed at the sheets as she awaited an invasion of her innocent body that was unimaginable, even to one raised by a promiscuous actress.

"Now you spread your legs apart, Miss Parnham. Wider. That's good."

She shut her eyes, wishing she could go to sleep. Better the nightmares of her dreams than that which she was living while wide awake.

Chapter 14

L ydia," Hugh said, his voice husky with emotion. Although the butler had announced his arrival, she did not seem to have noticed.

She stood, dressed elegantly in black, by a row of spring flowers that brightened the small, enclosed garden behind the house. The heady perfume of crocuses and nasturtiums wafted on the breeze. Beyond, the Thames slapped against the retaining wall at the edge of the property. Barges tooled by, and an occasional horn sounded. But they were distant distractions.

Hugh would be much more aware of the sweet smell of Lydia's unique and subtle essence than of all the flowers in Kew Gardens. How elegant she was. How strong. Her close-fitting black bonnet was tied at her throat with a scarf, emphasizing the daintiness of her slender neck. Her wide lips were set in a stoic smile. She was the most beautiful woman he had ever seen, and the only one he had ever loved.

"Lydia," he said a little louder. The wind must have carried his voice this time, for she looked up with a start. Relief washed over her features, and she seemed to take a quick step toward him, then caught herself.

"Hello, Monty," she said, sinking back on her heels.

He walked the distance between them, not stopping until he was too close for propriety. "I'm so sorry." He took both her hands in his and held them up to his chest, marveling at how right her skin felt on his. Her hands were so delicate. He almost laughed, remembering how firm her handshake had been when she was posing as the Midnight Angel. But the heat that flowed between them wiped away his inward smile. He had never felt so close to another. They needed no words. Their gripping fingers tethered them together like two souls lost in a storm at sea, lashed to a mast, forced to endure the worst the world could do to them, for better or worse.

"My husband was an extraordinary man," she said. "I shall miss him terribly."

She looked up with tear-filled eyes, as if measuring his understanding. She would see no jealousy, no possession in his face, for he did understand her love of Lord Beaumont. He understood everything about her. But he would not boast by telling her so.

"He was lucky to be able to share his last years with you," Hugh said simply.

"I suppose. But I was the luckier one."

He released her hands, sensing that he could not push intimacy too far too fast. "Reggie tells me that Mr. Morgan has hung up his cape for good. Is that true?"

She nodded and hugged herself against a cool breeze that sailed in from the river over the garden wall. "Yes. I must dedicate myself to finding Sophie. And then I must move on. There is no life for me here in London without Beaumont."

"Where will you go?"

She looked up, squinting in the sun to see him. "I don't know. But I cannot worry about that now."

"Will you marry me?" He could hardly believe the words had just popped out of his mouth. How incredibly rude of him to ask under these circumstances. Her husband hadn't been dead for more than a few days.

Lydia acted as if she had not heard. "We'd best get going if we're going to keep our appointment with Mr. Frances." She brushed past him and started for the house.

"Lydia—."

"Don't!" she said, whirling on him. "You don't want to know the answer to your question. You shouldn't have asked."

With that she walked off, leaving him to wonder why she simply hadn't said no.

They found Thurber Frances at his home, which was a cozy flat on Tottenham Court Road. "Welcome, welcome," he said when he opened the door. "You must be Viscount Montgomery. Ah, and this would be Lady Beaumont. My condolences, your ladyship. I read about your great loss in the newspaper."

Lydia was half in a fog, which was good; otherwise she might have begun to cry. But her desire to rescue Sophie had shoved aside all other considerations. Therefore, she was able to discuss her husband, even with strangers.

"Thank you, Mr. Frances. He was a great man. His death is the world's loss."

"Quite, quite," said the retired schoolmaster. He was a genial, portly fellow who looked to be in his mid-sixties. His eyelids drooped at an angle over his soft brown eyes, which matched the color of his tweed coat and vest. He was nearly bald but sported a few valiant wisps of gray. "Won't you come inside? I've just prepared some tea. I live alone and serve as my own housekeeper."

He led them into a parlor that smelled pleasantly of pipe tobacco and was filled from floor to ceiling with books. Lydia smiled at the sight of them.

"You like to read, your ladyship?" Frances said as he followed her admiring gaze.

"Yes, I read your book on pagan traditions some years ago. That's what brought us here."

She found a chair by a crackling fire and accepted a delicious cup of Earl Grey tea. Hugh seemed anxious, and she wondered with a worried frown if he was craving opium. She didn't know the extent of his dependence on it. Then again, he was always tense when working on a case.

"Won't you have a cup of tea, Lord Montgomery?" Frances said hopefully.

Hugh shook his head and sat on a settee by the older man. "Thank you, no. I wish we had time to chat, Mr. Frances, but we come on rather urgent business. I'm working on a very special case."

"I read about it in the paper," Frances said with obvious fascination. His soft, bowed lips sipped carefully at his tea. "You're looking for Lord Beaumont's daughter."

"Yes," Lydia said. "We need your help in deciphering some very important clues."

"Oh, dear me. I'm not sure how I can help."

"Take a look at these." Hugh pulled out the letters with the odd sequence of trees. "The Countess of Beaumont and I believe the kidnapper might have some special connection to nature. You see these notes are clearly written in code. We thought you might be able to point us in some direction or other based on your study of pagan lore." Hugh handed over the letters. "What do you make of this? Do you think it has anything to do with paganism?"

Thurber Frances reached for his spectacles perched on a pile of books on a side table. He propped them ceremoniously on his unremarkable nose and read the letters. As he scanned one and then the other, his cheeks flushed red and his eyes glowed.

"My!" he said. "Oh, my, my, my!"

"What is it?" Lydia moved to the edge of her seat, her tea

cup poised in midair. "Have you figured it out already?"

"Do you know what this is?" he asked, gazing incredulously from one to the other.

"No," Hugh said dryly. "That's why we came to see you."

"This is the tree alphabet!"

"The what?" Lydia looked to Hugh, who shrugged. "What is the tree alphabet?"

"It's a Goidelic alphabet, which was used in Ireland and Britain long before the Latin ABCs we use now."

"So it was used by the ancient Celts," Hugh said.

"Yes. But of course, this is the English translation. Were this to be written in the original Goidelic language, you would see very different words."

"I don't understand," Lydia protested.

"You see, ma'am, each tree represents a letter in the alphabet. For example, A would be represented by the silver fir, B by the birch, C by hazel. But were you to see the words used by the ancient people who created this form of communication, you would be reading Celtic words. The alphabet would read Ailm, Beth, Coll, Duir, Eadha, Fearn, Gort, and so on. But that is neither here nor there, because whoever wrote these notes used the Latin alphabet. That should make it simple to translate, assuming he knows what he's doing."

"Can you tell us what the letters say?" Hugh asked.

"Of course," Frances said with a confident chuckle. "I simply have to find my notes. It's been a while since I've had to translate from the tree alphabet."

He stood much too slowly for Lydia's liking and seemed to move at a turtle's pace toward his bookshelves.

"Now where did I stash those notes?" he muttered to himself.

Hugh stood as if his legs were spring-loaded. Lydia suppressed a smile, for she knew he wanted to throttle the information out of their kindly but all-too-retiring host.

"Mr. Frances, you called it the tree alphabet. Was this used by the Druids?"

"Oh, yes. Yes, the druids, or derwydd, as they were called in their time, worshipped trees, especially the oak. Derwydds were called oak-seers. They had three tiers in their social hierarchy." He groaned as he reached for a high shelf and grabbed at a thin portfolio until it was in his grasp and pulled it down. "Some were bards, who recorded history in long, allegorical ballads; some acted as seers and diviners; and finally some were priests and judges. The druids never wrote down anything that outsiders might be able to translate. They even created a secret sign language based on the tree alphabet to use when outsiders were present. That explains why there is so little known about the druids even to this day. Ah, here we are."

"Have you ever in your studies found any symbolism revolving around the butterfly, Mr. Frances?" Lydia inquired.

"Nothing in connection with the druids, ma'am, but it is an obvious sign of transformation. The butterfly starts its life as a caterpillar and changes within the cocoon. The idea of transformation, or rebirth, is very strong in the Celtic image of the cauldron of Cerridwen."

"I take it she is pagan goddess?"

Frances placed his portfolio on a small reading table and began to sort through it as he rambled on. "She is the great goddess of inspiration who stirs in her dark cauldron a tempting brew of knowledge and pain. She is the lovely blond and blue-eyed mother of wisdom. She is white like the new moon, full and bright, but she has a dark side. She can transform into a horse, a mare of the night. In some cultures she is the sow goddess. When her dark side is present, she is considered the lady of death."

Lydia's heart started to pound. She and Hugh looked at each other, both recognizing the truth. "Blond and blue-eyed? Like Sophie. And May."

Hugh growled. "My God, this is it! It's all coming together. Where is that blasted alphabet?"

Frances didn't seem troubled by his guest's impatience.

He was absorbed in laying out his fascinating tree alphabet. "Here it is."

Hugh quickly scanned the Goidelic alphabet and its English translations. He began to jot down the letters below the names of the trees mentioned in the newspaper.

Willow, Silver Fir, Hazel, Elder, Yew, Alder, Yew, Hazel, White Poplar
  S   A   C   R   I   F   I   C   E

"Sacrifice, Bel's 31," Hugh muttered. "The sacrifice will take place as planned on Beltaine."

"Yes," Lydia said over his shoulder. "That is surely what it means."

Then came the translation of the second note, which Reggie had found in the Diamond Forest after it had been stripped bare and abandoned:

Hawthorn   White Poplar   Rowan   Dwarf Elder   Vine   White Poplar,
   H   E   L   P   M   E,

Willow   Furze   Dwarf Elder   Hawthorn   Yew   White Poplar
  S   O   P   H   I   E

When the words registered, Lydia dug her fingers into Hugh's shoulder. "Heavens! It's from Sophie! She needs help."

"It can't be," Hugh said. "She wouldn't know the tree alphabet. But whoever wrote it wanted us to know he has her in his control and that she's in danger. What other purpose could this message have but to evoke sympathy?"

"Trevor Dobson," Lydia said with a sick feeling in her stomach. "That despicable man."

Hugh folded the notes and put them back in his pocket. "Thank you very much, Mr. Frances. You have been a great help to us."

"Excellent! Would you like more tea?" he asked, giving Lydia a bubbly smile.

"No, I'm afraid we must hurry along," Hugh replied for her as he stood and shook the old man's hand. "But I can assure you that if I crack this case, you will be mentioned in my next book."

"Thank you, my lord." Frances nodded. "It would be a great honor."

"What should we do next?" Lydia asked Hugh.

"We call Scotland Yard and have Dobson arrested. Before it's too late." Just before they departed, Hugh turned back with one last question. "Mr. Frances, does mistletoe have any special significance among the druids?"

"Oh, my, yes!" he said with an enthusiastic chuckle. "It is the very symbol of druidism itself. You see, the druids believed that mistletoe had a magical quality. It's a parasitic plant that grows on oak trees, among others. It was believed the very soul of the mighty oak dwelled in the dark green leaves and white winter berries. It was a great derwydd ritual to cut the mistletoe from the oak and, thereby, gain magical power."

Hugh nodded but said nothing. It was clear to him that Dobson had set a trail of clues, which began with the mistletoe found outside the Chamberlain Music Hall. Now he presented a cry for help, written in druidic code. But where would this latest clue lead? Instead of leading to Sophie, was it leading them into a trap?

T hey're coming after you, Cerridwen," Sophie's kidnapper said.

Sophie pressed up against the wooden wall of her subterranean prison, trying to put as much distance as she could between her weird visitor and herself. She trembled, partially from fear and partially from the chill. An hour ago Mrs. O'Leary had brought her a scandalous sleeveless black silk dress to wear, without a corset or petticoats. The cool cellar air seemed to cut through to her flesh.

Mrs. O'Leary had told Sophie to wear her hair down

straight. And when the hateful older gent had come down to see her again, he'd stiffened with excitement that made her feel cheap and ill-used.

"Oh, Cerridwen, you are so beautiful, my lady of death."

"You sick old sot!" she spat at him. "Get away! Leave me alone. Why did you bring me here?"

It had been bad enough that the doctor had violated her with that awful, horrible instrument simply to prove that she was a virgin. But to have this madman drooling over her! Never touching her, always hinting at some awful ceremony she couldn't even begin to imagine. It was enough to send her over the edge.

As usual, he didn't seem to hear her. He was in a perverse world of his own. He reached out with a shaking hand and stroked her hair. She slapped it away, and his other hand came fast to her throat, squeezing just hard enough to slow the blood flow to her head.

"They're coming for you, my darling Cerridwen, but they won't get you. Not before I take you to see the ladies."

"What ladies?" she managed to whisper, though she could scarcely breathe.

"The three ladies who will witness our union."

Our union! A dizzying sense of dread washed over her.

Suddenly there came a banging on the door at the top of the stairs. "Sir! Sir! I must speak with you, sir!" came Mrs. O'Leary's frantic voice. The door flew open and light flooded the cellar. The strange gent shielded his eyes with an arm. "Scotland Yard is at the house, sir. Mr. O'Leary just came down on a fast horse with the news."

"Damnation!"

Sophie knew this was her only chance. With an arch in her foot that would make her mother's dancing instructor proud, she shot her toe into the man's groin. *Thwomp!* She cringed at the muted sound, knowing the pain she'd caused him. He doubled over with a shocked cry, looking at her as if she'd stabbed him in the back. She lost no time over remorse, but bolted up the stairs, pushing

Mrs. O'Leary down as easily as if she were a domino.

I'm free! she thought as the luscious spring breeze sailed through her hair and her feet clomped madly over the ground in her frantic effort to escape. Unfortunately, they were bare. She felt the sting of twigs and leaves, but she pushed on. *I'm free. Run, Sophie. You can do it. Don't stop. Don't look back. Where am I? In the woods. But there's a light high on the hill. A house. Run there. No! That might be his house. But if Scotland Yard is there, that's the only safe place. Just run. Don't think. Run!*

And so she did—until her foot caught in her flowing, black dress. Down she went, slamming into the ground, knocking the wind out of her. She rolled on up onto all fours, determined to get up, but before she could rise all the way, she saw him looming over her.

"Cerridwen!" he said in a low, feral voice. "You bitch! You killing, nefarious bitch! Don't you ever defy Bel again. I am the god of the forest! You will obey me or die."

With that he drew back his fist and struck her a hard blow to her temple, knocking her unconscious.

Lydia met Hugh in her husband's study, and soon they were joined by Sir Todd and Lady Leach.

"Ah, Lydia!" Clara said. "You're looking well, my dear."

Lydia stole a glance at Clara's expanded waistline. She surely could not be showing a pregnancy this quickly, but her lack of a corset had filled her out a bit, as if she'd been eating too many *petits fours*.

"Thank you for coming," Lydia said as she kissed Clara's cheek. "We have a special favor to ask of you."

Todd shook hands with Hugh. "What is it, Monty? Your messenger said it was urgent."

Hugh pulled out a watch from his waistcoat. "Not too early for a brandy, I hope. You'll need one after you hear our convoluted tale."

Todd cheerfully acquiesced, while the women declined.

Together Hugh and Lydia alternated in an unrehearsed but efficient pattern, apprising the Leaches on all that had come to pass—from the first sighting of the mistletoe, to the notes written in tree alphabet.

"If the note you found in Dobson's club mentioned Sophie by name," Todd said, "then you have the proof you were looking for."

"Precisely. I shared the evidence with Scotland Yard. Detectives paid a visit to Dobson's townhouse this afternoon," Hugh said in conclusion. "Unfortunately, there was no sign of him."

"Good Lord! You've been busy," Todd burst out when it was all over. "What happens next?"

"I'm going to Tremaine Way—that's Dobson's country home. It's situated less than a mile from Windhaven. I'll stop there first. I just received a wire from the chief detective on the case. He visited Tremaine yesterday, and Dobson is not there, either. But I feel certain Sophie is. I mean to find her."

"When will you leave?" Todd asked, nursing his brandy as he frowned thoughtfully.

"Today."

"I'm going with him," Lydia said softly.

"But you cannot!" Clara blurted out, which was quickly echoed by an emphatic "No!" from Hugh.

Lydia raised her chin defiantly, daring them to deny her twice. "You will not stop me."

"But your period of mourning," Clara protested.

"I don't have the luxury of going through a superficial ritual for society's sake. My husband knows how much I grieve for him. No one else need be concerned."

"But your reputation, ma'am," Todd said. "I'm sure your husband would not want you to risk your social standing."

"You know as well as I do, Sir Todd, that Beaumont never cared what others thought. I'm going with Lord Montgomery, and that is settled."

Hugh swilled his brandy, and she frowned at him, wondering why he seemed so angry. She hated when he was

mad at her. But it was best that way. Not even grief would
protect her from her feelings for Hugh. Something remained
between them, something more than her past. That was
dangerous for her already-wounded heart.

"Here is what we need from you," Hugh said as he put
his empty glass on the sideboard. "Lady Leach, please go
back to the clinic where you found this girl they call May."

Clara looked up in surprise.

"You remember her, don't you, Clara?" Lydia prodded
her. "The girl with the odd butterfly scar on her wrist? I
pointed her out to you before we left."

"Yes, but what has she to do with the investigation?"

"We believe that she, like Sophie, might have been a victim of this strange cult of faux druids," Hugh answered.

"Do you mean Dobson's involved in one of the estab-
lished neo-druidic organizations?" Todd inquired.

"No. Most modern druid organizations are philanthropic
in nature. I've known members, and if they're guilty of
anything, it's their romanticizing of the druid culture—not
kidnapping. The fellows I know would be incapable of
snagging a virgin for a ritualistic rape. I fear Trevor Dobson
is much more cunning, far less intellectual, and certainly
more evil than the members of those cerebral organizations.
And from what I saw at his club, he's more than capable of
doing something outrageous."

Clara was obviously having a difficult time taking all
this in. "I don't understand how we could have found
May—a girl who was Dobson's victim—in such an
obscure place as the ladies' clinic. Doesn't it strike you as
an incredible coincidence? How could we happen upon
such a crucial potential witness?"

Hugh pondered the conundrum. He took a seat by Lydia
and wondered how he still managed to think properly in
her presence. Half his thoughts always swirled around her.
How long would he be able to resist her? Not as long as he
feared she would resist him.

"The girl may well have been planted there, Lady Leach,"

he said, forcing his attention back to the matter at hand. "Lady Beaumont was a frequent visitor and made no secret of her charity work at the clinic. Perhaps Dobson put May there to spy on Beaumont's wife, or to deliver a message. Or perhaps it was a coincidence. One must accept the notion of synchronous events. Sometimes it's almost as if the solution is given to one by a higher power."

"I'm surprised to hear you sounding religious, Monty," Todd said with amazement.

"By a higher power," Hugh shot back, "I didn't necessarily mean *the* highest power. An evil one will do just as well."

He thought about what his father had said in the club—that nothing happens by chance. How much was Trevor Dobson setting the stage on which they now acted? Was he pulling the strings that made them dance?

"Lady Beaumont and I will go presently to Windhaven. I don't know precisely what we'll be looking for, so we will need May's help, if she can give it. If she was a victim of the druid's Beltaine celebration last year, she might be able to lead us to the place where she was held."

"If she is able to talk," Clara added dubiously.

"If she will talk, interview her. If she won't, convince her to come with you to Windhaven. Whatever it takes. Money is no object."

"I might be able to employ my skills of oratory on your behalf," Todd said as he straightened his cravat with exaggerated self-importance.

"At least you'll be putting his hot air to good use," Clara said as she and Todd exchanged a look tinged with warmth and tenderness.

Lydia smiled for the first time since Beaumont's death. It seemed Dr. Smith's suggestions had been taken to heart, and the Leaches had resumed their attempts to create a family.

A pang tugged at Lydia's heart. How she would have loved to have had children. How she would love to have had anything in her life go the way it should. *But I can never have what the Leaches have. I must simply work hard. That is all that is left for me now.*

They discussed final arrangements. It was agreed that Clara would attempt to befriend May and that she would bring the girl to Windhaven if need be. There were two weeks left until May Day—just enough time to find Sophie if they were lucky.

When the Leaches departed, Lydia turned to find Hugh staring at her with faraway eyes. He was envisioning her as she had been long ago. She knew that instinctively. He was dangerously recalling a past that could never be revived.

While Beaumont had been alive, she could safely fantasize about reuniting with Hugh. But now that Beau was gone and she was free to love another, she was forced to face reality. She could never marry any man—most especially Hugh—not without confessing her time as a courtesan. She was no longer the innocent he once knew. Therefore, she felt certain he did not really love her. He loved the woman she used to be. Lydia would die before ever confessing the shame of her past, for then she would have to watch the love in his eyes turn to disgust.

"You're angry with me," she said.

His gaze darkened. "Yes."

"Why?"

He put his hands behind his back and sauntered forward, regarding her now as if she were one of the many pieces of the puzzle spread out before him. "You shouldn't go with me. I shouldn't let you."

He stopped only when he was close enough to tower over her. Perhaps it was because of her drained emotions, but his effect on her body was shattering. Lydia trembled with desire, aching with the need for him. She wanted ever so badly to lean into him, to press her face to his chest, to have him take her some place very private, unclothe her, and remind her that she was alive and very much a woman. With Beau she had been a companion, almost a child. But with Hugh, and only Hugh, had she ever completely shared both her body and heart.

Lydia knew she should turn away, but she couldn't. Instead, she met his searing gaze. She would never cringe from any man again, no matter the danger. "Why shouldn't I go?" she asked breathlessly.

"Because," he said deep in his throat as his hands came up to grip her arms very firmly, very intimately. "Because of this . . . ."

He pulled her close and pressed his lips to hers. They were closed but couldn't have been more penetrating than they were in this scorching, blissful reunion. Everything that had ever been between them, or could be again, joined at their lips. A great chasm of unfulfilled longing yawned and filled with his heat and warmth.

"I love you," he said against her mouth, his eyes open now and looking deep into hers, even as his mouth nestled against hers, brushing her lips, caressing and kissing them. "God, Lydia, I love you. I've never stopped loving you. Love me, please."

She was overwhelmed with him—lost in his gaze and hypnotized by his stroking lips, his intense kisses. And when he gently parted her mouth and his tongue tenderly probed inside her, she nearly fainted. A flash of desire piped through her, hardening her nipples, firing her skin. She opened herself to him, kissing with a completeness she'd long thought impossible.

I love you, she said with her kiss as he worked his spell on her. *My darling Hugh, I adore you. I always have. There's no one but you. No one.*

They had spoken without uttering a word. And then she felt everything come crashing to a stop. There was nowhere to go from here. No future for them. Too much had passed. There had been too many mistakes. Her mind knew this and abruptly put a chill on the heat that had nearly swept her away.

She pulled back suddenly and tried to catch her breath.

Tried to. Tears formed in her eyes. "I'm so sorry. What a fool I am."

"Foolish to think you can come with me to Windhaven," he said raggedly, pulling his head back with great effort but still not releasing her arms.

"There you're wrong." She pulled out of his grip and hugged herself, waiting for her desire to pass. "I would go to Windhaven with Satan himself if that's what it took to find Sophie. I've learned quite a bit in the last five years. I've learned the difference between lust and love, need and want. Sophie needs me. You merely want me. You'll simply have to control yourself in my presence."

When she turned to leave he called out in a pained voice, "And what if I need you as well?"

"Too late," she said, stopping at the door. "Your needs are no longer even a part of the equation."

With that, she was gone.

Chapter 15

The servants at Windhaven would have to be alerted that the viscount was on his way, so Pierpont and Reggie had gone ahead to make arrangements for their stay. On Lydia's insistence, Reggie secured a room in the village's only hotel for her and her small retinue. Colette would be coming the next morning with her wardrobe trunks. Pierpont contacted the local constable and made arrangements for him to meet the viscount and countess at Tremaine Way early the next morning. All was in order. They would not alert Dobson of their impending arrival. Hugh wanted to catch him unaware, if that was possible.

The railway trip from London was uneventful, but by the time they arrived at the station, Lydia's stomach was in knots. She was unusually quiet during the ride through the village. Then, when the carriage made a sharp right turn on the road that led to Windhaven, she broke her silence.

"Wait!" She looked at Hugh as if he'd just betrayed the country to the enemy. "Where are we going?"

"To the hotel. Eventually. But we haven't eaten since noon. You must be famished. We're going to eat at Windhaven. Pierpont told Cook to set a meal in the private dining room for two."

"But I'm not ready to go back there!"

"You never will be, Lydia. It's like falling off a horse. You have to get right back in the saddle, or you will be ruled by your fear evermore."

"I'm not afraid," she answered, then set her jaw at a stubborn angle. "I simply don't want to go back there."

"You're a different person now. You'll see the place with new eyes. And I doubt anyone will recognize you. Remember that you are the Countess of Beaumont. As you told me, Lydia, Addie Parker is dead. My father destroyed our lives because we let him. We can't ever again let anyone define who we are."

He hardly gave her a choice, for soon the carriage drew up on the front drive. She gave him a resentful look. "You knew I would agree. You knew I would not want to be defeated by this."

"Yes," he said, smiling sadly. "I know you well."

Ignoring his wistful expression, she responded briskly. "Very well. Let's get this over with. And then I'm going to the hotel. I don't want any part of Windhaven."

When Lydia descended the carriage steps and took Hugh's proffered arm, she paused a moment to straighten her riding cape and glanced up in awe at the many rows of windows in the Georgian mansion. Every one glowed with light. The staff had dutifully lit the rooms for the late arrivals. The housekeeper and butler stood at attention by the door, waiting to greet them.

As a spring breeze swirled refreshingly around her neck, she breathed deeply to still her jangled nerves. Would they recognize her? Would they look at her condescendingly as if she were the fallen angel only she knew she was? Was she still, in spite of all she had experienced, the foolish and naive woman who had begun her descent here five years ago with an impetuous love for the earl's son?

Hugh placed a comforting hand over her fingers where they were digging into his arm. "My father hired a new housekeeper last year."

"Oh." So she wouldn't have to face Mrs. Bertram, the old battle-ax who had so obviously gloated over Addie Parker's downfall. "Good."

"And young Mr. Harker replaced old Mr. Harker as butler. Practically a new staff."

She knew that wasn't true. Most of the employees who kept a great mansion like this passed their jobs down from generation to generation, as well as old gossip. But she had to remember that what anyone thought of her meant nothing. Her only purpose in coming here was to search for Sophie at nearby Tremaine Way. She hadn't come for redemption. If Hugh thought she needed to prove something by dining at Windhaven, she would do it and then she would go.

"Very well," she said. She glanced his way, and his concern warmed her against the chill of spring. She managed a thin smile. "I am ready."

The staff greeted them warmly, and Lady Beaumont received short bows and bobbed curtseys all around. They were good servants and kept their eyes downcast, except for the housekeeper and butler. No one seemed to recognize Lydia at all, and she realized at last that she was finally being herself—a widowed countess. That was no charade.

She had to remember that the strict social hierarchy that would never allow a governess to reach beyond her place would also give a countess every benefit of the doubt. It wasn't the person who mattered, but the title and position. Lydia was now the rich widow of a peer of the realm. All she had to do to live down her past now was accept herself.

At least that's all she would have to do unless the earl returned.

"Is your father coming to the country?" she asked as he led her up the grand staircase to the cozy golden dining room.

"No. I told him I was coming here. That guarantees he'll stay in town. He doesn't want to see any more of me than he has to."

Lydia let out an audible sigh of relief. "Good. You know, you're right. I am famished."

After an excellent meal of poached salmon with new potatoes and fresh spinach, the beaming cook brought out a charlotte russe and coffee with heavy cream. They enjoyed the rich dessert, although Lydia was not able to finish her portion. She was pleased to see that Hugh ate heartily. His addiction did not appear to be harming his appetite and for that, at least, she was grateful.

The coffee was welcome, because she felt her energy reserves faltering. When they'd finished, she asked Hugh to summon the coach. "I've faced my demons. Now I must go to the village and see to my accommodations," she told him.

"You had nothing to fear here," he said simply.

"But I'm glad you made me see that."

"You are far braver than you imagine, my dear."

He sent for his carriage, which took Lydia to Glennon Arms. It was a small, pleasant inn, and her rooms were clean if spartan. After the morning's exertions, both physical and emotional, she decided upon a brief nap to sharpen her senses for what lay ahead. As she drifted to sleep in the modest but comfortable brass bed, she felt a rare sense of contentment. Hugh had been right to make her visit his ancestral home before doing anything else.

She'd fantasized many times over the last five years about returning to the place of her ruin. In her fantasies, she was either chased from the mansion by scornful servants, or she married Hugh after the death of the earl and dismissed them all. Reality was far less dramatic. Now she could face Trevor Dobson with a clear and well-rested mind.

Tremaine Way was an Elizabethan cottage, rich in history and charm and deceptively large. It was nestled at the end of a narrow lane easily overlooked by those not native to the area. Entering the stone gates of the walkway, Hugh and Lydia found the cottage sitting in the shade like a grand old dame who wore old-fashioned flowers and whose spectacles winked warmly in the sun.

Hugh's pounding heartbeat belied the pleasantries of their surroundings. He hoped Dobson would agree to meet him and that their confrontation would not end in a violent manner.

"There's the constable," he said when they rounded a bank of blooming sweet woodruff and well-pruned boxwoods.

"Do you really think Dobson will hand himself over for arrest as easily as that? He'd have to be awfully agreeable. That old fellow there looks too kind to intimidate him into surrender."

"I don't want him to surrender. I want him to tell us where he's keeping Sophie. And I didn't invite the constable here for protection, although we might well need it. I've brought him as a witness. We learned long ago, you and I, that it's wise to have a third party to corroborate our accounts later on."

He looked penetratingly into her lavendar eyes, knowing she remembered all too well the standing stones that he had never been able to find again. They'd both seen them, but everyone else thought they were either lying or deluded. "Shall we? His name is Barnabas."

She nodded and warmly greeted Mr. Barnabas. He had broad muttonchops, a bulbous red nose, gentle eyes, and curly gray hair. He smelled of horse hair and hay. Hugh apprised him of their purpose and asked him to hang in the back as an observer unless he was needed to intervene.

Barnabas was in obvious awe of Hugh, and not just because of his notoriety. Hugh was the heir of the highest-ranking nobleman in the county, and his forebears had ruled over the lives of Barnabas's ancestors for centuries. Respect was inbred.

"Very good, sir, very good," he said, bobbing his head. "It's an honor to help in any way I can, though I have to say I'd be surprised if Sir Trevor had any part in such awful goings-on. He's a fine gent. But you know better than I, sir. You know better than I."

"Quite," the viscount said succinctly, and the constable fell silent with another subservient smile. Hugh exchanged a subtle look with Lydia. *You're right,* his eyes told her. *This old bloke wouldn't be able to rescue a fly.*

Hugh briskly tapped the brass knocker three times, and not long after, the arched door opened at the hands of an elderly woman in a mobcap. Hugh glanced at the telltale ring of keys at her waist.

"Good morning," he said, raising his bowler and smiling. "You must be the housekeeper."

"Yes, sir, the butler is gone for the day. May I help you, sir?"

"We are here to see Sir Trevor. I am Viscount Montgomery. This is Lady Beaumont, and with us is Mr. Barnabas."

The woman nodded a hello to the constable. In a small town like this, it was to be expected that she knew him well. "Come in, sir and ma'am. You, too, Mr. Barnabas. I'm Sir Trevor's housekeeper. Mrs. O'Leary's me name."

They filled the entryway, which Hugh remembered well from gatherings after riding to the hounds in years past.

"Won't you come into the drawing room?" the plump Irish woman said cheerfully. "Sir Trevor has been expecting you."

Hugh gave Lydia a loaded look. "Why do I feel as if I've just walked into a trap?" he asked out of the side of his mouth. They followed the housekeeper to a quaint drawing room that was lined with plaster and black timber beams along the ceiling. Hugh's eyes immediately focused on a large Elizabethan portrait hanging over the empty fireplace. The picture presented a man in a dark doublet with a six-inch-deep white honeycomb collar. He looked rich and royal, but Hugh could not place the likeness.

"Who is that?" he murmured more to himself than anyone else, but the housekeeper took it upon herself to answer his query.

"That? Oh, why that's one of Sir Trevor's ancestors. His mother was widowed very young, you see, and Sir Trevor treasures all the old things that are connected to his father."

Hugh suppressed a *harumph*. Dobson's mother had probably purchased this painting at an auction simply so she could create a fictional paternity for her son.

"I see," Hugh replied. He motioned to a comfortable chair, which Lydia took, and he remained standing. Mr. Barnabas hung back by a row of bookcases, browsing obliviously. "Is Sir Trevor willing to meet with me now, Mrs. O'Leary?"

"Oh, no sir," the flutter-breathed woman said. Her plump cheeks were pink as heather. "He's gone away for a few days. But he did leave a missive for you. It's right here on his desk. He told me to give it to you as soon as you arrived."

Hugh's gut tightened with disbelief and frustration. Had he been played so easily? He had thought coming here was his idea, but it had apparently been planted in his mind in a carefully orchestrated chess game by a player who seemed to have a considerable advantage over him.

Mrs. O'Leary handed him a sealed envelope that she'd extracted from a drawer in the desk. "Would you like some tea, sir? I'm sorry the master isn't here to greet you. But I know he'd like for you to have a spot of tea before you leave."

"Yes, that would be lovely," Lydia interjected. Hugh was already focused with single-minded intent, examining the handwriting and seal on the letter. She smiled encouragingly at the housekeeper, who bobbed a curtsy and departed on her errand.

Hugh immediately ripped open the missive and read:

My dear Viscount Montgomery,

What took you so long? I thought after your visit to the club that I would be seeing you promptly at Tremaine Way. As it is, I must away on business, so I will have missed you. What a shame. I would have enjoyed matching wits against you.

I do hope you did not bring with you that country bumpkin, Mr. Barnabas. And if you are planning to bring out Scotland Yard detectives, you will regret it. The moment I hear of the arrival of police from London, I will kill Sophie Parnham, mercilessly and without conscience. I have done it before and would not hesitate to do so again. If you doubt me, ask the milkmaid you found below Devil's Peak. So do take my threat seriously, dear boy. Or should I call you nephew?

I've been the poor bastard relation for too many years, Montgomery, living in the shadows of Windhaven. Now I am in charge. If you want Sophie back, you have to play the game by my rules. Here they are:

1. If you find her, you can keep her.
2. If you don't find her, she dies.
3. If you fail, she will be sacrificed on the eve of May Day.
4. You will be given a series of clues. The first series will be sent to Braemore Lodge three days prior. Each day for three days you will receive new clues.

Are you as clever as they say, Lord Clue? Will you be able to solve this mystery? Or will the stepdaughter

*of your lover die because of your incompetence?
Time will tell.*

   Dobson

*P.S. By the by, enclosed you'll find a letter Sophie
wrote to her mother. Consider it proof that I have her
and that she's still alive.*

Hugh folded up the letter, slipping it in the envelope.

"Well?" Lydia said breathlessly.

"I was wrong," he said. "You were right, Mr. Barnabas.
Sir Trevor has nothing to do with the kidnaping of Sophie
Parnham."

"What!" Lydia blurted out. "But he has to. He—"

"Nothing at all, Lady Beaumont. He's as innocent as the
driven snow, as pure as the whitest berries on the mistletoe
plant." He dropped his chin and eyed her pointedly beneath
his furrowed brow. "Do you take my meaning?"

Lydia bit her lower lip. "Yes, I believe I do."

"I knew he wouldn't be capable of any nasty business
like that," said Barnabas, chuckling with relief. "Why, he
holds a charity dance every spring. The missus and I
always have a grand time. A fine gentleman he is, Sir
Trevor."

"I'm sorry for troubling you," Hugh continued. "There
will be no further need of your assistance. If you see any
police detectives from London, please tell them I have
gone back to town and they needn't pursue the case any
further."

"From London?" Barnabas said, his eyes bright. "Must
be an important case."

"Oh, yes," Hugh said as he deftly steered the constable
toward the door. "I raised an alarm here for no reason,
though. I'll have to wire Scotland Yard and tell them there
is no need to send anyone all this way. And do me a favor,
if you will."

"Anything, sir."

"Do not mention this little embarrassment to anyone. I'm afraid I've made a bad decision, and, er, I don't want word of it to get in the newspapers."

"Oh, yes!" Barnabas said. "The great Lord Clue has a reputation to uphold. Not to worry, your lordship, you're our claim to fame here. The matter is as good as forgotten."

Lydia watched in tense silence as Hugh managed to ferry the constable out the door and then charmingly declined the tea Mrs. O'Leary brought for them, claiming to have just remembered urgent business. It wasn't until their carriage was safely down the road that Lydia turned on him.

"What did it say?" she asked with a premonition of dread.

"We've been played like a hammer dulcimer. Dobson knows our every move in advance. He has Sophie and freely admits it. He even says she'll be sacrificed on May Day eve unless I find her."

"What does he mean by 'sacrificed'? Her virginity or her life?"

"Both, I fear." His voice was grim as the slash of his mouth.

Lydia leaned back against the squabs and took a deep breath. "I assume he made some directive about involving police if he dared admit his complicity in this."

"Yes. He'll kill her immediately if anyone else is brought in on the search. He is going to give us clues. The first will be delivered three days before Beltaine."

"That means we have to wait five days for the first clue?" she practically cried in frustration. "Isn't there anything we can do?"

Hugh sighed. "I can think of nothing that has not already been done . . . and if we don't follow his instructions, he could kill Sophie just to spite us."

"Why is he giving us these clues?" Lydia frowned in frustration. "Surely he doesn't want to be caught."

"He wants to test my intelligence. I assume it has something to do with his status as my father's unacknowledged brother, my bastard uncle, if you will."

"Dobson can't expect us to sit around drumming our fingers until he sends us the clues."

"He's very confident that she cannot be found without his 'help.' And I daresay, he's probably right. He even included a note from Sophie just to make certain we don't do anything rash." He handed her the missive.

Lydia plucked it greedily from his hands and read it over several times. She shook her head. "Poor darling. She's obviously terrified. If only there was something we could do."

"I have to think," he said, rubbing his forehead. It pounded with the need for laudanum. He could never venture very far from that bottle. He was shackled to it, and for the first time in years, he actually felt a deep, abiding desire to free himself . . . if he could. Perhaps, with Lydia's help, it would be possible. Love did perform miracles. He'd given up on that until he found her once again.

But first, they must focus on saving Sophie. "The first clue will be delivered to Braemore Lodge. I was going to suggest you move there from the hotel even before this happened. It's in the woods and very private."

"Yes, I remember," she said softly.

That caught him short. He reddened and rubbed his forehead. "I'm sorry. Of course you do."

It was where they had consummated their affair. "It's on your property but near Dobson's. Not far from Devil's Peak," she went on in as practical a tone as she could muster, trying desperately to remove their past relationship from their present need to find Sophie.

He picked up his cue from her, saying, "I can visit you alone without creating a scandal. It would be an excellent place for us to think through whatever devilment Dobson plans to send our way. Do you mind leaving the hotel? It would be good to have someone at the lodge around the clock. We can't afford to miss a single clue."

He sounded so bleak that Lydia wondered if Hugh was capable of solving this particular, and very personal, mystery. For the first time, the consequences of his success or failure would affect him personally. Perhaps he was too close to do the job well.

"Of course I'll move to the lodge. But not without you."

He looked surprised.

"We can be discreet. I wouldn't feel safe without you."

He nodded. "You're right. I wouldn't trust your safety to anyone else. Not when Dobson is involved."

"Together, we can do this, Hugh," she said earnestly. Was she trying to convince him . . . or herself?

Hugh returned to Windhaven, where he wrote letters and prepared telegrams. He updated Todd and Clara Leach about the turn of events, and he asked Scotland Yard detectives to keep their distance until further notice.

Meanwhile, Pierpont spent the afternoon ordering servants to and fro between Windhaven and the hunting lodge, airing it out, stocking the kitchen, and changing the linens.

Colette had arrived with Lydia's trunks by train that morning, and Reggie took them to the hotel. It was decided that Colette would stay there and pretend that her mistress was taken ill and confined to her bed. Lydia returned in the early afternoon, complaining of a malaise, then made a surreptitious departure out the back door when the proprietor wasn't looking. Reggie would sneak her trunks out later when no one was about. The stage was set for her week-long absence, and she was keenly aware that it would be spent alone with Hugh.

Hugh felt that the fewer people who knew Lydia was spending time alone with him at the lodge, the better. She was still a new widow, and the scandal would be very harmful to her reputation.

Frankly, she cared nothing for what society said about her. That had been Beau's legacy . . . and Hugh's, too, if she were to be honest.

She wondered if he had other motives for being alone with her while they waited. And she blushed to realize that she hoped he did. Away from Beaumont House and back in the place where they had first fallen in love, Lydia's intense attraction to Hugh was already bubbling beneath the surface, especially during this strange time of limbo until Sir Trevor played his next hand.

Fortunately, there were distractions. Reggie pestered her with a million details. He had become confident in his role as her assistant and possessed a marvelous ability to organize. His instructions to the earl's servants were clear and delivered with authority. When he said it was time to leave Windhaven and take the convoluted route to the lodge that he and Pierpont had concocted for her, she climbed into the carriage unquestioningly.

After a very long drive that was designed to lose anyone attempting to follow, they arrived at the lodge just before supper. When Hugh's carriage brought them down through the wooded hillside drive deep into the valley where the renovated stone lodge nestled, Reggie gaped in awe.

It was really a castle from the Middle Ages, a small outpost built during the time of the Crusades. The square keep contained three floors. The first housed the traditional medieval great hall, with a vaulted wooden ceiling hung with banners, stone walls adorned with tapestries, and a stone slab floor that chilled bare feet in any season.

A round turret with arrow slits was attached to one side of the keep. It contained a winding staircase that led up to two more floors. The second level once stored armaments but presently served as a bunker for the earl's rustic hunting outings. And the top floor housed a bed chamber fit for a king, with an expansive four-poster bed from the Georgian era, an Elizabethan chess table, a fourteenth-century slab fireplace, and a medieval wooden washtub.

Utterly enchanted, Lydia readily moved in while Hugh spread out his notes on the wooden table in the great hall. Reggie set about making a fire to chase the winter from the eight-feet-thick stone walls that still hadn't managed to warm to the notion of spring. Pierpont proved himself yet even more indispensable by managing to start a fire in the small kitchen that had been built on to the lodge a hundred years before. Soon they were called to dinner. A shout up the stairs took the place of a dinner bell.

Lydia and Hugh dispensed with formalities and shared the meal with Pierpont and Reggie. Their mood was hopeful. By moving Lydia into the lodge, they felt they had accomplished something in their quest for Sophie Parnham. The light from two large candelabras added a warm glow to the dining table and an intimacy to the gathering, which was heightened by a very good bottle of red wine. The leaping fire flames played with the early evening's shadows and cast dancing figures on the stone slab floor.

Lydia felt almost as if they had been transported back into the Middle Ages. She half expected the men to go upstairs and don chain mail and armor in their quest to fend off an attack from a neighboring baron. What a simpler time that must have been, with no telegrams and trains, no polluting factories and sprawling cities. And yet it was a dangerous time. Life was shorter then. When the warmth of the wine faded from her cheeks, Lydia grew anxious for Sophie.

"I can't help but think we must search the grounds, Montgomery," she said. "Sophie is here. Sir Trevor confirmed that with her letter. How can we sit here and wait?"

"Aye, ma'am," Reggie agreed as he wiped his mouth with a napkin. "Let's search for her like we did the girls we took to Stone House. We'll find her."

"Don't be too sure, young man," Pierpont sniffed. "You

must learn to trust Lord Clue. Sometimes the greatest searching goes on in that head of his."

Lydia looked to see Hugh's reaction but was disappointed to find him staring pensively at the fire. He'd stretched his long, lean legs out and crossed them at the ankles. His knee-length coat spilled open, revealing his burgundy silk waistcoat, which stretched over his flat abdomen. His broad shoulders slouched against his thronelike chair. He leaned one cheek on an upraised fist and pursed his lips.

"Monty?" she said, putting down her empty wine goblet. "Why can't we go after her? Let's search the property."

He looked her way, and his heated gaze gave her a jolt. "You have always been very forthright, Lady Beaumont. I admire that about you. In this case, however, a random search would do no good. Trevor Dobson owns more than a thousand acres of land, which borders three thousand owned by my father. Alone we could search for weeks without finding her. If we bring in help, Sophie dies."

"Do you believe he would really kill her?" Lydia asked.

"I know he would," he replied without hesitation. "Remember what happened to the milkmaid I found at the bottom of the cliffs? I fear we must abide by Sir Trevor's rules, as he instructed us. Only if we play this game of his will we win her back. We know the time line he has given us will hold true. Everything he has done so far has been systematic, and in retrospect, even predictable."

Pierpont's mouth turned down and he shifted. "I don't see how one might have predicted any of this, sir. How could you guess that a nobleman would behave insanely? He's acting antithetically to everything his class stands for, no matter how brilliant his deranged mind may be."

Hugh's dark eyes glowed in the candlelight. "I concur that most of my noble counterparts are far from original thinkers." His tone was ironic as he reached for the bottle of wine and poured himself another glass, gathering his thoughts as the liquid tinkled against the pewter goblet. He leaned back in his chair and continued.

"Your problem, Pierpont, old chap, is that you still think there is truly a moral or intellectual difference between the classes. Sir Trevor has veered into the realm of ritual and religion. He has insulted our sensibilities by reminding us how barbaric our forebears were when this was still a dark island ruled by magic and myth, fire and human sacrifice. But you raise an interesting notion."

When he stopped to sip from his goblet, Lydia leaned forward and joined in. "I know what you're going to say. Is he truly insane?" Then she answered her own question with certainty. "He has to be."

"Does he? Or is he merely eccentric?"

"Bloody bastard," Reggie muttered. "All I know is he deserves to be hung from the highest tree."

"He will be, if we play the game correctly," Hugh replied.

"But if he's insane," Lydia persisted, "how do you know he won't change the rules? If we wait for the next clue, how are we to know that he'll keep his end of the bargain? She might be dead now for all we know."

"She's alive," Hugh said with finality, swilling the last of his wine.

"How can you be sure?" Lydia persisted.

"Because this time the game is different. It's not about the girl, or the rape, or the ritual execution that follows. This time he's expanded the cast of characters. We're part of the plan. And he knows she's the only bait that will keep us here. In fact, I expect he'll be sending us more evidence that she's alive."

"But why did it change? Why did he include us?"

Hugh shook his head and said with a look, *I'll tell you later.* "All I can say now is that I believe if we veer off of Sir Trevor's schedule in any way we will be endangering Sophie's life. We will have ruined the preordained plan. He is a man of habit and ritual. The first girl, I assume, was the servant I found at the bottom of the cliffs. Presumably there has been one victim every spring since. The girl in the clinic they call May has apparently become a regular pawn. From the knowledge you gleaned from her, Lady Beaumont, we can assume all the victims are marked with his self-appointed emblem—the butterfly. All but her were kidnapped, raped, and presumably murdered."

"At least we know what sort of bloke we're dealing with," Reggie said, supressing a shiver of revulsion.

"Yes," Hugh replied. "We have a great challenge ahead of us. We must prepare ourselves as best we can, for we must be in top form."

As Lydia nodded in agreement, she saw that Pierpont was melting into a puddle of gloom. So she wasn't alone in her concern about their prospects.

Something was wrong. Something in Hugh had changed for the worse. They had to talk, she concluded.

Alone.

Chapter 16

Hugh sent both Reggie and Pierpont back to Windhaven on a series of errands. He planned to sleep in the old armory, but Lydia listened for his footsteps in the turret and knew he had remained in the great hall. She unpacked some of her clothing and laid out her nightgown, but before she undressed, she crept back down the circular stairwell with a candlestick in hand.

She found him sitting in front of the fire in a winged-back easy chair, which looked incongruous in this rustic setting. His arm hung over one side of the chair in silhouette against the flames, cradling a brandy snifter. On a table beside him sat a bottle of laudanum.

As soon as she saw it, Lydia felt an invisible hand punch her abdomen. She sucked in her breath, realizing with sudden clarity that this bottle was his mistress. Jealousy stung her, which was followed quickly by scathing anger. And panic. This is what everyone had felt earlier. His pessimism and lack of self-confidence was owed to an addiction. Sophie could be lost because of it!

"So this is why you are afraid," she said to his back.

"Ah, Lydia!" he called out. She could not see his head, but she could tell he'd tipped it back, for his voice bounced off the rafters and filtered through the brightly colored pennons and medieval shields hanging above. "I was hoping you'd join me." He sounded oddly blasé, ignoring the anger in her voice, but she could tell it was forced.

"What's wrong? Haven't you drunk your fill of that drug? Doesn't it relax you?"

"Yes, it does. Would you like some?"

"No," she snapped. "Don't be ridiculous. Why would I want to risk becoming dependent on that dreadful substance?"

"It's not so bad when you get used to it," he said. "My doctor highly recommends it."

"Just because a drug is legal doesn't mean it's good for you. Sometimes doctors are wrong."

"Come join me." He motioned with his brandy snifter for her to come forward, and she walked around until she could see his profile.

She caught her breath again, but this time out of fear. He was white. His temples perspired. His cheeks were sallow, and his eyes were hard, black beads. They turned her way, and he smiled apologetically.

"I'm sorry, Lydia, that I'm such a disappointment to you." He finished off a generous portion of brandy in four loud gulps.

"I'm worried about you, Hugh."

"Don't be."

"You're not well."

He turned a tortured gaze slowly to the bottle on the small round table by his chair. He put down his empty brandy snifter and picked up the bottle, examining it in the firelight. "I hate this stuff. I absolutely hate it. I want to be free of it, but . . ." His words faded away into hopelessness.

"Then why did you ever start using it in the first place?"

He looked up at her with a start, as if he'd forgotten she were even in the room. He shook his head, smiling wanly. "Can't say, darling. It wouldn't be fair."

"Fair to whom?" she shot back. When he remained silent, she egged him further. "Wouldn't be fair to you?"

He held his hand out to her and said, feelingly, "Lydia . . . ."

Instinctively she took hold of him. He gripped hard, as if she were a lifeline when he had fallen overboard. It felt so natural that she covered his white knuckles with her other palm, smoothing over his cold skin. "Oh, Hugh, what has happened to you?" She knelt at his side. "Why are you like this? I thought your medicine made you feel better. You look like a ghost of yourself."

"I want to find that girl." He squeezed her hand so hard she nearly cried out.

"I know you do. And you will."

He shook his head. "No. I don't think I can. I'm not the way I used to be. I don't think as clearly anymore. And this is going to be a test of minds. May I sit by you?"

"Of course." She let her hips settle on the bearskin rug, and he lowered himself down in front of his chair, leaning back on it for support and stretching his legs out toward the fire. Some color returned to his face. She reached over to brush aside tendrils of hair that clung to his temples. He raised his face to her touch, savoring it, smiling.

"You always had the most lovely hands," he murmured, eyes closed. "Always so warm. I've missed that. Always remembered that. There's been no one else since you, Lydie."

When he opened his eyes, it was too much for her. She lowered her gaze and pulled her hand free of his, hiding it in her lap. She couldn't bear to touch him this way, or to think about the past now. "Why are you afraid of this case?" she asked, changing the subject.

"Because for the first time it's about me."

She gently scoffed. "Hasn't the whole world always revolved around you, Lord Clue? How is this any different?"

He smiled sadly. "Yes. But this time it's different. I didn't want to say anything in front of our men, but after studying that letter more closely, I had an epiphany. Everything surrounding this case has been planned to the smallest detail. And it all comes back to the same person—me."

"How do you know?"

"Sophie was kidnapped not at random, but because Dobson knew she was Beaumont's by-blow. By all accounts Louise Canfield was remarkably circumspect on the topic, so he must have gotten her as drunk as a top, or drugged her, for her to have confessed it. We know they were involved."

"Why Sophie?"

He regarded her with his intelligent eyes, and she saw in them her old friend, the one who had saved her life. "Because her father was married to you."

"To me!" She frowned. "I don't understand. He didn't know—you're not saying that he knew who I—."

"Yes, my love. Dobson knew that Lady Beaumont had once been called Addie Parker. He was a neighbor, remember? After our visit to the standing stones, there wasn't a soul in this county who didn't know that you and I were lovers. Sir Trevor knew that if somehow you were in trouble, or in need of help, that I would come running to save you, just as I did that day at Devil's Peak. I made no secret of the fact that I had searched for you for years after you left."

Tears sprang to her eyes as she recalled the past. Impulsively, she leaned forward and pressed her cheek to his, holding on to his shoulder. He pressed back, and warmth flowed between them. Comfort. Such sweet comfort. With great effort, she pulled away. "I want to understand this very clearly. You're saying that Sophie was kidnapped so you would be called in to help me find her."

He nodded soberly. "I'm sorry. As usual, it's all my fault."

"I don't blame you. At least not for that."

"Thank heaven." He smiled wryly.

"But how did he know who I was? My husband never called me Addie. We never socialized. We were virtual hermits."

"Obviously, Sir Trevor has many acquaintances from all walks of life. Perhaps he knew a mutual acquaintance of yours, perhaps someone you met just before you married Beaumont."

Heat seared through Lydia at that surprising prospect. She turned away, unable to face him. Did Dobson know about the time she'd spent at Ella Fenniwig's? Lydia shut her eyes, feeling as if the world were crumbling beneath her. She didn't ever want Hugh to know about her past. She'd lose not only all moral superiority, which she'd been lording over him unmercifully, but she'd lose the one thing in life she prized most—his respect.

"Have I upset you?" he murmured, running a finger along the side of her face.

She could feel his love in that simple touch. She shook her head. "No. I'm just trying to . . . put together the other pieces of the puzzle."

"Everything that has happened was by design. Dobson wanted us to find out he's holding Sophie. That's why he left the mistletoe outside the theater, and that's why he left the letter in the abandoned club."

"But we stumbled on the Diamond Forest Club quite by chance. If Reggie hadn't seen your mother's brooch, he would never have mentioned the place to you, and you would never have thought of stopping by that night we met Dobson."

"When did you hire Reggie?"

Her eyes widened. "You don't think Reggie is working for Dobson?"

"No, he's a good lad. But how long has he worked for you?"

"I hired him last week. Just before Sophie—" She stopped short. "Oh, Lord."

"How did you find him?"

"He was recommended by a benefactor at Stone House who suggested Reggie to Mrs. Cromwell when she mentioned we were looking for help."

"And who was this benefactor?"

"I don't know. He'd made a generous donation and asked that it be anonymous. Stone House is known for its discretion, not only regarding the women we serve, but for our benefactors as well." She looked at him, thunderstruck. "Do you think it was Dobson who recommended Reggie to the director of Stone House?"

"It was him or one of his cronies. Reggie admitted he frequented Dobson's club in his former life. He probably mentioned to someone there that he was looking for legitimate work."

"And Dobson knew I would stumble on May at the clinic, if your theory is correct. But to what end?"

"He wanted you to see the butterfly scar. He wanted her to lead us to him."

"But why? Why go to all this trouble simply to engage you in a battle of intellects?"

"He must hate me very much. I represent all that he can never have—legitimacy. He could have had my father's title and all his wealth and lands, but because he was born out of wedlock, he could have none of it. He had to settle for a baronetcy instead of an earldom. He's called 'Sir' instead of 'Lord.' He's not a peer. And everything goes to me, even though my father hates me, because I was the firstborn son of a legitimate firstborn son. The principle of primogeniture has caused more wars, murders, and mayhem in the history of this country than any other law, I daresay."

"So Sir Trevor wants to prove himself superior to you once and for all. Are you afraid of him?"

"No. But I'm afraid of this." He reached back and pulled the bottle of laudanum from the table and studied it once again. "Every month, every week, every night I feel the need to increase my dosage. I try to resist, but I don't think as clearly as I used to. I have to give this case everything I have, Lydia, and I can't do it without a clear mind. I refuse to let you down again."

With a spark of hope lighting her face, she said, "Oh, Hugh, I'm so glad to hear you say that. Then you simply must stop taking it."

"It's not that easy."

"I'll help you."

He looked up sharply, studying her, reading her determination. "I have no right to ask any more of you, Lydie. You've given—"

"Shhh." She reached out and placed a forefinger to his lips, then leaned forward and kissed his cheek. Lightning passed between them, burning away pretense. They were on the cliffs again, clinging to one another, with so much at stake. "You can do it. Do it now," she said with urgency.

When she drew back, he was smiling. He looked down at the bottle as if it were a friend on a dock and he was on a departing ship. "I'm afraid I'm going to miss this more than I can imagine." With that, he hurled it into the fireplace. Glass shattered. Liquid singed in the flames. Almost immediately he felt the first cramp in his stomach. He grimaced.

"You did not take any of it tonight?" she asked.

He shook his head.

"That's why you looked so terrible when I came down."

"Yes, the brandy helps, but not for long."

"We can get through this, Hugh. I promise."

He cupped her cheek with his hand and sighed. "Lend me your confidence. I'm going to need it."

Ahhhh!" Hugh's tortured voice roared in the darkness of the bed chamber.

Lydia bolted upright in the chair, where she'd been dozing by the fire. It burned low but still provided enough light for her to see that Hugh had sat up in the four-poster bed where he'd been fitfully sleeping. "It's all right, Hugh. I'm here."

"Ahh! They're crawling all over me." He frantically brushed at his forearms. "Get them off! Bugs, bugs! Get them off me."

She scrambled across the room to his side and placed her hands firmly on his shoulders. "Lay back down, darling. You're just imagining things. It's the drug, Hugh. Losing it does strange things to the mind."

"But—"

"There are no bugs. Now lie down and try to sleep some more."

"I'm cold." He shivered violently, yet he was drenched in perspiration. He said nothing for a long time, then seemed to see her clearly for the first time. "Lydia, oh, it's you. Thank God! I had the most horrible nightmare. I could have sworn—" He stopped, suddenly exhausted, and exhaled the weight of the world as he sank back against the pillow. "When will this end?"

"Not for days, my dear," she said and reached for a cloth, dipping it in the bedside washbowl. She wrung it out and dabbed the cool material against his burning forehead. "You can do it, Hugh. You're doing marvelously. I'm so proud of you."

He smiled, though he did not open his eyes. "Keep telling me that."

"I will."

His body remained tense. It would take time for it to learn once again how to relax on its own. But for the moment the hallucinations and cramps were at bay. That meant he might be able to sleep for another hour without waking.

"What did you ever see in me, Lydie?" he said in the silence.

"What *didn't* I see in you, you mean," she said with a raspy laugh. "I thought you were the most perfectly marvelous man I'd ever met. Now go to sleep. I won't leave you. I promise."

"Don't ever leave me again, Lydia. Never again."

She sat there for a long time, pondering his plea. It was strange how people saw the past from such different perspectives. He actually felt as if she'd left him, and she felt certain he'd rejected her. Of course she now knew they'd each made mistakes and erroneous assumptions, but that didn't wipe away the anguish they both still felt. What would it take to erase the horrors of the past from their memories?

When she was sure he had fallen back to sleep, she went to her smallest trunk and pulled out her diary. Then she returned to the chaise by the fire. She lit a candle, then riffled through the pages. She was not surprised when the diary opened to the exact entry she wanted to read. She simply dove in, swimming through the murky waters of yesterday that were begging to be crossed.

MAY 8, 1875

I haven't written in some time. If my hand is unsteady, it is because I am riding the train.

My last entry dealt with our discovery of the standing stones. I wrote it as soon as we returned. It wasn't until the doctor arrived to examine us that I realized the consequences of our wild outing.

Hugh and I were both knocked unconscious. We didn't revive until nearly sunrise. We hurried back to Windhaven, careful to arrive separately. But the damage was already done. Someone—perhaps many people—saw us returning and knew we had spent the night together. No one seemed to notice the gashes on our heads or realize they hadn't been acquired while making passionate love. Too many longtime servants had been suspicious and jealous of the viscount's obvious admiration for me. This indiscretion was just enough to seal my doom.

When the doctor was called in to examine our injuries, it seemed to give everyone permission to talk openly about our sojourn. No one seemed interested in the fact that we had discovered a new circle of stones. In fact, no one believed us.

Hugh was livid. He was angry at himself for letting me talk him into something that would ruin my reputation. And he was furious that no one would believe what we had both seen with our own eyes. Over and over again he returned to Devil's Peak and the hillside, bringing first the constable, then the land agent, the head gardener, and finally his father, who returned from a trip with Katherine four days after our debacle.

No matter how hard Hugh searched, he could not find the opening we had seen that night that led through the cave to the strange circle and haunting drum beats. He looked and felt like a fool, or a foolish young man who was desperate to cover up the fact that he had ruined the career of an otherwise perfectly good governess.

The day before his father returned, Hugh sent a note to my room: *Meet me at the goldfish pond at dusk.* I took my meal in my room, claiming the cut on my forehead still troubled me, though in fact I felt perfectly normal. When no one was looking, I donned a light hooded cape and slipped out into the west garden. He was there on a white horse that was barely visible in the fading light. He looked hard and determined, brash and handsome in his dark riding clothes. He reached down and easily pulled me up behind his saddle. And off we went.

We arrived about a half-hour later at a very mystical place in the valley he called Braemore Lodge. Inside, the ancient stone keep was aglow with candles and a blazing fire. Hugh had obviously prepared for our visit ahead of time. Two goblets awaited us at the table in the great hall, and a bottle of Spanish wine sweated in anticipation.

"Come," he said, extending his hand to me as he stood in the open door. As I entered, he glanced around the outside one last time to make sure we hadn't been followed. Then he shut the door and looked at me with guilt and despair etched on his face. His voice was determined as he said, "Take off your cape."

I wordlessly obeyed. We hadn't had any chance to speak alone since our encounter on Beltaine. I let the cape fall off my shoulders and tossed it over the back of a chair. Then I stood in the middle of the room shivering, for the night air had nipped me well. But it was more than that. This place felt almost alien, as if we'd stepped out of time into the brutal world of the middle ages.

But we could never escape the present. Or hope for the future.

The fact that he had invited me here alone confirmed what I had already suspected. My reputation was beyond salvation. There was no reason not to be alone together. It was just a matter of time before I would be sent away. The earl would no longer consider me an appropriate influence on his daughter. I would be dismissed without references, which meant I would never work as a governess again.

Suddenly our great discovery and the clues to the unsolved murder seemed inconsequential. "I've been a fool," I said.

"No," he replied, "I have been. I should have done this weeks ago."

"Done what?"

He knelt before me, and I was struck again by how tall and graceful he was. His eyes gleamed, and his beautifully sculpted mouth curved into an earnest smile as he looked up at my face.

"What is it, Hugh?"

"Will you marry me, Miss Parker? I love you. I am so sorry for what you have endured. But it doesn't take away the fact that I love you and want to marry you."

I held my breath. It was too much. All of it. I whirled away and found myself staring at the open bottle of wine. I reached for it as if it were life itself and poured a glass. I took a swallow, then coughed, unused to any kind of alcohol. I was a vicar's daughter. And he was an earl's son.

A viscount, for heaven's sake! This was impossible. All of it.

"No!" I declared, turning back, emboldened by the warmth the wine had brought to my chilled soul. "This isn't right. You can't marry me. I don't belong here. I am a . . . a humble person . . . a commoner."

"There is nothing humble or common about you," he said in that rich voice I'd come to love. "You are the most original, intelligent, and unconventional woman I have ever met. If I can't have you, Addie Parker, then I don't want anyone at all. Would you condemn me to a life of solitude?"

My doubts wanted to shrink at that, but I would not let them. "We are in two different worlds, Lord Montgomery, and if you did not know that before, you surely do now." I took another swallow from the goblet. The wine was becoming remarkably more smooth with each sip. It would give me courage to say what I must say, to do what I must do.

"We simply cannot marry. Your father will never accept me."

"You know I don't care what he thinks."

"I do."

"You won't. I love you, Addie. Say yes."

"No. I won't. I don't belong here. I should have stayed in my parents' village."

"You would have withered there. You're no country girl. You're smart and clever. Together we will solve cases, Addie. You can use that remarkable mind of yours."

I looked at him and blinked, amazed. "I've never met a man who wanted intelligence in a woman."

"I not only want it, I demand it." He winced. "Oh, hell, now will you please say yes? My knees are killing me."

I laughed. It sounded strange, for I had been mired in such gloomy despair until this very moment. I felt like a bird being let out of a cage, soaring just when I thought my wings had been clipped.

"Oh, Hugh." I laughed, and then I cried.

"Don't cry. Just come here and help me up."

I laughed again, this time giddily. "You're impossible, do you know that?" I went to him and threw my arms around him as he stood up. He wrapped his arms around me, and his heat burned me deliciously. Tendrils of desire spread over my breasts and down my body, twisting and stroking every nerve ending to life. "Oh, Hugh . . . ."

I pressed my cheek to his chest and felt him pulling the pins from my hair. My long black mane fell in a curling mass to my waist. He used his fingers to comb through it sensuously, then slid his hands around my face, gripping my temples with powerful strength. My eyes opened as he glared down fiercely at me. Expectantly.

"Well?" he growled. "Is this a yes?"

"Yes," I murmured. "Of course, yes!"

He smiled ecstatically and pulled me into a bear hug. Then his ardent mouth found mine, and the world began to spin out of control. We tumbled to our knees on the bearskin rug. He cushioned my fall with his powerful embrace and somehow never broke contact with my lips as we rolled to our sides on the soft fur.

He was a divine kisser. Not that I had anything to compare him to, but I knew heaven when I felt it. I slowly allowed my body to relax enough to feel and enjoy the long, hard length of him. Every inch of my body craved him. I immediately opened to him in a way I had never imagined possible. Every caress of his hands on my body was a tremulous gift, every stroke brought me joy and ecstasy. I responded with complete love and abandon, for this was my true love, my soul mate. This man was my destiny, and I his.

Every touch, every new exposure of skin, every bold joining of flesh was another new miracle, and so we went slowly and thoroughly to our ecstatic rendezvous. He was firm yet tender, skilled yet earnest. He was an incredible lover. Moments after he entered me, I exploded with a shimmering and shattering passion I could not explain or comprehend. I could only rejoice in it. And because he knew much more about this sort of thing than I did and stayed a long time where he was most welcome, I felt this peculiar explosion again and again.

"I love you, Hugh," I murmured when he had joined me in reaching his final fulfillment.

"I know," he whispered. "I love you. I love you. Never doubt it. Never forget it."

When Hugh's father and sister returned, I kept to the old nursery, where I taught young Katherine her lessons. She was delighted to see me again and full of stories about her trip to Europe. She clapped her hands together in front of her rosebud lips, and her eyes sparkled as she breathlessly said, "Oh, Miss Parker, have you seen the Louvre? It's heavenly!" and, "Miss Parker, I wish ever so much you could have been with me and Papa when we hired a gondola in Venice," and, "French pastries are simply divine!"

Katherine is a beautiful girl, as flighty as a butterfly, and the perfect distraction for me, as would be any vivacious twelve-year-old. I didn't want to go anywhere near the earl, so we resumed Katherine's studies. All the while I waited with dread for the inevitable summons that would mean my dismissal. As the day wore on, I began to hope it might not come.

But I was only deceiving myself.

That afternoon in the earl's study downstairs, the shouting raised by his lordship when he met with Hugh was the peal of doom. The house fell quiet as the two men roared like lions fighting for dominance in a pride. Eventually, Hugh stormed out, slamming the door after him. He came straight to the nursery.

"Monty!" Katherine cried when he appeared in the door. She jumped up in her bouncy white lace skirts and rushed to his side. She flung her arms around her adored brother, saying, "Monty, you haven't come to see me until now, and I've so wanted to tell you about my adventures with Papa."

He distractedly kissed her dark curls. "Not now, moppet," he said, his eyes gravely holding mine. "I need to speak with Miss Parker. Alone."

"Oh, Monty, you're no fun at all. I was going to recommend that you go to Paris. It's positively the most romantic city in the world!" She started for the door, casting him a teasing smile over her shoulder. "I think you're in love with Miss Parker, do you know that? Why don't you take *her* to Paris?"

"Moppet," he said with mock severity, glowering at her until she giggled and ran out the door. As soon as it clicked shut, he held out his hand to me and I hurried forward to take it.

"What happened?" I asked. "You sounded like animals at each other's throats."

"We very nearly were. But he knows. I told him we're going to be married, and there was nothing he could do about it."

"What did he say?"

"He said he wanted to speak with me in the morning, when I am capable of thinking more clearly. I don't want to go."

"I think you should. It will prove to him that you are thinking clearly. And of course, if you have a change of heart, it will give you a chance to back out of our marriage."

"I'm not going to have a change of heart," he emphatically replied. "If you feel prepared to meet with him, he wants to see you as well. Just before noon tomorrow, after my interview. I suppose he's either going to fire you as a governess or welcome you as a daughter-in-law. Or both."

I tried to laugh, but something in my heart told me the drama was far from over.

"Either way, I'll meet you at 12:30 at the fish pond. If he has not accepted you by then, we will leave immediately and elope. So wait for me at the fish pond where we met the other night, Lydia. Do you understand?"

I nodded.

* * *

I did not see Hugh the next morning, but at 11:30 I went for my appointment with the earl in his study. As I expected, he berated me for my indiscretion and said I was not fit to serve as governess for Katherine. That alone I might have taken well enough, but then he said Hugh had been in to see him that morning and that he'd changed his mind. After thinking it over a night, Hugh realized he didn't want my inferior blood to taint the family line.

I laughed out loud. That was so unlike Hugh. He would never think, much less say, something that patently shallow. Yet before the earl was through with me, he had planted the seeds of doubt. I remained confident, however, and headed to the fish pond as Hugh instructed me, certain that we would have no choice but to elope.

But he never came.

I waited there until midnight.

When I returned to the house in utter humiliation, no one would speak to me. It was as if I had ceased to exist. That was two days ago. Today when I was on my way to the station to take a train to my parents' home, I was finally able to learn what had happened to Hugh.

Mr. Deavers, the coachman, allowed as how he had taken his lordship to the train station yesterday afternoon. It seemed Lord Montgomery had decided to take his sister's advice and visit Paris.

Alone.

Chapter 17

Lydia woke to the sound of banging on the door to the great hall. The diary was still open in her lap. She'd fallen asleep reading and must have spent the duration of the night in the chair. Sunlight streamed in the windows now.

"Just a minute!" she shouted, running to the window and throwing it open. She caught Reggie just as he was about to begin another round of pounding. "Reggie! I'm up here. What is it?"

"Oh, there you are, ma'am! You received a telegram from Sir Todd Leach!"

"What does it say?"

"He says that the girl from the clinic—May, he called her—is dead."

"What?!"

"Run over by a carriage under suspicious circumstances."

"Oh, no!" She wanted to tell Hugh, but he was barely conscious. "Just a moment, Reggie!"

She went to the bed and looked closely at his face.

Curled in a fetal position, he was white as his sheets. "Poor Hugh. You need more help than I can give you." She hurried back to the window. "Come in, Reggie. I need your assistance. Viscount Montgomery is ill and must be taken back to Windhaven."

Reggie rode to the estate house on horseback and returned by carriage via the valley road. Lydia knew this route took longer, but Hugh was in no shape to travel up the quicker but narrower hillside roads on a horse. When the vehicle rounded the last embankment of trees and rumbled over the long gravel drive that curved around the front of the mansion, Lydia couldn't help but compare the last time she'd done this—return with Hugh after that night alone five years ago.

But this time she was a countess. And he was very ill.

She gave orders as if she were fully in charge. She instructed the housekeeper to set up the Renaissance Room. Hugh had always admired it for its luxury and tranquility. In addition, it was connected to the Blue Room, where Lydia planned to stay. She had no intention of letting anyone care for Hugh but herself.

Next she sent Reggie to the apothecary in the village to retrieve any sort of tonic that might relieve Hugh's suffering. He needed liquids, but he was unable to keep anything down long enough to hydrate his body. Then she ordered the groom of the chambers to fill a piping hot bath in the Renaissance Room.

Soon footmen and pages dragged in a portable porcelain tub and filled it with steaming water. When she dismissed them, they left without allowing their blank expressions to show their surprise that she would bathe him herself, but she had no doubt that tongues would wag below stairs. She didn't give a damn.

"Come along, Hugh," she said, going to the bed where he had been safely tucked in.

He managed to pry open his eyes and stared hard at her below narrowed lids. "We shouldn't have come back here," he said through clinched teeth. "They will talk."

"You're right. People will talk no matter what we do. I wanted you to be comfortable, darling. I was afraid . . . ."

"*You?*" He whispered the word with exaggerated incredulity. "I didn't think you were afraid of anything."

"Only of losing you." She stroked his face and kissed his dry lips. "Now let's get you in the tub. Your muscles are in contraction. You have to work them out with diligence. Try to walk, then we'll let the water do some of the work. Come along, then."

She threw back the covers and half pulled him up. He was hunched over like an old man. She put his arm around her shoulder and helped him hobble to the tub. Once there, she had to peal off his nightshirt and help him hoist one leg over the tub. She didn't in the least feel embarrassed by his nakedness, perhaps because just last night she'd read about the time when they were intimate, or perhaps because all she cared about now was getting him well.

"Ease yourself down now. Don't slip."

"Ah," Hugh groaned. "That's excellent."

"I couldn't do this for you at the lodge. I'm afraid hot water and servants to haul it weren't available there."

His body still was wont to curl, and she gently pushed his knees down. "Try to stretch out."

"Yes, ma'am," he said obediently, releasing some of his tension with a shiver. "Now if I'd only had a lovely nanny like you," he said, "my life might have turned out differently."

"Oh? Was your nanny something out of a Grimm's fairy tale?"

"You might say that. She had rotten teeth and a big wart on her nose and she was always threatening to check my fingers to see if I was plump enough to eat."

She chuckled. "Poor thing. All that going against her and she had to take care of you as well!"

She reached out to brush aside a tendril of hair plastered to his perspiring forehead, but he grabbed her wrist with more strength than she'd seen him display in the last twenty-four hours. She looked down and watched as he pulled her hand to his cheek and pressed it there.

"Thank you, Lydie. Thank you for being here. And thank you for taking care of Katherine. She never forgot you. She always talked about that delightful and intelligent Miss Parker."

"How sweet. She was a wonderful girl." They'd never really talked about her death. She wasn't sure now was the time for it, so she reached for a washcloth and lathered it with soap. "I think you're feeling a little better, aren't you?"

She grabbed his nearest arm and pulled it out of the water, running the soapy cloth over his muscular forearm, noting the fine dusting of dark hair on it. A tiny ripple of excitement stirred within her, but she tried to suppress it. Impossible. She remembered how fine his arms felt about her during their lovemaking. He was so strong, yet so gentle. She felt his eyes on her, watching her progress with keen interest, although exactly what his emotions were she could not even begin to guess.

"Ours has been a very complicated relationship, hasn't it?" she said as she lowered his arm in what she hoped was a brisk and professional manner and moved on to his chest. The white suds swirled over the hairy breadth of it, and she nearly dropped the cloth in the water. His answer to her question did not exactly calm her.

"Yes, it has. How are you feeling about . . . Beaumont's death?"

She sighed raggedly. "I haven't even thought about it. Isn't that terrible? I've been so intent on finding Sophie."

"That's what he would've wanted," Hugh reminded her gently.

"He was so careful to insist all during our marriage that he didn't have long to live. He wanted to prepare me for the inevitable. When he finally died, it seemed like the right thing to happen. Certainly it was what I was expecting."

When the cloth glided over his brown nipples she stopped suddenly, aware that the mood was changing. How odd to speak of her husband while she bathed her lover. Her former lover. And yet this was the only man she had ever truly loved in that way. He put his hand over hers, and for a moment she thought he was going to guide the cloth down farther. She could see his arousal through the sudsy water. Her cheeks pinkened.

"I do believe you are recovering," she said tartly, but there was a glint in her eyes that she could not conceal. "I think I'll watch you finish the job yourself. Just to make sure you don't drown."

"See?" he replied, "you're nothing at all like my former nanny. She would have tried to drown me."

"I'm not sure I would have blamed her."

He laughed, and she relished the sound. Yes, he would be his old self soon, but she still had to get some liquids in his system. She retrieved a glass of water from the beside table. "Take a few sips of this."

He obliged her, wincing as he swallowed. She could see the ridges of the muscles in his gut tighten with a cramp.

"Not too much. That's good." She retrieved the glass and sat on the stool while he finished washing. It was pure torture. Even if he was still ill, he was magnificently male. His muscles flexed as he glided the cloth over his powerful chest and down each long leg.

To divert herself from her shockingly inappropriate thoughts, she asked, "Whatever happened to your sister? Katherine was a marvelous creature, full of life and so innocent. And beautiful! How tragic that she passed away so young."

"It's been two years. I was on the Continent at the time. By then I had given up on my search for you. I felt as if I had nothing to live for, so I decided to travel. My father didn't even bother to inform me of her death until I returned at the end of August. She'd been dead for months. I was so furious I haven't really spoken to him since—except recently, when I questioned him about Dobson."

"I'm so sorry. It must've been a ghastly shock," she said, sorry to have brought up such a painful topic.

"I haven't even been to her grave to pay my respects. Every time I try . . . I can't bear to think of her there."

"Where is she buried?"

"In the family plot next to the old house. Next to Mother. That precious child doesn't belong in the ground. She was too alive. I still hate that I never even had a chance to say good-bye."

"How awful."

"Life can be awful, but it goes on. The longer I live, Lydia, the more I'm convinced that I must continue my work. If there is no justice in the world, then what's left?"

"I admire you for that, Hugh."

"Now, there's a miracle."

"No, it's only natural. You're brilliant and principled. That's why I fell in love with you five years ago."

"Fell. Past tense."

She took a deep breath and let it out slowly. "Aren't we too old to believe that love matters anymore?" She held her breath as he leaned back against the tub.

"Suddenly my head is killing me. Either the topic is too weighty or this damnable process isn't over," he groused.

Lydia let out a soft sigh. This was not the time or the place for them to discuss a future together . . . if indeed there was any hope of such. Considering her past, she knew she had no right to hope at all. She smiled at him and said, "Perhaps you need more nursing and less philosophizing. I'll ring for some beef broth and put you back in bed."

She fed Hugh the broth and the tonic Reggie had retrieved from the apothecary. When it became clear that he was well on his way to recovery, she let Pierpont take over his care. He had returned from London after making arrangements for Thurber Frances to join them in the country.

Lydia spent the day writing to the Leaches and arranging for Colette to move from the hotel to Windhaven. There was no point pretending anymore as to Lydia's exact whereabouts. She didn't think Trevor Dobson cared where she was, in any event. He clearly had his own agenda.

That evening she shared a meal with Hugh in the Renaissance Room. He was freshly shaved and washed and wearing a bronze-colored silk robe that lent some much needed color to his cheeks. He was thinner than ever, but at last boasting a voracious appetite. They ate from trays at a table by the window.

"Mr. Frances is coming in two days," she said as she updated him on the latest. "That will be the day we receive our first clue at the lodge. One can only assume it will be written in the tree alphabet, so he'll come in handy."

"Excellent. What news from Todd and Clara Leach? Anything?"

Lydia put down her fork and dabbed her mouth. "I didn't want to tell you until your strength had been restored, but they sent terrible news. The young girl in the clinic— May—has been killed."

Hugh shot her a disbelieving look, then shook his head sadly. "Poor chit. She might have helped us. I wonder if that's why she died."

Lydia looked up with a start. "You think she was murdered?"

He pointed the tines of his fork her way. "I don't know. There's so much I don't know. I'm beginning to doubt my skills as a sleuth."

"Well, they'll be much better now that you have a clear head."

"Thanks to you." He reached across the table and gave her hand a squeeze. A warm surge shot up her arm, and she carefully withdrew her fingers. But later, when he invited her to join him on the chaise, she did not protest. They sat comfortably turned toward each other, leaning back, sipping from small glasses of sherry.

"You know, Hugh, I realized that I never asked you how you enjoyed Paris."

When he didn't immediately answer, her heart began to pound. She had resisted talking about that terrible time, hating to admit how much she had been hurt. Lydia had always thought if she didn't admit it, the pain wouldn't be real. But there were questions for which answers were long overdue.

"You mean during my trip to the Continent two years ago? I didn't visit Paris then."

"No, I meant when . . . when I left Windhaven."

He raised one brow and pierced her with his perceptive gaze. "But I didn't visit Paris when you left."

"But you did. Katherine advised you to take a trip and . . . you left for Paris. The next day, I believe it was. And then . . . then I was sent away."

"Is that what they told you?" he murmured, leaning back. "That I'd gone to Paris?"

"Yes. Mr. Deavers, the coachman, told me."

"How ironic. The place I went was anything but gay Paris."

He drained his sherry and put the glass on a low table, taking her glass and placing it there as well. Then he gathered her into his arms and held her close, hugging her cheek to his.

"Oh, my darling Lydia, how can I explain? How can I ever make up for what happened to you?"

He was holding her so tight she could hardly breathe. He was trying to heal her. She could feel it in the heat and the completeness of his hold. Then he planted a very firm kiss on her cheek.

"I'm sorry, my darling. Lord, how I'm sorry." He kissed her mouth, then brushed his lips across hers. He cupped her cheek, then gazed at her, tilting his head as he smiled sadly. "Would you like to know what really happened that terrible, awful time?"

She swallowed hard and nodded. "Very much."

He leaned more fully against the back of the chaise, relaxing his hold on her slightly. He took one of her hands in his and caressed her fingers with his thumb. "I went to see my father that morning, as you had recommended. I told him that I had not changed my mind about marrying you, and that if he did not accept you as my fiancée we would elope. He told me he was glad I had stuck to my position and he was wrong, and he apologized. He offered me a drink to toast my proposed marriage. Giddy with relief, I tossed back the brandy, not realizing that it had been drugged."

"I don't believe it!" But she did. It all made such terrible, tragic sense now.

"It's true. I don't think I regained full consciousness for a week. By the time I did, I was thoroughly addicted to laudanum. A physician friend advised my father on the precise dosage required to subdue me, which, as it turns out, was just enough to make me develop a craving. I suppose I might have weaned myself off the accursed stuff if I'd been sensible about it, but I was wild with grief over the loss of you. I see now I was all too willing to numb my senses. In any event, now you know why I did not meet you at the fish pond and how I acquired my addiction."

"Damn him," she said quietly, then nearly shouted. "Damn him! He's ruined us both, Hugh. What a despicable man!"

"No, Lydia, he thought he was saving me from myself. He still thinks that."

"How can you defend him?"

"I'm not. I hate him for what he did to you. And to me. But I can understand his point of view, wrong as it may be. He is not an evil man, just misguided."

"I don't agree. I don't think you've fully come to terms with how much he has done to hurt you. And until you do, I don't think you will be fully yourself again."

His face turned to stone, and his jaw jutted out belligerently. "Since when did you know me so well?"

"Since the beginning," she spat back, jumping to her

feet. She wanted to run from him and pummel him all at the same time. Instead, she crossed her arms and began to pace. "I've known you ever since you reached for my hand as I tumbled over that cliff. I've known you better than you know yourself. There is something very wrong with your family, and I'm not just talking about your diabolical bastard half-uncle."

"Be careful what you say," he said in a low voice.

"I don't believe this! Will you defend dear Uncle Trevor now, too?"

"Of course not! You can't compare his aberrations to my father's mistakes. The earl wanted to maintain certain traditions, Lydia. It is not what I wanted, but he had spent his whole life trying to bring back honor to the family name."

"And honor is such an important thing," she said sarcastically. "So important he would send his wife to die in a sanitarium rather than have her embarrass him with her madness."

"He thought it would help her," Hugh said tightly. "He was wrong. But so were the doctors."

"She killed herself, Hugh. And you became an addict because of him. Lord knows why your sister fell ill. Perhaps she was tired of living in this house as well."

"That's not fair!" he shouted, jumping to his feet. "You can't blame Katherine's illness on the earl. Do you think the queen would listen to my father's counsel if he were so thoroughly rotten to the core?"

"I think family honor is highly overrated," she said, exhausted from the interchange. "I am stunned . . . stunned to hear you defend him."

"I am not defending him! I am simply saying I understand how the world works," he said wearily, combing his fingers through his hair. "I wasn't born with drew drops shimmering in my eyes and posies for brains."

Lydia was too stunned to reply, but merely stood there as he took a broad step forward and pointed a finger at her. "You weren't born into this world. You married into it.

There are some things you simply can't understand—such as what a burden an earldom is for a man who accepts the responsibilities like my father has."

"My father was a vicar with a whole parish to serve!" she replied hotly.

"That's nothing comparable to what my father dealt with. A priest's biggest concern is preparing the Sunday sermon, for God's sake."

"For God's sake is quite correct," she said icily, drawing back, stung by the insult. "How dare you!"

"Lydia, I didn't mean—"

Furiously, she cut him off. "So you finally admit we were born in different worlds and that it does matter. I was right. Love doesn't count at all, not when dealing with class differences. Yes, you were born into the peerage. And I suppose that makes you not only different but better because of your very blue blood. As you said, I merely married into it, like the whore I am."

"Shut up!" he shouted. "Shut up, Lydia. I will not have you demean yourself like that."

"I suppose you want to reserve the honor all for yourself!"

He raked his hands through his hair as if to pull it out. "Why won't you hear my point? I'm not superior. Quite the contrary. It makes me inferior because I am shackled even now by traditions that make no bloody sense but that I can nevertheless understand. And that understanding undermines my moral authority. Why do you think I spent so much time seeking justice in common law? Because I wanted something in this insane world of ours to make sense. I wanted logic, not privilege."

She covered her face with her hands, feeling cold and sick at heart. The gulf between them was insurmountable.

"What I'm trying to say, my darling Lydia," he added gently, "is that the damage has been done. To both of us. We have survived. You let my father defeat you once, and I'm telling you it's not going to happen again. He is not that powerful. No one is. No one will come between us again."

"*Us?* There is no us. There is you. There is me. But there is no we. I thought I had made that clear. For such an intelligent man, you can be remarkably dense at times."

She turned stiffly and marched toward her room. He lunged after her, and in a few quick strides passed her and blocked the doorway. She looked up incredulously.

"Goddamn, Lydia! When you are going to marry me?"

"Never!" Now she did pound him. She beat her fists against his chest and gripped his satin lapels, pulling him close until his face was mere inches from hers. "Listen to me. Never! I will never, ever—"

He stopped the tirade with a kiss. A hungry, hot, open-mouthed kiss. One touch of his tongue on her lips and she allowed him to enter with a groan. She let the monster in and the passion out. Suppressed desire coiled deep inside her, unfurling all the way down to her toes and up her back. Her head spun crazily. She flung it back limply, and his mouth roved over her throat, pressing to the pulse beating furiously there.

"Oh, my God!" she cried out as she lost her breath to his erotic nibbling. His tongue swirled over her delicate collar bone. "What are you . . . *doing?*"

"Kissing you," he murmured hotly as he worked his way back up to her ear, letting his tongue seductively caress that dark, secret place. He ran his hands up over her bare shoulders and into her hair, cradling her head and working his fingers through her soft curls. Unwittingly, he unfastened the pins . . . and ended up holding her hair piece in his hands.

"What the hell?"

Lydia realized what had happened and covered her shorn hair. She reddened when he examined the coils of false hair nesting in his palm. He looked at it in shock, then grinned teasingly.

"Well! If it isn't Mr. Morgan. Fancy meeting you here."

Her eyes were slitted with angry embarrassment for a moment, but then the absurdity of the situation suddenly washed over her and she smiled. "You're merciless. Do you know that?" Then she burst out laughing. "This is mad! I don't even know who I am anymore."

He laughed with her for a moment, then stroked her cheek with the back of his fingers while he tossed the hair piece away, pulling her close. "I know who you are. You are the same beautiful young woman I fell in love with just yesterday, it seems."

He pressed her forehead to his own and her laughter vanished. His touch was like a benediction. For a moment she was that innocent young governess again. She clutched his arms and felt the whole world going away. Here there was only the two of them.

"Oh, Hugh . . ." The words caught in her throat.

He swept her up in his arms with strength she couldn't imagine he still possessed after so many days of weakness. But it was emotion that drove him, not physical prowess. He carried her to her iron bedstead, knelt one knee onto the mattress, then lowered her to it.

As he sat beside her on the edge of the bed, he examined her nape-length hair with emotion-filled eyes, stroking it away from her face. "Your features are magnificent. I see that especially now when there's nothing to distract me from the obvious."

"But you always loved my long hair best."

He shook his head. "It was merely icing on the already exquisite cake."

She smiled and closed her eyes, basking in his unconditional love. Their hurtful, heated words meant nothing now. They were mere substitutes for the real dialogue between them.

I love you. I've always loved you. I always will.

He lowered himself to the floor, pulling her to a sitting position. Then he tugged her to the edge of the bed and knelt between her legs. "I want you to know, Lydia, that you are the most beautiful woman I have ever known, and you always will be. Even if you dress like a man," he added with a twinkle in his eyes.

"Will you make love to me?" she asked softly as her fingers caressed his face.

"Definitely."

She leaned forward then and put her mouth to his, feeling his tongue delve inside for a honey kiss. At the same time she reached for his lapels and pushed his robe over his shoulders, letting her fingers run over his muscular chest and back. His muscles tensed under her touch, and his kiss deepened in response. He reached behind and gripped her derriere, sliding her even closer.

"I have never wanted another man like I've wanted you," she whispered as she blazed a trail of kisses across his cheek and to his strong neck.

"How many have you wanted?" he chuckled.

She stilled a moment, realizing he thought she had only been with him. She mustn't show him just how much she knew about making love.

He brushed her collarbone with trembling hands, sliding the edge of her gown over her shoulders until he reached the top of her corset. Her breasts pooled there, and he kissed the cleft between them, breathing hot air against her already heated flesh.

She panted now and arched up in offering when his lips and tongue strained to reach the nipples hiding provocatively just beneath the edge of her corset. Frustrated, he returned to her mouth and gave her a rough kiss, squeezing her hips in his hands.

"I want you. I want all of you, Lydia." He leaned back, and she could see his magnificent, lean torso in the moonlight. It narrowed to lean hips. His muscles rippled, his forearms and chest covered with a velvety coating of black hair.

Hungrily, she reached out and smoothed her hands over the delightfully springy hair on his magnificent chest. He stood up and pulled off his robe the rest of the way, tossing it behind him. She looked avidly at his erection springing up from a nest of dark hair. She wanted to touch it in the way that Carlo had taught her, but she dared not. Hugh could never know she had done such things.

As Lydia swallowed her parching desire, Hugh pulled her to her feet and reached around the back of her gown, unfastening a row of buttons. Then he felt for the tie fastening her corset.

"You should follow Lady Leach's example," he murmured in her ear. "Do away with these silly contraptions."

"Don't talk, just kiss." She put her hands to his cheeks and claimed his mouth greedily.

Without looking, he pulled her gown down over her arms and somehow managed to loosen her corset just enough to get his hands inside. When his warm, hungry fingers wrapped around one breast and then the other, she felt that old familiar surge of desire. She had to have him or die. He played with her nipples, deftly flicking his thumbs over the taut beads.

Lydia groaned, "Oh, Hugh, don't make me wait."

"But I must," he groaned in return. "Until I've touched all of you."

"Do you want me to touch you?" she asked as her head swam with ecstasy.

"No," he said, chuckling. "I wouldn't ask that of you, darling."

She bit her lip with an ironic smile. *Ask,* she thought. *Please ask.*

His hands left her breasts and traced the indentations of her loosened corset. As he caressed downward over her skirts to her ankles, he knelt before her as if worshiping a goddess. Reaching under the hem of her gown, he touched her legs through her stockings at the edge of her leather ankle boots. She clung to his shoulders, emitting a hissing breath of excitement as his hands sensuously roved up her calves, to her garters just above her knees. She boldly widened her stance. With exquisite sensuality, he rolled the garters and stockings to her ankles one at a time, then smoothed back up her now-bare calves, kneading the muscles.

Lydia felt her legs begin to buckle.

"Oh, Hugh . . ." she moaned again. He stood and embraced her. He wildly kissed and laved her neck as he rocked his hips into her.

"Lydia, you drive me wild," he murmured as he urged her to sit on the bed and knelt before her.

I'm doing nothing, she thought as she lay back with languorous desire. *If only I could pleasure you as you pleasure me.*

Raising her skirts, he slid his hands up over her knees, over her drawers. His thumbs came tantalizingly close to the place that ached for him. He sobered and looked at her through sultry eyes.

"Please, love, sit up. I want to undress you." He tugged her up and reached around, further loosening her corset. He pulled the stiff contraption over her head. His face creased with an incredulous smile. "Lord, your breasts are gorgeous."

He gripped them again in both hands, lifting them up, toying with the nipples, then letting the wet heat of his mouth envelop each in turn. He sighed when she gasped with pleasure. "Lie back, darling," he commanded, pushing her shoulders until she lay prone, her legs still hanging over the edge of the bed. He stood and towered over her with his lean, naked body. He carefully removed her gown, pulling it out from under her, and tossed it aside. Then he unfastened her boots and tugged them off along with her limp stockings. All that was left now was her drawers.

He laid down beside her, gliding his fingertips maddeningly over her breasts, tracing a delicate trail to the tapes fastening her undergarment as if debating whether or not to remove it. He slid one finger provocatively under the edge, then it came free and his whole hand skimmed over her pelvis to the narrow place between her legs.

"Oh, darling, you're ready for me."

Yes, she wanted to scream. *Yes. Take me now.* But she wouldn't. She would do this like a proper lady.

Or as properly as she could manage.

She pulled his head toward hers and gave him a wet, hungry kiss. Urgently, his hand moved to the nest of hair that he'd been craving. He wanted to go slowly, to be respectful to her, and yet he was craven with the desire to fill her. He probed the slippery course. She was more than ready for him.

"I want to please you, Lydia," he whispered in her ear.

"You are," she whimpered. She quivered under his touch and arched against his hand. Just when she reached the point of near-climax, he stopped.

He slid back down until he was kneeling at the edge of the bed. He kissed her navel, his tongue swirling, then tugged her drawers over her hips, down, and off her ankles. This time he did let his hands smooth up to the top of her thighs, where he squeezed hard, eliciting another gasp— one of intense satisfaction.

He admired her pear-shape breasts, her smooth belly, and her dark thatch of curls. Able to wait no longer, he rose and slid into her. She sighed with satisfaction, wrapped her legs around his and kissed him deeply. With delicious slowness, he pulled himself out, then slid back in. Over and over he did this until she was quivering and desperate.

"Please, Hugh!" she begged him.

He smiled with satisfaction, then pulled her hips up off the bed and rammed into her with the fullness of his strength and desire. Hugh made love with his whole body, driving into her not only hard and fast, but with finesse, meeting her in just the right way so she soon exploded. It started where their hips met, but soon spread and pulsed through her entire body, leaving her completely limp and drugged when it was finally over.

He arched and shuddered with his own release, grunting in surprise from the eye-widening force of it. But the night was far from over.

He never left her . . .

Chapter 18

Lydia woke slowly and contentedly. She stretched in her deliciously comfortable bed and savored the warmth of sunshine on her cheeks. She yawned away the last remnants of tension she'd been holding tight for aeons. She never felt so completely at one with herself and the universe as she did after making love to Hugh Montgomery.

She reached over to touch him and felt only an empty place beside her. Her eyes flew open. "Hugh?" She sat up, looking for signs of him. "Hugh?"

She glanced at the window, now feeling betrayed by the sunlight. These were no early morning beams. The light was bright, signaling an hour as late as 9 or even 10 o'clock.

"Goodness, how did I sleep so long?" She threw back the sheet and jumped out of bed, retrieving her robe and fastening it as she hastened into the Renaissance Room. His bed was empty there as well. "Where the devil is he?"

A knock sounded at the double doors. "Your ladyship?" Colette called. "I have a tray for you, ma'am."

"Come in, Colette."

The maid entered, dressed in a black uniform and bearing a warm smile and a tray. "Here you are, ma'am. A hearty breakfast. You'll need it today."

"Why? What has happened?" She watched as Colette put down the tray on the small table by the window in her room. "Where is Lord Montgomery?"

"He's gone, ma'am."

"Gone? Where?"

"He was up early and dressed, feeling fit as a fiddle. It was as if he'd never been ill."

When Colette pulled off the silver dome from her tray of steaming food, Lydia's stomach gurgled and her mouth watered. Lovemaking certainly could create an appetite. Although she didn't want to waste time before pursuing Hugh, she couldn't resist the smell of fresh eggs and ham.

She sipped from a fragrant cup of coffee. "Where did his lordship go?"

"He went to Braemore Lodge, he said. That old gent, Mr. Frances, arrived this morning. They went off in search of clues, they said."

"Why didn't you wake me?" Lydia tried not to talk with her mouth full, but the food was so scrumptious she scarcely took a breath between bites.

"Lord Montgomery said to let you sleep."

Finally, Lydia slowed and tried to see herself through Colette's eyes. How thoroughly decadent and hard-hearted Lydia must seem to so blatantly take a lover scarcely before her husband's body turned cold in the grave. She dabbed her mouth with a napkin and took another sip of coffee.

"Colette," she said.

"Aye, ma'am?" the maid replied as she made the bed.

"Do you think I'm a thorough blighter?"

"What, ma'am?" She stopped her busywork and righted herself. "Whatever do you mean?"

"You know what I mean. Aren't you scandalized that the widow of your longtime employer is . . . well, here with another man?"

Colette smiled sympathetically. "Oh, no, ma'am. Lord Beaumont told me before he died that he hoped you would marry Lord Montgomery, and waste no time doing it."

"He did?"

"Aye. I could tell, ma'am, what sort of marriage you had with the earl. You were very good to him. But a young lady like you must go on. And as far as I can tell, you're fulfilling your husband's dying wish—to find his daughter. Not many a widow would risk the condemnation of society and doff her widow's weeds to dirty her hands seeing that her dead husband's wishes are fulfilled. I know you would have done anything for Lord Beaumont."

Colette's words made her eyes sting with tears. "What have I done to deserve you, my friend?"

"Tush, now, just you eat and regain your strength. Before this is all over, you'll be needing it."

"Thank you, Colette."

Lydia slowly resumed her dining while Colette put out a gown for the day. But now she merely picked at her food. How odd that Beaumont was so sure that Hugh was right for her that he'd even signal to his loyal servants that they should not condemn the arrangement after he was gone. Beau knew about her past. He knew that Hugh came from one of the most upstanding families in Britain. The scion of that family could not marry one of Miss Ella Fenniwig's former *girls*. The press would jump on the story like flies on a corpse. Lydia wished she could ask Beaumont precisely how he thought she could get away with it. Did he know something she didn't?

Well, that didn't matter now. She had to hurry to catch up with Hugh and Mr. Frances. It galled her that he would continue the investigation without her. She had exhausted herself taking care of him, and now that he was well he'd left her behind. He meant no harm by it. He was simply eager to find clues he was convinced that ultimately only he could find. The arrogance of the man! As she thought it, she smiled in that dangerously delirious way peculiar to those in love.

L ydia chose to ride on horseback to the lodge. It was much quicker than taking a carriage, and she wanted the exercise. The butler arranged for one of the groomsmen to lead the way. He led them to the lodge's stable and chatted with the man in charge while Lydia approached the great hall. She slowed when she saw a note had been pinned to the door.

"Oh, don't tell me Hugh has left already. Blast the man! Can't he ever sit still for more than a few minutes?"

She stopped when she reached the door. Her mind at first didn't want to register the chilling reality. This wasn't just any note. It was written in the tree alphabet. And it hadn't been nailed to the door. It had been pinned, along with a dried, dead butterfly.

"Oh, heavens," Lydia hissed, taking a step back. Knowing that the note had been left by Trevor Dobson sent goose bumps racing over arms. Was he still here?

Trying to look calm and collected, she slowly turned, scanning the surrounding greenery with sharp eyes. But there was no sign of him. She whirled back around and pounded on the door, taking care not to dislodge the evidence.

"Hugh!" She pounded with her fist again. "Lord Montgomery! Open up! Hurry! Are you there?"

The door swung open. Hugh looked at her in surprise, a wrinkle of impatience on his brow. "What's the matter, Lydie? Is the keep on fire?"

"Look!" She pointed to the note that still clung to the now open door.

"Good God!" Hugh shouted with uncharacteristic lack of composure. "He was here, Frances! We didn't even hear him."

The plump and tweed ensconced former teacher appeared at his side. "Why, look at that! And it's written in the tree alphabet. This will be a challenge!"

He sounded more excited than worried about the prospects of translating the note. There was a cluster of papers pinned together.

"You have your work cut out for you," Lydia said.

"I'll unpack my bag of books," Frances said, scuttling back into the hall. "I have everything I need."

Lydia took advantage of their privacy to give Hugh a sly, superior look. "No, Montgomery, the keep isn't on fire. But I'm glad I sounded the alarm, or you might have overlooked this obviously very important clue. Funny that you did not see it without me."

He broke into an unabashed grin. "Don't be mad, Lydie. I wanted you to catch up on your sleep. You worked too hard caring for me." He gripped her arms and kissed her cheek. "Did you sleep well?"

She nearly melted in his arms. "Too well. Now let's get busy. We have only three days to save poor Sophie."

"You're right," he said grimly, turning to the door and carefully unfastening what turned out to be a broken hat pin. Then he slipped the attached notes from it. He handed her the still-impaled butterfly. "Hold this."

She did so gingerly and glanced over his arm as he shuffled the papers. "What else is there?"

"There also appears to be some sort of map. And another note sent in Sophie's handwriting. I knew he'd send us more evidence that she's alive. And there's another letter in a very different sort of code. I hope Mr. Frances can help us. Let's go in and have a look."

They went into the great hall and joined Thurber Frances, who was spreading out his books on the long dining table. Hugh went to the other end and put out each missive with great care.

"Here you are, Frances. More than enough to keep you busy."

"What does the note from Sophie say?" Lydia asked, close on his heels.

"Here it is," he said, bending over so as not to miss a single word.

Dear Lord Clue,

I cannot tell you how relieved I was to hear from Dr. Keeley that you are searching for me. I wish I could tell you where I am, but even if I knew and told you, I'm certain this letter would not be delivered.

However, I want to assure you I am still alive and healthy. Do not give up on me. I desperately await your arrival.

Miss Sophie Parnham

Hugh read the letter aloud, then fell into gloomy silence. Lydia crossed her arms. "Who is this Dr. Keeley?"

"He is the local physician," Hugh said in a low, angry voice. "The same one who kept me from coming after you."

Lydia looked up at him in horror. "He was allowed to continue practicing medicine after what he did to you?"

He chuckled cynically. "Oh, yes. He was greatly rewarded by my father. Although, the earl might have second thoughts now if he finds out that the good doctor has stooped to treating kidnap victims. He must have been bought by Dobson. Keeley is beyond conscience now. I'm not surprised. He's an opium eater whose only concern is feeding his addiction. I only pray he has not fed the drug to Sophie."

"Now this is interesting," Frances muttered to himself as he poured over the other missives.

"What?" Hugh was at his side in an instant.

"Do you know what this is?" He pointed to the letter

with the other code. It appeared to be a series of dashes in varying clusters, as if someone had grouped twigs together in parallel formations—in twos, threes, fives, and fours.

"No, Mr. Frances. If I knew I wouldn't have sent for you."

"This is the Ogham, another way in which the druids communicated. There is no alphabet as we know it. But each group of markings represents a letter. I'll get to work on it presently."

Hugh went to the fireplace and lit two more candles, adding them to those already burning on the table. Although the shutters had been thrown open to let in air and sunshine, the rafters above cast long shadows. Hugh sat down near one of the candles and pulled the remaining item forward.

"It's a map," he said.

Lydia pulled up a chair beside him. "What of?"

"I cannot tell. It's a small area. There is no perspective. No indication of north or south. Frances, look at this, will you? Does this look like anything to you?"

"Let me see." Frances joined them and frowned at the crude ink map, adjusting his glasses from one end of his nose to the other and back again. "Uh-huh. Uh-huh. Ah-ha."

"*What?*" Lydia was at the edge of her seat.

"Huh?" Frances looked up with a start.

"What is it? It sounded as if you recognized something."

"Well, of course I do." He smiled benignly.

"What, Frances?" Hugh said with admirable patience. "What did you recognize."

"Well, of course it's a Celtic burial ground."

Lydia swallowed thickly. "I see."

"It probably dates back to the third century," Frances continued, pointing to the map. "You see, here you have the circle temple, which doubtless consisted of little more than an earthen embankment or natural stonework of some sort. The circular temple was quite common. These dots scattered about—there are four of them, it would appear—indicates votive shafts."

"What were they used for?" Lydia prodded when he began to make more thinking noises.

"What? Oh, it's unclear what they were used for, actually. But archaeologists who've excavated these shafts have found some to be as deep as twenty-five feet. One was even found to be one hundred and twenty feet deep and eight feet in diameter. They're often filled with pottery, logs, and various debris, as well as human and animal bones. It's believed these shafts were considered to be old-fashioned telegraphs."

"What?" Hugh said with an incredulous look.

"They offered a way for the ancient Celts to communicate with underworld deities. And of course, sacrificial offerings were one way of speaking to the underworld."

Lydia pointed to three rectangles that dominated the map. "What about these?"

"Those doubtless represent the actual burial pits themselves."

"I hope it doesn't mean that Sophie is dead." Lydia bit her thumb, her eyes never leaving the map. "Would that awful man have buried her there?"

"No." Hugh placed a large, strong hand on her shoulder. "Don't worry, Lady Beaumont, that is not what any of this is about. And I'm sorry to disagree with you, Mr. Frances, but these aren't burial pits."

Lydia looked up to find him turning her way with a look of long-awaited triumph gleaming in his eyes. "What is it, Hugh?"

"These are the standing stones." He jabbed the map with a forefinger. "These are the stones we saw! At last! Here is proof. By God, they all thought we were mad. I knew they were here. You see, Mr. Frances, Lady Beaumont and I stumbled on three megalithic stones some years ago, and we could never find them again. But they were in the middle of a circular ritual site, just like this. That's why Dobson sent this to us. He's taunting us. He's telling us that he knows we discovered the stones, but he still won't tell us where they are."

Thurber Frances wandered back to his Ogham translations. "It's impossible to tell, of course, until you find out where the map is placed in the grand scheme of things. Right now I want to get back to this letter. I suspect it will hold vital information, perhaps even pertaining to that map."

Hugh leaned back and put his elbows on the arms of his chair, interlocking his hands. "This is it, Lydia. Three rectangles representing three megalithic stones dating back centuries. I'm going to send the groom back to Windhaven and have Pierpont wire my father. He must come. He cannot imply that I am mad any longer."

"Don't call on him," she pleaded. "It doesn't matter what he thinks."

He reached and grabbed one of her hands. "I will abide by your wishes. But consider this—he has stored away, in Lord knows what drawer or attic, the surveys of his entire estate, some of which date back hundreds of years. I know they exist, but I don't know where. This map here is the only proof I need to enlist his serious support in this investigation. Unlike London detectives, the earl could come to help us without raising Dobson's concern. I know you do not want to see him, my darling, but we might not be able to find Sophie without being able to put this map in perspective."

"But we know where it is! We were there. We simply don't know how to get into the circle again. How frustrating! It's as if that cave opening disappeared."

"If this drawing exists, I can almost guarantee another one exists that will show us the entrance. If anyone has such a map, it would be the earl. He might not even be aware he possesses such a treasure. These documents have more historic value than anything else. What do you say?"

She thought of Sophie writing that note, hoping against hope that the infamous Lord Clue would rescue her. She nodded slowly. "Very well. We cannot turn down any help. Wire him at once."

"That's my girl. We'll face him together, darling. I promise."

Lydia tried to feel soothed by his words, but she did not succeed.

They tried not to hover over Thurber Frances while he finished translating the Ogham document, but it was difficult. It took him an hour. When he was finally finished, he looked up as if he were in a fog.

"Well, it's done."

Hugh and Lydia returned to his side and read what he had jotted:

Lord Clue,

Let the game begin. Three days. She is now ready for Beltaine. She will be waiting for you in the belly of the cauldron. She has food, water, and candles to last three days. Kill me and she will die of starvation—unless you are smarter than I think and find her first.

You know who

"The belly of the cauldron," Lydia said. "Would that be Cerridwen's cauldron of transformation and rebirth, as you mentioned in your book, Mr. Frances?"

"Dobson is not referring to the goddess's cauldron," Hugh answered for him. "He's talking about the cave we found. It's pitch black, like a witches cauldron. It's round. And never forget, that before rebirth, there must come death. We simply must find it."

A re you ready, Cerridwen?" came the deep voice of Sophie's kidnapper.

He held her close to his body. She didn't know where she was because she was blindfolded. All she knew was that they stood at some point in nature where a fantastic breeze whirled around them. She savored the touch of the sun on her cheeks. She was afraid she'd never feel that again.

"Do you know where you are, my darling goddess?" he whispered in her ear. His old man's belly pressed against her, not fat, but flaccid. Much lower he was quite firm. His hot breath spread over her ear. She could feel his lust now like a sword of Damocles hanging over her head. It would drop soon, and it would kill her.

"He's not coming for me, is he?" she said, her voice devoid of emotion.

"Who, my darling Cerridwen? Who is not coming? Your consort? Your God? Your co-Creator of the universe?"

"Lord Clue," she whispered.

He laughed. She felt it more than she heard the rasping sound. "No, he's not coming. He thinks he is, but he's not clever enough to find you. I've always been smarter than he is. He always thought he was better than me. But he was wrong."

For the first time in days Sophie began to weep. Her body convulsed, but no sound would come. There was no point.

"Don't cry, Cerridwen. Our wedding day is coming. Say! You haven't answered me. Do you know where we are?"

He fumbled at her hair and then pulled away the blindfold. He quickly put his hand at the back of her neck to keep her from turning around and seeing him. "Look! You're at the cliffs, my love."

She blinked against the light, and in spite of her desperate circumstances, joy leaped in her heart. She could see the sun, the bright, blinding sun. "It's beautiful."

"I knew you'd like it. Now look down."

She did and gasped. She stood only inches from an enormous drop-off. She could see treetops far below. Imagining herself free-falling toward them made her queasy. She tried to push back, but he stood his ground.

"Are you afraid, my beloved? You should be. This is the place where the imposter died."

"What imposter?"

"The other girl who pretended to be you."

"There was another?"

"Yes. Many others." He let his hand rub intimately over her belly. She nearly retched. "But they were all liars. They cried out in pain when I broke the virgin's gate. The real Cerridwen would cry out in ecstasy. I know you will, my love, because I know you are the true and only goddess of creation."

"No," she protested, beginning to cry in earnest. "No, no, no!"

"Come along, my dear. It's time for you to purify yourself." He half-dragged her to the middle of the semi-circle that surrounded them.

She saw three enormous stones. They were so tall and wide they blocked out the sun's rays as they passed.

"These are the three ladies I told you about. One represents you in the spring, one is you in the summer, and one is you in the winter. But don't fear. You will never be the old crone, the old hag that she is. When you and I make love, we will both be immortal."

When she realized he was heading for the entrance to the dark cave in which she'd spent the morning imprisoned alone, she tried to dig her heels into the ground. "No, no more darkness. I want to see the sun!"

He ignored her pleas and yanked her into the blackest black she had ever seen. It was cool, and she could hear water dripping. After following a convoluted path, she saw the light of the torch he'd left earlier. It burned and hissed, offering blessed light. But it would not burn forever, and she would once again be left in darkness.

He pulled a box from around the corner. "Here is cheese and bread. Water, too. I'll put it in reach. And here are enough candles to burn for three days. If you're smart, you won't let the flame go out."

He forced her to sit against the stone wall, then he shackled her to chains driven into the stone, as he had earlier in the day. At last she looked up and saw his face in full light. It was not terribly remarkable. He was a fine elderly gentleman, though there was a mad look in his eyes, and his silver hair fell in an unruly mass over his forehead. He smoothed it back as he caught his breath.

"Who are you?" she whispered, truly curious.

"You may call me Trevor."

She shut her eyes, realizing that he had just given the first indication that she would not live. Otherwise, he would not have told her his name.

What is this all about?" Boxley snapped as he marched into the library.

Hugh and Lydia were having coffee in lieu of late tea at the Chippendale table beneath a portrait of the third earl. He looked to have been an amiable fellow with a paunch and a penchant for King Charles Spaniels. Lydia looked up when the sixth earl made his arrogant entrance and was almost too tired to feel nervous about seeing him again.

With the map in hand, she and Hugh had exhaustively searched Devil's Peak all afternoon, looking for an entrance to the cave, but to no avail. They'd returned just in time to change clothes and snatch a bite to eat before the earl arrived unexpectedly early. He explained that he had already been on his way to Windhaven.

"We're glad it worked out this way," Hugh said, giving him a conciliatory handshake. "Won't you join us for coffee?"

Boxley was dressed in a gray tweed suit. He put some papers down on his desk and joined them at the table. When Lydia rose, so did her heart, stopping at the base of her throat, it seemed. She could scarcely breathe. Facing this man was like stripping naked in front of a row of courtroom judges. She had never felt so condemned by anyone before. She had never been hated by anyone before this man, and all because of the circumstances of her birth.

"Lady Beaumont," Hugh said, "I'd like to introduce you to my father, Charles, Earl of Boxley. Sir, this is Lydia, Countess of Beaumont."

The earl's keen gray eyes focused on her for a full second before he said, "It is a pleasure, madam. I am sorry for your loss."

She swallowed hard. "Thank you." She could not tell whether he had recognized her. *It's me,* she wanted to shout. *Me. Addie Parker. The woman you destroyed. And I survived in spite of you!*

"Thank you for coming," Hugh said.

"As I mentioned, I was on my way already," he replied with his usual air of refinement and ingrained snobbery. "What was so urgent?"

"I'll explain. Coffee?"

"Yes."

Hugh poured him a cup and refilled his own. Lydia retrieved her cup and saucer.

"Shall we?" Hugh led them over to a grouping of furniture on the rich red rug. The men sank down into brown leather chairs while Lydia sat erect on the edge of the divan. "As you know, sir, I am searching for Lady Beaumont's stepdaughter."

"No luck?" The earl was shorter than his son and stockier, but still fit for a man his age and good-looking in spite of the pouches beneath his eyes. He was humorless and lent an air of sobriety to every occasion. Hugh had never heard his father crack a joke in his life. "I'm sorry to hear it."

"We now know it is Sir Trevor who has her. And we know that he's keeping her in the cave near the standing stones."

When the earl's cheeks puffed with a patronizing smile, Lydia gripped the handle of her cup firmly, willing herself to remain cool.

"Haven't we been over this before, son?"

"Yes." Hugh smiled confidently. "Unfortunately, at the time I did not have proof. Therefore, you doubted me. Now I have this. Dobson gave it to me as a clue."

When Hugh procured the small map from inside his waistcoat, the earl examined it from several angles.

"This proves nothing," he said at last. "It could have come from anywhere."

"That's why I need you to dig out the surveys and maps of the estate. I believe we will find that this is a piece of a larger puzzle."

The earl gave him back the map and picked up his cup and saucer from the coffee table at their feet. He sipped thoughtfully, then turned to Lydia. "What do you think, Lady Beaumont? Are you, too, convinced that your step-daughter is being imprisoned by Trevor Dobson?"

"Most assuredly." She met his eyes. His were intense. She was sure that any moment they would widen in recognition. Her heart beat faster. The suspense was killing her. "He has admitted it in writing, sir. I would be most grateful if you would assist us in this matter."

He nodded. "Very well. I have my doubts, as you well know, Montgomery. But I will do whatever I can to help find this poor girl. I will contact my land agent tonight. I'll go through the old documents as soon as I am able." Boxley sighed heavily and leaned back. "If you are right and Dobson has done this horrible thing, why do you suppose he has done it?"

Hugh said, "I believe he might have murdered a number of young girls—all virgins—as part of some sort of base pagan sexual ritual."

"Good lord!"

"I know it sounds far-fetched. In this instance, I believe he wants to match his wits against mine. It might have something to do with the fact that you are legitimate and he is not."

"Yes, that's a burden," Boxley said not without sympathy. "I won't believe it, though, until I see proof. I trust you've called in the appropriate authorities."

"No. We have to do this alone or Dobson will kill her. That's why I . . . need your help."

The earl had the good grace not to gloat over this admission.

"Monty, I want to say something . . . ." His voice trailed off, and he exhaled a quick, strained breath of air. "This is very difficult for me. I want to say to you and Lady Beaumont that I am so very sorry."

When he looked at her with a naked expression of remorse, her heart skipped a beat. She'd never before seen emotion of any kind in his mask of a face.

"Thank you, sir," she said, "but I am sure we will find Sophie."

He shook his head sharply. "No, that's not what I mean. I am sorry that I sent you away. Five years ago."

So he did recognize her. The anxiety boiling in her belly burst into flames that scorched their way up her throat. She couldn't speak. It hurt too much.

"I was wrong. Very, very wrong. I hurt you and Montgomery. And all for pride. I hope one day you will be able to forgive me."

Her heart lightened at this, but her mind could not accept these words. Old hurts fed new doubts. Was he sincere? "I hope so, too," she said simply and carefully studied the flower pattern on her cup.

From the corner of her eye, she saw father and son exchange a significant look. Was this the first step toward reconciliation? Perhaps Hugh was right about his father—he wasn't evil, simply misguided. Either way, was she magnanimous enough to accept this olive branch?

Chapter 19

Lydia was too exhausted to worry much over the earl or anyone else. Earlier in the day Colette had moved her belongings to the Peking wing of the house. She chose it because it was far from the master's quarters and, thereby, as far from the earl as she could get. It would take time for her to digest what he had said to her.

The room's chinoiserie décor was luxurious in the extreme, but the turquoise and imperial red bedspread and curtains adorned with silver and gold embroidered Chinese dragons scarcely registered in her overwrought mind. She collapsed into the ornate four-poster bed, almost as physically exhausted as mentally.

It seemed as if she and Hugh had walked every square inch of the cliffs that bordered the Boxley property. Her feet ached, and her legs were sore. She wanted to get plenty of sleep, for they would leave at dawn to return to the lodge for the next clue. She hoped the earl would be able to help them. And she hoped Sophie had not given up hope. The poor darling. Imprisoned in a cave.

I'll find you, my dear girl. I promise.

As she fell asleep, she realized that rescuing Sophie meant as much to her as it had to her husband. Somehow she sensed that if she could save Sophie, she could save herself. Maybe then there would be a bright future for all of them. But her troubled dreams made that appear a distant hope.

Just before Hugh began to undress in the quarters, he was interrupted by a knock on the door. Pierpont informed him that Reggie waited in the main drawing room with urgent news. Hugh hurried to find that Trevor Dobson had returned to Tremaine Way late that afternoon. Reggie had very adeptly acquired a network of local spies—heretofore upstanding if humble members of the community who had somehow fallen under his boyishly charming spell. At least that's how he explained it to Hugh. More likely the clever lad had bribed Dobson's servants. Either way, he had done his job well.

At 11 o'clock that night, Hugh called for a carriage, then traveled to Dobson's cottage with Reggie. He didn't want to disturb Lydia, who was clearly exhausted, nor did he want to endanger her. He could only conclude that Dobson had returned in broad daylight because he was ready for some sort of confrontation. Perhaps he wanted to personally deliver the next clue. If this assumption was erroneous, however, their meeting might turn ugly, or even violent. In any event, he owed it to Sophie to approach her captor. Just because he had agreed to play the game by Dobson's rules did not mean he could not try to reshuffle the deck, and carry a small pistol hidden in his coat.

Hugh and Reggie were greeted at the door by the butler. Although he didn't act surprised by the late-night visit, he nevertheless said that the master of the house was not receiving guests at this hour. He was immediately contradicted, however, by none other than Sir Trevor himself. He staggered into the entry hall waving a gun.

"Well, if it isn't Viscount Montgomery," he said boisterously, then broke into staccato laughter. "Welcome! Welcome!"

When he waved the gun, motioning them in his direction, Reggie stiffened.

"Do you want to leave?" Hugh asked sotto voce.

"Not if you're staying, sir," he whispered in reply.

"And that would be young Reginald Shane, wouldn't it?" Dobson said, slurring his words. He was clearly foxed. "I recognize that young man from my club." He gave Reggie a lascivious smirk. "You're welcome, too, Shane. Come have a drink."

"Don't mind if we do," Hugh said, handing his hat and cane to the beleaguered butler. "Come along, Reggie."

They followed Dobson's staggering lead down the hallway to his private study. The walls and ceilings were timber and plaster, and rows of dark bookcases filled the room. It was a charming place filled with antiques. The bright floral Victorian furniture made it seem oddly incongruous for a madman such as this to inhabit.

"Make yourself comfortable," Dobson said, then nearly tripped over an ottoman. He grabbed for his desk to catch his fall. "Whoa! I didn't see that. Shane, get the great Lord Clue a drink, will you? Be a good lad." He pointed vaguely toward a small oak table in one corner upon which sat a number of bottles. Several were empty. Trevor had apparently been tippling for some time.

Reggie followed the instructions, his watchful gaze never leaving Dobson for long. Hugh was touched by Reggie's sense of duty and his urge to protect. Hugh was also mindful of Dobson's every move, especially the ones involving his gun. Dobson dropped it on his desk with a thud and stumbled back into his chair.

"There. That's better."

While Hugh waited for his drink to be delivered, he

studied Dobson carefully. Now the likeness to his father seemed blatantly obvious. They both had a generous head of classic silver-gray hair. Both had mustaches and the same aristocratic nose. But Dobson's eyes were a warm hazel, where Boxley's were cool gray. And Dobson had always possessed an easier personality. He appeared to be a likeable fellow, whereas the best one could hope to feel for Lord Boxley was respect. Hugh had been blind all his life. How often one sees only what is expected or desired, while the truth is patently ignored.

At last Reggie delivered a brandy and water. Hugh took a small sip, more to please Dobson than to relax. Relaxing was the last thing he could afford to do now. He had not expected to find Dobson drunk. It didn't fit in with the game. It was the first thing that gave Hugh hope the plot might be unraveling. Why would Dobson risk his meticulously masterminded plot by getting drunk?

"Where is she, Sir Trevor?" he said calmly, as if asking about the weather.

Dobson produced a slow, deep frown. "Who?"

"Sophie Parnham."

"Oh, right."

"You've made it clear she's here. Now I need to find her."

"So you're not as great a detective as you would have the world believe."

"I don't give a bloody damn what the world thinks. I just try to solve crimes. And as you well know, this one is particularly near and dear to my heart. I can solve it now if you'll simply tell me where she is."

Dobson leaned forward and put his elbows on the desk. He covered his face with his hands. "I've been wanting to talk to you for a long time. You found her. You knew. You knew something was wrong and someone was to blame."

Hugh exchanged a baffled look with Reggie, then said, "I haven't found Sophie, Sir Trevor. That's the problem. I can't find the cave entrance. If you'd just show me—"

"You found her at the bottom of the cliffs. The milk-maid." He lowered his hands and slumped back against his chair. "It was an accident."

Hugh tried to remain calm, but he sensed he was about to get the confession he had wanted to hear all his life—some accounting of why a poor, innocent, humble girl had died prematurely without explanation, without justice.

"You're saying that she fell over the cliff? She wasn't pushed?" Hugh prodded.

"It was my fault," Dobson whined in drunken remorse. "I admit that. I tupped her, and I shouldn't have. Then she scrambled away from me and ran right over the edge of the cliff. It was dark. She didn't know there was a drop-off. Or she didn't care. You have to believe me—it was an accident."

"Some accident," Hugh said. "Things like that always happen when you kidnap young girls and rape them in a Beltaine ritual. That's what it was, wasn't it, Dobson? A pagan ritual."

Dobson nodded as he struggled with his emotions. "You have to believe me when I say I never intended for her to die."

"How comforting. Especially for her family."

Dobson focused on Hugh with a drunkard's intensity. Then he seemed to sober as hatred bubbled to the fore. "I hate you, do you know that?"

"Yes, I believe the obtuse Lord Clue has been able to figure out at least that much," Montgomery said bitterly.

"I hate you because you're his son. He ruined my life. And I looked up to him for so long. What a fool I was! I just thank God my wife is dead now so she doesn't have to see this."

"See what?" Hugh sat forward. "Look here, Dobson, enough with the histrionics. A girl is terrified, imprisoned in a cave, for God's sake. That's where she is, isn't it? And here you are blubbering about your half-brother. Grow up! Now, where the bloody hell is Sophie Parnham?"

All emotion wiped clean from Dobson's face, as if an

unseen hand had sluiced it from his deeply lined but still handsome features. He looked at Hugh with jolting clarity. "Do you really want to know?"

"Yes!"

He smiled ironically. "Then ask your sister." He reached for the gun.

Reggie flew to his feet, but it was too late. Dobson pointed the barrel at his temple and pulled the trigger.

"No!" Hugh roared, futilely jumping up and lunging to stop him.

As the ear-ringing explosion ricocheted around the small room, Dobson slumped over on his desk, blooding oozing from a small hole in the side of his head.

Reggie ran around the desk to examine the wound. "Oh, Christ have mercy! He's dead. He has to be. Oh, Christ, the blood!"

Hugh stood a moment in stunned silence. "But the clues!" he cried out, raising a fist to his forehead. "God almighty, we needed the clues!"

Hugh sank back into his chair, pressing his fisted hands to his pounding head. Without Dobson's clues, Sophie might as well kill herself, too. For they might never find her now. She would starve to death in that cave.

Sophie hugged herself tight in her blanket, trying to ward off the cave's pervasive chill and damp air. She was exhausted and so longed to sleep the night through. But she couldn't. She had to keep the flame burning. She had plenty of candles, but no matches. If she let her candle burn out, there would be no way to light the others. Then she would be condemned to utter and total darkness. She couldn't bear that. Then she would surely lose her mind.

Already she had endured so much. Why? Why was God punishing her like this? She had done her best to be a good girl, a good worker at the theater. She had kept to herself, spurning the attention of the lecherous actors at Louise's theater. But still, she must have done something very wrong to deserve this.

Sophie was now convinced her captor was going to kill her. He was utterly mad. Whatever he planned to do to her, he would not want her to speak about it afterward. He would doubtless have a reputation to keep. All gentlemen did. She would be expendable. He probably wouldn't even feel remorse.

She laid her head down on the crook of her arm and watched the yellow flame burn. In the absence of noise, she could hear it eating the air. Fire was fascinating. Reassuring. Hypnotizing. She watched, her eyes growing heavy. She could not sleep. Could not sleep. Could not.

Hugh burst through the front door of Windhaven shouting orders. He handed his cane and hat to the butler, who had been waiting for his return, then took the grand staircase two steps at a time, with Reggie close on his heels.

"Wake up the earl!" he shouted. "Send for Lady Beaumont. Tell her to dress and meet me in the parlor. Pierpont!"

"Yes?" Pierpont had been waiting in the parlor on the upper level and hurried into the hall. "What is it?"

"I need you to go immediately to fetch the constable."

"What has happened, sir?"

Hugh pushed past him and went directly to the sideboard. The parlor was a cozier, more feminine version of the downstairs drawing room. This was where Hugh's mother used to sit with her friends and do her needlework. It was where Katherine used to play the piano for the earl, and where Hugh used to recite poetry for his parents. It held fond memories but had been mostly empty since Katherine's death. Hugh poured two neat glasses of brandy and handed one to Reggie.

"Here, old chap. Drink up."

Reggie looked momentarily nonplused that the viscount was offering him a drink in formal circumstances. Reggie would be just as happy to have a nip of gin below stairs with the servants. But before he could humbly decline, his hand reached out and he tossed back the liquor.

"There's a good lad." Hugh followed suit. The liquor burned deliciously down to his belly. It helped erase the horrible image of blood flowing from Dobson's head. He looked at Pierpont, who stood practically on the tips of his toes, waiting to hear what had happened. "Dobson is dead," he said without preamble.

"Dead!"

"That's right, Mr. Pierpont," Reggie said, wiping his mouth on his sleeve. "Killed himself right in front of our eyes. Never seen anything like it, I haven't. Don't want to again, either."

"He shot himself," Hugh said and shook his head disbelievingly. "Now we have no one to show us where the cave entrance is. We're on our own."

"Why did he kill himself? I don't understand," Pierpont said. He sank down into a chair. "This is frightful."

"I believe he did it because his conscience caught up with him," Hugh replied. "He admitted killing the milk-maid, though he said it was an accident. That's what he seemed most interested in talking about. Not Sophie . . ." He appeared lost in thought for a moment, then snapped his attention back to his trusted servant. "Look here, old man, go find Barnabas and report Dobson's death. Tell him the baronet confessed to murder before killing himself and that we searched his office for clues about Sophie but found nothing."

Just then the earl appeared wearing a robe. His lips were thinned and he scowled. "What's the meaning of this, Montgomery?"

Lydia came in a moment later. She had managed to jump into a plain black day dress, but her hair lay in unruly curls surrounding her face. A small cap hid the back of her head. Hugh held her gaze a moment and realized how difficult it would be to tell her the bad news. He so wanted to be her hero and rescue Sophie. Now that task would be much harder.

"Go on, Pierpont," Hugh said. "Quickly now." When Pierpont exited, Reggie followed discreetly, leaving the viscount, the earl, and the countess to their privacy.

"I just returned from Sir Trevor's cottage," Hugh said, smoothing a hand over his tousled hair as he searched for delicate words. None would come to mind. "Dobson is dead."

"What?!" the earl thundered.

"Oh, no!" Lydia said, sinking onto a chair.

"He killed himself in front of my own eyes."

"How? Why?" Lydia asked.

He turned her way. "Don't worry, Lady Beaumont. This is a terrible setback. It means no one knows where the cave entrance is to be found. But it also means that we don't have to play his game anymore. He won't be able to move her or change the rules."

He faced his father, who had turned ashen. "I went to see Dobson tonight, sir. He was drunk and waving a gun. I told him I knew he had Sophie Parnham."

"Did he admit it?" the earl said in a low, gravelly voice.

"Not in so many words. But he didn't deny it. He did admit killing the milkmaid I found at the bottom of the cliffs. And I know the two cases are connected."

The earl shut his eyes and shook his head. "My God, you were right. I had no idea he was so . . . so unstable. Did he say why he did it?"

"It was part of the pagan ritual I told you about—the Beltaine fires. The ritual rape. He had many perversions. His London club was just one of them."

Boxley raised a brow as he regarded his son. "It would appear I have failed you in yet another matter, Montgomery. I should have believed you when you said that girl was murdered. Well, I can't rectify the past, but perhaps we can prevent another tragedy. Let's go to my study and take another look at the surveys and maps."

"We should call in Scotland Yard," Lydia said. "Prepare a telegram and send Reggie with it."

"I suppose we can now that Dobson is dead." He looked at Boxley. "Sir Trevor said he would kill Sophie if I brought in the authorities."

"Are you sure you want to do that now?" his father said. "What if Dobson was working with an accomplice? You said he conducted pagan rituals. Did he do it alone?"

"He probably had some of his perverse friends involved—the ones from the Diamond Forest."

"What if one of them is keeping watch over Miss Parnham? If he finds out that you broke this edict about the authorities, she might still be in danger."

Hugh looked to Lydia. She clearly did not trust the earl, and yet she was obviously stymied by his logic. "Lady Beaumont, he has a good point. We could use help, but I don't want to put Sophie at risk."

"Why don't we have a closer look at the maps?" the earl suggested. "You might see something I haven't. Bring down that professor friend of yours."

"Mr. Frances," Lydia offered. "Yes, he might be able to help." Her voice did not hold conviction.

"Let's start now. I don't think we can afford to wait another moment," Hugh said grimly.

They roused Mr. Frances and examined maps for the next hour and a half. Although he found evidence of possible pagan burial grounds and ritual sites, none of them correlated specifically to the area where Hugh and Lydia had stumbled onto the cave and circle temple. It was obvious that the site was the only remaining ritual ground still being used. So why didn't the maps show the location? Had they been tampered with?

The earl called it a night by suggesting that they get some rest and travel to the cliffs area at first light, which was only a few hours away.

Lydia did not want to disturb Colette, so she laid back on the bed without undressing. Her gown was loose and flowing and, owing to her haste in dressing, she wore nothing beneath it. She could sleep in relative comfort. Pulling off her cap, she sank onto the pillow. Her hair was growing quickly, and little curls framed her face. She ran her hands through them, liking the feel of her hair when it wasn't drenched in oil, wishing Hugh were here to feel it as well.

No sooner did she think it than the door cracked open. She saw a shadow and held her breath.

"Lydie?" he called. His voice was uncertain.

She propped herself on her elbows. "Come in," she replied in a hushed whisper as per pulse raced.

He shut the door quietly behind him. Her skin tingled all over at the sight of his tall figure cloaked in darkness. "I can't get enough of you," she said, urging him to approach and sit on the edge of her bed. He did so, and she could see him through the thin shaft of silvery light emanating from a nearby window.

She took hold of his wrist as he reached up to cup her face in his hand.

"You know I've never been afraid before during an investigation."

"But you are now." She simply knew it, just as she knew him. And loved him.

He nodded. "Yes."

"Are we making a mistake doing this on our own? Should we have sent for detectives?"

He sighed heavily. "I don't know. I just feel that I must be the one to solve the mystery here. Boxley was right to be cautious, though."

"Why is he helping us, Hugh?"

"Probably because he doesn't want to be embarrassed by his half-brother's crimes."

"I always wanted you to hate him as much as I did."

"And I did."

"But you don't now."

"Frankly, my love, I have no feelings for him at all." His hand curved around the nape of her neck and pulled her toward him. He bent and pressed his lips to hers. Then he raised his head. "The only feelings I have left are for you. I love you. I love you, my darling Lydia. You are my strength, my inspiration."

He hesitated for a moment, and she arched toward him, giving him permission. His other hand glided down her body, feeling her bare skin beneath the gown. He let out a growl and was rewarded with a small gasp of pleasure from her as he gently cupped her breast. His thumb rubbed the pearly bud of her nipple.

"We need to sleep," she said, even as her hands roamed up his arms and gripped his shoulders, pulling him closer, arching against his firm chest.

"I need you," he said in a rough voice that sent a shiver down her spine. "Move over."

She obeyed, and he laid down beside her, fully clothed. He tucked his arm under her shoulder and leaned on his elbow while his other hand skimmed lightly over her.

"You're my life's breath, Lydia," he murmured desperately.

She was aware of every place his hand went. Her body unconsciously strained to meet him. She loved this man. She trusted him. She wanted him. Her breath hitched every time he touched a tender place. Soon she was breathing hard.

At that moment he let his hand swerve downward and Lydia shivered, gripping the sheets in her fists.

He reached down and pulled up her gown until he could touch her skin. She inhaled his hot breath, cherished the intimacy and offered her lips in a deep, luscious kiss. His hand seemed to vibrate as he returned to that place of ultimate pleasure. Lydia quivered and inhaled a gasping breath. This time there was no material to keep him from her dark, wet depths. He felt until he found what he wanted. What she wanted, too.

"Oh, Hugh . . ." Lydia bit her lower lip and gripped him close. That the one person she loved best in all the world could give her so much pleasure seemed like a miracle.

"Come for me, Lydia," he rasped against her ear. And she did.

She groaned and undulated in a tidal wave of ecstasy that had been building far out at sea. And that was just the first wave. When she could take no more of his skillful massage, she sank back in luxurious surrender.

He bent down and kissed her, a quick peck. Then his lips touched hers again, and his tongue delved deeply into her mouth, claiming her with heat and determined sexuality. Lydia wanted to be claimed and to claim him as well. Could that be done when he didn't know her?

She needed for him to know everything about her. And what she could not tell him—not without losing him—she would show him. For if she could not live happily ever after with the man she loved, she at least wanted to be known—fully known—by him. How sad to live a life without ever experiencing that.

When he pulled away, not sated, but momentarily satisfied by the kiss, he whispered, "Oh, my angel."

She smoothed her hands over his forehead and played with this thick hair. "I might be an angel, but I'm not the kind you think I am."

Like the fallen angel she was, she deftly unfastened his trousers. His whole body tensed. As he watched in stunned amazement, she lowered his garment to his knees. She returned to his side and caressed his staff—it was velvet over steel. Then she lowered her head and took him in her mouth. He stiffened all over and sucked in a hissing breath.

"No, Lydia, God—no, you can't." He pushed at her shoulders, but she refused to be put off. He sank back, surrendering to the ecstasy.

"Who taught you to make love like this?" he gasped at last.

She raised her head, caressing him with her hand as she replied, "You taught me to love."

"No," he whispered, "not like this . . ."

"Are you accusing me of something, Hugh?" A tremor of alarm touched her, yet she did not relinquish her hold on him. *Why don't I just tell him the truth?*

"How could I accuse you?" He groaned again as she tightened her grip around him. "You're my perfect angel."

Angel.

Guilt seared her. Yes, Adelaide Parker had been an angel, all right—a fallen angel. She didn't want him to know she had bedded, much less enjoyed, others. It was her secret. Her shame. Instead, she resumed her ministrations.

"Oh, Lydie . . . you don't have to do this."

Ignoring his perfunctory protestations, she worked slowly, with utmost love and skill. She led him right up to the moment of no return, pausing to look up at him, savoring the incredulity, the shock, and the adoration that mingled in his face. She wanted this to be a moment he would never forget.

Hugh trembled and groaned, even growled with the need for release. She felt him ready to explode, felt him lengthen and harden greater than he ever had before.

Supreme satisfaction washed over her as he lifted his head and stared at her with glazed eyes. "You're better than opium," he rasped through gasps for air.

She felt a small surge of triumph. "You're mine, Hugh. All mine. No one else, nothing else matters. Not here. Not tonight."

She rose to her knees and moved forward to straddle him. She guided him inside, then put her hands on his shoulders and sunk slowly down, impaling herself until she'd taken him in entirely.

"My darling," he said hoarsely, cupping her breasts. "You *are* a perfect angel . . . my own angel."

He thrust upward then as she tightened around him. It was her turn to groan and gasp. They made love, rocking as one, until they were wild with need. At the last moment, when neither could stand to wait longer, they rolled over so he could thrust harder and faster. They came together, pleasure sheering them into shreds, until they collapsed in a heap of blissful union.

As they cooled, Lydia realized she was at last content. Hugh now knew everything about her. He knew her unlady-like desire. Whether he would still love her tomorrow, she could not tell. She could not even dare to consider. But they had known each other. That was the best she could hope for.

Chapter 20

At noon the next day, the search party broke for a meal at Braemore Lodge. Pierpont ordered servants to put a picnic lunch on the long table in the great hall while the others greedily consumed water from the well. A half-dozen men in the earl's employ had joined the search through the woods near the cliffs above the lodge. Hugh and his father, along with Lydia, had paid special attention to the rock formations, searching for the cave entrance. Reggie watched after Mr. Frances, who was more intent on looking for archaeological signs of pagan worship than he was on looking for Sophie.

Pierpont had stayed behind at the lodge to act as go-between, in case any of the groups found anything of importance or needed to communicate. He was glad he had, for Todd Leach arrived just before noon. He said he'd wanted to help search because he'd been unable to find out anything beneficial in London. Pierpont told him about

Dobson's suicide and the fear that Sophie would starve if they didn't find her soon.

Hugh was relieved to see Todd. It bolstered his flagging spirits. But nothing could quite settle the uncomfortable feeling gnawing in his belly that warned him he was over-looking something very significant. Tired, hungry, and taut with anxiety he could not identify, he stood by the open door of the great hall while the others eagerly sat down to Pierpont's portable but delicious repast.

"Join us, darling," Lydia whispered as she passed him on her way to the table after washing her hands.

He shook his head and returned his focus to the grounds. The servants ate at an outside table by the stable. It was a glorious spring day. His mind registered that fact—the warm breeze, the sound of birds nurturing their young, the smell of wild flowers—but inside him it felt like winter. He was numb. His senses were cold and slow. What was he missing?

"The gate outside this lodge was obviously part of a gatehouse at one time," Todd said, amiably directing the conversation because everyone else was too tired to talk. "Have you ever seen a medieval castle, Reggie?"

"No, sir," Reggie answered. He sat by himself in a cor-ner, eating with his legs stretched out.

"There used to be great gatehouses that completed the circle created by enormous walls—or curtains—that enclosed castles in the Middle Ages. The porter stood above the entrance in a little stone house, watching as strangers approached. Often they'd have to cross a drawbridge over a moat, and the porter would raise the portcullis if they were deemed friendly. The portcullis looked like a giant iron grate with wicked arrows pointing downward, ready to impale trespassers at a moment's notice. It was connected to a wheel and pulley system, which would raise the patch-work of iron, allowing entrance. Much too heavy to raise by hand. Quite an operation."

Hugh listened half-heartedly. An image of Dobson flashed in his mind.

"Where the bloody hell is Sophie Parnham?"

"Do you really want to know?"

"Yes!"

"Then ask your sister."

Ask your sister. What the devil did he mean by that? Hugh turned slowly and watched Lydia conversing with the others. The subject had turned from medieval castles to the Inquisition. Hugh remembered his conversation with Lydia about Katherine. She seemed surprised that he hadn't yet visited his sister's grave, as well she might be. It was really unconscionable that he hadn't paid his respects. She'd been dead and buried for two years. The only reason he hadn't was because of his own sense of unjust loss. He hadn't wanted to think of her as dead. Ever. And now Dobson had mentioned her.

In fact, it was the last thing he said before he'd killed himself.

The nagging feeling nearly choked him now. He went to the table and snagged an apple. "I'll be back in about an hour," Hugh said.

Todd looked up. "Do you want me to come, old chap?"

"No. I'd like some time alone." He felt as much as saw Lydia's worried expression. He gave her a secret smile of reassurance. *Don't worry. I'll be fine.*

If only it were true.

Hugh grabbed a fresh horse from one of the grooms and took the shortcut up the side of the valley. Then he cantered over the estate road to the site of the old house. It was a gothic monstrosity that had burned to the ground in the early part of the century. All that remained was the blackened chimney and the family graveyard just beyond near a grove of oak trees.

Hugh dismounted a stone's throw from the wrought-iron

fence that surrounded the small cemetery. He tied his horse to a beach tree that rustled sweetly in the breeze. Then he pulled his apple from his saddlebag and bit into it with great care. It seemed the most important thing in the world, far more significant than the emotions roiling inside him. He was vaguely aware that he was starving, and even more aware that he now faced the difficult good-bye he'd been avoiding for so long.

When he finished the apple, he dabbed the corners of his mouth and pitched the core into the bracken and wildflowers that dotted the ground in the shade of the tree. Then he took a bracing breath and headed for the graveyard.

He found his mother's headstone immediately. He had placed flowers there often. He knelt in front of it, and an image of her bright and lovely face filled his mind.

"Help me, Mother. If you live beyond the grave, help me find this poor girl." His gaze wandered to the smaller headstone sitting next to the countess's. "Katherine Elizabeth Montgomery."

Still exhausted from the search and lack of sleep, and heavy of heart, he sank down between the two graves, crossing his legs. He sullenly plucked at grass blades, angry still that she had died. What kind of God would allow a perfectly charming and happy girl of fifteen to die of a fever? He didn't want to look at the grave. She wasn't there. The effervescent Katherine was in heaven. Surely, if anyone had made it there, she had.

He shut his eyes. "I'm sorry, Katherine. I'm sorry I haven't come sooner. Sorry I wasn't there when you died. And most of all, I'm sorry I let you die. If I had been here, I might have saved you somehow."

The words rang hollow. He knew he wasn't omnipotent. He didn't have the power to save a young girl with a raging fever. The doctors hadn't even been able to do that. But just acknowledging his feelings of guilt over her death made him feel lighter. He was glad he had come. Dobson's urging, though clearly the ravings of a madman, had served a purpose. It had forced Hugh to come and face a painful part of his past. He was better for it.

But time was wasting. With a groan, he forced his weary limbs into action and stood, dusting off his trousers. That's when he looked at the headstone closely and realized why Dobson had sent him here. Suddenly, everything became horrendously clear.

Lady Beaumont," the Earl of Boxley said as they headed back out into the stable yard. "Since Montgomery is not here, I propose that you and I return to the place where we searched earlier. I have an idea that occurred to me while we were eating. I'd like to pursue it."

Inwardly she cringed. She wanted to spend as little time as possible with him. But Hugh hadn't returned, and if they went without him, he would know where to find them. She gave him a thin, brief smile. "I suppose that would be in order, sir. I'll do anything to find my stepdaughter."

He smiled, something she had rarely seen him do. His obvious attempts to make up for past hostilities were awkward at best. *Just give up,* she wanted to tell him. *I've thought about it, but I cannot forgive you. I will declare a truce for Hugh's sake, but I will never be comfortable in your presence.*

"Good," he said, adjusting his hat. "You can help me judge the success of my theory. If I'm right, Miss Parnham might be in your care before Hugh even returns."

Boxley had dressed in khaki as if he were hunting lions in Africa, but he still looked as hard and unyielding as he did in his gray suits. She realized something important about the earl. Nothing came naturally to him—not love, not familial relationships, not even his offer of assistance to help search for Sophie. He had adopted the costume, and he had been searching energetically, but Lydia didn't sense that he cared in any way about Sophie's plight. He couldn't empathize with the girl's undoubted terror, couldn't feel sorry for her mother, didn't understand why Hugh cared, and certainly would feel no relief upon finding her, other than satisfaction that he had avoided a scandal by not having her die on his property.

Yet if he had an idea of where to find her, Lydia would willingly follow him to the ends of the earth.

They mounted up and rode along the cleared path from the lodge to the cliffs. Under Todd's instructions, the others decided to work in the opposite direction, looking for a possible manmade prison buried underground. Mr. Frances also warned them to look in the trees. If Dobson had been true to druid lore, she might be suspended from above in a hanging wicker basket. Sparse historic accounts claimed that the druids imprisoned human sacrifices in wicker baskets and lowered them into blazing fires.

It was an image Lydia quickly cleared from her mind. She and the earl arrived back at the spot where they had spent the morning.

"I don't see what good this will do," she said.

He dismounted, hobbled his horse, then came to give her a hand off her sidesaddle. He practically lifted her from it, and she was struck by how strong he was for a man in his sixties. When her feet landed, he didn't immediately let go.

"Steady?" he asked.

"Yes." She stepped from his grasp, frowning. She put some distance between them while he tied up her horse. The mount whinnied. A stream trickled nearby. She hadn't heard it before. She was too intent on finding something. How could she not have noticed the trickling, gurgling sounds before? A hawk cried overhead. She craned her neck to look at it.

"You're very beautiful, Addie."

She snapped her head his way. The gurgling water sounded in the silence. She wanted to see some sign in his face that she had misheard him, but all she saw was blatant lust. That rigid mask of his had somehow peeled away, leaving a leering expression that chilled her.

"I see why my son allowed you to seduce him so many years ago."

"It wasn't like that," she said in a clipped manner.

His gray eyes sneered with derision. "Ah, I see. Yes. He is a rather romantic sort. Foolish and romantic. Did you really think you could sleep your way out of your class of people?"

"I won't listen to this." She marched to her horse and searched for the knot in its reins. What a fool she'd been to come with him here.

"Tell me, Addie, how many men did you bed while you worked in Ella Fenniwig's parlor?"

She froze, gripping her mount's mane. He came up behind her and pressed himself against her backside. She could feel his arousal. She whirled around, but he trapped her in his arms.

"Why don't you give me a quick fuck, you little tart, before my son returns? You fooled him. You even some-how tricked Beaumont into marriage. But you've never fooled me. Come along, slut, I can take you here without any fuss. I trust you weren't fool enough to catch syph from your husband, and I know Mrs. Fenniwig takes the greatest care with the health of her girls."

He started fumbling with his pants, and his mouth lunged for hers. It was wet and just sickening enough to rouse physical strength Lydia didn't know she possessed. She shoved him off with a fierce roar of outrage.

"You bastard!" she screamed. "You haven't fooled me, either."

"Lydia!" Hugh's voice cut through the woods.

Her heart leapt with relief. The earl glanced irritably over his shoulder.

"Bloody bad timing," he growled, then stepped forward, drew back his fist, and slammed her hard in the temple.

"Ah!" she cried out in pain as she staggered back from the force of it. Then all went black.

* * *

"Hugh? Are you there?" Todd called out. He came on foot through the woods, sweating and winded. He found three horses tethered, but only one person. "There you are! Any progress?"

Hugh whirled on him. "He's got her!"

"Who?" Todd pulled a kerchief from his waistcoat and dabbed his florid cheeks. "Sophie? Good God, did you find her?"

"No!" Hugh raked his hands violently through his hair. "Boxley! My father has Lydia. I'm sure of it. I found both their horses tethered here, but no sign of them."

"Perhaps they took out after us in the other direction. I still believe we might find her in a cellar or some sort of natural underground prison, though we haven't had much luck. A note arrived from Pierpont. The constable told him there was a well-equipped cellar behind Dobson's cottage, and it looked as if it had been used recently. I'll avow she was being kept there until you arrived."

"Christ, shut up, Leach! You talk too bloody much."

"Well, I say, old chap, I'm just trying to—"

"You don't understand! The earl is the one! He is the kidnapper."

Todd frowned slowly. Hugh could see the disbelief in his eyes. It made him so incredibly mad that Boxley had fooled the entire world. No one had known his true nature, except for Dobson.

"My father was here just moments ago with Lydia. I believe he's kidnapped her, too."

"Oh, come now, Monty. Are you sure you haven't been smoking from the golden bowl again?"

Hugh turned on him, grabbing Todd's lapels and thrusting him against a tree. Glaring into his face, he muttered, "If you weren't my best friend, Toddy, I'd bloody well strangle you now."

Todd looked truly terrified. He swallowed hard. "Very well. What happened?"

"My father . . . my father . . . ." He was suddenly nauseous.

He let go of Todd and gripped his shoulder for support with one hand. "I just visited my sister's grave for the first time. Boxley told me . . . he told me she had died of a fever in the spring. I didn't find out until August. It never occurred to me—"

"*What?*" Todd pressed, gripping his arm in support.

"The date she died. It was May 1." He took in several breaths, willfully collecting himself. "She didn't pass from a fever. She died during a Beltaine ritual. I told you Dobson raped young girls every May Day. But that wasn't the whole story. He wasn't alone. My father was the one behind it all."

"You mean . . . he sacrificed *his own daughter* in this horrible pagan rite?"

Hugh couldn't bring himself to answer. "What day is it? I've lost all track of time."

"April 31," Todd whispered.

They looked at each other.

"He has Sophie and Lydia," Hugh said. He began to pace along the edge of the sunken grounds. "And they're somewhere in there. Goddamn! There has to be a way! There has to be!"

"What if there isn't just one entrance?" Todd said as he scratched the back of his blond head. "In medieval castles, there was the gatehouse, but there was also the postern. The main entrance was used by guests and merchants—"

"Yes, yes, yes. I understand."

"But the postern was a small back door used as a quick getaway and for easy access."

"And your point, Todd?" Hugh prodded impatiently.

"If this ritual site has remained a secret for all these centuries, there would have to be various ways to reach it—all which could be hidden depending on the circumstances—and all which were highly secretive in nature. With all these sinkholes, there are doubtless many ways in, equally convoluted and potentially dangerous. They all appear to be blocked, but somehow they can be opened under the right circumstances."

Hugh looked at him hard and felt a surge of immense affection. "I'm glad you've come. At least one of us is using his head. I'm too bloody close to this case. I've been fixated on my own recollections and trying to find the entrance I used five years ago. I should have known that the doorway would have been obliterated as soon as it was breached. But what can we do? It would take an army to push aside the boulders that are apparently blocking the entrances from inside."

He looked at the rocky hillside, where more than a dozen small entrances led to labyrinthine networks of pitch-black passageways. Just when he was about to speak again, he heard the cock of a revolver. He and Todd turned in the sound's direction. There stood Lord Boxley, aiming his gun at Hugh.

"Now will you admit you are not as clever as you pretend to be?" he asked. Hugh had heard this noncommittal, vaguely condescending tone of voice before. *Care for a cigar, Montgomery? Are you going to the races today?*

"Yes, I admit it," Hugh replied without hesitation. "Where is she?"

"That's not good enough."

"Nothing I do is good enough, Father. Tell me what you want to hear and how you want to hear it."

Like a chisel on fine china, this cracked the earl's stony facade. The veneer of indifference shattered and fell. A strange, feral light of deep passion and hatred shone from his eyes, transforming his features.

"Don't patronize me, you pathetic, precious excuse for a man." He held the gun higher and stalked toward Hugh.

"What's this all about, Boxley?" Todd inquired with remarkable affability.

"Go frig yourself, Leach," the earl growled without glancing away from his son. He stopped only when he was close enough to press the barrel to Hugh's temple. "Tonight is the night."

Hugh swallowed audibly. "You mean the Beltaine ritual?"

The earl nodded. "Yes, that's right. Finally I can initiate you into the brotherhood, and I don't mean the Botanicals." He laughed in his throat. "You were stupid enough to suspect them at one point."

"Yes, Father, I was stupid. Now take me to the girls."

"I don't like your lack of genuine humility, son," he said close to his ear. "You're still humoring me. You don't seem to understand. If you don't do this right, you and that whore of yours won't live through the night."

Suddenly he stepped backward until he was well out of Hugh's reach. "Go now. Come back tonight when it's dark. Once again, the sound of drums will lead the way. You'll see the fire. It will lead you to your precious whore and the girl. But come alone. If you bring anyone with you, I'll kill them both."

He started backing away into the woods.

"No!" Hugh shouted, lunging forward. He stopped when the earl pointed the gun at his forehead. "Don't do this, Father. I have to see them now."

"You can't, Montgomery. You're too busy now." He swung his arm around until the gun pointed at Todd. "You have to take your friend to the morgue."

He pulled the trigger. A bullet exploded into Todd, knocking him to the ground.

"Hell!" Hugh cried out, rushing to Todd. The barrister grimaced and clutched his shoulder. A button of blood bubbled up beneath his hand. Hugh put an arm under his head. "Toddy! Are you all right?"

Todd nodded and grimaced. "Hurts like hell."

"I have to get you back."

"No, go after him."

Hugh looked up. The earl was already gone. "It's too late. Besides, he's not going to hurt the women until tonight when I'm there to witness it. It looks like he hit your shoulder. He was always a lousy shot, thank heaven. Let's go. Easy does it now."

"Ohhhh." Lydia groaned as she regained consciousness. Her head pounded unmercifully. She felt a strange moistness on her forehead and tried to touch it, but something got in her way. It took a moment to realize it was a delicate hand holding a damp kerchief. The hand removed the material, then gripped her fingers reassuringly.

"Don't worry," came a young, feminine voice. "He's not here. You're safe with me."

Lydia's eyes shot open. At once she recognized the uneven dome overhead as a cave. The cool, dank air confirmed it. She blinked in the darkness, but she could see enough by the light of a single candle to focus on the person hovering next to her. It was like looking at a feminine version of Beaumont.

"Sophie?" she whispered.

"Oh!" the girl whimpered. "You know who I am? Oh, you . . . you came for me! I knew someone would."

Lydia sat up, and the girl flung herself into her arms. "Oh, my darling girl, I am so glad to see you." Lydia hugged her fiercely. "We've been looking for you. We were so worried."

Sophie sobbed. "Thank you. Oh, thank you."

Lydia crooned reassurances, and when Sophie quieted, she offered the girl her handkerchief. Sophie's was sopping wet after using it to mop Lydia's forehead. She was obviously a caring child. Beaumont would be so pleased.

"There, there, Sophie. May I call you that?"

"Of course." She delicately blew her nose and dabbed at her eyes. "You have no idea how lonely it's been. And last night I fell asleep. The candle burned out. I've been in complete darkness ever since. That is until he brought you here. Then he lit another candle. I've been making sure it didn't burn out while you slept. We'll have to be careful not to blow it out with our movements."

Lydia looked at her as closely as she could in the shadowed light. She was a lovely girl, with long, flowing hair, her father's handsome nose, and her mother's wide and beautiful eyes.

"Do you know who your captor is?"

Sophie shook her head. "A gentleman. He said his name was Trevor."

"Did he mention a Lord Boxley?"

"The only others I know of are Mrs. and Mr. O'Leary. And Dr. Keeley." At Lydia's prodding, Sophie explained their roles in her recent life.

When she heard about the doctor's examination, Lydia felt sick to her stomach. She didn't think it was possible to hate the Earl of Boxley more than she already did. But after hearing what he had instructed Dr. Keeley to do, Lydia was seething with outrage.

"I am so sorry, my darling girl," she said, reaching out to tuck a fallen strand of hair behind her delicate ear. "You should not have had to endure that."

Sophie sniffled and nodded quickly. "I know. I've put it behind me."

"You're strong, aren't you?"

At this vote of confidence, Sophie looked up with curiosity. "Who are you?"

Lydia took in a deep breath. She had been so intent on finding Sophie that she'd given little thought to what she would say once she did find her. Perhaps honesty was the best policy. It was important for Sophie to know just how much Lydia cared about her well-being, and why, just in case they didn't make it out of here alive. She wanted Sophie to know that her father had loved her. Lydia knew how painful it was to lose a father's love. She could only imagine how much worse it was never to have had it at all.

She took one of Sophie's hands in hers. "I am your father's widow."

Confusion played over the girl's china-doll-smooth forehead. "You mean . . . he's *dead?*"

Lydia fought a sudden surge of tears. She bit her lower lip and nodded. "I'm afraid so."

"I'll never get to meet him?"

She burst into an unpretty wrack of tears. Lydia cried, too. They held each other as they rocked. The child mourned the father she had never known. The widow still mourned him, too, and all the loss of innocence. They quieted in each other's arms until all that could be heard was the slow drip-drip-dripping of water from a stalactite into a pool below.

Lydia pulled herself together. "Now then. I want you to know, Sophie, that your father would have loved you very much if he had been given the chance. But until a few weeks ago, he did not know you even existed."

"Louise," she said sullenly. "My mother likes to run her own life. She never believed I needed a father."

"And she was wrong, wasn't she?"

Sophie nodded, her eyes connecting fully with Lydia's now. "Who was he?"

"His name was Adrian Tyrell. He was the Earl of Beaumont. He had no other children, and he wanted me to make sure you knew he had planned to claim you as his daughter and heir. He has left you a great fortune. I'm sure it doesn't seem like a consolation at this moment, but you are a very wealthy young woman."

"He was going to claim me?" Her smooth, young fingers pulled at a long blond hair that had fallen in front of her eyes. "That is wonderful. Thank you. Thank you for telling me. I know you didn't have to."

"But I did have to, because I loved your father very much. And I know that when he died, he cared about nothing more than finding you and making you safe."

"I don't think he'll get his wish," Sophie whispered, looking down at her hands.

"What makes you say that?"

"He's crazy." She shook her head, as if trying to squeeze out the horrifying memories.

"Lord Boxley? The gentleman who brought me here?"

"He's mad. He thinks I'm some goddess or something. He wants to sacrifice me."

"He won't. I promise you that. I'm working with Lord Clue. He received your letter. He knows I'm somewhere in this vicinity, and I know he won't give up searching until he finds us."

"How can he?"

Lydia looked at the flame, flickering steadily. She had no idea how he'd find them. This time, she decided not to be entirely honest. "He has a plan, Sophie, and it will become clear to us in the proper time. But one thing is certain. Lord Clue will find us. I have complete faith in him."

Chapter 21

Hugh and Reggie stood for hours in the woods near the caves. They waited as dusk descended and then by moonlight for the sound of drums, but all they could hear was the gurgling of the stream and an occasional owl.

Farther back into the woods the constable and a phalanx of men employed by the earl waited in case they were needed. Although they would prove useful as witnesses, they would be of little help in any confrontation with the earl. He had been their lifelong employer. They had agreed to come on this bizarre mission, but they were clearly unconvinced. The only reason they would go along with someone who questioned the earl's activities at all was because of Hugh's fame as an investigator.

Hugh was standing by a large oak tree and Reggie was leaning against its trunk when the first faint pulse of a drumbeat sounded. They both stiffened and cocked their heads. Silence. Hugh shut his eyes, listening hard. Finally, there came a *boom, boom, boom.*

"There it is," he hissed.

Reggie bolted upright. His freckled face hardened. "I'm ready."

Hugh put a hand on his shoulder, silently thanking him for being here. Pierpont would be in London by now, transporting Sir Todd for surgery to remove the bullet from his shoulder. The wound was thankfully in as benign a place as possible. The loathsome Dr. Keeley had been called to Windhaven to stop the bleeding, but there was no way Hugh would allow Keeley to operate on Todd.

That had left Reggie as Hugh's right-hand man. "Now, remember, Reggie," he said, "stay hidden as long as you can. I'm certain the women are no longer in the cave, but out in the open in the semi-circle temple area where the ritual will take place. Two-thirds of the circle is bordered by rock. The other third opens to the air and drops off into the valley."

"Yes, yes, I have it in my mind."

"Don't come into the temple area unless I'm in dire straits. There might still be a chance that I can reason with my father. And don't do anything quickly. You don't want to startle the women. If they flee in the wrong direction, they'll plunge over the edge of the cliff to their deaths."

Reggie nodded soberly. "I understand."

"And don't do anything the earl tells you to do. Take your cue from me. I fear I shall have to improvise as I go along."

"Yes, sir," the young man answered gravely.

"Very good, then. Let's proceed."

They followed the sound to several cave entrances, but backed off when the primal drum beat seemed to fade. When at last they reached the right entrance, the drum grew louder. They crawled through a small passage that took a sharp turn. Hugh would have thought it was a dead end, but the opening soon widened and they were able to stand. There were two paths that forked almost immediately.

"Our choice is easy," he said, nodding to the right. "I see a flicker of light. He has lit the path for us."

They traveled a surprisingly long and convoluted path that was not always easy to traverse. At several points they had to crawl and squeeze through precarious angles of rock. When they finally reached the cave's exit, Hugh paused to adjust the gun tucked inside his coat and looked on while Reggie prepared his weapon and nodded.

Hugh stepped out into the temple circle, quickly scanning the scene. There was a thronelike chair to one side, overlooking a blazing bonfire in the center of the circle. In its flickering light he saw the three standing stones off to the side that he had seen five years ago. The women were bound to two of them with ropes around their waists.

He spotted Lydia immediately. She looked worn and battered but very much alert. She didn't cry out. She knew better. Hugh then spied the girl bound to the standing stone next to her. It was Sophie. He'd memorized her likeness from the photograph he'd seen. She looked to Lydia for guidance, and Lydia pursed her lips in a silent *Shhh*.

Hugh was tense, still waiting like a cat with its back arched and its fangs beared, wondering where his father was in this tableau. Yet he also felt deep satisfaction that he had found Beaumont's daughter. He had promised Lydia he would. He had not let her down, although technically she had found Sophie first.

He stared at his brave Lydia's lovely face. She looked past him and shook her head frantically. At the same time a premonition made the hair on his nape stand on end. Hugh whirled around and gasped. Not a foot away was a haunting figure wearing a white hooded robe. More to the point, he was aiming a rifle at Hugh's chest.

"So you finally found her, Montgomery," his father said. He pulled back his druid's hood and grinned darkly at Hugh. "Took you long enough."

"Yes, I have found her. And you led me to her. You won the game, Father. It was you who lured us here with your elaborate clues, wasn't it?"

"Yes, with a little help from Dobson."

"You've proven your superior sportsmanship. Now let's call it a night and all go home safe and sound."

The earl chuckled. Hugh didn't recognize the broad smile or the loose timbre of his normally rigid voice. This was a different man than he had ever known.

"The game is far from over. You are not leaving until you make love with Cerridwen." He gestured in Sophie's direction. "I went to great trouble to procure a virgin just for you, my son. You are so used to your whores that I thought it might be a nice change for you. I have found that virgins are very tight. A bit difficult to breach at first, but well worth the effort."

This last, leering comment left Hugh completely speechless. The words coming out of his father's mouth were so utterly out of character they were beyond comprehension. Here was the man who had been one of the prime forces behind the Contagious Diseases Acts in Parliament. He had campaigned to rid the world of prostitution and vile sexual trade. He had been a proponent of family and fidelity, even a favorite of the queen's because of his moral stances and his devotion to his wife. When she'd died in an asylum, he'd been an object of sympathy.

Had it all been an act? Had Boxley supported the Contagious Diseases Acts because he was offended by prostitution and its accompanying horrors, or because he wanted to wipe out syphilis so he could safely have sex with impunity himself?

"I do not believe I've ever seen you at a loss for words, Montgomery. It's rather refreshing."

"Who are you?" Hugh rasped, his face distorted with incredulity.

The earl tossed back his head and laughed. "Tonight I am Lugh, god of the forest, consort of the Great Goddess herself. I don't know or care about tomorrow."

"That much is obvious. You're mad. You know that, don't you?"

The earl sobered. His straight, silver eyebrows puckered.

For a moment he looked like the emotionless, proper gentleman Hugh had always known.

"Am I mad?" His eyes filled again with that odd foreign light. "I don't think so, Montgomery. I think I am finally very, very sane. Is it wrong for me to want this?" He swept his arm around the circle. "Here I'm happy at long last. Now," he said, shifting from the dreamy tone in which he was speaking and turning practical. "This gun is getting rather heavy. Remove whatever weapons you've brought, and I'll put this down. Then we can have a meaningful discussion."

Hugh hesitated. Was there any reasoning with this man? Or would he have to overpower him? He was not yet sure. But having this clearly unstable man pointing a rifle at his head was an unacceptable risk. He reached slowly into his coat and withdrew his pistol, placing it on a tree stump that looked as if it was used as a table. The earl placed his rifle beside it.

"That's a sensible chap. Now, let's have a drink." Boxley went to a cauldron near the first and ladled a cup of steaming liquid. "I highly recommend it. Very relaxing."

"One of Dr. Keeley's recipes?" Hugh asked. "No, thank you."

"You don't know what you're missing." He took a drink himself and eyed Hugh. "What is it you wish to know? Now that I've bested you in your little contest, I feel magnanimous."

"If you are not mad, Father, how do you explain the children you've raped and murdered?"

Boxley frowned and smoothed the edges of his silver mustache. "You mean the milkmaid?" he asked. "That was Dobson's fault. Besides, she was just a servant, Hugh. I've always said you carry your notions of equality to the extreme."

"How many others have you killed?"

"None but the girl in the clinic."

"You mean May?"

The earl shrugged impatiently. "Don't bore me with the details. I neither know nor care what her name was. She had to be dealt with before she recovered her wits and talked."

"How did she get to the clinic?"

"A year ago she escaped after the Beltaine ritual. She refused to be bought off. She managed to get on a train back to London and wandered into the clinic. Dobson tracked her down and took care of her. She had gone mute and posed no threat. I told him to take the chit back to the clinic a few weeks ago, knowing Lady Beaumont was a frequent visitor. After you gleaned enough information from her to get you here, she'd served her purpose and had to be dispensed with."

As his father spoke those chilling words, Hugh glanced quickly at Lydia. She had a bruise and cut on her temple, but otherwise she looked well. When the old man paused, he asked, "How many others have there been?"

"Let me count." The earl wandered back toward the fire as he thought. "I suppose it would be one virgin a year for the last, oh, two hundred years or so."

Hugh was stunned by the enormity of it. "You can't mean that."

The earl tilted his head sideways, regarding his son as if he were the butterfly impaled by pins. "It must distress the great Lord Clue that this has been done by your ancestors for so long, and you have never had the faintest notion of it."

"You mean these barbaric rituals have been passed on from father to son—that my grandfather—"

"Yes, but I fear the fifth earl was not worthy of our family tradition. He occasionally maintained the annual rituals, but his heart was never in it. He preferred whores." Boxley's voice was flat and vicious as he looked over at Lydia for a moment. Then he quickly returned his attention to Hugh. "I have been far more dutiful than he. There is wisdom with the ancients. Unlike Lord Beaumont, I'll never die of syphills. And I did not have to resort to murder, either. In most cases I paid their families handsomely for the privilege of deflowering that last child in a large brood for whom they couldn't afford a dowry."

"Like the Botanicals."

The earl stiffened angrily. "Really, Montgomery. The Botanicals are so pedestrian. They simply molest young girls. I worship the girls. And because of my largess, they're happily married after I finish with them."

"Except for May," Hugh shot back. "And the milkmaid. What about them?"

"Both of those were Dobson's mistakes. I should never have initiated him into the rites. I wanted him to continue the family tradition, but he was never a true believer, merely a pathetic sycophant who wanted my approval." The earl added with a sneer. "As if that would make him legitimate."

"Constable Barnabas told me something quite shocking earlier tonight," Hugh said. "An examination by the coroner revealed that Trevor Dobson had been castrated. And not recently. It had apparently happened years ago." He waited, watching this monster who was his father, wondering how this would all end as he attempted to outwit a dangerously cunning madman.

The earl scoffed nastily. "That silly diamond leaf of his covered up a considerable lacking, did it not?" He walked over to his throne and sat down. "Dobson deserved what he got. I feel no regret whatsoever, if that's what you're expecting." His voice was flat, without effect at all now.

"He was your brother, for all he was born on the wrong side of the blanket. Why did you hate him?"

The earl leaned forward and shouted, red-faced, "Because the bloody bastard bedded my wife!"

Hugh stood stunned. "My mother! So they *were* lovers!" The fury and pain behind the madness in the old man's eyes confirmed it. "So you castrated him for it." It was not a question.

Boxley did not bother to deny the remark, but continued

on his rant. "As if tupping my countess would not have sealed his fate, he allowed that milkmaid to escape. She was hysterical and ran in terror until she fell over the cliff. Then you found her body and wouldn't stop asking questions. You've ever had this unhealthy, obsessive curiosity, Montgomery. And you know what they say about curious cats." Boxley's voice was a deadly purr as he sipped from his chalice.

Hugh studied the old man's glazed eyes. What sort of drug had the drink been laced with? Perhaps he could use this to his advantage. He began to draw out more old memories, asking, "Do you honestly believe my mother and Dobson were lovers?"

"I know they were. Trevor and I argued after the girl died. In a fury, he taunted me with the fact that he and your mother were in love. Why do you think I had her put away?"

Hugh's knees nearly buckled. "Then she wasn't mad. You had her committed to an asylum because she had an affair." He could barely get out the words.

He looked at Hugh as if he were unutterably dense. "I had my reputation to consider. The only thing my father and I had in common was the Beltaine tradition. He was a drunken debaucher who ruined our family name. I devoted my life to restoring it. I couldn't have your mother ruin everything."

He was speaking as if the countess's death was insignificant compared to his supposed sterling reputation. Hugh lost control, fisting his hands at his sides as he cried out, "She killed herself in that asylum, you bloody bastard!"

"She was unfaithful to me. She deserved to die." The flat, toneless voice again. "Besides, I don't think she wanted to live after her lover lost his ballocks. She was never the same after that, and after learning about the pagan rituals."

Hugh took a deep, steadying breath and wiped his hands over his face. "How . . . how did you castrate my uncle without killing him?"

The earl smiled now, saying casually, "That required the services of Dr. Keeley. It was quite a bloody mess. I observed, of course. As the cuckolded husband, that was my right."

Hugh stepped back as nausea churned deep in his gut. He could see Lydia's face had gone ashen, but he forced himself to concentrate on this devil in druid's clothing sitting calmly before him. "You cut off his stones because he had bedded your wife?"

"Don't forget that dead girl you were so obsessed with. Trevor threatened to compromise a centuries-old family tradition. My great-grandfather might have gotten away with sacrificing a servant or two, but with newspaper reporters and *detectives,*" he paused and glared at Hugh, "one must be more careful now. We have to pay off the girls. Dobson risked everything when he let that one get out of his grip."

"You brought Dobson here to rape her! You undoubtedly drugged him. It was your fault, not his."

Boxley stood and pulled off his white cloak with a dramatic flourish. All he wore beneath was a buckskin loincloth. Tattooed on his chest in a blaze of colors was a butterfly. Its wings stretched from shoulder to shoulder and covered most of his torso. His gray-haired chest sagged with age. Hugh realized that in spite of his brilliance and chilling madness, the earl was really pathetic.

"Behold the butterfly," he said in sentorious tones. "She has emerged from her chrysalis. She who dies in the name of the goddess lives forever."

He went to the fire, reached into a small pot, and scattered a handful of its contents on the flames. They roared high in the air in a blaze of blue and red.

"Very theatrical," Hugh sneered.

"I go to church every Sunday," Boxley said, looking back at Hugh. "It's enough to wither one's soul. This god who was crucified says he offers life everlasting, but first your earthly existence must be a misery of self-sacrifice and propriety. I did not know true bliss until my father initiated me into the druid religion. The pagans of old believed the body is to be celebrated, while our society requires that we pretend it doesn't even exist. Do you know that your mother wept every time I took her?"

"No wonder she sought solace from your half-brother," Hugh whispered.

The earl shot him a look of seething hatred. "How dare you defend that adulteress and condemn me? I have found here the love she never gave me."

"Love!" Hugh snorted. "From whom?"

Boxley glided over in his drug-induced euphoria to the second standing stone. "This is my lovely Cerridwen." He lifted Sophie's chin with a finger. She looked so innocent, yet she did not weep. Her gaze kept traveling to Lydia, who nodded silent reassurances. Clearly they had already formed a bond.

"Isn't she breathtaking? And she's pure. My white goddess. You see, Hugh, with her I will never die. She is immortal."

Hugh stole a glance at Lydia. She returned it, silently saying, "He *is* mad."

"Her name is Sophie Parnham," Hugh said with calm emphasis. Was there any use trying to reason with him? "Sophie is not Cerridwen. You kidnapped her. You're going to rape her, too. Call it what it is."

"You're a fool possessing no understanding," Boxley said disdainfully. "She will want me before the night is through. She will drink from the cauldron and understand what ecstasy really is."

When he let his hand skim over Sophie's breast, Hugh took a step forward, then forced himself to stop. Before he put an end to this ghastly charade, he needed to know one more thing. "What really happened to Katherine?"

The earl's shoulders hunched with pain. He suddenly looked very old, his face as gray as his hair. "Who?" he asked distractedly.

"Katherine! Your daughter! My sister!" Hugh stalked him now. "Or was she Dobson's daughter? You told me she died of a fever, but that was a lie, wasn't it? She died on May Day! Did you kill her because she was Dobson's child?"

Lydia gasped aloud with shock. It was the first sound she had made since he'd arrived. "Oh, Hugh . . . ."

Boxley shut his eyes tightly. "Cerridwen only has one name, and she is eternal. She has many forms, but only one name. She transforms from an Earth-bound creature to one who flies from this despicable world. Don't talk to me about death."

Hugh took the last steps forward and lunged for the earl's neck. "You bloody loon! What did you do to Katherine?"

The earl staggered back from the force of Hugh's attack, then stumbled and fell. Hugh was on him in an instant, choking him.

"Be careful, Hugh!" Lydia cried out.

He scarcely heard her. He was only vaguely aware of how close they were to the edge of the cliff. "Did you take her, you bastard? Did you rape her?"

Boxley choked and struggled for air. "No! I swear! She was my child. I would never have touched her."

"How did she die?" Hugh ground out.

The earl made a gurgling sound. His gray eyes bulged. Hugh loosened his grip.

"Now talk, damn you!"

"She followed me here. She watched. When I saw her, I tried to reach out to her. She was frightened and ran from me. She . . . she ran over the edge of the cliff."

"Just like the milkmaid," Hugh rasped. Picturing the horrifying event, he grew even more queasy. He was only a foot away from the cliff's edge now. He wondered how many people had fallen to their deaths here over the centuries. Heartsick beyond words, he rolled away from his father and rested his head on one upraised knee. "Oh, Lord, Katherine . . . I left you here with . . . with *this!*"

"Hugh!" Lydia cried out. "He's getting the gun."

He glanced up just as the earl grabbed his rifle from the tree stump. Hugh froze. His father came forward with wide, measured steps until the barrel of the gun touched Hugh's forehead. He cocked the weapon.

"If you move so much as a hair, I will pull the trigger, Montgomery. I swear it. So listen closely. I am going to give you one chance to see the light. You and Lady Beaumont either join with me in the Beltaine celebration tonight, or I'll kill you both."

"You want me to join in this perverse rite so you can blackmail me, just as you did Dobson. Is that why you went to such effort to get me here?"

"The tradition must continue. You have disappointed me in so many ways, but I will not let you disappoint me in this. I knew I could show you how incompetent you were at finding her. Now you will give up your amateurish obsession with police investigations. You will devote yourself to family traditions as I have."

"If you kill us, Father," Hugh said, ignoring the barrel pointing at his forehead, "you will be charged with murder. Your druid practices will be revealed. Your reputation will be obliterated."

"No one will find out. I'll leave your bodies here for the vultures."

"But the constable and your servants are waiting in the woods for me. I told them you had kidnapped Sophie and Lady Beaumont. They'll wonder why you return and we don't."

Boxley remained impassive. "I can deal with Barnabas and my servants. They'll want to believe me, not you. A handful of my employees share my secret, just as their fathers shared my father's pagan predilection and our grandfathers before. They will join us later to celebrate your initiation. I thought you might want to consummate in privacy the first time."

"Scotland Yard detectives—"

"I'll convince them as well. I'll say I'm very worried

about you and Lady Beaumont. You were investigating a
crime committed by Sir Trevor, who unfortunately took his
own life in a fit of guilt. You lost your way during the
course of the investigation and never returned. They'll look
for you, naturally, but no one can see the temple circle
from the ground below. The path you took tonight will be
closed over. Even if they suspect foul play, they'll never
dare to accuse me. That's one of the advantages of an
impeccable reputation."

"You don't care at all about continuing the family line?
I'm your only son. Your last living child."

"A man can always have more children." The earl
glanced quickly at Sophie, and Lydia emitted a low growl
of rage as she futilely strained at her bonds.

"Very well. You win," Hugh agreed, slowly rising. "But
you don't really believe any of this. Do you? It's just . . . a
form of diversion, isn't it?" Hugh asked as he covertly studied the rifle barrel, estimating his best method for seizing it.

"You lack true understanding, Montgomery. You always
will. I have never desired a mere female body. I have
longed for the perfect woman. And at last, I have found
her. How ironic that it was an accident. The only reason I
abducted her is because she was related to the one woman
I knew you would come after. I knew your former lover
had married Beaumont. But I couldn't devise a plan to
entrap you both until Dobson revealed to me that Beaumont had a bastard daughter." He lowered the rifle and
turned to Sophie with a moonstruck look. "And here she is.
My darling Cerridwen, tonight we will anoint our love."

When the earl looked to Sophie, Reggie stepped out
from the dark mouth of the cave. "Put the gun down, your
lordship."

Boxley glanced at the intruder, then said to Hugh, "Stupid
boy. He'll have to die."

As he spoke, he turned the rifle and fired at Reggie.
Hugh lunged at his father just as the weapon went off. Reggie
crumpled to the ground. Father and son went down at the

same time, locked in mortal combat. Hugh wrenched the rifle away from the old man, who fought with amazing strength. Boxley kicked and punched as if he were a twenty-year-old, then broke free as they rolled near the tree stump on which Hugh had placed his pistol. The earl reached one long arm up and seized it, bringing it crashing down on his son's temple.

Hugh was able to deflect the worst of the blow, but his head rang with a sickening ache as he grabbed hold of it with both hands, wresting it from the old man's gasp. Boxley butted Hugh's head with his own as the weapon went flying into the dark mouth of the cave. Taking momentary advantage of Hugh's dazed state, Boxley jumped to his feet and ran for the rifle, which lay gleaming in the firelight near the edge of the cliff.

Before he could reach his prize, Hugh scrabbled after him, wrapping his hand around the old man's ankle and bringing him down. They rolled over and over, nearer and nearer to the edge of the cliff. The earl came up on top. This time he did the choking.

"Wouldn't it be ironic," Boxley rasped, "if you were to die like the milkmaid?"

Hugh could hear Lydia's scream echo in his ears. He flung his arm out and felt the drop-off. He could not die this way and leave her and Sophie to face this evil. *It has to end now!*

"What is your answer, Montgomery? Tell me before I choke you to death. Will you join in the family tradition or will you die?"

"Neither," Reggie said. "Now get off of him, sir, and do it carefully." Although bleeding profusely from his left arm, the young man held his pistol to the earl's temple. In spite of his injury and chalk white complexion, his young freckled face had never held such determination.

"It's over, Father," Hugh rasped. "You're going to pay for your crimes. There is justice in this world, if good men stand up against evil."

"Shoot me, boy," the earl dared Reggie as he released his hold on his son.

"You're going to prison, Father," Hugh said as he rose to his knees. "Just as a commoner would. You'll be tried and convicted for your crimes against all the young girls who have suffered here."

With the same superhuman strength he had earlier exhibited, Boxley stood up as he replied, "There you're wrong, Montgomery. I'm going to fly from here, like the butterfly. Fly free into the arms of Cerridwen."

With that, he leaped over the edge of the cliff with out-stretched arms, as if he were diving into a pool of water.

Both Lydia and Sophie screamed, but Lugh, god of the forest, made not a sound as he fell.

Hugh looked down into the moonlit abyss and watched until his father's heavy body thudded on the rocky ground below.

Chapter 22

Hugh had a great deal to take care of after the death of his father. There were endless explanations to the local authorities and to the press, not to mention to the longtime members of the staff at Windhaven. He was sure no one would have believed him if he hadn't been able to show them the druid circle temple and the standing stones and had the corroborating witness of Lydia, Sophie, and Reggie.

After his father's suicide, Hugh sent Lydia and Sophie to London, promising to return himself soon. It hadn't come soon enough. But that made the reunion all the more poignant and welcome.

When he arrived at Beaumont House two weeks later, he was led directly into the drawing room, where his well-wishers awaited him—Todd and Clara Leach, Sophie Parnham and her mother, and of course, Lydia.

"Here he is!" she said, rushing forward and offering him both hands. "My dear Lord Montgomery, it is such a relief to see you here in London."

He took her hands and squeezed firmly, marveling that he could gaze down into her beautiful amethyst eyes with all the horrors now behind them.

"I cannot tell you how wonderful it is to be here, Lady Beaumont."

"I've invited a few friends for tea. They were all eager to see you."

He glanced around and his gaze fell on Sir Todd Leach. He wore a dapper suit as always, and a warm smile, but this time he also sported a sling around his arm.

"Hello, Todd," Hugh said, stepping to him and shaking his hand. "I'm so glad to see you alive."

Todd chuckled. "It was just a scratch, old boy. Gave me something to talk about at the club."

"It had me worried to death," Clara said. She stepped beside her husband. Her auburn hair was swept up in its usual prim quaff, but she wore a scandalously loose gown. "Lord Montgomery, I certainly hope you aren't planning on involving my husband on any more dangerous missions. I want our son to have a father when he grows up."

Todd and Clara exchanged a tender look. "Now, darling, I told you I would be just as happy with a girl."

So Clara Leach was going to have a child. Fast work, Hugh thought, but he would never say so in mixed company. She must have conceived as soon as she'd visited the clinic. She could only be a month along at most. Time would tell if her body had restored itself enough to carry this one to term. He prayed so.

"I wish you the very best, Lady Leach, and I promise I will not embroil your husband on anymore intrigues."

"He won't need to," Lydia said as she offered Hugh a cup of tea. Their hands brushed as he accepted the cup and saucer. Just that touch made his mouth go dry with desire. He wished desperately to be alone with her. She seemed to understand, for she gave him a longing look, then smiled briskly for the others, saying, "I have proven myself to be a great asset to Lord Clue. I hope we can continue to work together in some capacity in the future."

"I think that can be arranged," he said slyly, his suggestive gaze never leaving her as he sipped from his cup.

"I certainly have you both to thank for saving my daughter," Louise Canfield said. She wore a surprisingly modest dove-gray gown, a string of pearls, and a smart gray velvet pillbox hat tilted to one side over her luxurious coils of red hair. "What can I ever do, Lord Montgomery, to repay you for saving Sophie?"

Hugh smiled as he turned his gaze to Miss Parnham. She was dressed in a very fine and proper gown he was sure Lydia had purchased for her. Her blonde hair was pulled back in a pink ribbon that matched the color in her cheeks. She looked genuinely happy.

"I think I already have my payment, Miss Canfield. Seeing your daughter safe and contented is all I have ever wanted." That wasn't entirely true. He had cared deeply about Sophie and all the other girls, but he might never have done so much for them if not for Lydia. "Are you happy to be home, Miss Parnham?"

Sophie glanced self-consciously at her mother. "Well, sir, I'm not precisely home. I'm staying here with Lady Beaumont, at least for a time. And I'll be going to school."

"Miss Canfield was kind enough to let Sophie stay a while at Beaumont House," Lydia explained. She went to Louise's side and tucked her hand inside the actress's arm. "Miss Canfield understands how important it is for Sophie to learn about her heritage and to prepare for her fortune. She will be going to a collegiate day school here in London. Of course, she'll see her mother every week."

"I'm going to buy Miss Canfield a theater as soon as I understand more about my inheritance." Sophie slipped her arm around the actress's waist. But in spite of their obvious affection, she still could not bring herself to call her mother.

"Why didn't you bring Mr. Pierpont?" Clara asked. "I was hoping I could thank him personally for taking such good care of my husband after he was injured."

"I wanted to, but he and Reggie are conspiring on a top-secret project. It would seem that Pierpont has become a mentor of sorts to young Shane. Do you know what they're up to?" he asked Lydia.

"I haven't any idea. All I know is that they both should be knighted for their service to us. Now won't you have a seat and enjoy some tea cakes?"

The gathering remained merry until the very end, when it was time for the guests to go. Without a word, Lydia knew Hugh would stay. She walked her company to the front door, bade farewell, then returned and found Hugh leaning against the mantel. When his eyes met hers, she knew he had something important on his mind.

Closing the doors behind her, she glided forward and stopped only when she could wrap her arms around his waist. "I'm so glad you're here. I was worried about you."

He wrapped his arms around her shoulders and kissed her forehead. "The danger has passed, my dear. We have nothing more to fear from my father."

"Yes, but I was afraid he might have one last surprise left. I thought he somehow might have fixed blame on you in a note left behind."

He gave her a slow half-grin. "Don't you believe there is justice in this world, my darling?"

"I do now. Everything seems perfect."

"Almost perfect." He frowned and gently gripped her shoulders. "Lydia, I won't ever truly be happy until I hear you say you will be my wife."

"Hugh, I—"

"It doesn't have to be now. We can wait until your period of mourning is over."

She shook her head. "It's not that. It's . . . ." Her voice trailed away. She let her arms drop and folded them across her chest. She turned away, suddenly panicked. How could she tell him? How could explain why she could never marry him? Not unless she told him the truth. No, that was simply too unbearable to consider.

"I cannot marry you, Hugh."

"Haven't you forgiven me yet?"

"I have, my darling. I truly have. I cannot explain further. I simply know that we cannot wed."

"I refuse to accept that. If you won't marry me, you'll have to give me a good reason. And I cannot believe there is one."

"I can't explain it." She tipped up her chin. "If you truly love me, you will not ask me why. You will simply accept my decision."

Instead of growing angry, as she had anticipated, Hugh simply took one of her hands and led her to the sofa. He nudged her shoulders down until she sat. Then he knelt on both knees and grasped both of her hands in his. She felt the warmth of his lips when he removed her gloves and pressed kisses on her sensitive inner wrists. His heat immediately penetrated her flesh, and she suppressed a gasp. How she longed to hold him close.

But he would think that she was accepting his suit, and she couldn't, not without revealing her past. It wouldn't be fair. If his father had found out about her work at Ella Fenniwig's parlor, it wouldn't be long before the whole world did. Not only would Hugh have the horrible scandal of his father's madness and suicide to live down but a wife who was a former courtesan as well.

"Marry me," he murmured, then leaned in and pressed a kiss to her lips. "Marry me."

"No. I . . . I cannot . . . Please, Hugh . . ." *What am I pleading for? What do I want?* She did not know herself, and he was breaking down her resistance. She could not think.

Hugh seemed to sense her weakening, for he leaned his hands against the back of the sofa and lowered his mouth to her shoulder, nibbling softly. "Marry me, darling. I won't take no for an answer."

She tried to resist his lure. She really did. But he was so skillful, so attuned to her every desire. All Lydia could do was tilt her head sideways, inviting more of his hyponotic kisses. He trailed a blaze of them up her neck until he reached her ear. "Marry me. We'll always be happy."

She leaned back suddenly, as if ice water had been dashed against her face, bringing her to her senses. "No! This must stop. You can't seduce me into marriage. That would be a terrible mistake."

Hugh sighed in resignation and sat beside her. He took her hand in his and gently caressed it. "I was hoping to avoid this conversation, my dearest Lydia, but you leave me no choice. I must ask you a very delicate question. And as I do, I want to remind you that I love you with my whole heart and being. I have never loved another."

She looked at him tremulously. "What? What is it?"

"Are you saying no to me because of your time with Mrs. Ella Fenniwig?"

Lydia froze. Then the heat of shame quickly thawed her. She flushed. "How dare you? How dare you know that about me and not tell me?"

"I don't care, darling. That's all that matters. I don't care about your past."

"Who told you? Tell me! Who told you?"

He looked at her so sympathetically that she felt like a fool. "Your husband told me."

There was a long silence as Lydia tried to comprehend this. "My husband? When? Why?"

"He told me that first day I came to your house. I went to his room briefly. Remember? You took me there and left us alone. He told me that you still loved me deeply, and that I should not trifle with you in any way. He wanted me to know how you had suffered for me, and he said if I could not accept your past, I should leave and he would find another investigator to search for his daughter."

Lydia's shoulders sagged. She looked up at him forlornly. "You've known *all this time?*"

"Yes, and the only one to blame for what you were forced to suffer is me. Lydia, whatever you did to survive you wouldn't have had to do if not for my mistakes."

She thought back to all that had taken place in recent weeks, recounting all the significant conversations they'd had, recasting them all with this new information. One memory stuck out in particular. When he'd asked her who had taught her to make love with such skill. It apparently hadn't been a rhetorical question. He knew about her lovers, even if he didn't know their names.

"I was a whore, Hugh. You come from a great family. You cannot marry me. You must have an heir. He can't live with my legacy. Beaumont never cared because he never expected me to provide an heir. But your wife must do so. You must care. And someday you will."

He cupped her cheeks, and his eyes met hers with an earnest gaze. "My father was a madman, but he wasn't entirely without wisdom. He said our society requires all sacrifice and gives no pleasure in return. He was right. I will do my duty to my family and to my title, but I will not give up the woman I love for anything. You might as well accept that now, Lydia. I'm not giving up. If I can't have you, I'll have no one. Do you want me to go to my grave a sad, old, and lonely man?"

Her chest constricted with a painful pang of love. She threw her arms around him and squeezed his neck, weeping against his collar. "Oh, Hugh, I love you. I always have. I never stopped loving you."

"I know, my darling, I know.

"Yes, yes, of course I'll marry you."

"Thank you," he said, rocking her back and forth in his arms with more joy than he had ever known in his life. "Thank you."

She pulled back suddenly. "But what of Stone House? I can't simply abandon the girls on the streets who need me."

"What about me? I need you as well. I'm not sure I'm capable of resolving any more cases without that astute mind of yours, my dear. Can't you let someone else carry on the great tradition of the Midnight Angel?"

"You really want me to work with you?"

"I don't want you to. I need you to. I've always needed you, Lydia. Do you understand at last?"

She nodded. "I do."

He grinned. "That's my girl. Those were the words I wanted to hear."

They called him the Midnight Angel. The prostitutes chattered about him endlessly as they waited in the mists of late-night London for their next customers. Some said he picked up girls and took them to his harem, where they were taught to make love like women in the Far East. Others said he had a home for wayward girls, and those lucky enough to go there could put their lives back in order and return to respectable work.

Young Paul Bellam didn't know what to think of the legendary figure. The clerk sat across from the Midnight Angel in his carriage. The gentleman had introduced himself as Mr. Morgan and said he'd been doing this for years and needed a new clerk, as his old one had been promoted. But Mr. Morgan didn't seem that old. There was something odd about him.

"Where are we going, sir?" Paul asked.

"We're looking," Morgan answered cryptically. "Just looking."

"What exactly will my duties entail, sir? Mr. Pierpont didn't say much, except that this was very important work."

"You'll help me pick up young girls before they fall from heaven."

"Eh?"

Mr. Morgan smiled slyly. "Before they become fallen angels. Then you take them to Stone House and hand them over to Mrs. Cromwell." They rode a while in silence until Morgan turned to Paul and said, "You're staring at me, Mr. Bellam. Is something wrong?"

Paul reddened. "No, sir. You just look . . . familiar. I

used to know a young bloke by the name of Reginald Shane. He was about my age. We used to . . . well, sir, we went to the same clubs."

"Reginald Shane?" The freckled-faced Mr. Morgan shrugged. "Never heard of him."

Then he spotted a girl and rapped the carriage ceiling. He grinned with sheer joy and satisfaction. "Here we go, Bellam, it's all in a night's work."